Praise for Spirit of Lost Angels

EFestival of Words 2013,
Best Historical Fiction category, Winner.

Historical Novel Society Conference 2013, Recommended in
"Off the Beaten Path" recommendations.

Writing Magazine Self-Publishing Awards 2013, Shortlisted.

.... I LOVE, LOVE, LOVE when a book sucks me in and is so engrossing that I get ticked when I have to put it down. As a reader, it made me feel as though I was being written into the pages of the book. I simply love when that happens. I always say to people that those who refuse to read indie published books lose out on dynamic novels and this book is definitely an example of why I feel that way. I would not be surprised if this is a book I find in the collection of a large publishing house in the future – Naomi B (A Book and A Review).

... an historical book about enduring, accepting, regret, love, loss, family, hope, coming home, and an angel pendant that held it all together for each of the women who wore it. 5/5 – Elizabeth of Silver's Reviews.

An incredible page turner ... Spirit of Lost Angels is an exciting novel to read with its many plot twists and high degree of conflict and emotion – Mirella Patzer (Historical Novel Review).

... impressed with Perrat's knowledgeable treatment of the role of women during one of France's most tumultuous times, as well as the complexities of insular village life – Darlene Williams (Darlene Elizabeth Williams Historical Fiction Reviews).

The writing is superb, the sights, sounds and smells of a city in turmoil is brought vividly to life – Josie Barton (Jaffareadstoo).

... a tale to lose oneself in ... Liza Perrat persuasively combines fact and fiction in this engrossing novel. The peasants fury, the passion building up to the Bastille storming, and the sense of political explosion are just a few of the vivid illustrations in Spirit of Lost Angels – Andrea Connell (The Queen's Quill Review).

... a truly astounding book that will have you reaching out to the characters, feeling for them, and fiercely cheering them on ... a book not to be missed ... perfect for fans of historical fiction – Megan (Reading in the Sunshine).

... escapist fun — Francophiles will want this one and those who enjoy historical fiction that doesn't focus on royals ... great fun for the summer read — and I can't wait to see what Perrat does next – Audra (Unabridged Chick).

Liza Perrat brings to life the sights and sounds of 18th century France. Her extensive research shines through in her writing, from the superstitions of the villagers to the lives of the more sophisticated Parisians – Anne Cater, Top 500 Amazon reviewer (Random Things Through My Letterbox).

Liza Perrat
Spirit of Lost Angels

TRISKELE BOOKS

Cover design: JD Smith.

Printed in the United Kingdom by Lightning Source.

Published by Perrat Publishing.

All enquiries to info@lizaperrat.com

First printing, 2012.

ISBN 978-2-9541681-0-4

To Jean-Yves Perrat, for believing in me

The people are like a man walking through a pond with water up to his chin. At the slightest dip in the ground, or the merest ripple, he loses his footing, sinks and suffocates. Old-fashioned charity and new-fangled humanity try to help him out, but the water is too high. Until the level falls and the pond finds an outlet, the wretched man can only snatch an occasional gulp of air and at every instant he runs the risk of drowning.

The Origins of Contemporary France, Hippolyte Taine

Prologue
July 1794

The early light burns Victoire's cheeks, like a beacon warning her this summer day will bring something special. She hears the cries of the villagers long before she reaches the square of Lucie-sur-Vionne.

'Robespierre is dead!' Léon shouts, dancing about la place de l'Eglise with the others. 'Guillotined!

'They say the Parisians are frolicking on the streets,' the baker cries. 'For the death of that bloodthirsty dictator!'

'Cheering as when they guillotined fat Louis and his Austrian whore,' a silk-weaver woman shouts.

Victoire had not relished the Queen's beheading. No matter how scornful; how wasteful with money, Marie Antoinette was but a scapegoat. Victoire believes we are all such victims, simply shuffling the hand of cards dealt at our birth.

'Come and celebrate with us, Victoire.' Léon takes her hand. 'They're saying this reign of terror is over.'

'Let's hope we'll have peace now,' she says, looking away from him, at the coach rattling along the cobblestones of the square. 'Far too much blood has stained our earth.'

Snagged in the revelry of the crowd, Victoire doesn't pay much attention to the first two people who alight from the public coach, but then a young girl steps down.

She is about fifteen years old, and her grey-green eyes remind

Victoire of the Vionne River in a storm.

The girl gazes around the square, her ribboned curls, the colour and sheen of a fox, bobbing in crests and peaks. One of her hands folds over a pendant, hanging from a strip of leather about her neck.

Victoire cannot move, or speak. She can only stand there, staring at the girl, terrified she is simply a wicked trick of her imagination—a spirit-like illusion she might have glimpsed that terrible day on riverbank.

Her heart begins to beat wild, like the wings of a bat trapped in a hot attic.

'No, surely not, it cannot be …?'

She falters, and stumbles towards the girl.

Lucie-sur-Vionne
1768–1778

1

Père Joffroy flung his arms about, his cassock swishing, as we settled on the benches, quietening the animals we'd brought for the priest to bless.

'Sorcerers and sorceresses, wizards and witches, leave this church so may begin the Holy Sacrifice!'

Grégoire said some of the villagers thought our mother was a witch, but I didn't believe my brother. How could anyone who helped babies get out of their mother's belly be a witch? Besides, as well as birthing the babies, Maman was our healer-woman, which is a truly unwicked thing to be.

I was still afraid though. My heart skipped and I held my breath, waiting to see if Maman would get up and walk out of the church, but nobody moved; not a single person left Saint Antoine's. The fear faded. There were no wizards or witches at all in Lucie-sur-Vionne.

Grégoire also said our mother was an angel-maker. I glanced across at Maman and felt all warm inside. How lucky I was to have a *faiseuse d'anges* mother. I hoped when I was grown up, Maman would teach me how to make angels too, like she was teaching me to read and write.

Maman said if I was to succeed in this harsh world I must learn the letters, and I looked forward to the end of our day in the fields when she'd read from *Les Fables de Jean de la Fontaine*— exciting tales of snakes, dragons, princesses and treasure. I dreamed of finding that glittery treasure for myself one day.

She said now I was six, I was old enough to turn the pages, so gently—fearful of damaging them—I flipped over each page, staring at the words, which were like magic. I could never imagine being able to understand them.

Mass went on too long and was mostly boring, but I didn't mind being inside the church. I loved the rainbow of colours that danced on the walls in the sun, the smell of candlewax and the cool, flagstone floor.

There were statues in each corner, with shiny golden curves, and colourful paintings hanging on the walls. The biggest one was of Jesus nailed to the cross, blood dribbling down his hands and feet where the nails were stuck in. There were others of naked women showing their bosoms, with cloth covering the part nobody is supposed to see.

I jumped at the first crack of thunder, far away across the wheat and corn fields. From my spot in the last pew, I stretched my neck to look at the congregation before me. The farmers did not get up and run from the church, so this could not be a storm to worry about, even though the grey cloud made shadows behind the coloured windows. I twisted around and looked behind me, through the open door, as the first raindrops wet the cobblestones.

I remembered I wasn't supposed to move, and turned back towards the priest. I swung my legs and looked up at my favourite painting—a man with a long beard and brown robes. He held a stick with a bell on the end and a pig sat at his feet.

'Saint Antoine, patron saint of our church, was a hermit monk who embodied all virtues,' Père Joffroy once told me. 'The pig represents his victory over the demon of gluttony.'

I did not know what the gluttony demon was, but it must be something as terrible as the speckled monster sickness that ate your face away, or blinded or killed you.

Maman leaned across my twin brother and sister. 'Pay attention, Victoire. Stop your dreaming.'

I wished I could still stand next to my mother in church and clutch the warm hand that used to hold mine before Félicité and Félix came. My father always stood at the end of us—my older brother, Grégoire, me, the twins, then Maman—watching to make sure we didn't fidget, which was forbidden in church.

Papa said each time we behaved badly in church we drove the nails of the cross deeper into Our Saviour's flesh. I didn't want that to happen so I looked back at Père Joffroy, whose voice still boomed from the pulpit.

'We simple folk must rid ourselves of these superstitious notions: amulets, evil eyes, exorcisms at full moon. It is my duty to dispel such heathen beliefs that persist hundreds of years after the establishment of our Christian religion!'

Père Joffroy's voice grew louder and he shook his fist. I never understood what our priest seemed angry about, but I lowered my eyes like everyone else and sat as still as a cat watching a mouse.

Père Joffroy was blessing the sheep when the first lightning lit up the church like a thousand candles. Everyone jumped and glanced outside. The goats bleated, the cows mooed and the sheep baaed, their legs shivering.

I turned again, looking through the doorway, beyond the village square. The rain was falling faster and the countryside looked like someone had drawn a grey sheet across it. Thunder cracked again, closer, louder, and the families began murmuring and wriggling.

Some of the farmers slapped on their hats and ran from the church. Père Joffroy did not scold the farmers or the fidgeters even though he had not finished blessing the animals. Instead, the priest rushed from his pulpit and started ringing the bell.

'We must pray as the holy church bell tolls,' he said. 'Your prayers will be heard more easily by God.'

I knew he would have to ring the bell long and hard to chase away the witches who were bringing the dark clouds, and to call on the angels to take the storm away.

Père Joffroy was supposed to fix everything that went wrong in our village, including storms. So why did the thunder still crack, the rain still fall in silvery curtains, as he clanged the bell over and over?

The animals shook and made nervy noises, and as we knelt before the altar of the Blessed Virgin and asked for her protection against storms, sickness and poverty, I saw they'd all made stinky messes on the flagstones.

My father tightened his grip on the rope holding our two sheep and hurried us all out of the church and into the rain.

'We must run home, out of this storm,' Papa said, dragging the sheep that kept bleating and trying to dart off the wrong way. Maman gathered the twins in the folds of her cloak. I took Grégoire's hand and we dashed across the square of Lucie-sur-Vionne.

It was fun, skipping through the rain together, past the post-house, the clog-maker, the blacksmith and the baker. I jumped into puddles around the gallows post and squealed as muddy water sprayed about, laughing as my hair slapped my cheeks. I lifted my face to the sky, closed my eyes and let the rain tickle my eyelids.

The twins were giggling too, stumbling on their short legs, my mother half-dragging, half-carrying them beyond the old stone wall that, Papa said, defended Lucie from the plundering hordes.

'Victoire!' my father shouted. 'Hurry.'

My eyes snapped open and I saw my parents were not laughing—they were frowning and shaking their heads at each new zigzag of lightning.

All of us breathing fast, we scurried up the hill, past Monsieur Bruyère's farmhouse, which sat on the ridge above the Vionne River.

I covered my ears against the boom-boom of the anti-hail cannons Monsieur Bruyère was firing at the clouds, whose bellies seemed to sit right on his fields. By the time we slithered down the slope to our cottage on the riverbank, the wind was shrieking, the rain coming down sideways from a sky as black as a moonless night.

Everyone dripped water across the floor, quickly turning it to mud. Maman lit a candle and handed around bits of cloth for us to dry off. Papa pushed the sheep behind the partition, with the chickens.

My father's brow creased as he rushed outside, and back in again.

'Mathilde, the oak's on fire!' he shouted at my mother. 'The lightning must have struck it.' His eyes grew as wild as the madwoman who lived in the woods—the witch they forbade us to approach.

'We'll get water from the river to put it out?' Grégoire said.

'Not a chance, my son,' Papa said. 'The flames have taken hold. We can only pray to God the fire dies out on its own.'

Maman gripped my father's arm. 'Let us all pray then, Emile.'

Our heads bent, we huddled together in silence. I knew fire was the most frightening thing of all; worse than the sickness that ate your face away, or the one that made you cough blood. Lightning fires had destroyed whole villages.

Outside, the trees moaned as the wind whistled through the woods, but the rain had slowed. The twins were bored with the praying and scampered over to pet the sheep.

My father frowned, and stroked his chin; my mother fiddled with her cap.

Wood cracked, and splintered. Maman and Papa glanced at each other.

'Leave the sheep, Félicité, Félix,' Maman said. 'Come here to me.' I could tell she was worried but my little brother and sister didn't listen to her, and kept tugging on the wool.

A great roar and a rush of air made my ears pop, as the oak tree crashed through the roof, right on top of the sheep and chickens.

Maman screamed and threw herself at the fallen tree.

'Run, children, go!' Papa said.

Through the noise and the mess, I tried to reach my mother. 'Maman, Maman!'

I wanted to hold her hand but Papa was pushing me away. 'Go!' he said. 'Go, now!'

Terrified, I stumbled outside with Grégoire. Flames spurted from the roof like great orange fingers reaching for the sky, and inside, my father was still shouting at Maman.

'Mathilde, we must get out now!'

Papa staggered from the burning cottage, dragging Maman behind him. My mother's head whipped around as she pulled against him.

'No, let me go. The twins!' She dug her nails into Papa's arm. 'My babies ... must ... save my babies!'

Papa pushed her to me but Maman was heavy, and we both fell to the ground. My father ran back inside. Grégoire was brave too, tearing in after Papa, even though smoke was puffing out of the doorway, and from the hole in the roof.

'No, Grégoire, come back.' Maman's voice was faint against the whooshing flames. 'Emile, are you all right? Have you got the twins?' she kept saying.

The villagers came running down the slope, shrieking against the noise of the fire—all talking at once so I couldn't understand what any one of them was saying.

'... fire start ... lightning?'

'Is everyone out ...?'

'Quick, get water ... river!'

'The will of God ... a terrible thing.'

I covered my ears, Père Joffroy's voice roaring inside my head. 'Water and fire—embrace those symbols of purification!'

I did not understand how we could embrace a thing that was destroying our home.

Papa and Grégoire staggered outside, clutching their throats and gasping. My father lurched towards Maman, tears rolling down his face. I had never seen him cry, and it frightened me.

Papa was shaking his head and falling into Maman's arms, but she couldn't hold him up and he collapsed on the ground.

The rain stopped. The storm was over, but it was hot, so burning hot that the villagers had to drag Papa further and further from the dragon fire that was feasting on our home.

Very quickly, there was nothing left, only the fireplace standing in a mess of black wood, stones and branches. The ground was a carpet of twigs, leaves and small birds, their necks bent, their eyes wide open.

I took my mother's hand. It was floppy and cold.

'Where's Félicité? And Félix?'

Maman did not answer me, and her fingers closed around the talisman she wore on a strip of leather around her neck—a little bone angel carving.

2

'When is Papa coming home?'

'Your father will return any day soon, Victoire,' Maman said. 'Now the harvest is over and the season of hedgehogs is upon us.'

'Why does he always have to be away?'

'As I have told you, there isn't enough carpenter's work in one village to earn the money to rebuild our cottage,' Maman said with a sigh. 'I gain a few sous from birthing the babies but many people are too poor to pay a thing. Your papa earns a little extra as a journeyman knife-grinder, just like the travellers you see passing through Lucie—those pedlars, soothsayers and merchants.'

Maman kept telling Grégoire and me we must look ahead; we were never to think or speak of the storm, and it was God's will that made the oak tree crash through our cottage and burn it down to a tangle of black wood and stones.

But I couldn't help seeing that terrible day over and over; the fire stealing Félicité and Félix, and it made me feel sick, as if the ashes were sitting in my belly and floating up into my throat. I tried too, not to feel guilty about the happiness I felt holding Maman's hand in church, since I was, again, the youngest. I never told her that when the breeze caught her skirt she no longer smelt of musky lavender, peppermint and wild thyme, because the fire that scorched her beloved herb garden and her medicinal stores also burned my mother's smell away.

No matter how long Père Joffroy had rung the church bell, the angels didn't come and chase away the witches and their storm clouds. The priest must have felt bad about not doing his job properly because he'd lent us a small parish room to live in until Papa and Grégoire could rebuild the cottage. Père Joffroy also let my mother use a patch of his garden to grow her herbs and vegetables.

But this church room was damp, with no hearth, no windows and not a stick of furniture. It was a sad place; as miserable as Maman when Grégoire or I spoke of Félicité and Félix.

'Come now, Victoire, or we'll be late,' Maman said, wrapping her cloak around her shoulders. 'And lift your hood, the wind is harsh.'

For as far back as I could remember, when the first frosts announced the season of long nights, and icy north winds brought the pink snow clouds, the villagers would gather around the great hearth of Monsieur Armand Bruyère.

Winter was long, dark and unfriendly, but I was glad the season of hard field work was over for another year. With Papa gone half the year, there was only Maman, Grégoire and I left in Lucie, and my brother and I were often alone when Maman went to birth a baby, to heal a sickness with her magic potions, or to make an angel.

Grégoire went to open the door for us to leave for Monsieur Bruyère's, but it opened on its own, and my father stood there, stamping the cold from his feet, a smile lighting his sun-darkened face.

'Papa!' I threw myself into his strong arms and felt I would burst with the excitement of having him home.

Papa gripped my shoulders. 'Look at you, *ma fille*, lovelier every year.'

'Yes, our Victoire is eight now,' Maman said. 'Another one to pay the salt tax for, but *Dieu merci* you've come back to us safely, Emile.'

'I can read and write now, Papa,' I said. 'Well, nearly. Maman's teaching Grégoire and me. She says it is the only way to rise out of poverty.'

I was not certain exactly how knowing the letters would get us out of poverty, but I kept learning, and hoping the answer would come to me.

'Your maman's a wise woman,' Papa said.

He turned to my brother and patted Grégoire on the back. 'I hope you've been working the wood, my son? You will have eleven summers next year—ready to be a carpenter on your own.'

'Well … yes,' Grégoire said. 'But you promised I could journey with you next time, *n'est-ce pas*?'

'Oh no!' I said. 'Who'll throw snowballs with me in winter, and jump off the hay stacks in summer?' Of course, I didn't mention playing in the river or spying on the witch-woman in her hut in the woods.

'Think of the exciting stories I'll bring home,' Grégoire said. 'Just like Papa.'

'Quickly, come and warm yourself and tell us everything, Emile,' Maman said. 'Did you find work? Were your earnings good?' She ladled a bowl of soup out for my father, who sat on one of the two chairs Grégoire had made.

'What's it like to be a traveller?' my brother asked.

'I'd imagined exotic places, exciting people, but mostly I saw misery,' Papa said with a sigh. 'A journeyman leaves his village, his family, in the coldest month, tramping across the country with only the bare necessities on his back. Work is rare, not only for knife-grinders, but for every traveller—the wine and corn broker, the quack doctor, the hair-harvester collecting for wigs.'

Papa ran a rough hand through his hair, which I noticed had grown silvery threads. 'But it is not only hard for the journeyman. I have seen men and women at the plough with no shoes or stockings, children with swollen bellies and people as thin and ragged as scarecrows.' He drank the last of the soup.

'People here complain about bread prices, taxes and lazy nobles,' he went on. 'But in Lucie, a mason might earn forty sous a day, a labourer twenty, the silk-weaving women about half that. At least we can survive here, which is not so for many others.'

'But we still don't have the money to rebuild the cottage?' my mother said.

'I don't care how many francs you got,' I said. 'I am just glad you're back, so you can come to Monsieur Bruyère's with us. You'll come, won't you?'

'Of course,' Papa said, with a wink. 'And I have such a story to tell you all.'

***

We hastened from the gloomy Saint Antoine's parish room, our breath escaping in steamy puffs. The November sun was a pale lemon ball sitting on the ridge of the Mont du Lyonnais as if it couldn't decide whether to stay or go. An owl's hoot rang across the fields and the wind crept beneath my cloak. I tried to shake off the fingers of cold clutching me, my teeth chattering in time to our clogs clunking across the cobblestones of la place de l'Eglise.

I bent my head against the gusts snapping at my cheeks, skipping to catch up with my father's long strides. I took his hand. 'Why do you tell your tales to the villagers, Papa?'

'Because, Victoire, most of the peasants here have not the slightest notion of the outside world. They yearn for tales from beyond.'

'Where is beyond?'

'Outside of Lucie,' Papa said. 'Before the village gates are locked at night, the people simply move from field to street. Never any further. They know only what they need to survive from one season to the next, and their minds conjure up mysterious lands and curious people, who they imagine as dangerous barbarians.'

My mother drew her cloak around herself and leaned close

to my father, taking his arm. 'If it weren't for storytellers like your papa,' she said, 'learning things from fellow travellers and pilgrims, we might never hear of Charlemagne or Jeanne d'Arc, or even of the word "France".'

'Or those ancient people who named Lucie-sur-Vionne,' I said. 'Who were they again?'

'The mighty and rich Romans,' Grégoire said. 'The soldier, Lucius.'

'Is Monsieur Bruyère rich, Papa?' I said.

'Well, yes, the man is quite well off, for a peasant.' He waved an arm across Monsieur Bruyère's domain. 'He owns his farm and the land, unlike most of us who must lease our land from the noble lord.'

'And he hires peasants like us as day labourers,' Maman said. 'So we may have wood for our fires and food for our bellies.'

'And he has crops and scores of animals,' Grégoire said, as we reached the woods, which protected us a little from the wind. 'He makes wine too, and his wheat is used for all the village bread.'

That sounded like a lot of things to own. As we hurried through the scarlet, orange and yellow mass, I vowed I would concentrate harder on my letters so one day I too might own so many things.

***

'I bring news of the fireworks,' my father announced as the men slapped him on the back and Monsieur Bruyère poured wine into beakers.

The adults lined the bench seats: Monsieur Bruyère, Papa and Maman, the silk-weaver women and their husbands, the clog-maker and the blacksmith with their wives, and the baker on his own because his wife was dead birthing the last baby.

Grégoire and I settled, cross-legged with the other children, while Monsieur Bruyère's wife nursed her latest baby.

I rubbed my hands, holding them close to the flames. I loved being at Monsieur Bruyère's hearth. It was a happy and safe place, as if the old stones were wrapping strong arms around me, protecting me from all the terrible things—lightning, fire and death. I imagined angels in the candlelight shadows of the stone walls, batting their fragile wings hard, to keep away the evil witches.

Léon Bruyère, Monsieur Armand Bruyère's oldest son, came to sit beside me. Léon was fourteen and often swam with Grégoire and me at our secret spot on the Vionne River.

'What is this fireworks story, Emile?' the clog-maker asked, as the men pushed aside their card game. They spoke no more of the moon, of hunting, or of the news picked up at the last fair. The women ceased chatting, but the sewing women kept on with their lavender packets, and the knitters' needles went on clicking as the stockings grew longer, falling from their laps.

'The fireworks display to celebrate the marriage of our future rulers, Marie Antoinette and Louis-Auguste,' Papa said, placing one clogged foot before the other—a true orator's pose, Maman said. 'But it turned into a disaster. Another omen, the people say, hanging over this foreign alliance!'

Papa waved his fist and raised his voice against the gales that shrieked outside. 'The omens that began at Marie Antoinette's birth, when an astrologer proclaimed she would meet a terrible end.'

Maman had always read the stories to us, and even though the words of *Les Fables de Jean de la Fontaine* still seemed like magic, Papa's travelling tales were more exciting. Maybe because his stories were real and his voice was like the sound of a flute.

'Why *does* this foreign girl marry our future king?' the baker said.

Papa's eyes flitted across the people. 'The Austrian empress, Marie Thérèse, arranged for her princess daughter to marry our Dauphin to cement the new alliance with France.'

I had only seen pictures of princesses, but one day I hoped

to meet a real one, and touch her beautiful gown and watch her servants waving pretty fans across her powdered face.

Papa told us what he'd heard of the royal wedding. 'Marie Antoinette received the magnificent jewels of a French dauphine, worth two million livres.'

Two million! I could never imagine so much money.

'*Oh là là*,' the blacksmith's wife said, as backsides shuffled about on the wooden benches.

'Then,' Papa went on, 'this terrible fireworks tragedy. Several of us had found carpentry work in the attic of a Parisian mansion. From the roof, we had a grand view of la place Louis XV. So many people filled the roads, the coaches could barely advance—all of them going to the grand fireworks honouring the Dauphin's wedding.'

He took a breath and exchanged his orator's pose foot.

'And the noise! Carriages, the pushing crowd trying to reach la place Louis XV, the cries of coachmen stopping to light lanterns.'

I tried to imagine so many people together. Perhaps like at Midsummer feast, Carnival, or harvest time.

Papa gazed upwards. 'The first stars were twinkling, the lights of Paris shimmering on the waters of the Seine, and, with a muffled explosion, the display began.'

His eyes rested on me and my heart swelled. We may not have the francs to rebuild our cottage, and sometimes there wasn't enough food to fill our bellies, but how proud I was of my storytelling papa, who knew far more than the others of Lucie.

'But the trouble soon started,' he went on. 'A rocket rose into the air, tipped over, nose-dived and exploded on the pyrotechnician's bastion. This bastion split and fire and smoke spewed out!' My father flung his arms about, as always when he got to the exciting part.

'The magnificent colonnade they'd built before the King's statue became a huge inferno,' he said. 'In all that smoke, the people became confused, then the whole thing collapsed and those falling into the ditches shrieked like wounded animals.'

Everyone made sympathetic, clicking sounds and Papa took a gulp of wine and rested his beaker on Monsieur Bruyère's great long table.

'The pump wagons came to put the fire out but the noise panicked the horses and they bolted, trampling everyone in their path. Then the thugs came out of the faubourgs brandishing swords, and attacked the terrified people and stole their belongings. So many fell into the Seine, trying to avoid being crushed.'

He spread his arms and shrugged. 'But to descend into the crowd would be to get sucked into it all. I could do nothing but listen to their screams as the coaches ran down and crushed them.' He tapped his nose. 'My nostrils were clogged with the terrible mustiness of fire, damp and blood.'

I did not quite understand why the people gasped and shook their head, but it must be something awful, so I gasped and shook my head too.

'And there, in the middle of the square, that bronze king crowned in smoke looked down upon them all with a scoffing, careless air,' Papa went on. 'Most of the dead, naturally, belonged to the humblest classes.'

We all looked at each other and, behind me, my mother squeezed my shoulder. I knew we belonged to the humblest class, even Monsieur Armand Bruyère who owned his land, his crops and all those animals.

'As always, it is unjust that only the strongest and richest survive,' Monsieur Bruyère said.

'Hear, hear!' a silk-weaver woman cried, raising her beaker.

Everybody else raised their beakers and cried, 'hear, hear.'

'When I awoke the next day,' Papa said, 'a grim mist, like some shapeless bloodstain, covered Paris, and when news of the disaster reached Versailles, it cast a terrible shadow over the wedding of the young Dauphin and Dauphine.'

'A bad omen surely,' the blacksmith said.

Everybody nodded, and outside, the wind howled around the farmhouse like something in pain, and desperate to get inside.

3

It was early in the autumn of 1772 when Léon Bruyère tapped on the church room door. I was practising my letters, and supposed he'd come to tell us another journeyman was passing through Lucie with more tragic tales of the thousands dead from the famine.

Destroyed by hail, the crop had been disastrous and Père Joffroy seemed in a constant state of fatigue as he hurried about the village performing the Last Rites, then burying those who had succumbed to the starvation. Of course, our bellies grumbled too, but Maman's edible plants and flowers did stop us from starving.

But Léon had not come to tell us about a traveller.

'It's your father,' he said, panting hard and looking from me to Grégoire. 'I came across him out along the road.' He waved an arm northward. 'On his way home but he is feverish, so I left him resting in a hay shed along the roadside.'

A rush of heat, then ice cold, struck me. 'Is he all right?'

'It must be the hunger got to him,' Léon said. 'I'm going to get the cart, my father and I will carry your papa home. Where's your mother?'

'Out birthing a baby,' I said, my voice tight.

'We're coming to help,' Grégoire said.

***

'We're almost there.' Léon waved towards the old stone shelter up ahead.

'I hope Papa is all right,' I said. 'Nothing can happen to him.'

'We'll take care of your father,' Monsieur Bruyère said. 'Don't fret, child.'

'Look, there he is!' I cried, pointing to a bent figure shuffling along the roadside on the crest of a small slope.

'Your father is a proud man,' Monsieur Bruyère said. 'I'm not surprised he is trying to get home unaided.'

Puffs of dust, thrown up by the hooves of horses that came galloping over the hill, clouded our view. The coach appeared, and as it careened along the road towards us; towards my father, I could see its gilded decoration.

'Get out of the way, Papa!' Grégoire yelled, over and over.

'No, Papa, no!' I screamed.

'*Mon Dieu, mon Dieu.* Move, run!' Monsieur Bruyère shouted.

Papa must have been so weak and sick that he didn't hear the hammering hooves behind him, or our frantic shouts before him. I don't even think he realised we were there, so close to him.

My eyes widened in horror as the coach drew closer to my father. We kept waving our arms and shouting. Surely there must be some way to stop it?

My breath caught in my throat, strangling me so I could no longer breathe, as the horses ran down my father without even slowing.

Monsieur Bruyère swerved the cart sideways to avoid the coach thundering past us. I gripped my brother's arm as I caught the unmoving gaze of the noble, from inside.

The cart came to a stop beside Papa's bloodied, broken body. I was numb with shock, and the pain slicing through my breast—a thousand swords at once—was so great I was certain it would kill me. My quivering legs could no longer hold me, and I sank to the ground.

'No! No!' I clutched at my brother's legs, dug my nails into his flesh, and beat my fists against his calves.

***

Even before any of us spoke, I think Maman sensed something was very wrong.

She said nothing though, as Monsieur Bruyère told her of the accident. Her face a milk-white mask, her green eyes wide and staring somewhere beyond, her fingers groped about her neck for her angel pendant. She rubbed the old bone between her thumb and forefinger.

'Death came instantly, Madame Charpentier,' Monsieur Bruyère said. 'Emile did not suffer.'

Still Maman did not flinch; the only movement was the angel pendant rising and falling with her shallow breaths. My mother's tears came only when Grégoire told her the noble didn't even stop; he hadn't descended from his decorated carriage to check on the commoner he'd run down.

My tears came too, burning my cheeks, and I wept long and hard for my father; for the fascinating stories he conjured up to entertain me—tales of werewolves, of flying snakes with boils for eyes, and of green men who looked frightening but were harmless. I sobbed for his stories from the far-off coast—of mermen who broke fishermen's nets and of horned men who stole young girls, because there were no horned women. I cried for the touch of his tender hand, which seasons of carpentry and knife-grinding had roughened and calloused.

***

'*Dieu n'existe plus!*' Maman cried, as we buried Papa beside Félicité and Félix.

The villagers gasped in horror. How could their healing

woman, their midwife—whose skilled hands saved the lives of mothers and babies—no longer believe in God?

'I will never again enter the church!' Maman said.

'Maman shouldn't say such things,' Grégoire hissed at me. 'She only ignites the fires of rumour as if she herself were holding the blazing flambeau.'

'She's shocked and sad,' I said. 'Maman does not mean what she says.'

Grégoire and I too, were shocked and sad, and my anger at that murdering baron wouldn't leave me, the pain like all of Maman's sewing needles jabbing into me at once.

'We'll find the villain,' Grégoire said, his dark eyes grim, his face pale with the rage. 'And throw rocks at his head until he too leaks out all his blood.'

'I'll kill him myself,' I said, feeling the first stirring inside me—a bitter hatred of every noble person.

4

The following year Maman decided I was old enough to attend my first hanging.

'No,' I said. 'I don't want to go; I cannot see such a terrible thing.'

'Don't be an idiot, hangings are fun.' Grégoire said. 'And there is always such a crowd.'

Maman snagged my arm. 'You have eleven summers now, Victoire—quite old enough to see what happens to wicked people.'

I kept tugging against her grip as she hustled me across the village square, where the wooden frame of Lucie's gallows stood opposite Saint Antoine's, the looped rope hanging from a high beam.

It seemed all of Lucie gathered on the square that sunny May afternoon to see the boy die: old people and babies, the women who wove silk from their homes, the families of the baker, the clog-maker, the stone-masons and the blacksmith. Even the day labourers had stopped their field work.

I'd seen this boy before. Grégoire told me his family had recently come to Lucie from a village two leagues distant. Nobody had any idea why they would leave their own village, and we didn't know their names, so we simply called them The Foreigners.

'But what has he done?' I asked.

'The boy is accused of celebrating black Masses on the naked body of his sister,' Maman said.

'Black Mass?'

'The most evil blasphemy,' Maman said. 'The worst mockery of the Holy Mass.'

I frowned, still not understanding.

'They bleed a baby to death over the body of a woman who lies naked on an altar,' my brother said.

'Grégoire! Your sister does not need to know every detail,' Maman said. 'And where did you learn of this?'

'Shush, it's about to start.' The blacksmith's wife tapped a finger to her lips. The crowd fell silent, all eyes on the boy whose tears rolled down his cheeks.

Surely he was too young to die. Then I remembered Félicité and Félix were only three when God called them.

Two big men were pushing the boy up the steps because he wouldn't go on his own and kept screaming, 'No, no! I am innocent.'

Père Joffroy stood beside the struggling boy. 'Repent my son, before it is too late!' he said in his loud priest's voice, the great cassock opening in the breeze as if trying to swallow up the boy's cries for mercy.

The executioner tightened the noose around his neck. A large stain appeared on the front of the boy's breeches. A few people laughed.

'Ha, he's pissed himself!' a man cried. 'A sure sign of guilt.'

The boy seemed stiff with terror, his eyes opening so wide I thought they'd burst from his skull.

'Why doesn't Père Joffroy save the boy, Maman?'

My mother said nothing; she simply gripped my hand tighter, the fingers of her other hand folding around her bone pendant. She slid the angel back and forth, along its leather thread.

The boy's screams had died down to moans. The villagers were quiet again. The birds stopped singing and I imagined even the flowers and trees stopped growing for this one moment—

the end of the boy's life.

The square was silent, as if everyone held their breath. The executioner pushed the boy from the platform. I wrapped my arms around myself and turned from the body writhing and flipping like the fish we caught in the river.

'Watch, Victoire.' Maman's firm hands pivoted my shoulders around. 'Public punishment is an important lesson to deter people from committing crimes.'

'But how can we be certain of his guilt? What if he is innocent, and dies for nothing?'

I kept trying to avert my eyes from the boy, who was still twisting about. How long did it take to die?

'Hush.' Maman frowned at me. The executioner took hold of the boy's legs, and stretched them out backwards.

I flinched as his neck snapped like a summer twig. Maman pulled me close and held me tight, and from far-off, a woman's keening cry echoed deep and mournful through the valley.

'I know a boy's passing is a terrible thing to see, but death is part of life, Victoire and, apart from unforeseen tragedies, you now know it comes early to those who do not obey the ways of the Lord.'

I nodded, thinking of the boy who had not repented in the end. I pictured him falling fast, deeper and deeper, until he reached Hell. The devil was waiting for him—a scarlet, horned creature surrounded by great flames. The devil's fangs drooling spittle, it gobbled the boy up, and he disappeared into everlasting darkness.

A small girl with tangled hair appeared beside us, and startled me from my thoughts of the devil.

'Madame Charpentier, the baby is coming.' She was tugging my mother's skirt. 'Maman sent me to fetch you.'

'Grégoire, Victoire, go straight home,' Maman said. 'No wandering off in the woods. Those beggar people are so wild and poor they will steal your clothes and clogs one day, and remember, no going near that dangerous river.'

We nodded. 'Yes, Maman.'

'Prepare the soup, Victoire, and Grégoire, light the fire under the pot please. This is her fifth babe, I shan't be gone long.'

Our village had no physician, so my mother alone cared for the people. She looked serious with her hair pulled back like that, in a chignon sitting low under her cap, but I understood Maman had to look serious when she was birthing babies and healing the sick of Lucie.

Our mother was not always serious though. She often smiled when we were alone in the evenings, reading a funny tale together, except when something reminded her of The Day of the Storm. Then Maman would stop smiling, and shadows darkened her green eyes as if she was seeing right up to Heaven to check on Félicité and Félix.

***

'Let's go?' Grégoire said.

I nodded, glad to get away from the boy's body swaying in the breeze like someone's forgotten scarecrow.

We hurried from la place de l'Eglise, out across the fields, through corn and wheat as tall as me, the green already speckled with gold. Cherry and pear blossoms floated from branches like snowflakes, as we flew past. Fat crows circled and squawked overhead, as if eyeing us as prey. We reached the woods and slowed down, breathing fast.

'We're safe,' Grégoire said. 'Nobody will see us here—no tale spinners to tell Maman we didn't go straight home.'

'There she is, the mad witch!' I pointed through the trees to an old wooden hut, so well hidden between the large oaks that you could easily mistake it for some tangle of branches, leaves and ivy.

'Not too close, Grégoire, she'll see you and cast spells on us.'

But I was certain the witch-woman had already spotted us. A dark eye, rimmed in red, stared from around the open doorway.

'No such thing as witches.' Grégoire rolled his eyes. 'That's only another stupid peasant story. You'll learn, Victoire, when you're as old as me.'

Witch or no witch, I was glad we hurried on, breathing more easily when we left the woods, on the side near Monsieur Armand Bruyère's grapevines.

Léon Bruyère, bent over the vines, was seventeen now, and when I'd watched him weed and plough the earth, this spring, I saw he was as strong as a man.

Léon smiled as we waved, the sun shining off his skin the same bronze colour as the King's statue on la place de l'Eglise. Léon stuck his thumb up, which meant he could sneak away and meet us on the riverbank.

Grégoire and I continued on, past the Bruyère farm perched on the ridge like a king surveying his great domain. We somersaulted down the grassy slope, shrieking all the way to the riverbank. Fingers of sun tickled my cheeks, my nostrils flared with the scent of spring grass and damp earth, and the Vionne River twisted like a green serpent through the valley of the Monts du Lyonnais.

We walked the opposite way from where our cottage had stood. Since The Day of the Storm, Grégoire and I avoided the pyramid of stones and rotting beams that had been our home. Even if I caught a glimpse of the fireplace, the only thing left standing, my belly heaved and I felt sick.

'A hearth without a home is worse than a home without a hearth,' Maman had said.

We rounded a bend, to where a group of women were washing clothes and sheets in the river.

'Quick!' Grégoire pulled me behind an oak tree. We leaned against the trunk, listening to the women chattering about what their husbands made them do in bed.

'... bend over like a dog,' one was saying.

'Tie ... rope around ... neck,' another said, giggling. '... lead him ... like a pig!'

I nudged my brother and we cupped hands over our mouths to smother the sniggers.

As much fun as it was listening to their stories, we tramped on until we came to our secret place where the water flowed fast around a bend, sweeping across ferns, and boulders with mossy faces, emptying acorns, twigs and leaves into a deeper pool.

From the pebbled shore, we skimmed stones, breaking the smooth surface, waiting for Léon. Grégoire was showing off, boasting he could skim pebbles better than I could.

Léon soon sauntered towards us, and as he pulled off the boots he now wore instead of his old clogs, I saw Grégoire eye them, and I knew he would love to have such a pair.

Perhaps, if we found that golden treasure from the fables' book, my brother would have a lovely pair of boots, and I might have a princess dress.

The boys rolled their breeches up and waded into the river.

Grégoire grimaced. 'Ah, freezing!'

I knotted my chemise and petticoat on the side and followed them into the icy water.

I never understood why Maman worried so about the river. Grégoire and I had come to know every ditch and hole in which you might lose your footing; we were aware of every twist and bend where the current snagged and became a swirling whirlpool. We paid no attention to the villagers who called it *la Vionne violente.*

If Maman discovered we actually swam in the river, she'd have worried even more. The river was for scrubbing clothes, for cooking and drinking. Nobody wanted to swim, or even wash, in it.

Grégoire always said we must not tell people we came here; that they believe the river is bad for you, even deadly if you get your skin wet. He said they would treat us as if we had a curse.

Tiny fish darted like fireflies, moss glowed the brightest green, and the sun's rays stretched right down to the smooth, rounded stones on the riverbed. I flicked water at the boys and laughed, longing for the hot summer days when we would swim and lounge beneath the waterfall.

'This is the loveliest place in all the world,' I said.

'That's because you've never been out of Lucie,' Grégoire said.

'Oh but I will, one day, Grégoire. I'll journey across the country like Papa did, and see exciting places.'

'I don't see why you'd want to do that,' Grégoire said with a snort.

Léon's large hand wrapped around a trout, and as he held up the writhing fish, the poor hanged boy flashed through my mind.

'Your supper,' Léon said.

'Keep your fish,' Grégoire said. 'Or our mother will know we've been at the river.'

Léon pushed the trout towards me. 'Tell her I gave it to you, it is the truth.'

Grégoire shook his head. 'Keep it, I told you. I'll catch one for us.'

Léon lit a fire. We danced around the small blaze, and when our feet were warm, we fell into a heap on the grass, giggling. I never knew what we found so funny, but something always made us laugh until we were breathless, and clutched our sides.

Léon plucked a poppy, lifted my cap and wove it through my braid. The afternoon sun lay across my shoulders like a warm stole and my father's words chimed in my head.

You have your mother's tresses, Victoire, that gleam like a fox in the moonlight.

How I missed him, and how the rage bubbled in me each time I thought of that noble baron and how a peasant could do nothing to punish such a person.

'Stop touching her hair,' Grégoire said. 'You're not supposed to play with girls' hair.'

'Wherever did you hear such a thing?' Léon said. 'Anyway, your sister doesn't seem to mind.'

'She's only eleven—not old enough to know what she minds.'

Grégoire grabbed my arm and pulled me upright.

'Come on, we have to get home before Maman.'

I wondered why Grégoire didn't talk to me all the way back, and why I had to run to keep up with him.

***

Maman lit a candle, which threw long shadows onto the walls. I shivered as I mopped up the last of the pea soup with rye bread. It was not really cold but after five years in the damp church room, I still shivered, remembering our cosy cottage hearth.

'Be thankful for what we do have,' Maman had said. 'We are lucky to have a roof; blessed we don't have to live like really poor beggars in open huts in the woods.'

Maman opened the copy of *Les Fables de Jean de la Fontaine*, which Père Joffroy had given us when we lost everything The Day of the Storm. I sat beside her, following each word with my finger.

'*Maît-re Cor-beau, sur un ar-bre per-ché…*'

'You are reading so well now, Victoire,' she said, as I started on the next story.

'How strange,' she said, pressing her nose into my hair. 'It smells like the river.'

I stole a glance at Grégoire, sitting on her other side. Even in the dim light, I could see my brother's face had darkened. He sniffed and looked away, as if studying the candlelight shadows.

'And what's this?' Maman plucked a scarlet petal from my braid. 'A poppy petal? I haven't seen poppies anywhere besides the riverbank slope.'

The *tap-tap* on our door saved me. 'Madame Charpentier?'

'Who's there?' Maman asked.

'Françoise, the clog-maker's daughter. Maman told me to come for you. The chest sickness has got my father again.'

Maman gathered garlic, dandelion, thyme and some other things from her stocks, which had taken us all those five years to replenish. She was thankful for the few shelves Grégoire had built, though they were nothing like the light and airy place in the cottage she'd stored her herbs and flowers, her special mortar, pestle and bowls. She kissed us and disappeared into the darkness with Françoise.

'I hope they've got doves,' Grégoire said.

'What for?'

'Because, silly, don't you know how Maman heals the chest sickness?'

I shook my head.

'You slice a white dove down the middle—a live one.' Grégoire grinned. 'Then you put the two shuddering halves on the man's chest.'

'That cannot be true! Maman would never kill a lovely bird. Our mother could never kill anything.'

'She kills babies,' Grégoire said.

'Maman does not kill babies, she births them! I could slap you, Grégoire, for saying such a terrible thing.'

'What do you think an angel-maker does then?'

'Well … makes angels, of course.'

I knew Maman needed three different herbs and flowers to make her special angel tea, but after that, I really had no idea how the angel came to be.

'No stupid,' Grégoire said. 'An angel-maker gets rid of a baby from its mother's belly. She kills it.'

My hand flew to my heart and I thought I would pass out with the shock that our kind and gentle mother killed babies in the womb.

5

'He's dead, the old King is dead!' As the voice skittered over the sun-warmed cobbles, I hurried out onto the square.

'Gather, gather, let me tell you the story of the old King's death,' the journeyman said, the familiar traveller's rags hanging from his ragged body.

As word passed around that a pedlar had arrived with a tale to tell, the people of Lucie scuttled from their homes. After all it was a Friday so we were not busy doing anything—the baker's oven was cold, the silk-weavers' looms still, the clog-maker and the blacksmith's hammer quiet. It brought bad luck to do business on Fridays, dig a grave, give birth, bake food or change your clothes. Nobody began the harvest, sowed seed or slaughtered a pig, and the worst thing you could do on a Friday was wash clothes—garments washed on a Friday would become shrouds.

'How is the old King dead?' a silk-weaver woman asked, as the villagers crowded around the mountebank, who stepped onto an upturned crate.

Once the man had everyone's attention, he held up a dark-coloured bottle.

'My elixir to heal aching joints,' he said. 'It works like magic.'

'Tell us about the King first,' one of the quarry men said.

'The old King is dead from *la petite vérole*,' the traveller said.

'The speckled monster got him!'

'*Oh là là*,' the clog-maker's wife said. 'The speckled monster chooses from all classes.'

'The aristocrats may believe us commoners ignorant,' the pedlar said, 'but we are all, sadly, too familiar with this smallpox, which fills our graveyards and turns our babies into changelings their own mothers shudder at.'

'Well I have a remedy for the smallpox,' Maman said.

'Your mixture of viper flesh and sweating paste no longer heals us,' the blacksmith said.

'Madame Charpentier's remedies no longer seem to heal much at all,' another silk-weaving woman said, clicking her tongue.

'No, this is an entirely different treatment,' Maman went on, ignoring the taunts. 'Something far more efficient—the variolation—a procedure the royal government wishes all doctors and midwives to learn, to treat the smallpox.'

'Hmm, this *variolation* sounds suspicious,' Monsieur Bruyère's wife said, cradling another new baby.

'Not at all suspicious,' my mother said. 'Why as far back as half a century ago, an English lady living in Constantinople said the smallpox there was harmless, with the use of ingrafting. It was an operation performed after the great summer heat abated,' she explained. 'An old woman came with a nutshell full of the matter of the best smallpox. She ripped open a few veins, injecting as much matter as could lie upon her needle head. The fever began and they took to their beds, but after eight days they were quite well again.'

'So why was the King not variolated?' the clog-maker's wife asked.

'Ah, the King wrongly thought he'd already had the smallpox, so was immune,' the mountebank said, retrieving his story from my mother. 'Besides, despite some advocating variolation, our country is much opposed. Our great thinker, Voltaire, had seen it practised while exiled in England and begged his fellow

Frenchmen to variolate "for the sake of staying alive and keeping our women beautiful".

'How did the King catch the smallpox?' Léon said.

'It is said he caught the speckled monster from a girl child delivered to Versailles for his pleasure,' the man said.

'Ha, serves him right,' cried a quarry man. '*Qu'il aille au diable!*'

'Why did we hate the old King, monsieur?' Léon said as the people cheered the defunct king gone to Hell.

'Because he was a bad king,' the man said. 'We peasants suffer the most taxes—roads, salt, cloth, bread, wine …'

'Not to mention those lazy nobles who charge us *banalités* to use their flour mills, their granaries, their oil and wine presses, even the community ovens!' a stone-mason shouted, his eyes blazing. He pulled a morsel of rough grain bread from his pocket. 'The price of a loaf of this wretched stuff has risen to eleven sous—half the daily earnings of some. I heard it will be up to fourteen by next spring, but do our wages rise? No!'

'I don't know how we are to keep paying the lord's rent, or buy candles and fat to cook with,' the clog-maker's wife said.

Everybody nodded.

'And what goes on at Versailles?' the pedlar continued. 'Court society passing its days devising intrigues to catch the King's favour and feasting on banquets of meat, fish and candied fruit.'

'Tell us about the old King's death,' the baker said.

'Well,' he began. 'The King spent a pleasant evening dining with his mistress, Madame du Barry, at Trianon. The next day he woke with the fever.' Nobody spoke as the man paused.

'The King got worse so his six physicians, five surgeons and three apothecaries decided to bleed him, but that didn't help. On the fourth day, the face rash broke out. He became delirious and received the last sacrament. The court assembled in the Œil de Bœuf antechamber and waited. His face became swollen, and the hue of copper. A single black scab covered the face of our once-handsome ruler, as if he'd been burned or severely scalded.

They say the smell was foul.'

We all wrinkled our noses.

'One month ago, at three o'clock on the morning of 10 May, 1774, his candle was snuffed out. The old King was dead.' He paused, running his tongue over his lips.

'And since his death, people all over are welcoming the new rulers—the fair-haired, blue-eyed King Louis and Queen Marie Antoinette,' he said, 'in streets decorated with flowers and triumphal arches.'

'Long live the new king and queen!' chimed several people.

'But,' the traveller said, holding up a hand. 'Many say we must be wary of a young simpleton king who tinkers with locks, and a foreigner queen with expensive tastes.'

***

The sun dropped westward, behind the Monts du Lyonnais, throwing its amber light across Lucie.

As the sky turned a darker blue and the villagers gathered in the meadow, Père Joffroy held back his cassock with one hand and, with the other, touched his blazing torch to the stack of dried sticks and wood. The flames lapped at the kindling, quickly building to a noisy crackle that vied with our cheers.

'Gather all, for this celebration of the solstice,' the priest said, beckoning us closer. 'Let us rejoice in our Midsummer bonfire we have built together, to protect us. For, as the sun turns southward yet again and the veil between this world and the next thins, evil spirits roam free.'

Wearing the wreaths we had made from the yellow, star-shaped Saint John's flowers that covered the meadows like thousands of tiny suns, everyone began to circle the fire, leading their animals in the sunwise direction.

'On this Midsummer night—Holy day of Saint John the Baptist—we embrace fire and water, symbols of purification,' Père Joffroy chanted as he blessed the horses, cows, sheep, goats and pigs, so they would bear more young and have longer lives.

Grégoire and I each took one of our mother's hands.

'Come and dance,' I said, trying to coax her to join in the celebrations. Even though she held our hands and feigned happiness, I sensed, as I often did since that day she'd claimed God no longer existed, Maman had stopped believing in everything—especially things that were meant to ward off evil and misfortune.

Tragedy had visited us twice. Félicité and Félix, and our home, had been gone six years. My father had been dead for two, and even as Maman said we must not think of those things; we must get on with the living, it seemed she, herself, could not forget them. It was as if those cursed accidents had broken something inside her—a thing nobody could fix. She continued to teach me to read and write; to explain the birthing skills and instruct me what plants and flowers to use for the different sicknesses, but she seemed to trudge through each day, eternally sad.

'I hope you're dreaming of me?'

Startled, I jumped. Léon adjusted my floral crown and took my hand. 'Come and enjoy this night with me, Victoire, and forget our work, the hunger and sickness, for a moment.'

I gripped Léon's hand and together we circled the flames, watching them leap closer towards the darkened sky, which would not go entirely black on this longest day of the year—only deepen to the inkiest blue before paling again.

'The firelight makes your eyes the same dark green as the Vionne,' Léon said. 'That's what I'll call you from now on— Mademoiselle *aux yeux de la rivière*, eh, Grégoire?' He looked across at my brother. 'Your sister's new name, Miss River Eyes?'

Grégoire, holding the hand of the clog-maker's daughter, Françoise, threw Léon and me dark looks, but I couldn't help feeling flattered. My cheeks burned and I was aware of the buds of my breasts tingling as they pressed against my chemise; of my hips brushing the coarse cloth of my skirt.

When Léon paid me attention, I forgot my mother's sadness,

my brother's jealousy. All I felt was the warmth that started in my ankles and crept up my legs, the heat peaking at the top of my thighs. It was that same strange but pleasurable sensation as when I removed my cap at night and brushed my hair out, or when I lifted my chemise and ran my hand across the patch of light brown fuzz below my belly.

Firelight made macabre shapes of the wrinkled, toothless faces of the old people. The younger faces—scrubbed clean for the festival—glowed pink and smooth as ripe peaches. Flames threw shadows onto fat oak trunks, and I conjured up horned beasts with drooling jaws and ravens with hooked claws. I loved this time of year, when we all laughed, danced and made jokes together, giddy with the scent of flowers, the pulse of summer sweat and dirt.

People leapt higher and higher, Léon the highest of all.

Armand Bruyère beamed. 'That is how high this year's harvest will be then!' he announced, and we all clapped and cheered.

The flames began to lose their force, and the fragrance of grilled sausages, mushroom and cheese-filled crepes, *pâté* and sweetbreads filled the night air. Baskets brimming with fruit appeared. The dancing slowed and people began to drop, exhausted, to the ground.

We washed our feast down with blessed water from the Vionne and wine from Monsieur Bruyère's grapes, and I beckoned to Maman, standing alone, to come and sit beside me to listen to the stories people had saved up for this special night.

'What of this *Bête de Gévaudan* the journeymen speak of?' Grégoire asked.

'Ah, the Gévaudan beast was an unusually fierce and daring wolf-like creature that roamed for two years, killing twenty people!' Monsieur Bruyère said.

'*Oh là là*,' several people cried.

I felt something creeping up behind me. I shivered and spun around, staring into the woods, dark in the waning firelight. I imagined the Night Washerwoman hidden amongst the greatest oaks, washing the shrouds of all her children she'd killed; the woman you had to be careful not to come upon, or she'd ask for help and you too would be covered in the blood of her infants. The trees were still though, nothing moved.

The stories were over, and I had eaten more than I normally would in a week. I patted my swollen stomach and, with the other villagers, Maman, Grégoire and I curled up beside the glowing embers and closed our eyes.

I awoke some time later, rubbed my eyes and stood, tugging down my crumpled petticoat. Maman was gone, probably to the church room where she liked to sit, alone. Grégoire was gone too, back to his wood-working.

'See, the sun also dances with joy,' Léon said, as I bathed my bare feet in the sacred, early dew. I looked to where Léon pointed, beyond the village, at the stripes of pale sunlight throwing soft lavender shadows across the hillsides.

'As if we have washed the world clean and it shines like our very own diamond,' I said, as Père Joffroy sprinkled more holy water for the crops.

We scattered the bonfire ashes across the fields and, blessed, I went home feeling safe and protected.

At least until the next storm.

6

Dawn still darkened the countryside when I ducked outside to empty our chamber pots. Geese honked, a flock of doves scattered like ash and birds swooped and shrieked watery notes, as if announcing this summer day—the beginning of the harvest.

I skipped up the steps of Saint Antoine's. From the top step of the church, I looked out beyond the fields, and the vineyards boasting their new grapes, to the Monts du Lyonnais, westward boundary from where the clouds brought storms and rains—our allies and enemies. Grégoire had convinced me by then, angels and witches played no part in the coming of storms.

Planted by the farmer in October and November, then nurtured like a baby for seven months, I knew a single rain or hail-storm could destroy the entire crop. I relaxed when I saw the early sky was cloudless—a distant pale blue where the sun was rising; not the slightest hint of a storm.

We washed our bread down with water, Maman and I caught our hair under our caps and we set off with Grégoire up to Monsieur Bruyère's farm.

'I don't care about the hard work, or if the day goes on for hours and hours,' I said. 'Harvest time is so much fun, I wish it would last all the year.'

'That's true, Victoire,' Maman said, 'but don't forget we must still work hard if we are to rebuild our home.'

I stared at her. 'Rebuild the cottage? It has been six years, Maman—six winters in that damp church room. I don't believe we will ever have our own home again.'

My mother didn't reply; I knew she had no answer. She merely put her head down and fell easily into the same circular movements as the other adults, all swinging their scythes in perfect rhythm.

The fields hummed and ticked with insects, and as the morning wore on, the sky turned a sharp blue, the sun slanting in low slices along the dry grass, and forming haloes around the hedges.

The other girls and I gathered handfuls of the cut wheat, breathing in its familiar summery smell, as we tied it into sheaves others would flail, to remove the grain.

When sweat plastered our shirts and chemises to our backs, and our throats were parched, we sank down in the shade of the hedges and slaked our thirst with water and wine.

Small boys chased about ferreting out hedgehogs, which they then burnt to stop them sucking out all the cows' milk.

'Surely they don't truly suck the cows' milk?' I said to Léon, as he sat beside me, his smell of earth, hay and horse filling my nostrils.

'Do you still believe in silly peasant legends?' he said with a knowing grin.

'Well those silly little boys will only grow into silly big men,' I said, feeling a little pulse of something like fear or nervousness, but it was neither of those.

'And how would you women fare without us silly big men?' he said.

'You really believe we need men, Léon Bruyère? Who, I ask you, are all those earth-coloured figures working in the fields for months on end like a herd of beasts, even when they are sick, or blind, or with child? Women plough, we sow, reap and thresh.' I swiped the sweat from my brow. 'We gather firewood, cook and feed families, clear snow, milk cows and fetch water. Who makes the cheese and bread, spins the cloth and washes the clothes?' I spread my arms. 'And you men come prancing along at harvest time, pretending to have done all the hard work.'

Léon smiled. 'Ah, a man can tell a girl is no longer a girl when she starts complaining about women's chores.'

I slapped his arm. 'Get back to work, you.'

When the hot sun reached its peak, work stopped again and everybody sat in the shade and munched on bread and *saucisson*, and raspberries and gooseberries from Monsieur Bruyère's baskets.

Afterwards, the young children frolicked about playing hide and seek. The men lay down, covered their faces with their hats and were soon snoring. The women whispered and giggled, apart from my mother, who sat, as always, on her own, her shoulders taut, her gaze rigid on the Monts du Lyonnais.

'Do it to Léon,' I said to the whispering women. 'Please, choose him.'

Several women rose and crept over to the dozing Léon. Three of them held him down while a fourth stuffed his pants with cow dung. Léon was soon wide awake and fighting them off, and we all squealed, tears of mirth streaking our sunburned cheeks.

I laughed so much it pained my belly. Léon grinned, shook his head and went back to work.

Grégoire strode towards me. 'You only look like a fool,' he hissed, 'throwing yourself at Léon Bruyère. You know you'll never have a decent enough dowry to marry him.'

I smarted against the sting of my brother's words. 'Who are you to tell me what to do, Grégoire? You're not my husband or my father.'

'A brother takes care of his sister,' Grégoire said.

'I can take care of myself,' I said. 'Besides, Maman will help me get a dowry.'

'Our mother isn't much help to anyone these days,' he said waving an arm towards the lone woman, on the edge of the group. 'People are gossiping about her more and more, since she claimed there is no God, and stopped going to church. They say, with her potions, floral remedies and cataplasms, our mother is no more than a common witch.'

'No, Grégoire, that can't be!' But I sensed my brother had not spoken in jest for once.

'I heard some talking of magic spells she casts on swollen wombs,' he went on, 'the infant coming out hideously deformed, or dead.'

'Poor Maman. How unjust they are.'

'And remember what Papa told us?' Grégoire went on. 'Father Debaraz was the last person burnt for sorcery thirty years ago, but people are still persecuted for witchcraft, even for such a thing as blighting cattle with their evil eye.'

'But Maman is a healer-woman, a midwife,' I said. 'She's no witch … not at all!'

'And didn't Papa say the midwife and the healer-woman have always been associated with witchcraft?'

A twinge of panic coiled inside me, waves of pain catching me low in my gut. Nothing could happen to my mother. With our father gone, we needed her more than ever.

A flush of heat swamped me and I needed to get away. I got up and wove a silent path away from them all, past the Bruyère farmhouse and down the grassy slope to the Vionne River. Sweat prickling my back and dampening my underarms, I threaded through the ribbon of willows lining the bank until I reached my special place.

I braced my aching stomach and rested on a rounded stone. The sun shone through the transparent water, lighting up the rounded rocks on the riverbed, but where the bands of light cast shadows, the water was dark and furtive.

A bird sang a deep and mournful, *peow, peow, peow,* as I knelt at the edge, cupped my hands and gulped down the cool, fresh water.

I sat back on my heels and looked around. Save the birds, I was alone. I heaped my cap and apron, my petticoat, and my chemise on a rock and waded into the river, careful not to slip on the mossy stones. I drifted across to the deep pool until I was under the cascading water. I closed my eyes and threw my head back, letting the water seep into my skin until I felt refreshed from the inside out. The pain in my belly and lower back waned a little, and I shivered with the pleasure of my bare skin against silken water. As I lost myself in the birdsong, the rushing water like strong hands kneading my shoulders and back, I wondered however anyone could hate the water.

I remembered I was supposed to be raking the cut wheat; they would surely miss me. I swam to the bank and as I stepped onto the dry grass, something prickled across the nape of my neck. I looked up into the grinning face of Léon Bruyère.

Mortified, I bent over, trying to hide my nakedness. 'What are you doing here, Léon?'

'We always swim and fish together, Victoire. Why didn't you ask me to come with you?'

'Go away. Go! Stop staring at me.'

'Besides, I hope you've not been fishing today?' he said. 'It is Sunday, remember? Your future babies could be born with the heads of fish.'

'Give me my clothes. Please, Léon.'

'That is, of course, if you believe all those silly peasant tales?'

Then I felt it—a warm trickle. I glanced down at the dark pink liquid running across my thigh. Blood.

'Whatever is wrong with me?'

I looked up, but Léon was not gasping, or recoiling from me and whatever terrible sickness had struck me.

'Welcome to womanhood, Mademoiselle *aux yeux de la rivière*.' He threw me my clothes and turned around while I got dressed. 'I know about the bleeding. I have five sisters, remember?'

Bleeding? Then it came to me—the curse of which Maman had spoken.

'The church allows girls to wed at your age … at twelve,' Léon was saying, his head still turned. 'But my father says they're mostly too young to know all about wifely dutie—'

'What? Why do you talk of marriage?' I pressed a clutch of grass between my thighs. Flushed with embarrassment, I wanted to slide back into the river and disappear under the water forever.

'Not now,' Léon said, 'but one day, you know, we could …'

'You want to marry *me*?'

My cheeks burned again. Like every village girl, I dreamed of wedding and having my own family to care for. I could hardly believe my good fortune—the strapping and handsome Léon Bruyère, whose father owned land and animals, wanted my hand. In that moment of exhilaration, I ignored what Grégoire had said about my scanty dowry.

***

'The bleeding came today,' I told Maman that evening, when the weary harvest workers had headed off to the tavern to drink ale, listen to village gossip and tell jokes my mother said were vulgar.

'Quite normal. You are twelve years old. It will come every moon until you are an old woman,' Maman said. 'Unless you are with child. Because now the curse has come, you are able to have babies.'

My own child.

Maman was always telling me about the dangers of childbirth; how women often died—the infant too—while she was birthing them, but it was still such an exciting, incredible thing that was happening to me.

'To be born a woman is not favourable to long life, Victoire,' Maman said. 'Especially a peasant woman.' She waggled a finger at me. 'And you must be careful not to let a man have his way with you. In a flash he will charm you and lift your skirt and pull his breeches off, and do to you what you've surely seen those dogs doing, up on Monsieur Bruyère's farm.'

I did recall my surprise, my curious shock, when I'd first seen one dog mount another. I had known, instinctively, that it had to do with having young, even though I'd wished the dogs were simply playing.

'Because if you do,' Maman went on, 'your maidenhood will be torn and you will never be able to hide it from your husband the night of your wedding. He would disown you immediately.'

'I will never let any man do that to me, Maman. Besides, I know who my future husband will be.'

She glanced at me sharply. 'Léon Bruyère? Surely you cannot imagine your dowry is decent enough to wed a well-off landowner's son?'

'But ... but I thought you could help me gather a dow—'

'I am rightly sorry, Victoire, but you will never be good enough to marry that boy.'

'I will! I will find a way to marry the man I love.'

'Marry for love? You must be joking. Here,' she said, handing me a beaker of warm liquid. 'Lime-blossom and sorrel,' she said, obviously dismissing any further talk of my marriage. 'For the pain in your belly.'

I wished Maman wouldn't act as if my curse wasn't the unbelievable thing it was to me. She seemed not the least moved, though she did give me scraps of cloth and tell me what to do with them.

When the pain eased a little, Maman told me how I would now accompany her when she birthed the babies. 'You are old enough to be my apprentice midwife, to learn the skills.'

'Will you teach me how to make angels too?' I said.

'Haven't I told you never to mention that word, Victoire? It will only lead to trouble for many people.'

'But it is true, Maman? You do kill unborn babies?'

My mother sat beside me. 'You must understand it is difficult for country midwives. In the cities, a midwife takes in a pregnant girl and lodges her in secrecy until the baby is born. No one is the wiser, but here, that's impossible. Girls do not have the money to pay for such things, and a pregnancy out of wedlock only causes a scandal—a curse on the girl, the child and her family, forever.'

I nodded. 'Yes, I understand.'

But as my mother snuffed out the candle, threw her cloak about her shoulders and curled up on our straw bedding, I was still confused. Père Joffroy always said it was a sin to take a life, even an unborn one.

7

'The stone-cutter's baby has been born with the elephant head!' a woman squealed, scuttling past me on the square.

My mother had been called away to birth the stone-cutter's baby not a few hours ago, so when people began murmuring to each other, I put my copper cistern aside, leaned against the fountain wall and listened.

'The cretinous child may bring good luck to the family,' the blacksmith's wife was saying. 'And it will never have to work or leave home and earn money to pay the tax-collector, but who has the time to care for an idiot child?'

'The midwife is a witch,' one of the silk-weaving women said.

Another woman nodded. 'A charlatan. Remember the baby of the quarry man's wife last month? Born dead and already cold.'

'And what of the infant born with a gap in its top lip and a hole in its mouth?' the silk-weaver said. 'The child couldn't suckle properly … the milk came back out through its nose. 'Mathilde Charpentier has cursed the village of Lucie with the black magic only a *sage-femme* is capable of,' she went on.

My dismay rose as I caught their murmurings of burnings and funeral pyres, and my heart heart beat against my breast like the wings of a trapped dove.

'How can they say such things, Grégoire?'

'Come on, don't give them the satisfaction of listening to their vicious lies,' Grégoire said, tugging me back towards the church room.

'They speak of burning witches. Surely they would never burn our mother?'

'But it's really not surprising,' Grégoire said. 'You know how they have been gossiping about her. For eight years, since Papa died, our mother has claimed God exists no more, and she has never returned to Mass. The people's suspicions have swelled so much over time that they fester now, like some great pus-filled sore.'

'Maman is a smart woman, Grégoire. She taught me to read and write, and instructs me on the birthing and healing skills. The bailiff would never have her burned.'

'Well let's hope her blasphemy only costs her a simple fine.'

***

I was right; they did not burn our mother at the stake.

'Mathilde Charpentier will be swum in the Vionne River,' the bailiff said.

I felt giddy, recalling one of my earliest memories, even before The Day of the Storm—the swimming of the previous village midwife, also accused of black magic. We had all lined the banks of the Vionne to see if, as a servant of the devil, the water rejected her and she floated, or she was guilty, and sank.

I gripped my brother's arm. 'No, they cannot, Grégoire. They cannot do this. It is so unjust. She's only a poor peasant woman!'

My brother's eyes clouded. 'We must not go there, Victoire. We'll stay home until it's over.'

'I am not staying in this awful parish room a minute longer!' I said. 'The Church has failed my mother, and God has failed us all.'

'Don't say such things, or the same thing may happen to you. There is nothing we can do, it will only be torture to watch,' he said.

'I must try and stop them.'

'You cannot, Victoire. They'll never waver from their decision.'

'At least I have to try.' I tore myself from my brother's clutch and rushed outside, through the chill mist, up to Monsieur Armand Bruyère's farm and down to the river.

A crowd had gathered around several men who were carrying my mother, screaming and thrashing, towards the water.

I rushed to Maman, trying to hold her; to touch any part of her, but the men kept pushing me back, and her face was a blur behind my tears.

'Maman, Maman, no! They can't do this!'

My mother's eyes sought mine, as the men dumped her onto the riverbank, not far from a place where ten years of growth had all but concealed a tumble of blackened wood and stones. I averted my eyes from our old hearth rising like some macabre tombstone. I could not look at that memorial to happy times as tragedy was set to strike me, again.

Maman tore the angel pendant from her neck and pushed it into my hand.

'Wear it always, Victoire. It will give you strength, and courage.'

As the men shoved me away from her, I felt the heat of my mother's hand for the last time. Or perhaps it was the warmth of the bone angel that took the chill from me.

They held my mother still and stripped her naked. I was aware of Léon, beside me.

He covered my eyes. 'Don't look, Victoire.'

The sobs catching in my throat, strangling me, I prised Léon's fingers apart, watching through the gap as they tied Maman's right thumb to her left big toe and vice versa.

The men secured her with ropes and threw her into the deepest part of the swirling current. Nothing happened for a moment, as she bobbed in the freezing water, and I saw the despair in her eyes, more grey than green as they emptied of all hope.

'Maman!' I tried to break free from Léon but he held me tight as the raw, chaotic grief clawed at my heart. My mind flashed back to the day I'd witnessed my first hanging, and the injustice of it—of this—speared me like the blade of a bayonet.

The men were using long sticks to push Maman's head under the water while others, holding the ropes, dragged her to the surface. They continued, up down, up down.

'Maman, Maman!' I shouted, on and on, until my voice cracked into a hoarse whisper and, finally, no more words came.

Léon released his grip and I sank to the muddy riverbank in a limp curl, my fingers still gripping Maman's angel pendant—my angel now.

Through my tears, I saw Père Joffroy performing Extreme Unction and, amidst a blur of autumn browns, reds and yellows, I lay amongst the leaves that had fallen, thin and brittle, to the ground.

I never saw my mother's head dip below the ivy green water for the last time.

***

We buried Maman with haste, in the cemetery of Saint Antoine's, alongside Félicité, Félix and Papa.

Both of us wrapped up in our own grief, Grégoire and I could barely speak, or comfort each other. I did not sleep that first night, and I refused the wheat bread, the gruel of grains and the dried peas Léon Bruyère and his mother offered us. Never could I have imagined a loneliness so utter, so complete.

The following day, the clog-maker's wife—Françoise's mother—came with more soup.

'Your parents are gone, Victoire,' she said. 'Grégoire promised your mother he would care for you, but he is only eighteen, earning but a pittance from working the wood.'

'We'll manage somehow,' I said.

'But you have no dowry,' she went on. 'You understand you cannot marry Léon Bruyère? If you stay here in Lucie, you'll never have any means of getting a husband to set up your own household. You're sixteen, you must go to the city—to Lyon or Paris—and find work in the domestic services.'

I did not answer her, and kept my eyes on the earthen floor, clasping the bone carving between my thumb and forefinger, desperate for the courage my mother said the little angel would give me.

When Françoise's mother left, I shuffled outside into the autumn dusk, climbed the church steps, and looked out across the valley.

The view over Lucie and back to the Monts du Lyonnais had always comforted me but I felt only emptiness, trapped as I was in this place of no light, no happiness, no hope and no love. Especially not the love of Léon Bruyère who, it seemed, was lost to me forever.

I understood that everything was different now. A snap of time had reshaped me, and nothing could ever be as it was before.

I shivered in my thready clothes and looked up at the moon. In its pale light, I glimpsed a tawny owl on a branch, starting his night hunt. He glided down in silence, dropping onto the bird, frog or insect, and extended his wings over the luckless victim.

***

A week later, Grégoire opened the door to Père Joffroy—to the church room in which, of course, I'd had no choice but to remain.

'I've been meaning to speak with you, Victoire, since your mother's death.'

'The death you might have stopped?' I said my voice tight. 'The death that, had we been rich or noble or *anything* besides poor peasants, might not have happened?'

The priest shook his head. 'I am so sorry for your loss, Victoire, but I am only a lowly parish priest, with no influence on those types of decisions. I know the accusations against your mother were untrue. She was a healer-woman and a midwi—'

'My mother was no witch, Father.'

'I also believe,' he went on, 'it was simply some temporary madness; an unfortunate melancholy of the blood, which turned her back on the Church and God. She never deserved to die for that, and you, Victoire, must guard against this same type of affliction. I have heard a mother can pass it to a daughter.'

He ran his tongue over his lips. 'My brother is a priest in one of the parishes of Paris,' he went on. 'He tells me of a noble family in the suburb of Saint-Germain whose scullery maid is dead of the dropsy.' He thrust a sealed letter at me. 'I have written you a recommendation letter, Victoire. The family is expecting you.'

Stunned, I stared up at the priest. 'I'm to go to a noble family? After what a noble did to my father? Besides, I don't know a single person in Paris, and I am sure it is such a big city I would only get lost.' I breathed fast, grappling for more excuses. 'Maman told me they don't even speak as we do in Lucie.'

'Your mother taught you well,' Père Joffroy said. 'And gave you the taste for learning. You will accustom yourself to the French language of Paris, and the ways of the city. Besides, you must not generalise about the aristocracy, they are not all like that baron.'

I glanced at my brother. 'Grégoire is all I have left, and I am all that he has. How can I leave him?'

'Go, Victoire,' Grégoire said. 'You've always dreamed of rising above our peasant roots; of seeing the world beyond the gates of Lucie, *n'est-ce pas?* Go, little sister, and take this chance.'

Paris
1778–1779

8

Accustomed as I was to the smell of unwashed humans—mouths of rotting teeth, clothes stained with grease and sweat, the cheesy odour of the sick and dying—nothing in Lucie had prepared me for the stink of Paris.

Stiff from a week of bumps and jolts in the cramped public carriage and the squalor of roadside inns with their hard bread and bland gruel, I finally stepped out onto the streets of the capital on a thickly-misted November dawn of 1778.

Against the din of church bells chiming for morning Mass, roosters crowing and dogs barking their replies, I skirted a line of women waiting for a bakery to open: servants, working women, the wives of labourers, I supposed. Mingled with the delicious aroma of fresh bread in the bakers' ovens, the scent of hot coffee from the carts of roadside vendors flared my nostrils.

Through mist rising from the cobbles, which swallowed ground-floor windows and shrouded shop signs, I had little idea where I was going. Clutching Père Joffroy's letter, I tramped up and down streets with no names, the ache in my feet deepening as I searched for the noble house.

'M'sieur, m'sieur, *excusez-moi*,' I said, stopping a passing man. 'Please, in what direction is the district of Saint-Germain?'

'Saint-Germain, eh?' the man said, baring dung-coloured teeth, his eyes hovering over my breasts. 'What would a nice girl like you be wanting with those *sang bleus*?' He raised his eyebrows. 'Ah ha, domestic service I bet?'

'Please, m'sieur, which way?'

He pointed vaguely, bending so close to me I thought his nose would touch my face. 'You be careful, young thing, those aristocrats think they can do what they like with us commoners.'

As I hastened through the fog, I realised the noise of the capital was even more shocking than the smell. I was used to Lucie's church bell tolling when it was time to rise, at noon for the hour of break, and in the evening for vespers, but here, church bells from what sounded like a hundred different belfries, deafened me.

As dawn gave way to day, the streets filled with more people, who looked like labourers, on their way to the workshops. I snatched whiffs of stale beer, roasting meat, and cheese from the *fromageries*.

I found myself in a narrow street that went nowhere. I retraced my steps, gagging on the stench of piss and shit, rotting vegetables and animal fat, and holding my skirt up as I stepped over the slaughterhouse blood streaming into the sewers. I stumbled into a blind alleyway and reeled from the odour of congealed tannery blood and damp featherbeds.

I shrank from a man defecating in a courtyard, and recoiled from ragged beggars squatting in roadside filth, pawing at my skirt and pleading with their mad city eyes.

It came lighter. I crossed a bridge, the river below teeming with barges and so wide it made the Vionne look like a stream. The Seine River, I imagined. Ships smelling of coal, hay and damp ropes lined the gravelled riverbank, and, from the grisly spectacle unfolding before my eyes, I assumed I'd reached la place de Grève.

Spectators were throwing mouldy vegetables at a poor wretch attached to a cartwheel on the square. A group of children played with balls and spinning tops, while others waved sticks about.

To the crowd's gleeful shouts, the executioner raised his iron club and brought it down onto the victim's limbs, stretched along the spokes of the revolving wheel. I flinched as bones cracked, one after the other, his screams carrying far across the Seine.

Over and over, the executioner bludgeoned until finally he dealt the fatal *coup de grâce* to the man's chest, for which I was certain the victim was grateful. I gasped as blood spurted from his mouth and his head fell, limp, sideways.

The executioner braided the man's shattered limbs through the wheel spokes and hoisted it up a tall pole. As the birds swooped to peck at the remains, I clenched my eyes shut but I still saw the bloodied face, the mouth open in a soundless scream. The horror—the fury—of my parents' senseless deaths tore through me again.

I hurried away from the gruesome square, and came upon a vast market place. The stench of decaying fruit, vegetables and meat flared my nostrils, along with the odour of the excrement of hundreds of horses and mules. The vulgar cries of the fishwives—the *poissardes* who seemed loathe to part with the smallest scale or fin before it began to stink—filled my ears. Grains of all kinds overflowed from sacks and the pink carcasses of skinned hogs, speckled with black flies, hung from hooks. Never could I have imagined such an expanse of produce and wares in one place, not even at the village fairs.

The smell only worsened as I trudged on, not the stink of rotting food, but a powerful stench rising from a shocking expanse of tombs and charnel houses.

'Careful, lovely, you don't want to end up in there.' I spun around to a toothless man, his gaze travelling across my face and down to my breasts. 'The Innocents Cemetery. They've been stacking the dead here, bone upon bone, for eight hundred years.'

I quickened my steps, anxious to be away from both the man and the cemetery. Above the street noise, I didn't hear the thundering coach until it was almost upon me, the velvet-nosed horses so close I could see the sweat glistening on their flared nostrils. I flattened myself against the sooty wall of the narrow street and held my breath as the coach screamed past me.

The liveried footman hanging from the back waved his arms. 'Out of our way, whore!'

On impulse, I picked up a stone and hurled it at the footman. 'I hope you fall off the back of your murderous coach!' I screeched, but of course, he didn't hear me, and my stone dropped well short of the disappearing vehicle.

I took deep breaths and looked about me. The street was seething with women opening their garments for passing men, who snagged them against the wall and groaned and thrust into them. Nobody seemed to have noticed my outburst, or paid me the slightest attention.

Where were the grazing cattle, the clucking hens, the perfume of spring flowers and new grass; the soft sigh of trees swaying in the breeze sweeping off the Monts du Lyonnais? I had been in Paris only a few hours, but already I missed the kiss of country rain on my face, the warmth of fresh sun on my cheeks, the silence of snow in the woods. I wanted to fall in a heap and cry.

But I knew homesickness was a luxury I could ill-afford; this awful place that killed the poor and was trampled upon by the rich was now my home—the home in which I would tear out the roots of my peasant poverty.

Père Joffroy's words came back to me.

The suburb of Saint-Germain is on the left bank.

I realised this was the right bank, and I had crossed the Seine needlessly. I cleared my throat, held my head high and pushed on, recrossing the river on the first bridge I reached.

I soon began to glimpse neat gardens and handsome coaches, through elegant wrought-iron gates. Over high walls came whiffs of coach leather, the powder of pages' wigs and the scent of hedges, freshly trimmed for the coming winter. Faint with fatigue, thirst and hunger, I felt relieved to have found the district of Saint-Germain.

***

Columns boasting the sculpted faces of wild animals decorated the front of the house. In the courtyard, I glimpsed two sleek horses hitched to a crimson-lacquered carriage bearing a black and red coat of arms with a wolf crest.

A maid opened the door and as she closed it behind us, the crystal beads of a chandelier jingled with the light sound of small bells. She led me up a wide staircase into a parlour, where a straight-backed woman in a pink gown sat in a tapestry chair.

'Mademoiselle Victoire Charpentier, your Ladyship,' the maid announced with a curtsey.

Never had I seen a room like it; never could I have imagined people living in such luxury. Paintings of richly dressed aristocrats—ancestors I imagined—hung from the walls and the faint smell of coffee, powder, and some cloying perfume hung in the air. Gold-embroidered drapes of silk framed two tall windows. Patterned paper the colour of green apples hung on the walls. A marble fireplace bearing the same wolf crest as the carriage occupied the centre of one wall. Bookcases covered most of the other walls.

I swallowed hard and curtseyed, bowing my head as Père Joffroy had instructed me. 'Your Ladyship.'

'You are hired on a yearly basis with lodgings and board,' the Marquise said. 'You will receive twenty-five livres per year, one pair of clogs and two ells of cloth.' Her eyes roved across my crumpled peasant rags. 'And you shall wear my cast-off clothes, which are at the disposal of all servants. That way at least, the Marquis and I are certain our domestics maintain an acceptable appearance.' The hint of a smile curved the corners of her painted lips.

'You are granted one half-day off per week,' she continued, 'and providing your work is completed, you may have an hour at your leisure each afternoon.' All the time she spoke, her head never moved, nor did the layers of ringlets jutting from each side of her head.

A man in yellow satin breeches and a heavily embroidered

white vest appeared, a sword dangling from his side.

'Ah, my husband,' the Marquise said. 'Alphonse Donatien Delacroix, Marquis de Barberon.'

The Marquis de Barberon's powdered wig was brushed back and tied with a black silk ribbon, revealing a small scar on his left temple. His hooked nose, high brow and grey eyes reminded me of a regal raptor.

'Welcome, mademoiselle, I hope our humble abode is to your satisfaction.'

He took a pinch of snuff from an engraved box and his smile showed a complete set of white teeth. Nobody I knew had all their teeth, especially such white ones.

'Your Lordship.' I curtseyed, my head bowed.

The Marquis drew so close to me, I almost jumped backwards.

'Don't be afraid, my dear,' he said, taking my angel pendant, the signet ring on his left little finger glinting in the chandelier light as he turned it over.

'What a strange, but delightful thing,' he said.

'It was my mother's, monsieur.'

The Marquis smiled and let the pendant go, patting it against my skin.

Of course, I'd heard the stories of rascal lords who treated their servants worse than dogs, but this marquis seemed friendly and charming. Besides, I had promised Père Joffroy I would not judge every noble like the baron who killed my father.

As the maid reappeared and led me from the parlour, I already felt much better about my new life in Paris.

***

In the centre of the kitchen stood a solid wooden table. Pots and pans hung above it, and a rack of knives and several cabinets for other utensils and tableware lined the walls.

'This is Cook,' a young girl said. 'And I am Marie, the kitchen maid.'

Cook held a plucked chicken by the fire, burning the remaining feathers off. She looked quite old—forty perhaps— with silvered hair and a wide, wrinkled face. A fat orange cat crouched on the floor beside her.

'*Bonjour,* madame.' I nodded to the woman and bent to stroke the cat. 'What's his name?'

'Roux. Best mouser in all of Paris,' Cook said. 'Not a single live mouse has been seen here since the Marquise ordered the carpenter to put in swinging panels for *mon petit* Roux.'

As I petted him I realised Roux—true to his reputation—was toying with a limp mouse.

'You are poorly paid and not of high rank,' Cook said, cutting the chicken open and removing its giblets. 'But watch and learn from me and you may make something of your wretched life.'

I nodded, meeting her black eyes that I sensed hid a wealth of wisdom.

Roux bit hard into his prey, breaking the mouse's neck in a sharp snap, and as Marie took me through to the scullery, the cat stalked from the room, the rodent dangling from its jaws.

9

I rose from my attic bed at five-thirty, as every morning. I slipped out into the December gloom to empty the chamber pots, my breath forming icy jets of fog, which vanished quickly.

The edges of the wind snapped at my face as the hooves of mules pulling produce-laden carts towards the market squares clattered on cobbles stained with churns of snow, dung and soot.

I smiled at the boy I saw most mornings, a water-carrier hurrying up from the river, leaning into the weight of his brimming buckets. He gave me a nod.

Two sous a load, he earned. How was anyone to cast off the shackles of poverty on such a miserable wage? I was barely better off.

My fingers numb, the piss quivered as I emptied the pots, and scurried back inside to light the fires and fix breakfast—coffee, chocolate, jam, cream or gruyere cheese, sausages, bacon, biscuits and pastries—whatever their noble appetites craved that particular day.

Later in the morning, Marie and I took vegetables from the sand bins in Cook's cellar, which also housed her jams and liqueurs, and where hams hung in the dark corners.

'Have you heard, Victoire? Finally, a royal baby,' Marie said, as we cleaned and chopped vegetables, plucked fowl, and gutted fish—our usual morning work to prepare the main meal of the day. 'Eight years it took them. What a scandal. They say Louis couldn't get it up. *Un mauvais fouteur*! Can you imagine, the King of France a hopeless fuck?' Marie shrieked so loudly that Cook scuttled in to see what the hilarity was about.

'Perhaps it is not the King's fault,' I said, recalling Maman's tales of barren ladies. 'Maybe the Queen can't have children, like the Marquise?'

'Ah, the reason the Marquise has no children,' Marie said with a snigger, 'is because she refuses her husband.'

'Refuses her husband? Surely that's not allowed?'

'Maybe not,' Marie said, 'but the Marquise refuses her husband because she is a *tribade*.'

I frowned. '*Tribade*?'

Marie's tongue curled about her teeth. 'A woman who loves the sex of another woman.'

'Oh … oh!' I shivered with gooseflesh, finally understanding.

'But the Marquis doesn't care a bit,' Marie went on. 'There are hundreds of places for the pleasure of a noble man—mistresses, bordellos …'

Marie flicked her gaze from me as we sat down to eat at the kitchen table, and to keep an eye on the family's simmering meal of roast beef with chestnuts.

Cook dined with the other servants in the communal dining hall, while the Marquis de Barberon and his wife took their meal, as always, in the oak-panelled dining parlour, except when the Marquis dined out.

They sat at the fireplace end of the long table lit by two candles, the Marquis reciting *le Bénédicté* before they ate.

'Such a grand table for only two people,' I said to Marie, waving a hand in the direction of the dining hall. 'They dine like the King and Queen.'

'Oh, you think *that's* extravagant,' Marie said. 'Well let me tell you, it is *nothing* compared with the meals of the King and Queen. Don't you know anything about Versailles, Victoire?'

'All I know of Versailles is the stories my father would bring home from his travels, or what passing journeymen told us.'

'Well,' Marie said, her eyes glittering, 'their tablecloth is of damask, their crockery silver, with gilded cutlery, and the meal—five courses—begins when the *maître d'hôtel* enters the room holding a long staff crowned with a *fleur-de-lys*.'

'*Five* courses?' I could not imagine such extravagance. 'How can they eat so much?'

'They don't,' Marie said. 'Well, not the Queen. She eats only a sparrow's portion but the King, well he gobbles the lot. I'll have you know, one morning before going to his stables he ate four cutlets, a whole chicken, a plateful of ham, half a dozen eggs and drank a bottle of champagne. You'd think all his reckless galloping through forests, hunting stag and boar, might keep the King trim, but no, he eats like the worst pig and is getting fatter and fatter!'

'*Oh là là*,' I said. 'What gluttony. When thousands across the country are starving.'

'Don't be silly, Victoire, he's the King! But you know what I would really love,' Marie went on, a dreamy look in her eyes, 'is to wear one of the Queen's dresses. Just for a day.' She smiled ruefully. 'You know she buys a hundred and fifty different ones every year, from the great Rose Bertin's boutique.'

I shrugged. 'However can one person wear a hundred and fifty different gowns? Besides, court dress must be like a walking gaol, with those hoops and trains and stiff brocades. They even have to walk sideways, to get the panniers through doorways.'

'Oh I wouldn't mind, I really wouldn't,' Marie said. 'Give me armoured trimmings any day, over these shapeless aprons and unflattering caps.'

Once the family meal was over and we'd washed dishes, scrubbed work benches, scoured stoves, sinks and pots, and swilled the floors, I was relieved to have my free hour. Marie flitted off to flirt with one of the coach boys and I traipsed into Cook's small room, off the kitchen.

Cook sat, darning, on one of the two chairs at her small

wooden table, the only furniture besides a narrow bed, which occupied the rest of the room. Roux was crouched on the wide sill of a tiny window, his head cocked at birds swooping by.

'Who taught you the kitchen skills, Cook?' I said, as she got up and poured tea for us.

'I've told you, my child, call me Claudine. My father taught me. He worked at a grand hotel. I took his place when he died.'

'You have no other family?'

Claudine shook her head and went back to her sewing. 'Our only child was dead in my womb.'

'How sad. I'm sorry for you.'

She shrugged. 'It happens.'

I blew on my tea. 'And what of your husband?'

'Dead.' Claudine's eyes didn't waver from her needle, jabbing in and out of the fabric. 'A good man he was—a hard-working carter. A duke's coach rammed his flimsy two-wheeled cart and killed him outright.'

'Just as my father! How can they get away with such things?'

'Nobles do as they want, my child. They don't care for us commoners.' She pulled her yarn taut, twisted it into a knot and bit off the thread. 'Not that I can complain. I have food and shelter here, Roux to keep me company, and the Marquis never comes to the kitchen to bother me.'

'Yes, the Marquis seems a pleasant man. What is the scar on his temple?'

'Oh, some silly duel. Over a woman, most likely. What else? Women are all he thinks of. Now, my child,' she said, eyeing the clock. 'It is time we thought about supper.'

***

After supper, at nine o'clock, all the servants gathered in the dining hall and knelt, along with the Marquis and his wife, for prayer time.

Careful not to lapse back onto my heels, which was forbidden whilst praying, I stole a glance at the painting that always entranced me—a nymph-like creature splayed in forest verdure. Vine leaves draped across her pale, curvy body, and clusters of grapes swathed her pubic mound like forbidden fruit.

The Marquis caught my stare, the white teeth flashing in an engaging smile. I blushed, and lowered my eyes.

At last, two hours short of midnight, the Marquis stood, signalling everybody to rise. I trudged up to my attic room— little more than a closet with a table, chair and chest of drawers— and dropped onto the straw mattress.

I was drifting in that cottony place just before sleep when the sound of soft footfall on the stairs startled me. My eyes flew open. The footsteps stopped. A powdery smell flared my nostrils, and the Marquis de Barberon towered over me.

He did not look at me, but somewhere beyond, at the splice of moonlight snaking through the dormer window. I started shaking beneath my coarse blanket, prickling with a sense of danger. The Marquis still did not meet my eyes as he tore the blanket from my grip and threw it on the floor.

Still he said nothing as his finger traced the curves of my face, my neck, and across my shoulder. I gasped as he clutched my breast and squeezed hard.

'Wha-what …?'

The cotton of my chemise sheared apart in his hands. The scar on his temple blanching white against red, his wine-stained lips stretched in a leer, the Marquis jerked my legs apart with his knee. The breath caught in my chest and Maman's words batted about inside my head.

Be careful not to let a man have his way with you … his way with you.

'No, no! Please, no!'

He locked a clammy paw over my mouth and without the least forewarning, speared into me with a single thrust, which rippled from my thighs up to my face.

'No, stop, you're hurting me!'

He tightened his hold over my mouth and I took frantic, short breaths through my nose.

I closed my eyes and tried to tear myself from his clutches as he hammered my flesh—a solid, unrelenting pounding that seemed to reach right to my womb with every stroke.

My body tightened into a single, rigid spasm as he battered me, my thighs aching more with each fresh stab. His breath came, hot and fast on my cheeks, and rancid as sour milk.

One hand scrabbled about, trying to reach my angel pendant, but my fingers wouldn't work properly, my skin slippery with droplets of his sweat and drools of his saliva.

The Marquis held his breath. He gripped my hair and forced my head back to open my eyes and meet his, glowering with furious triumph. The signet ring with its wolf-crest engraving winked at me in the slant of light. He gave a single grunt and slumped, sweat-drenched, on top of me.

When his breathing slowed and I no longer felt his heartbeat racing against mine, he pushed himself off me, took my blanket and wiped a sticky sheen from his dark fuzz.

He left the attic room without uttering a single word. I was too shocked, too numb and hurt to move, as if he had flipped my body inside out and emptied me onto the floor.

As my quivering hand finally drew the blanket over me, I knew Père Joffroy had been wrong—every noble was a monster, as hateful and arrogant as the baron who had killed my father. I pledged to myself the Marquis would pay for this; they would all pay.

10

It was a clear spring day, the streets dry but the traffic congested, as always. These weekly half-days off kept me sane. As I escaped the stifling blue-blood house, I forgot, for a few blissful hours, the limp creature that waited for soft footfall on the stairs with the fatality of defenceless prey.

I strolled along the rue du Bac towards the river, eyeing fashionable ladies bent under the weight of elaborate head-dresses. Some of the decorations soared over a metre high, and were fortressed with wire, cloth, horsehair and the flour so many peasants needed just to survive. All of Paris was copying the Queen's hairstyles but I did not envy them, especially the ones who rode along with their head sticking out the carriage window like a dog. I laughed at those ladies.

Instead of crossing the river on the Pont Royal, I continued along the left bank until I reached the Pont Neuf—a more lively bridge where swindlers, beggars, thieves, magic healers and entertainers gathered.

A dentist mountebank stood high on a dais, accompanied by a drummer and a trumpet player. Teeth and jawbones embossed the dentist's gold-trimmed, purple gown. A live cockerel was perched atop his silver hat, and his magnificent horse boasted a necklace of teeth.

The patients' knuckles white as they gripped the chair legs, the dentist's assistants extracted their rotten teeth with great long tongs. I hurried along, thankful I had no dental ailment, for now.

'Messieur Dames, make your eye-glasses for you?' a man called.

'Wooden legs to fit all ex-soldiers,' another cried.

'Buy my magic luminescent herb,' a pedlar said. 'Never again shall you be fooled.'

'Ma'moiselle, ma'moiselle!' a man sang out to me. 'A powdered gem to beautify your lovely face even more?' he said. 'To stop the wrinkles and give you long life?'

I smiled and shook my head. I had no sous for such a thing. The small indulgence I allowed myself, I saved for the place where booksellers laid out their books and the public letter-writers had their booths.

As I rifled through the books, the trader handed me one from the bottom of a pile.

'I recommend this, ma'moiselle,' he said.

I read the title: '*L'Ingénu*. What does it speak of?'

'It tells the story of an Indian who comes to our sophisticated capital,' the man said, his eyes wide with enthusiasm, as always when he told me about a book. 'The author, the enlightened Voltaire, pokes fun at our religion, our justice system, our corruption.'

'Oh, right,' I said. 'Yes, that does sound interesting.'

It would be difficult to understand the words of this Voltaire, but I knew I must persist if I was, one day, to escape the humiliation of the diabolical Marquis in whose home I was a prisoner as sure as if he shackled me to my attic bed.

'A most valuable work,' the man went on, 'because, *naturellement*, the police have censored it, and for you, lovely ma'moiselle, I'll make a special price.'

'I will buy your book, monsieur,' I said handing him the coins.

My illegal purchase concealed beneath my cloak, I stood on the bridge span, gazing up the river at heavily-laden ships, rowboats and fishermen's punts ploughing the dirty brown water. Barges emerged from under the next bridge ahead, the Pont-au-Change. A flower market burst with colour, floral perfumes mingling with the smell of the great sewers flowing into the river.

A barefoot beggar woman holding a filthy child held out a palm. I shook my head. The child was probably not even hers. Claudine had told me begging was a well-known profession, where people borrowed diseased and deformed children, and manufactured realistic sores from egg yolk and dried blood, working the yolk into a scratch to produce a crusty effect. They made fake humpbacks and clubbed feet, and blacked out eyes to give dramatic impressions of blindness. Beggars were also masters at mimicking epilepsy.

Once on the opposite side of the river, I avoided what must be the most horrible district of Paris—that great stinking central market, and the slaughterhouses, from where rivers of curdling blood and discarded innards flowed into the sewers. Instead, I strolled down the rue Saint-Honoré, gazing into luxury furniture and clothes shops.

I weaved back towards Saint-Germain, through the street vendors selling tobacco, matches, ribbons and paste jewellery, and men waving pamphlets from café doorways—pamphlets printed on illegal presses. My gaze strayed to their portrayals of the Queen in unnatural positions with the King's brother, and others depicting Marie Antoinette in sexual acts with her friends, the Princesse de Lamballe and the Duchesse de Polignac, along with the caption:

These two ladies help the Queen widen la porte de Cythère so that her husband's jeanchouart, always soft and bent, can more easily enter it.

I crossed the river, pausing again on the bridge as the dying sun angled itself above the water, the sunset tapering across the slate roofs. How different the city light was to that of Lucie. Perhaps it had to do with so many buildings, but at times the light was so bright I felt it burned the flesh right from my bones.

The boats had disappeared, brief gusts sawing jagged notches across the river's surface so that the Seine glittered like a scattering of thousands of louis d'or. I imagined all those golden coins were mine—riches to flee the noble home of Saint-Germain, return to Lucie and, perhaps, become Madame Léon Bruyère.

I gripped the book close to my chest, casting my despair, my helplessness, aside, and dreamed of the day I would punish the Marquis de Barberon. I was not yet certain how, but the brute would not escape chastisement.

***

Claudine stood at the stove stirring a pot of lamb ragout. Its rich, garlicky aroma sailed up my nostrils as I rubbed my hands before the fire crackling in the hearth. The copper kettles glimmered orange in the firelight and Roux, curled in a chair also gleamed orange.

I set my book on the table. 'Look what I bought.'

'Ah, Voltaire,' Claudine said. 'Didn't the police censor that?'

'So it must be interesting, *n'est-ce pas*?' I said with a knowing smile.

Claudine shook her head. 'You young people … your new ideas.'

'I must improve the literacy skills my mother taught me, Claudine. I will not be a servant all my life.'

'Your maman sounds like a wise woman. My father too, taught me a few letters.'

'Well you must practise with me then.' I opened the book at a random page.

'*L'Ingénu, plongé dans une sombre et profonde mélancolie, se promena vers le bord de la mer…*'

Claudine bent over my shoulder, reading with me.

'*… et souvent tenté de tirer sur lui-même.*'

'So, does he kill himself, this *ingénu*?' Claudine said.

'How would I know? I haven't got to that part yet. Besides, I need to copy out the difficult words, to learn them.'

'*... maudissait ... ravager ... compatriotes...* '

'Such beautiful handwriting you have, my child,' she said. 'You might one day be a writer yourself.'

'What a dream,' I said, flexing my fingers, cramped from gripping the quill. 'You know, I think it is easier to write what a person feels, than to tell it to someone.'

I set the paper aside. 'Tell me more about Versailles, Claudine. If I am ever to get anywhere in life, I must know what is happening with our rulers ... I need to understand how it all works.'

'Well,' she began, blotting sweat beads from her brow, 'a great man named Turgot became the Controller General four years ago.'

She left the lamb to stew and began melting sugar and cream to make her delicious caramel. 'He told them all at Versailles to stop spending, and refused to grant favours to the Queen's cronies. Marie Antoinette had even bought a cabriolet and drove it herself, very fast!' Claudine giggled, a chubby hand covering her mouth. 'Of course the court was shocked and the Austrian woman became his enemy.'

I smiled; it was like listening to Papa's stories again.

'Two years ago,' Claudine went on, 'Turgot got rid of the *corvée*. You know the *corvée*, my child?'

'Oh yes, when they drag peasants from the fields and force them to build bridges and roads ... free labour for the crown.'

'Well nobody liked that decision,' she said, 'except, naturally, the voiceless peasants. So our weak King sacked Turgot.'

'Why is the King weak?'

'He is a jolly, but childish man,' she said. 'He behaves not like a king, but like some peasant shambling along behind his plough. Even his wife teases him, calling him "poor man". He can't hear, can barely see and spends his time playing silly jokes like tripping up pages with his *cordon bleu*, pulling faces and scampering around with his breeches dangling around his ankles. All he ever thinks about is his next meal.'

Claudine slid a bowl of eggs towards me. 'You wanted to learn how to make meringues,' she said. 'Well, start by separating the eggs.

'They do say he's good with his hands though,' she went on, as I separated the whites from the yolks. 'Beating out bronze and copper, carving wood, making locks. The man should have been an artisan, but never a king.' She nodded at the egg whites. 'Keep beating, yes, like that. Don't stop.'

She shuffled back to the stove. 'And I have heard, Victoire, the word "Revolution" is simmering on the lips of every Parisian.'

11

My dearest Rubie,

    You may wonder about your mother for a long time. I have penned this letter for the day you will finally dare to ask about me. Had I not been blessed with a wise mother, I may have remained illiterate my entire life, and you would have only been able to guess about me. On this day of your birth—the feast of Michaelmas—it is as if I mastered those skills for the sole reason of telling you the truth. Because I want you to know, my child, that I had no choice.

You must have been conceived soon after I came to this noble house in Saint-Germain, as I first felt you move—a quivering butterfly—in the spring. Though I had suspected before, that you were there, my private warmth through the coldest part of winter; a dear little friend to help me endure my bleak existence.

You remained small right to the end—a tiny bump secreted beneath the mistress's cast-off clothes. No shameful, swollen womb to brand me as a sinner against modesty and have the Marquise cast me out into the filthy streets. I thank you for that.

You came tonight, in the dark, by the sallow taper light. Claudine—that's Cook, my friend—squeezed my hand and pushed the rag into my mouth. She told me to bite down, to hush my cries.

She held a beaker to my lips and told me to drink; said it was her own brandy, made especially for the Marquis.

I drank her brandy, which helped the pain, a little.

I gnawed on Claudine's rag and rocked, wanting to scream as the waves rushed faster and faster, rising to stabbing peaks. I never yearned to cry with the pain, though. No, that was bearable; I wanted to yell at you to stop, to stay where you were because once the agony was over, I knew you would be gone from me.

In the hollows between the pains, Claudine mewed softly, close to my ear, telling me I was doing well; you would soon be here.

I wallowed in those blissful moments of peace when I could imagine it might all be different and I would be able to hold and suckle you; to watch you grow.

Then, with that final, uncontrollable urge to bear down, when the sweat soaked me and I thought I'd burst, you slid from my warmth into the cold night.

Claudine cut the cord with her kitchen scissors, severing, forever, our ties. She wrapped you, still mottled from the womb, in my sweat-damp scullery rags and lay you in a wicker basket, as one might a litter of kittens.

She urged me to go, to hurry off right then, before it became light. She said Marie would cover for me until I returned.

Yes, yes, I told her, I would go, but first I had to write your letter; to tell you your name is Rubie, because you will always be my precious, elegant and hardy gem. On this feast day of the archangel Michael, of 1779, I pray that most angelic warrior will protect you through the dark of night and grant you luck, health and wisdom.

Claudine is pressing me now, to leave. So I shall fold this paper, Rubie, and slip it behind your sleeping cocoon.

I unclasp the pendant too, from around my neck—the little bone angel my own mother pressed into my palm. I slide it in the basket, beside you. It is yours now, Rubie, to give you strength as you begin your journey through life, alone. One day you will hand it down to your own daughter, when she needs it.

As I told you, with the Marquis's threats to throw us both out on the streets, I have no choice but to hurry through the dawn, carrying your basket across the cobblestones shiny with dew. Once

I have laid your basket on the church steps, I will wrest my eyes from your wizened gaze—fewer memories to torture me through the void.

But don't fret, I will not abandon you on those church steps. No, I'll retreat to the shadows and wait and watch for Matron to arrive from her foundling hospital. I will stay until I am sure she has found you, and knows to call you Rubie when she carries you to the wet nurses, who'll come morning and evening to feed you their rich milk.

I think of those wet nurses gathering in a corner with their rows of foundlings, bartering their milk for sous and swapping news. When it is my Rubie's turn at the breast, you'll drink in their stories—perhaps the one of your mother, a child scullery maid of seventeen, and your father, a distinguished marquis from the rue du Bac, who bears a duel scar on his left temple.

Your needs are only primitive now and you'll not understand the wet-nurses' tales, but one day you'll want to know. I hope Matron will find this letter and, when you are old enough, she'll tell you your story.

As I leave you, my sleeping jewel, I know my heart will be torn from my breast, the place in my belly where you'd been, burning with my unquenched desire for you.

As I unfurl my fingers from your basket, I will leave behind a part of me. Perhaps that is what Père Joffroy calls the soul?

I hope, as they feed, clothe and educate you, then give you back to the community as a marriageable girl with a modest dowry, you will understand and forgive a mother who, besides love, could afford you only misery and poverty.

I am your ever-loving mother.
V.C.

***

Matron arrived with her orphans. In puffs of thin white fog, she barked out orders at the two orderly columns of children, graded from smallest to tallest.

From the dawn shadows, I watched her herding the children into church for the Michaelmas sermon, though my eyes did not stray far from the basket.

One of Rubie's tiny fists freed itself from the wrapping, and flailed about in the cold air, as if she was beckoning me to go back for her. She began to cry, the feeble mewling carving great gashes through my heart, and I cried too—silent tears of agony.

A cart arrived in the square, bringing vegetables for the Michaelmas feast, the clatter of wheels and the horse's whinny startling me.

No, I couldn't do it! I could not leave my Rubie. I hesitated, the breath catching in my throat.

I must get back to the house; they would be rising, washing. I had to boil water, light fires and prepare the goose for today's banquet.

An orphan girl pointed to the basket. Matron scurried over. I lurched forward. Too late. Matron grasped the basket and, as she carried it off, my tears fell, unheard, onto the hard cobblestones.

***

Rubie gone from me, I could not bear the Saint-Germain house any longer. Of course, I had no choice but to remain, so I tried to forget my grief; to bury my melancholy in reading the Voltaire book, and in writing letters—skills I was convinced would, somehow, help me flee this noble prison.

I wrote to my brother. I knew someone would have to read the letters to Grégoire, and that my brother would not reply. Rather than pursuing our mother's literacy lessons, Grégoire had preferred to master the wood-working skills.

Despite my bitter memories of Lucie-sur-Vionne, I felt the tug of those familiar childhood things; of a time I was blissfully unaware I was only a poor peasant girl.

I wrote to Père Joffroy too. I did not tell him about Rubie, no, I avoided this grim event and spoke rather of my friends—Claudine and Marie—and about the gossip of the streets of Paris.

The Queen styles her hair in more and more ornate poufs. One I find especially amusing—la pouf à la jardinière—with artichokes, radishes and a head of cabbage piled on her head! I do find it odd that people are so obsessed with hair and clothing when everybody says our country is on the brink of bankruptcy.

Do not worry for me, Père Joffroy. Even as I long for the day I can return to Lucie, I have shelter, clothing and nourishment here in Saint-Germain.

With God's grace,

I am Victoire

As much as my quill itched, I stopped myself writing to Léon. If he'd grown fond of a village girl in my absence, or worse, become engaged, the embarrassment would be too much to bear, but when Père Joffroy's replies arrived, I tore the letters open, scanning his words for any mention of Léon Bruyère.

One afternoon as I sat at the kitchen table reading the priest's words, the Bruyère family did indeed figure.

My dear Victoire,

I hope this letter finds you well and content, for the life of a scullery maid is harsh. I write to tell you of Armand Bruyère. You remember, everyone gathering around his hearth to hear your father's stories? Well, the honest farmer has lost his wife—dead birthing the thirteenth child. The infant too, passed on.

Armand now looks for a new wife to care for him and his remaining children, the three youngest having succumbed to the speckled monster.

Aware that you are only seventeen—still quite too young for a commoner to marry, younger even, than three of Monsieur Bruyère's own children—I have recommended you to the good farmer.

On a happier note, your brother, Grégoire, wishes me to share his joy with you. With the fine carpentry skills your father would be proud of, he has succeeded in building a sturdy cottage. He is much excited at the prospect of seeing you again, and showing off his fine work.

I write with God's grace,

Père Joffroy

I felt the rush of blood to my face. A new cottage. A husband. Escape from the Marquis's attic visits—so much excitement at once.

'I'm going back to Lucie!' I shrieked at Claudine, waving the letter at her. 'I am going home!'

Thoughts of Léon startled me from my rapture at fleeing the Marquis. I inhaled deeply, trying to still my trembling hands; to push away the tug in my breast when I pictured Léon Bruyère.

Claudine's little raisin eyes held mine. 'You're not dreaming, surely, of this boy you speak to me of—your childhood love from Lucie?'

I stared at the tiled floor. 'He is the son of this widower. If I marry Armand I can never be with Léon.'

'Listen to me, Victoire.' She took my chin in her hand. 'You may think love is a wondrous thing but it is only a passing fantasy; nothing compared with the fondness and attachment of a blessed marriage. Besides, the only paltry items of bed linen you own make for such a miserable dowry. True, I could gather a few clothes for you, undergarments, toiletries, but what better could you hope for than to marry a stable, ageing widower? Besides,' she said, 'he would more likely accept you, than a young boy.'

'Accept me? What do you mean?'

'Your husband will realise things, Victoire, on your wedding night. Things you cannot hide from a man.'

I stared at Claudine in dismay. 'Oh ... oh yes, I hadn't thought of that.'

The despair swamped me again, my hopes tarnished.

'But I must get away ... I can bear it no longer, Claudine. You know, I hear the Marquis and his wife talk, saying how they, the authentic ancient nobility, hate the vile bourgeoisie. But I am certain now, those aristocrats are the vile ones, *n'est-ce pas?*'

Claudine clasped my hands between her pudgy ones. 'I understand you must flee the Marquis. So go, my child, but you must tell your future husband about … about everything. If he has a nasty surprise on your wedding night, he'll throw you out of the nuptial bed. We can only pray he is an understanding man.' She smiled and pinched my cheek. 'Now, promise you will write to me?'

Lucie-sur-Vionne
1779–1785

12

I arrived back to Lucie in the winter of 1779. As the public coach approached the snow-peaked Monts du Lyonnais—white bastion guarding the village—my heart beat faster with excitement, and fear, like the rising panic of a hare snagged in a trap.

During the long, cramped journey, the carriage full of people cradling baskets, parcels or dogs, I had convinced myself I would say nothing to my new husband about the sullied scullery maid; I would not mention Rubie. Maybe Monsieur Bruyère would not notice anything on the wedding night.

As I cast my eyes across the Bruyère farm—the familiar vineyards and fields—I thought about seeing Léon again, and the blood pulsed through me, warm and thready.

I forced my gaze down the riverbank slope, to the damp place I'd last seen Maman. They had murdered my mother, and I despised them for that injustice, but I didn't hate those men personally, only the system under which they'd acted. I also knew, from my time in Paris, such things did not only happen in Lucie, but in every village and city across the country.

I walked on, eyeing the tumble of blackened stones and wood, and the fireplace, rising from new foliage like some dark tombstone. Even as I tried to blot out the memories, the searing heat of the flames scalded me again, and I choked on the smoke. I felt my mother's tremble as she pressed my face into her skirt so I wouldn't see the horror, but seeing it anyway, and feeling Maman racked with grief and sobs. I smelt once more the stench I was certain would linger forever at the back of my nostrils—the odour of small, charred skeletons.

I looked hard, past those memories—the remnants of the day that brief, horrifying lapse of Nature had stolen a part of our lives—and I saw Grégoire's new cottage. It was small and simple, yet held my gaze like some great visual banquet and my heart soared with a special gladness.

My brother appeared from behind the cottage, carrying an axe and a lump of wood. He was nineteen, and taller—a younger version of my father.

The smile spread across my face. 'Grégoire!'

He looked up, dropped the wood and the axe and waved his arms, both of us laughing as I ran down the slope and into my brother's arms.

***

At forty-eight, Monsieur Armand Bruyère was elderly, but he still had a healthy smile and a sturdy body. I had known this pleasant, honest farmer since I was a child, but it was different now, and I was afraid of this husband-to-be; terrified he would beat me as I'd heard most husbands did, and force me to do unspeakable things at night. Not to mention the problem of my torn maidenhood.

'I can read and write,' I said. 'And count. I will help you make the wine. I am a good cook and thrifty with money.' The words poured from me in a gibber, so anxious I was to please him.

'Welcome back to Lucie,' Armand said with a smile. He took my quivering hand. 'I hope you will be happy. Come now, my children await you.'

My eyes flickered along the line of them, from the youngest aged nine to the eldest, Léon, who was twenty-three. But Léon was not at the end of the row. Where was he? My breaths quickened.

Léon came then—strong, sun-bronzed and as darkly handsome as I remembered—and stood beside his siblings. He simply nodded, saying nothing, which seemed worse than any words he might have said.

I felt my cheeks flush and averted my eyes, aware Armand was speaking again.

'You too, will have many children, Victoire. Just as my son, Léon. He also, is engaged and will shortly marry.'

Engaged, marry.

Armand's words hung in the air, as frozen as the icicles hanging from the roof of the farm.

It felt like someone had dealt me a blow with a cold axe-head, and I concentrated hard, to keep my face calm and unperturbed.

***

With the shock of his intended marriage, I avoided Léon, fearful my face would betray my heart. I stayed inside Grégoire's cottage, only venturing into the village when necessary.

I threw myself into my own wedding preparations, refusing to dwell on what could have been; on what was lost.

'I did warn you,' Grégoire said, as if he read my thoughts, 'that you could never marry him.' Spoken without a trace of his old scorn and possessiveness, my brother's words still stung, with their ring of truth.

'Don't worry for me, Grégoire. I am fortunate Armand wants me for his wife, and I will devote myself to making him happy.'

'And you'd do well to remember just how fortunate you are,' he said with a curt nod. 'Armand Bruyère is a good man. He gave me the carpentry tools to supplement Papa's meagre supply, and let me stay on his farm while I built the cottage, but you can't fool me, I know you'll never forget Léon Bruyère.'

Anxious to shift the conversation away from Léon Bruyère, I pored over the two ells of cloth and the Marquise's cast-offs

Claudine had bundled into my bag. 'And you, Grégoire, who will you marry? I know you are still too young for marriage but you have a fine home now.' I waved an arm about the clean, whitewashed walls and the simple, but solid furniture with which Grégoire had furnished his home. 'Surely you have your eye on a girl?'

I splayed the fabric out on the table, to fashion myself a black wedding gown. Claudine had advised me a gown of black cloth was sturdy and would see me through funerals, weddings and any other formal event.

'You remember the clog-maker's daughter, Françoise?' he said with a grin. 'Well … perhaps in a few years.'

'Oh yes, of course I remember Françoise, she's a pretty girl, and young,' I said, my voice dropping to a whisper. 'And … pure. She will make you happy.'

***

All nine of the groom's surviving offspring were present in Saint Antoine's Church as Père Joffroy wed Armand and me. As my new husband took me in his arms and kissed me, I vowed he would never discover my impurity.

In Armand's bed that night, I curled on my side, away from him, wrapping my arms around myself to stop the trembling.

I felt his rough fingers brush the nape of my neck. 'Don't be nervous, my dear.'

I reeled from his touch and bolted from the bed, hurtling to the farthest corner of the room, where I crouched, holding my chemise tight over my knees.

'Sorry, I can't. Don't touch me, please.'

Armand strode towards me. My pulse beat faster with his every step. He bent down. I cowered behind my folded arms, sure he was about to strike me. I squeezed my eyes shut, waiting for the blow.

'I know you are my husband,' I said. 'This is your right, but …

please don't beat me.'

'Don't be afraid, Victoire.' He sat on the floor beside me and stroked the hair from my face. 'Père Joffroy's brother, the Parisian priest, told him of this marquis, and of an abandoned child left on the steps of his church. That's why he did everything in his power to bring you home to Lucie.'

I opened my eyes, and lowered my arms. 'You know about the Marquis ... about Rubie?'

'That sort of thing is, sadly, a common occurrence with domestics,' he said. 'If I had the chance I'd rip his sword from its hilt and slit his ugly throat, and I'd cheer as his blue blood stained his fancy parquetry floor!' He crossed himself. 'May God protect the innocent child.'

'I wanted to tell you, Armand. Forgive me, but I feared you would send me ba—'

Armand held a coarse finger to my lips. 'Hush.' He took my hands and led me back to the marital bed.

Once I was lying down and no longer shaking, he turned and took his knife from the bedside dresser. I slithered away again, to the edge of the mattress. Had I mistaken his understanding, his compassion, for some cruel joke?

Armand held the knife against the hairs of his sun-beaten arm and sliced clean through his skin. He flipped his arm over and smeared the blood across the sheet.

I could not believe my luck in finding such a good man. 'Thank you, Armand. I will devote my life to making you happy.'

'You deserve happiness too, Victoire, after the tragedies you have borne.'

'Isn't it also tragic to lose four children and a wife?'

'*C'est la vie*, my dear. God never meant for our lives to be simple, or easy. We must rejoice with what we have and not waste time sobbing for what is gone.'

He wrapped me in his arms and in that instant I understood what Claudine meant by the affection and comfort of a good marriage.

The next morning we hung the nuptial sheets from the window and the people of Lucie smiled and clapped.

13

'The King should never have sacked Turgot,' the journeyman from the north said. 'This Necker is turning accounting tricks to hide the country's enormous debt.'

Despite our contentment, our easy companionship, Armand and I could not ignore the chatter passing travellers brought to Lucie.

The journeyman went on about the many enemies this new finance minister—Necker—had made at court. 'The Queen being his most formidable,' he said. 'Of course, the King will sack him. That man does everything his foreigner wife commands him.'

'I have been thinking, my dear,' Armand said. 'It seems the finances of our country have declined to a pitiful state, but I have an idea to help our village, at least.' He caressed my arm in long gentle strokes. 'As you know, the nearest fair is six leagues far from Lucie. A fair in our village would benefit us all. I propose we make a request to hold our own fair, which Père Joffroy will send to the King.'

'What a grand idea, Armand. Of course, a fair in Lucie would help us too,' I said, patting my swelling stomach. 'We may be thankful for extra income soon.'

We drew up a letter, Armand dictating as I wrote.

The people of Lucie, the peasants, merchants and artisans, have all kinds of animals, vegetables, cheese and eggs to sell, as well as grain and cloth. As there is no fair close enough to conduct business, we thus request five annual fair days in the village of Lucie-sur-Vionne.

***

The heat hit me like a blast from Claudine's oven as I left the blacksmith's that summer afternoon.

In a bid to remove heat—that humoral excess ascribed to pregnancy—I'd lain on the blacksmith's vibrating anvil as he swung his hammer and sparks flew about. People had advised me this would make the birth of my child less painful.

A hot breeze gusted and the beginnings of dark cloud scudded across from the Massif Central. Something—an untouchable magnetism, or simply the promise of coolness—lured me away from the direction of the farm and down the slope to the Vionne River.

I'd not been back since they drowned Maman, but the clear water, the gushing cascade, beckoned me as if the river had missed me as much as I had longed for it.

I wove through the willow trees lining the riverbank like languid courtesans, and beyond the beggars' hut. I no longer feared the woman as a mad witch, but was simply sorry for her wretchedness—too poor even to dwell in the village with the others.

I sat on a boulder and removed my shoes—the Marquise's cast-offs that cut into my hot, swollen feet.

As the fat grey clouds gathered over the foothills, I felt a prickle, like a cluster of spiders scrambling down my backbone. I jumped and twisted around.

'Are you going to take off all your clothes again, Mademoiselle *aux yeux de la rivière*? I suppose it should be Mrs River Eyes, now?'

'Léon! What are you doing here? Why aren't you with your

new wife?'

'My new wife.' I reeled from the arc of his spittle; from the anger that ploughed his lovely face.

'You should have been my wife. How could you marry my father, then face me again? Why?'

'Don't make it harder than it already is, please.'

'Why did you have to come back to Lucie and torture me with your presence?'

'I had no choice, Léon.'

He took a step forward, standing over me and I felt I would choke on his familiar heavenly scent of horses, hay and sun-baked soil. 'What do you mean, Victoire, no choice?'

I moved aside and stepped into the shallows, and as the sharp coolness of the water jolted each nerve in me, I told Léon about the Marquis, and Rubie. 'You would not have wanted me, a woman with a bastard child. You deserved a fresh young girl of your own.'

Léon edged into the water beside me, and bent his face close to mine, though not a hair of his touched me. 'I wouldn't have cared,' he hissed. 'I loved—love—you!'

'I had no dowry, nothing to offer you, and when your father proposed, I had to accept, and put you out of my mind.'

'Put me out of your mind? How could you?'

'Please try and understand. I must devote myself to your fath—'

'No, Victoire, I will never understand. Surely there must be some way … divorce, I don't know.'

'You know divorce isn't allowed. There is nothing, Léon, *nothing* to be done.'

He clamped his lips over mine, so tightly I could not budge, his warm breath rushing into me, stealing my air. I saw the red sunburst behind my closed eyelids, then the shadow as the clouds covered the sun.

His tongue darted in and out of my mouth, licking, caressing my own, and the heat rushed to the top of my thighs until the place between them burned.

Léon pulled me from the shallows and down onto the sun-bleached riverbank. Blades of dried grass dug into my back and I felt the first smattering of raindrops.

I did not move, and as the clouds opened, emptying their load on my bared legs, Léon eased himself on top of me, gently, so as not to hurt the tiny person inside me—the life I had begun with his father.

Thunder blasted, louder, closer, but I didn't care that we were getting drenched. I knew I should scream at Léon to stop; push him off me and scamper from the storm, back to Armand with my head bowed low.

Raindrops snaked between his lips and mine, as his hand cupped my breast, his fingertips kneading my nipple.

Lightning painted luminous veins in the sky and thunderbolts Nature only utters in her wildest mood cleaved through the valley as I arched myself towards him, his hardness pressing against me.

Léon's fingers fumbled as he tore his breeches off. I felt I would burst if I could not have him, right then.

In a single jerk, I felt Léon's weight lift off me, and I looked up into the glowering face of my brother.

'*Mon Dieu!*' Grégoire stared from Léon to me. He jabbed a fist at the bleak sky. 'Someone up there, besides me, is angry.'

He swung his other fist into Léon's face. 'Get away from my sister! And don't go near her again. You know she'll never be yours.'

My brother turned to me, still lying, half-naked, on the soaked earth. 'And you, get up now before I hit you too. I've a mind to go and tell your husband what you do down at the riverbank with his son.'

Angular sheets of sleet pummelling the trees like tap-dancing horses, I scrambled to my feet, my belly like some guilt-laden weight throwing me off balance. 'I'm s-sorry, Grégoire.'

I felt the tremor in my voice, faltering and tinged with

premonition, and I found my fingers feeling about my neck for the smooth, comforting bone of the angel pendant.

My tears came fast. 'S-so sorry. It w-will never happen again. Please say nothing to Armand.'

Grégoire was no longer looking at me, or listening to my pleas. Sodden and scowling, he faced Léon, as if preparing for a duel on the banks of the Vionne River.

***

The rain fell incessantly for weeks. It destroyed the harvest.

'Nature's punishment, *n'est-ce pas*, Victoire?' Grégoire said one day, casting a grim look at the storm pelting the fields and flattening the crops.

My brother kept punishing me with his words, but thankfully he'd not said anything to Armand. My belly swelled more. I didn't speak to Léon, and avoided his eyes and those of his wife, as we sat around the hearth in the evenings.

'This autumn cold has destroyed almost all my wheat and vines,' Armand said. 'I fear too, the price of wood, chickens, beef, eggs and butter is rising beyond our means.' He sighed. 'And nobody can afford to buy my barrels of wine.'

I patted his arm. 'Don't worry, Armand, together we will think of something.'

In November of 1780, as my husband continued to knit his brow over our financial plight, I gave birth to our daughter, Madeleine, just fourteen months after Rubie had been born.

Where are you now, my child—that little girl I can only speak to in my dreams? Are you walking yet? Who are you smiling for? I pray she's nice, your new mother, and that she might read to you from *Les Fables de Jean de la Fontaine*, as I will, to Madeleine. I hope she'll teach you to read and write, because Maman always said it is one of the best gifts a parent can bestow a child.

Despite his happiness over the birth of our daughter, graced with the dark Bruyère beauty, Armand grew steadily more concerned about our finances.

'What with the Church tithe, the royal and seigneurial taxes, saving seed to plant next year and having enough to fill our bellies, I don't know what we are to do, Victoire,' he said. 'The harvest was so poor we have barely any flour to make the bread.'

Perhaps it was my guilt over Léon, or maybe Rubie, that decided me to try and help our dire finances.

'I can do something, Armand,' I said on impulse. 'I could sell my milk to the rich people.'

So, like many commoners, I became a wet-nurse.

***

'Hush, my child,' I soothed, when Madeleine shrieked with the hunger, as the babies of the wealthy suckled all my milk.

She began to cry less and less. Her little limbs shed their womb fat and the roses in her cheeks paled.

Armand flung an arm in the air. 'Our daughter is wasting away! You must feed her, Victoire.'

'What if the agent comes?' I said, thinking of the people who came to check the wet-nurses were not giving the babies animal milk, or water thickened with mouldy bread. 'You know if they find my own child at my breast we'll lose the money, and you will be fined by the courts as much as you could earn in twenty days at harvest time.'

The next day I found Madeleine listless, and whimpering.

'Perhaps it is this cold weather?' Armand said. 'Or some other infant sickness. God only knows there are many. We must pray for her health, Victoire.'

By evening Madeleine's forehead burned, as I pressed it against my cheek. As I'd seen Maman do, I laid cool cloths over her hot, limp body. I crooned and whispered into her ear, and smoothed the dark hair from her flushed face, willing the fever to break. Her heat persisted though, and Madeleine made no sounds, apart from her raspy breathing.

'The child is very ill,' Armand said. 'We must call Père Joffroy.'

'No, Armand! She will recover … she cannot die.'

But the priest came with his white cloth and candles, and solemnly performed the Last Rites.

'Thank the Lord she is baptised,' Armand said. 'Madeleine's soul will pray for our family, from heaven. Don't be sad, Victoire. You are young, not yet nineteen. God will bless us with many more babies.'

Sad? I could barely speak, could hardly breathe, the grief— the guilt—drowning me like an overflowed well. I could not understand this resignation my husband seemed to have acquired, over dying babies. Was it because he'd already buried four infants, or simply that, unlike a father, a mother remains forever bound to the child she has carried; as if the umbilical cord had never been severed?

'If we were wealthy she would not be ill,' I said, 'and Rubie would not be gone from me. Isn't it so unjust the babies of the rich live and the poor children perish? How can you simply accept that? Don't you see it is all wrong, Armand?'

'That may be the case, but I don't know what we can do about these things, except to rejoice in what we have; in the living,' he said. 'Don't feed your sadness on ghosts, Victoire, they will only haunt you until *la mélancolie* strikes you down.'

I sat by Madeleine's crib through the night, listening to her quick, shallow breaths. I kept reaching across and touching her all over to gauge the extent of the heat in her body. I patted her with the cool cloth, and, my eyelids, heavy, I sank into the chair beside her crib and fell into a restless sleep.

In my dream, I saw Armand's farm, but it was more than a simple farm. It was a grand inn, nestled just off the main road, above the woods. I watched bedraggled travellers approach its charmingly crooked thatched roof and moss-coated stone walls. As dusk fell upon their coaches and their horses slackened with thirst, I saw them smile at the golden glow of lamps from the many tiny windows, thinking they'd come upon an enchanted paradise.

The church bell striking five startled me from sleep. I felt an odd sickness rising from my belly, and I lurched from the chair. I steadied myself with a hand on Madeleine's crib and leaned over my sleeping daughter. Madeleine was white and quite still.

No, no! A foul-tasting liquid shot into my throat, and my head spun so much I thought I would pass out.

'Madeleine!' I touched the ivory-pale cheek, dreading the cold touch of marble.

Nothing. Then she blinked, her eyes flickering open. I picked her up. She was cooler to touch. The fever had broken. I wept into her soft skin, and latched her onto my breast.

'*Dieu merci*. Thank you for this miracle.'

Madeleine was still drinking thirstily when Armand came into the room.

'Victoire, wha—'

'Armand, it's all right, we'll no longer need those wet-nurse sous, the health of our child is far more important.'

'But—' Armand started.

'You know the King has accepted our demand for a fair in Lucie, well those merchants, traders and visitors coming to the fairs, and the travellers—more and more, between Paris, Marseille and Lyon—will need somewhere to sleep,' I said. 'We could turn the farm into an inn.'

Armand's coal eyes brightened, and shone, as I continued.

'Adélaïde and Pauline could help me cook and clean and fix beds. The boys will help you make the wine and till the soil. An inn could be the answer to our problems.'

'Innkeepers?' Armand's face spread in a smile.

'We'll call it L'Auberge des Anges,' I said taking my husband's hand. 'The Inn of Angels.'

'For all the angels who have flown from us,' Armand said. 'My children, my wife, your family.'

I nodded, stroking Madeleine's dark curls from her forehead.

***

Once she was suckling my own milk again, Madeleine thrived. I never stopped thanking the Lord for sparing her but Armand was right, God did send me more children—twins, a boy and girl—just a day after my twentieth birthday in March of 1782.

'Look, Armand, how lovely and healthy they are—our little Blandine and Gustave.'

Their father ran a hand through the twins' chestnut wisps of hair.

'*Dieu merci* they survived the birth,' he said. 'And I thank the Lord you survived it too, Victoire.'

I held a baby to each breast and felt the tingling rush as my milk flowed for my children—for them alone. I pushed away the pain of my lost sibling twins, Félicité and Félix, as I nursed my own babies.

Never again would I have to feel the guilt of risking my own child's health for a few miserable sous—the unjust lot of a peasant woman.

14

I held two-year old Madeleine up to the window. 'See how lovely the dawn is, my pretty girl.' The sky was just coming light that May morning, streaked with pale blue ribbons, and over the snowy Alps a pink ball of sun rose, like heaven set on fire.

'And look at all the people, Madeleine,' I said, as the countryside came alive with fair visitors, horses and loaded carts.

'Don't you love this first day of the fair, Armand, of the crowds flocking to Lucie from all over? How the streets fill with people, and every house turns into a shop.'

'Such a grand day,' Armand said, breaking off a hunk of bread. 'L'Auberge des Anges will be overflowing, with even more guests bedding down in the stables and barn,' he said, joining me at the window and wrapping his arms around my waist. 'I know you work hard, my dear, sweeping out the inn and preparing beds. It is relentless, but how important the fair is, to help our meagre income.'

'Oh but I don't regard it as work, Armand, our inn is my greatest pleasure.'

I kissed his weather-worn cheek. 'So, what should I serve them for the meal this evening? A tasty lamb ragout?' I said, memories of Claudine's kitchen smells teasing my nostrils. 'Or perhaps beef with chestnuts?'

'Nothing surpasses your *médaillon de veau* with vegetables,' Armand said with a wry smile. 'If only we could afford to be so extravagant, but your creamy herb omelette from our best eggs will suit famously.'

My husband kissed us both and left with Léon and his brother, Joseph, to set up their brandy and wine stall at the fair.

When I had finished preparing L'Auberge des Anges, I left the twins with their half-sisters, and took Madeleine down to the meadow, which was fast becoming crowded with booths. Stallholders, recognising acquaintances from previous fairs, shouted and clapped one another on the back.

I hurried across to Grégoire, who was displaying his finely crafted furniture, engraved boxes and trunks.

'Hello, my favourite princess.' My brother kissed his niece, who giggled and tugged at his hair.

'You'll never guess, Victoire ... Françoise's parents have agreed to our marriage.'

I clapped my palms together. 'I'm so happy for you, and I wish you a cottage full of lovely babies. I only wish our parents could see how successful you've become,' I said. 'They would be proud of you. I am proud of you.'

'You've not done so badly yourself,' my brother said. 'You have three healthy children, and Armand Bruyère is a good man. One of the best.'

'I know, Grégoire, and I am being a good wife.'

'I'm glad to hear that, sister ... very glad.'

Madeleine and I walked on, amidst the noise of the people exchanging ideas, news, rumours, and organising seasonal work.

'Look at these pretty dresses, Madeleine,' I said, admiring the merchant's garments of muslins and painted silks, the scents, pomades and liqueurs. 'I hope you might wear a gown like this one day.'

Baskets of eggs and rows of goat's cheese, their rinds rolled in ashes, sat beside sacks spilling grain, rice and sugar, the edges rolled back to boast the quality of the merchandise. Rabbits and chicks of all kind huddled in cages. Lambs, mules and cows were bought, bartered and sold as écus, sols, livres and louis d'or coins jangled against the thud of measuring weights and the swing of scales.

Dogs barked, children darted about, horses whinnied and booth-holders laughed and shouted as they bantered awful jokes back and forth.

A mountebank touted his magic elixir from his position on an upturned crate. 'A cure for all eye problems, Messieur Dames!' the charlatan proclaimed. To attract attention, a woman was dancing, a young boy juggling. 'Treats skin ailments too, stomach problems, even bad breath.'

Another magic healer had set up a large pool with a statue of a mermaid, which had captured my daughter's gaze.

'Ladies, gentlemen,' the man shouted, 'gather and sample my special potion to change the colour of hair, beards and eyebrows!'

I laughed, wondering why ever someone would want to change their hair colour.

I had no idea what the mermaid was for, but the grand spectacle of it all made me smile, as I recalled Maman telling me their magic potions were probably only harmless vegetable juices and herbs.

For lunch, we feasted on grilled sausages, crêpes and fruity wine with the other villagers and fair-goers, our chatter and trills of laughter chiming across the meadow in concert with birdsong.

Oh yes, my life was certainly charmed these days, and a contented warmth coursed through me as I returned to the inn for Madeleine's afternoon nap.

***

'Best turkey I've tasted,' the merchant from Marseille said, wiping his mouth after the evening meal. He raised his beaker. 'To m'dame's succulent food and m'sieur's full-bodied wine.'

'Hear, hear!' cried the inn guests gathered around our long wooden table. Everyone lifted their beakers. 'A toast to the food and wine of L'Auberge des Anges.'

'You wait till you taste madame's orange and lemon marmalade *à la bergamote* at breakfast,' the man from Normandy said, kissing his fingertips through his thick red beard. 'Or her moist *macarons*, buttered brioches and strawberry jam.'

'I believe m'dame's *escargots de Bourgogne* are the talk of all the travellers,' the Marseille merchant said, beaming at me. 'As is her reputation for *fricassée de boudin* with *petite grise* apples.'

I smiled at our guests, silently blessing Claudine for her instruction on stewing and roasting meat, preparing vegetables and *pâtés*, and whipping up creamy desserts.

'What I truly appreciate here is the dry storage for my wares, and the stables for my horses,' a large man from Clermont Ferrand said. 'I've had the misfortune of staying in inns with not a strand of fodder!'

'*Oh là là*, I could lie on your soft feather mattress all day long,' his wife said to me.

'Unlike many a villainous hole I too have encountered,' the red-bearded Normand said. 'With rude hosts, food burnt to a crisp, abominable wine and kitchens black with smoke.' He patted his paunch and pushed his empty plate aside. 'Not to mention beds of wooden planks in draughty rooms.'

He swallowed a last mouthful of wine. 'So, I imagine everyone has heard the latest news from Versailles?' he said, looking around the room. 'The Austrian has birthed a son. Last October—the Dauphin Louis Joseph. An heir to the throne, finally, after twelve years. That's if there is still a throne by the time he inherits.'

Everybody laughed. It was time to serve dessert, so I lay Blandine and Gustave in their crib, smoothed down their shocks of chestnut hair and stroked their pink cheeks.

The Clermont Ferrand trader handed his empty plate to Pauline, who was clearing the table.

'The Queen, that daughter of fortune, is bored and unhappy,' he said, raising his eyebrows in mock concern. 'Bored with her homely husband who devotes his time to hunting, clocks and his workshop.'

'It is rumoured she threw herself into the skin pleasures with the Swedish count, Axel Von Fersen, before he left for the war in America,' his wife said with a smirk. 'Apparently she can't keep her eyes off his breeches. Of course, everyone knows it was the Swedish scoundrel who sired the little Dauphin.

'All the Queen cares for is fashion and masked parties,' she continued. 'The people hate her more and more and the gossip at Versailles is vicious. *Madame Deficit*, they are calling her.'

'*Oh là là,*' Armand said as he poured the brandy—another of Claudine's recipes—while I served the *crème brûlée*. 'What a sin to waste such money on gambling and diamonds, when our country faces economic ruin.'

'Well,' the Marseille man said. 'Gambling and diamonds aside, we all know the commoners' condition—the tithe, the *corvée*, the dreaded salt tax—is wretched and unjust, but what can a man do when our so-called thinkers advocate passivity?'

'The people *are* reacting,' the Normand said. 'And without violence. Our recently deceased enlightened scribblers ... Rousseau, Voltaire, have reached all of society with their sheer delight in discontent, their questions, and their prying scrutiny.' He paused for a mouthful of brandy. 'It is no longer enough for a man to say something is so, or for the Church to continue enslaving the human mind.'

'And you think this is a good thing?' I jumped as the Marseille man thumped his fist on the table. 'That without the least embarrassment people can question the authority of God's Church?'

He nodded at the Normand. 'You speak of Voltaire. Did you know, on his deathbed, the priest asked him to renounce the devil and turn to God? And what did Voltaire say, my friends?' He gazed around the table. 'He said, "For God's sake, let me die in peace!" *Dieu merci* the man was denied a Christian burial.' He swallowed his brandy in a single gulp.

'People dare to describe God Himself, the Almighty, as dispensable and claim the maintenance of order and morals could be conceived of without Him!' He shook his head. 'What has our world—our spiritual existence—become?'

'But people are seeing it as their right not to blindly accept things, like the church, any longer,' the Clermont Ferrand man said. 'Wherever you look there buzzes this sort of hectic excitement. People are reading books, women even.' He glanced at his wife.

'The commoners are, at last, fighting their poverty and the capital seethes with the fury and energy of people marching in the streets!' He tapped the side of his nose. 'Revolution will soon be hammering on the gates of Paris, my friends.'

Revolution.

The word arose in me a timorous kind of excitement; the longing to atone all those slights to myself, and my family.

15

It was late in the spring of 1783, but the rains had not yet come across the Massif Central to Lucie. Square patches of meadow, still brown and greyed from winter, bordered the flanks of the hills rising behind—naked and thirsting for new cover. Few birds flew overhead, and none shrieked with the joy that usually heralds fresh growth.

I headed towards the Vionne River with Madeleine, Blandine and Gustave, waving at Grégoire and his wife, Françoise, bent over in the cottage garden. They smiled back, Françoise massaging her lower back and arching with the awkward gait of the heavily pregnant woman.

Madeleine jumped up and down, her curls bouncing around her face like hundreds of black coils. 'I want to stay here,' she said. 'Will Uncle Grégoire tell me a story?' It seemed my daughter loved her uncle's tales as much as my father's had enchanted me.

'We won't be long,' I said to Grégoire. 'I must gather bugle flowers for the infusion. Armand's poor children are sick again.'

I left with Blandine and Gustave, gripping their hands as I helped them cross the river at its lowest point, where the Vionne was so sluggish my petticoat barely got wet.

'Hold my hand tight,' I said, leading them along the riverbank, through the willow trees, until we reached the bend in the river, and the place where the water rushed into the deeper pool in which I'd so loved to swim as a girl.

I'd not returned to my special place since that stormy afternoon with Léon, but the heat rushed through me as I remembered it, the guilt and shame shrouding me as I felt the same stab of desire for Léon Bruyère.

I barely thought of him these days though, because Léon was busy, and happy with his new wife, who awaited the birth of their first child. When I saw them in the evenings, we exchanged only the minimum of conventions.

I gripped the children's hands as we crossed a clearing where, on rising ground, a woman and her three sons were building a simple hut, the boys cutting and driving stakes in.

I recognised her as the woman who'd come to the farm the previous day, Noëmie, whose husband was travelling the country in search of odd jobs. They could ill-afford to rent a house, and had to build a hut in the woods. They'd been sheltering in the old witch's hut, but it was draughty and leaked when it rained. She asked for the loan of an axe and a mallet.

I thought of my journeyman papa and I warmed to the woman and her boys. After all, what could a destitute peasant child become? Only poorer than his absent father and his mother, already halfway to the grave. Was there coarser, cheaper cloth than they wore? Was there anything worse for the feet than rope? What was more tasteless than boiling up nettles and bark for meals?

I handed Noëmie the tools, and a basket, and when she saw the bread, wine, cheese and eggs, her hand flew to her toothless mouth. 'You are too kind, good Madame Victoire.'

'*Bonne chance*, Noëmie,' I said, because good luck was about the only thing a beggar woman could count on.

I led Blandine and Gustave up the opposite bank towards another wooded area that bordered the Monts du Lyonnais, to a place where, as a child, I'd gathered bugle flowers with my mother.

Bent over around the shaded trunks of trees, I filled my basket with the cobalt blue petals with which I would make an infusion for three of Armand's children.

As I plucked the flowers my thoughts drifted back to Léon and his pregnant wife, and I forgot, for an instant, the twins playing nearby.

A fly settled on my forehead, jolting me from my thoughts of Léon. I swiped at it and realised I could no longer see the twins. I was not yet anxious, but my pulse quickened and my head whipped around, left and right.

'Blandine, Gustave!' However could they run off so quickly? True, they had begun walking at scarcely ten months old, but they were slow and ungainly.

I dashed about, calling their names, my heart lurching. The river flashed through my mind; how they loved playing at the edge, as if the moving water bewitched them. The river was running low but there were still ditches and holes into which they might stumble out of their depth; twists and bends that caught the currents and transformed them into whirlpools.

La Vionne violente.

I had always scorned those words of the villagers, but now I raced back towards the river my breathing faster and more ragged with every step.

I stopped to catch my breath, at the spot where the people were building their hut. Noëmie was bent over, collecting twigs from the brushwood. I saw she had already assembled a pile of moss from the roots of trees and rush from a pond margin.

'Have you seen my children?' I said. 'A boy and a girl, only one year old.'

'Sorry, Madame Victoire.' She shook her head and threw her handful of twigs onto the pile. 'But I will help you search.'

'Blandine, Gustave!' I kept calling. No sign of them. I tripped on my skirt hem and stumbled. Noëmie took my hand and helped me to my feet.

'Don't be afraid, we will find them, Madame Victoire.'

Gripped with a heavy dread, my breathing laboured, we reached the ridge of the slope that led down to the river.

'There they are!' Noëmie cried.

Blandine and Gustave were on the riverbank, wobbling about on their stumpy legs and throwing handfuls of shore gravel. 'Luck is with you today, Madame Victoire.'

'*Dieu merci, Dieu merci.*' I held a palm against my sprinting heart, my fingers groping for my angel pendant. The empty place felt warm, as if it was still resting against my breastbone; as if the little sculpture was still protecting me.

16

Exhausted from his journey to the produce market eight leagues far, Armand slumped into a chair before the fireplace.

I handed him a beaker of wine. 'Drink and rest, my merchant husband.' It made me smile, how he insisted we call him a merchant innkeeper now, instead of a lowly farmer or winegrower.

A plume of smoke leaned into the room as Armand drank the wine. He took my hand. 'A small profit was made. Minimal, but every bit counts, n'est-ce pas, my dear? All in our effort to overcome this impoverishment gripping Lucie and every other rural place around.'

I thought back to Noëmie and her beggar family and, once more, I blessed my good fortune to have such a man—a man who, despite lacking youth, rose in the four-o'clock cold to ride off and bargain good prices at the surrounding markets for our eggs, vegetables and poultry. What luck to have a husband also clever enough to understand a smattering of every dialect—the language of the river people, the butchers, the silk-workers and fishwives.

I left my hand in his. 'I fear your children are worse, Armand. Their brows are feverish and they barely eat because of the coughing. This morning they began spitting blood. I keep giving them the bugle infusion and I have moved them from the others.

I had to use one of the inn rooms.'

'You separate them from the family?' Armand looked up from the crackling fire, his eyes red-rimmed and bleary from the long ride home into the brunt of a south wind.

'Maman always said a child with the speckled monster sickness smells like horse manure, one with scarlet fever smells like old apples, but the tuberculosis child has the odour of onions.'

'And my children smell like onions?'

'I'm sorry. Maman also told me *la tuberculose* is contagious. I must keep the other children safe. We cannot have more of them fall ill, and Madeleine, Blandine and Gustave are young ... so vulnerable to sickness.'

Armand gave my hand a faint squeeze. 'I know you'll take care of my children—our children—and make them well again.'

I left my husband by the fire and, as Maman had shown me, I boiled up linseed and mustard for a poultice. I returned to the sick children and placed it on their hot little backs.

I held the beaker to their pale lips. 'Come now, just a little more,' I said, coaxing them to sip the minty-smelling bugle tea— my only hope to stop the bleeding inside.

I had been with the children only a few minutes when I heard voices. I listened closer. It was Léon's voice, hushed and urgent. I put the beaker on the bedside table and hurried out to them.

Léon was sitting at the table, his hat in his hand, fiddling with the brim.

'What's wrong? What is it, Léon?'

For someone I thought I knew so well, I had no idea what to read on that grim face. I looked from him to Armand, the panic rising in my chest. 'What is it?'

'They are dead, Victoire,' Armand said. 'Léon's wife and child. Dead birthing the first son.'

My first instinct was to run to Léon's side to hold him, to smother him with kisses and rock his pain away.

I felt my husband's eyes on me and I did not move, only

lowered my head to hide my blush. 'I'm sorry, Léon. So very sorry for you.'

***

'Water drips down the windows again,' Armand said, as I prepared the morning coffee. 'How peculiar, for a summer day. Quite as odd as this smoky haze that persists across the countryside.'

He nodded beyond the window. '*Mon Dieu*! Look, Victoire, frost covers the ground! Whoever heard of thick frost in a month of June?'

'And the sun is the colour of blood again,' I said, watching it rise, as it had done these past weeks, into that strange, smoky fog. A flock of birds heeled sideways, catching the first sun's rays. They wheeled and dipped like crazed things, as if trying to dodge the fog, seeking fresh air in that great bowl of singed, scarlet light.

'Whatever is happening, Armand?'

'I have never seen such a thing,' he said as he washed down a hunk of bread with coffee. 'God must be enraged, my dear.'

He kissed me and strode outside to begin the farm chores. Through the rusty haze, I watched him—a bleak figure looking across his frosted fields, and shaking his head as his gaze lifted to the sky.

Busy with the twins and preparing the inn for the evening guests, I pushed the worry of the queer weather aside, until Armand came stomping back inside.

'The new oats are brown and all withered. The wheat looks mouldy and the water has turned a strange, light blue.' He shook his head. 'How are we to make the bread, Victoire? We, and our inn guests, surely have the right to decent bread?'

Léon appeared in the doorway. 'That's not all, Papa. The snouts and feet of the livestock are raw and have turned a bright yellow. The fruit trees have all shrivelled up, as if a fire had burned beside them.'

As always when Léon spoke, I busied myself at the stove or the fire. Still we avoided each other's eyes, as if afraid of what we might see. Nor did we mention the loss of his wife and child, especially after the joyous birth of Gregoiré and Françoise's healthy baby boy—Emile Félix Charpentier.

'What poison does God send us from the heavens?' Armand said, flinging his arms skyward.

'Witches' revenge!' Pauline said.

Adélaïde shook her head. 'We have enraged the angels.'

Over that whole summer, the people of Lucie tilted their heads towards the sky. They looked with suspicion and fear, but nobody could explain the frequent, violent thunderstorms which affrighted and distressed us, and which struck down cattle and men across the country. We had no idea why people had trouble catching their breath, some choking to death on the bizarre, ever-present fog, which covered the sun and stopped it warming the earth.

***

'It is because of a volcano,' our inn guest—a silk trader from south of Lyon—explained one morning the following autumn.

'A volcano?' Armand said.

We rarely heard of such things, and we all fell silent, still mourning our lost harvest.

The man nodded. '*Eh, oui.* So the scholars say. From a far-off land. Apparently this volcano, Laki they call it, began erupting in early June, and spews out great clouds of volcanic ash and lava, covering our sun with its poison.'

All eyes stayed riveted on the man. 'This cloud has killed thousands and made the living even poorer, and more destitute.'

Before their afternoon sleep, I took a moment in my busy day to read to Madeleine and the twins from *Les Fables de Jean de la Fontaine*. I would teach them to read and write when they grew older, as I had promised Grégoire I would teach little Emile, but for now, the children were content to listen to the tales and gaze at the pictures.

The door flew open. 'Come quickly, Victoire, Papa's had an accident with the plough!' Léon cried. ' … gone through his leg, the blood gushes out. Grégoire is with him.'

I hustled the children from my lap. 'Stay here with Adélaïde and Pauline,' I said, grabbing strips of cloth.

Léon and I hurried across the half-ploughed field to where Armand lay, the wound on his leg bloody and gaping.

'*Mon Dieu,* poor Armand. Let me look.' As Maman had instructed me, I pressed on the wound until the bleeding ceased, then bandaged it with the cloth. Between Léon and Grégoire, Armand hobbled back to the farm.

By the time my husband had crossed the courtyard and laboured up the steps, his face was grey as a storm cloud, and sweat dusted his pleated brow.

'Go quickly,' I said to Pauline. 'Fetch *la guérisseuse.*'

Lucie had no residing physician or barber-surgeon, and apart from the blacksmith who set bones and helped women prepare for less painful childbirth, the healing woman was the only one who could help the sick.

La guérisseuse probed and cleaned Armand's injured leg and applied a poultice. 'Yarrow flowers leaves, to staunch the bleeding and close the wound,' she said, applying a binder fashioned from thick leather strips.

'Give him this for the pain, madame … willow-bark tea. Then make him rest. I will return tomorrow.'

'Rest now, Armand,' I said, helping him to our bed. 'Tomorrow you'll feel better.' As he closed his eyes, I tried to quell the foreboding swelling inside me.

'Armand must get well,' I said, accompanying Grégoire outside. 'He has to recover.'

My brother kissed my cheek. 'I know you're a good wife, you'll take great care of your husband.'

As my brother left to return to Françoise and little Emile, the hairs on my arms bristled in the late afternoon chill.

17

My dear Victoire,

Thank you for your wishes. Marie, Roux and I are well. The lecherous Marquis found new prey quickly—the young scullery maid who replaced you. The poor girl must have resisted him and Marie found her strangled in her attic bed. Quelle tragédie! Of course, the Marquis, ever the fawning toady to those who matter, claimed it was some intruder—a thief come to rob the silver and jewels.

I have an urge to upturn my vat over his powdered wig and watch the burning oil run down his frock coat and soil his satin breeches and white stockings.

So caught up he is, in his own high and mighty self at the Palais-Royal, he never notices me observing from the throngs of commoners at the Camp des Tartars; watching him strut around the expensive arcades, eyeing the fancy ladies in their paste jewellery and striped gowns. As he goes up to the gambling casinos and plush houses of pleasure, I am plunged into sorrow for that dead scullery girl, as I was for you, Victoire.

He will go unpunished no doubt. As you well know, justice is a dream! Those of the blue blood are above crimes and we commoners are powerless against them.

I was relieved to hear of Madeleine's recovery. I hope the twins are also in good health. They must be eighteen months old now? Healthy children who survive infancy are true gifts from God.

I imagine you experienced this terrifying volcano down south? The foggy rust-coloured air over Paris killed many throughout summer, and the scholars predict thousands more will perish in the freezing winter this volcano is sure to bring. We must prepare ourselves, my child, for this unexplained punishment God sends us.

So as not to cloud this letter with bleakness, I have some news that will make you laugh. Did you hear of the brothers Montgolfier, who invented an enormous balloon filled with hot air? Well, they have flown this giant balloon before a huge crowd at Versailles. You could never imagine such a spectacle! A rooster, a duck and a sheep were inside to check its safety. This trio travelled a short distance and landed unharmed, except the sheep had kicked the rooster! The fat King watched it all through his telescope, and has made nobles of the Montgolfier family. Humans flying in the sky, whatever will men think of next, Victoire?

I close now, my child, the kitchen awaits me. I hope all is well with you and Armand at L'Auberge des Anges.

Affectionately yours,
Claudine

***

I immediately took up my quill.

My dear Claudine,

I beg a thousand pardons for not answering your letter earlier. Several reasons, the first being that some months back, three of Armand's children succumbed to la tuberculose. *Despite all I could remember of my mother's remedies, theirs were terrible deaths, all within days of each other, and it seemed we were constantly calling Père Joffroy out for the Last Rites in the morning, then again in the afternoon to lay the children to rest.*

I am desperate for my poor husband, and try to comfort him. He has now lost seven children. Dieu merci *Madeleine and the twins were spared the sickness.*

Alas, this is not the only bad news from our hearth. Two weeks previous, the plough pierced Armand's leg. The healing woman comes daily with her marshmallow cataplasms, but the wound is surrounded by an angry halo of swelling, and causes him dire pain.

Since Armand is no longer able to work the farm, his children— Léon, Joseph, Adélaïde, Pauline and even the two youngest boys— and I are working harder than ever. Everyone is anxious. I am terrified.

As in Paris, and all over we are hearing, the weather has been unkind to us too, made even worse as the previous spring rains never came to Lucie. Along with the great drought, this volcano killed much of the vines, fruit trees, animals and crops. The price of hay, wine and wheat is elevated. With little stock, some days I wonder how I will feed my family, let alone the inn guests. Though travellers are far fewer these days. As if, since they witnessed its fury, people are afraid of Nature, constantly staring at the sky and fearing what poison it will rain on them next. Or perhaps it is simply that the burden of feeding and sheltering families has become too much for men to stray far from their own hearths?

Finances are desperate once more and I fear la mélancolie *stalks me again. As when I left Rubie, the darkness crouches on my shoulder like a feral cat whose hunger has driven it from the forest, wild and searching for prey. I am less and less able to fight it. Some days I can no longer even find joy with my sweet children.*

It angers me to hear of the Marquis's terrible crime. He must be stopped from killing more girls. As a simple scullery maid, I could do nothing, but I am a free woman now, helping my husband run a respectable inn, and thus able to ponder over such injustices.

I know you value your position in that noble house, Claudine, but do you not feel vengeful for your poor carter husband? After my time in Saint-Germain, and the murder of my father at the cowardly hand of a noble, I can no longer passively accept this kind of behaviour. The day I am able, my friend, my revenge shall be savoury, my hand steady, my conscience uncluttered with guilt.

I must hurry back to my husband. It comforts me to know you will be praying with me for his recovery. We cannot lose him.
Yours affectionately,
Victoire

***

Armand was too ill to accompany us to *la fête des morts* in the cemetery that November, to commemorate our dead.

'We should not leave him alone for long,' I said to Léon, as we cleared and groomed the family tombs. 'I am afraid the fever comes upon him.'

I knelt before the resting place of my siblings and my parents, and crossed myself. 'We must hurry.'

Back at the farm, I took wormwood tea to Armand for his fever. 'Sorry we had to leave you,' I said.

He took sips from the beaker I held. 'It is only right you tend to our dead, my dear,' he said in a voice that seemed to come from some distant place.

His wound was still inflamed, and the edges shone a dusky crimson, as if left for days under a hot sun. I recalled what Maman used when a wound became like this, and hurried back to the hearth.

I peeled garlic cloves into boiling water with thyme, then added strips of old linen. As I dabbed around the wound with the garlic solution, I could see he was trying not to flinch with the pain.

I swabbed the sweat from his burning brow, though the poor man shivered under the covers.

'Pray I die soon, my dear,' he said, his eyes glittering with the fever. 'For I have become a burden. With barely enough food for the living, the mouth of the dying is but an obscenity.'

I held his limp hand and we sat in silence.

'Do you regret returning to Lucie and marrying me, Victoire? You, so young and lovely.'

'I regret nothing, Armand.' I squeezed his damp, frail hand. 'You are a hardworking, pious man, who shows me nothing but kindness. We have a good, happy life together, and for that, I feel only fortunate. Hush now, save your energy to fight the sickness,' I said, stirring the air about him with slow waves of my fan.

'I die in comfort, Victoire, knowing you and my son will not be alone. Léon is a good man; he will take care of you.'

My pulse quickened. 'Don't speak of such things. You are my husband.'

'Léon needs a new wife.'

The heat rose to my cheeks. 'My loyalty to you has never wavered, Armand.'

With what little strength remained in him, Armand clutched my hand. 'You have been the perfect wife; I couldn't have asked God for one better.'

***

My dear Victoire,

Oh là là, my child, you must show prudence with your mind of revenge. The Marquis is respected and well connected. To fight against a blue blood is to invite disaster. I would hate to watch the spectacle of your public execution on la place de Grève. I hope you are not serious and you'll stay safe in Lucie with your good merchant, innkeeper husband.

It bereaves me to hear of the death of Armand's children. I know you cared for them as if they were your blood, and the love and attention you showed them deserves a high place in the character of the Good Wife. Here in Paris too, many are dead from this outbreak of la tuberculose.

Marie and I pray constantly for Armand's recovery. Please send me more news soon, but I understand the children, the farm and the inn must occupy all of your day.

We are all still shocked at the murder of the scullery maid. Marie can't sleep and Roux chases his tail like a mad thing.

Another young girl, Margot, who will no doubt lose her innocence before long, replaces the maid.

I have some news I hope brings you a smile. An apothecary by the name of Monsieur Parmentier is, would you believe, trying to convince folk to eat potatoes! "The flesh is good and healthy," he says, of that suspicious root. He says grain is easily destroyed in wartime, and from storms, hail, even volcanoes (!!), but the potato, growing below ground, is safe.

But doesn't this apothecary man realise that digesting such root vegetables will only invite some awful phlegmatic disease? Mind you, he must have great influence. He has persuaded the King to give him two acres of land outside Paris on which to grow these potatoes.

If this food situation worsens, Victoire, we may all have to succumb to M. Parmentier's humble potato, and every other root the good earth pushes up!

Yours affectionately,
Claudine

***

Armand's fever never truly broke. His wound turned the colour of a toad and gave off a pungent odour. He screamed when the healing woman tried to touch it.

One afternoon a grey mask dropped over his face, one I was afraid no human could lift.

'What about the hospital, Léon?' I said.

'That filthy, airless place, with so many crowded onto the one straw mattress seething with lice and fleas.' He sighed. 'If we were wealthy enough to make a charitable donation, we could get my father a bed of his own. Apart from the very rich, Victoire, hospital is only a gateway to the grave. I fear it is time we called Père Joffroy.'

The priest came with his white cloth and candles. Léon brought in the twins and Madeleine, to kiss their father.

Armand's children came too, to say goodbye—a circle of pale faces and watchful eyes full of sadness. Grégoire and Françoise were with them, and I saw how each of them respected his piety, admired his strength and now lamented his death.

Léon was the last to take his father's hand.

'Look after her, my son,' Armand said, his voice no more than a whisper. 'Take care of them all.'

'Yes, Papa.'

The two men kissed tenderly and the son left, unable to stay and watch his father die.

For a time, there was no sound, save Armand's spasms of breath, as he slowly lost his hold on life. His limbs grew cool, his lips white, and his face damp. Yet, through the painful hours, my husband's eyes never lost their tranquillity, and it seemed I was staring straight into his bared soul.

Scarlet streaks of dawn creased the blue-grey night sky. Armand raised himself slightly, turned his head and gazed outside to the rising sun. His face creased into a strange smile, and he slumped back on the pillows and never spoke another word.

I held his hand until the end, so tightly that when he was asleep at last, I could not draw it away and I remained sitting there, clasping my husband's cooling hand.

'Come, Victoire, he is gone.' Léon's hand rested on my shoulder. 'You know it is unsafe for the dead and living flesh to touch each other for long.'

I didn't reply and I shrugged off Léon's touch. I could not cry. I could not think, or move. The numbness paralysed me. I felt I had gone somewhere beyond grief, beyond pain. I kept my hold on Armand's hand as if, that way, he wouldn't truly leave me.

Madeleine and the twins came running to me; towards their dead father, their cherub faces tilted, their arms outstretched. I didn't have the strength to pick them up, and I looked away as Léon gathered my children into his arms and took them from the room.

Later, when Léon prised my hand from his father's, Armand was cold and stiff and marble-grey.

18

Several weeks after we buried Armand, I was sitting in his chair by the hearth, scribbling down my thoughts. I hoped it might take away some of the loneliness, the sensation of being so utterly lost. Now I understood the wretchedness Maman felt when Félicité, Félix and Papa died—*la mélancolie* that turned her from religion and, ultimately, cost my mother her life.

Slow footsteps approached, but I didn't have to turn to know whose they were. I recoiled from Léon's breath, close to my ear.

'Why do you tremble, Victoire, when I come near? Since Papa died, you're like some hovering ghost, not with us at all. You must master this grief.'

I shook my head, trying to shrug off the clutter that fogged my mind and made the edges of everything cottony.

'Adélaïde and Pauline are taking care of the household and your children. The boys and I work the farm, so you have no need to concern yourself about that. As for the inn,' he said. 'Well there are so few guests I fear L'Auberge des Anges must close its doors.'

In some chamber of my mind, so distant I could reach only a thread of it, I knew I should be concerned about that, but I felt no sadness. All I felt was something slipping away from me, like when I'd caught a river trout with my bare hand and no matter how tightly I clutched it, the fish slithered, slowly, from my grasp.

'He's gone, Victoire,' Léon said. 'We are both free now—free to be together. Papa even said as much. That afternoon … at the river, you spoke of divorce. Did you mean if divorce was allowed, you might have considered being with me?'

I could not answer him, and the fervour in his black eyes seared a hole in my flesh.

'Papa gave us his blessing. What is wrong? You remained loyal to my father—to your affectionate, comfortable marriage, but you cannot deny your real love has always been with me.'

Still I said nothing.

'You believe you no longer care for anything, Victoire. If only you would let me, just once, into your bed. Let me lie beside you and give you comfort, you might not feel so bereft.'

I did not know what made me rise from my fireside place, and cast my nonsensical jumbles of words aside, but I let Léon guide me to bed.

As I, I did feel some of the burden slip away.

'Thank you,' I said, leaning into the circle of his arms, inhaling his soft whispers. 'It does feel less … less painful.'

'I promised my father I'd take care of you, remember?'

Léon smiled, and I could not bring myself to tell him that beyond the sensation of unburdening myself, there was nothing more. The passion, the unbearable ache, I'd always felt for him had vanished along with his father.

***

The snow stole into Lucie one early December night like a silent seductress. It sculpted the Monts du Lyonnais into a dizzying snowscape. It embraced the vineyards, draped itself across fallow fields and vines, and kissed the naked limbs of the trees. Seven days of heavy falls took us into 1784.

When the snow stopped, a violent north wind flared up and blew for three weeks. I'd never known such cold that split large trees like flimsy paper and froze wheat and oat seeds underground.

The air crackled and froze the Vionne River so deeply that carts crossed it with no fear of breaking the ice. Birds hit by the chill in mid-flight plummeted to the ground and the frigid air struck down passing journeymen, soldiers and beggars, along the roadside.

Madeleine, Blandine and Gustave gave me great comfort through that winter as I read to them and watched them play together, warm and safe beside the hearth.

'Two of the cows are dead,' Léon said. 'We must bring the rest of the animals indoors, even the barn and stables are too cold.'

So we hauled them all into the house—the two remaining cows, the horse, the pigs, the fowl and the sheep.

'Villagers help each other through hard times,' Léon said, and just as Armand would have done, he brought the newly destitute people from the countryside around Lucie, whose unheated homes were exposed to the wind. He also brought Noëmie's family from their hut in the woods.

It made me think of Père Joffroy, when he gave us the church room, and I welcomed those worse off than us into the warmth of our spacious inn room.

'The *savants* say it is all because of this volcano,' the blacksmith said, as man and beast huddled around our fireplace. 'They say the temperature has gone as low as it possibly can and predict the harshest winter, with permanent frost.' He spread his fingers and rubbed his hands close to the flames. I would have liked to offer him, and the others, a beaker of wine, but our stocks were all but gone.

'Some are now down to making bread from acorns, bracken, even pine bark,' a silk-weaver woman murmured. 'I've seen people so hungry they eat the bark off trees and what grass they can dig up from beneath the snow and ice.'

'Many are dead from the dysentery,' Noëmie said, 'so they have to bury them in shared graves.'

'Not that those spoilt royals are doing anything for our wretched situation,' the blacksmith said. 'What with the tithe we must pay the priest.'

'It is not our overworked priest who profits from the tithe,' I said. 'Père Joffroy is as poor as his flock, living beside the Church and surviving on the pittance he earns from weddings, baptisms and funerals. No, it is the Church that benefits from the tithe, and everybody knows the Church pays no taxes and that its leaders come from the aristoc-'

'*Oh là là*, don't talk to me about the loathsome *sang bleus*,' the baker said with a scowl. 'Always worming their way out of taxes.'

'It doesn't help them much,' Grégoire said. 'The travellers tell us the bourgeoisie—the merchants, doctors and lawyers—are far better off these days than the aristocrats.' He looked around the gathered villagers and I felt the same pride as when Papa had narrated his stories.

'All I know is, at the end of the day we keep less than a fifth of our earnings,' the silk-weaver woman said. 'And we are told the silk looms of Lyon will soon be at a standstill.' She waved an arm. 'While our country's finances are in a state, the Queen amuses herself going to horse-races, operas and balls, and, they say, buying three or four new dresses every week!'

'She has birthed another son,' the quarry man said.

'Ha, the gossipers whisper that once again, the King is not the father,' the weaver said. 'But the Queen's lover, the seductive Count Axel Von *je ne sais quoi*.'

She sniggered and I laughed along with the others.

In those instances of camaraderie, surrounded by friends and family, the warmth of those village bonds abated my distress; the creeping misery I could not truly shrug off.

19

Grégoire's second child was born just days after my twenty-third birthday in March of 1785.

'We'll call her Mathilde,' Grégoire said, his voice brimming with tenderness as he stroked his newborn's soft pink face. 'Mathilde Félicité Charpentier.'

'What a fine, strong name,' I said.

Mathilde's rosebud lips pursed, and if I hadn't known better, I'd have sworn she was smiling. 'Come, Madeleine, Blandine, Gustave, say hello to your new cousin,' I said.

'Isn't she the loveliest child God sent to this earth?' my brother said.

Françoise smiled, latching the baby onto her breast.

I laughed. 'Of course she is. They are all God's loveliest children, and I hope you will let me teach her to read and write too, like Emile. Remember what Maman said—it is equally as important for a girl to know the literacy skills.'

'You shall teach them the letters,' Grégoire said. 'And I'll tell them the stories—every one of their grandfather's legends.'

'Oh yes, uncle Grégoire, tell us another story,' Madeleine said. 'Please, Maman let me stay here while you get water.'

'All right,' I said, 'but I won't be long.'

I held a twin's hand in each of mine as we continued on, to the river. The Vionne was running high and proud with the spring thaw. Scores of daises and poppies dotted the slope, the breeze randomly orchestrating their faces, and trees, pregnant with buds, bristled with birdsong.

The sun warming my face, I knelt beside the mill that turned the grain into wheat and rye flour and watched Blandine and Gustave play. I smiled at their squeals of glee as they plucked daisies and tumbled about on the fresh grass.

Once I filled my copper cistern with water, I put it aside, cupped my hands and drank the clear water, the same emerald green of the jewels in the house of Saint-Germain; the colour of my eyes, so Léon had once claimed.

Such a long time since he'd called me Mademoiselle *aux yeux de la rivière*, it might only exist in my imagination.

I tilted my face to the sky, a blue so sharp it almost hurt my eyes. I inhaled the scent of willows, spiced primroses and the fruity odour of fresh grass. Nature's perfumes filled the void a little, but no matter how deeply I breathed, my chest remained tight as a drum, as if the air couldn't get in properly.

I began plucking the young dandelion greens with which I would make soup for our evening supper, our single daily meal since the disastrous winter. The hunger a permanent ache in my stomach—or perhaps it was this desperate sadness—I tried not to think of food as I watched the twins frolicking like new lambs.

'Stay away from the edge,' I warned.

Trapped in the updraught of the breeze, my voice trembled like a frightened heartbeat as I recalled the recent rumours of desperate land-workers casting their young into the river like unwanted kittens—mouths they could ill-afford to feed.

My basket full of dandelions, I sat for a moment, the young grass caressing my bare feet. My cheeks felt flushed from the day's sun, Armand's earthy smell tickled my nostrils and my skin prickled, as I imagined my husband come to sit by my side.

'The fatigue beats me like some relentless whip, Armand,' I said. 'I fear I can't go on. There are no eggs for the market, no vegetables. I don't know what will become of the children and the farm.'

I'd not brought my cloak, but its weight pressed on me as if it were slung across my shoulders. Shadows crossed and darkened my mind, my eyes ached with the sunlight, the lids hanging so heavy I had to fight to stop them closing. I felt an urgent need to keep them open, or Armand might leave me again.

A twittering bird startled me. I must have closed my eyes, perhaps even dozed. Surely it could have only been for a moment. At first I wondered about the silence, then I realised the twins were no longer beside me.

'Blandine, Gustave!' I jumped up. 'Where are you?' I squinted into the setting sun and saw them, down by the water's edge.

I beckoned, calling them to come back, but Blandine didn't answer, and kept throwing pebbles into the water, skipping closer to the swiftly flowing river with each new pebble. Her brother was crouched on the shore, beside her, playing with the gravel.

I called again, louder. 'Blandine, Gustave!' I picked up my basket and the cistern and hurried towards them.

***

My legs are so heavy I have to drag my feet for every step. Why do the children not heed my calls? Do I speak too softly? Do I speak at all?

The twins are near the water's edge. So close. Too close now. Blandine skips in, then her brother. Deeper, deeper they go. Up to their knees, their waist, their shoulders.

But the river is too icy for swimming. Why are we all standing in the freezing water?

White smocks swirl beside me, and rush away, a giant hand tugging them downstream. Further, faster. Chestnut curls darken beneath the blur of green. The birdsong ceases. Willow leaves trap the breeze and the air is still. The river flows no more.

***

'However did Blandine and Gustave get away from you?' someone said, but I didn't know this person.

'How … it happen?'

'Terrible … tragic …'

I gazed up at the circle of faces, not recognising any of them. Those faces without names pored over mine, so close I smelt their rancid breath and felt the spittle droplets of their chatter wet my cheeks. They were asking so many questions I couldn't concentrate on any single one. I turned my head, the tears pooling in my cheeks and leaking onto my bed.

'The water be-bewitched my Bland-Blandine,' I said in a voice that was not mine. 'Come back … come back. I called … kept calling. She walked right in.'

'And Gustave?' I recognised Grégoire's voice, and his face, an odd milk-white mask. He held Madeleine, who stared, wide-eyed, as if she was terrified of something. Even as I desperately wanted to take her, I couldn't hold my little girl.

'I don't know. I don't know.' I couldn't stop shaking my head. 'G-Gustave wouldn't listen … I beg-begged him to come back … not to follow her. Went into the river … beloved sister. St-stumbled.' I swallowed my sobs. 'Everything they did, together. Always together.'

I could no longer bear their stares, and flung my forearms across my face. 'Babies—my angels—I couldn't reach them.'

People kept patting my arm and asking more questions, but still I could barely answer them.

I didn't know how I left my bed, or got to Saint Antoine's.

'Another tragedy of *la Vionne violente*,' the villagers said, as Père Joffroy buried Blandine and Gustave in the same grave, leaving the world as they had entered it—together.

The grief, the darkness that had begun when Armand left me, rushed in torrents and swamped my ragged senses. I could not even weep for what I had lost because I too felt dead.

'You must eat, Victoire. Adélaïde and Pauline have made *potage* for you. A little dark bread?' I think it was Léon speaking, and I supposed we were back at L'Auberge, but I couldn't answer him, and turned away. I wanted to ask where my twins were but when I opened my mouth, no words came.

Adélaïde and Pauline rubbed the kettle with lard, boiled water and chopped bits of bread into it, but still I couldn't eat. I shivered and dragged the hood of my cloak further over my head, and in the mirror above the hearth, I no longer recognised the face veiled in a gaunt white nothingness.

Adélaïde and Pauline shook their heads, muttering things of which I made out only snatches, '... madness got her ... *mélancolie* ... drowned ...'

'*La guérisseuse* has come for you, Victoire,' Léon said.

The healing woman held a beaker to my lips. 'Just a little tea, Victoire, to drive this terrible demon from you.'

Demon?

I pushed her hand away. I did not want her poison.

'A little of this one then?' She held a different beaker to my lips. 'Your maman used to make this remedy, you remember?'

I stared at her. No, I could not remember. I could not recall a single thing.

'She would make it from Saint John's flowers, before the Midsummer feast.' I shivered at the touch of *la guérisseuse's* hand. 'Drink, Victoire, it will chase away this demon madness, and give you back gladness and courage.'

'Where are my children?' I sprang from the chair and scurried around searching for Blandine and Gustave. 'I must go to them ... too young to be alone.' But when I couldn't find them, and I felt exhausted from looking, the heartache pushed me down to the cold floor.

At first I didn't realise the surging sound—a pure sound from Hell—came from within me. I only understood they were my screams when the people clamped their hands over their ears. I covered my ears too, and I felt the noise moving away from me, seeping beneath the floorboards and echoing from the cracks in the stone walls.

Why were they all reeling from me and gazing, wide-eyed, as if I was some monstrous stranger? Even Grégoire and Françoise, clutching my Madeleine, and little Emile and Mathilde. But I did not want to look at their children, whose names only made me think of my lost parents.

Léon too, seemed wary, hesitant. 'This cannot go on, Victoire.'

He helped me up from where I lay on the ground and pushed a folded paper into my hand. 'A letter from your cook friend. Maybe that will cheer you.'

Through the confusion beleaguering my mind, I could barely read Claudine's words.

My dear Victoire,

Still no news from you, my friend. It has been such a time. I am beside myself with worry and pray your lack of correspondence is simply the fault of our terrible postal service.

I hope Armand recovered from his plough injury and that you all, and L'Auberge des Anges, survived the terrible winter.

I don't know if the news reached you in the south, but all of Paris is talking of the diamond necklace affair. An impoverished aristocrat, Jeanne de Valois-Saint-Rémy, devised a plan to regain what she says is her family château, stolen by the Crown. Pretending to be one of the queen's most intimate confidants, she tricked the Cardinal de Rohan into believing the Queen wanted to buy this very expensive necklace.

They have arrested the Cardinal and thrown him into the Bastille. The woman too, was arrested. People are jumping with excitement as this scandal has damaged the Queen's reputation beyond repair!

I hope to receive your letter soon.

Yours affectionately,

Claudine

My tears plinked onto the page, spreading the ink like damp flower petals. I slid from Armand's chair to the floor, closer to the fireplace. The page quivered in my hand as I held it over the flames. I stared, dry-eyed—because there were, suddenly, no more tears—as the flames curled and blackened the letter I knew I would never answer.

I bent my legs up, hugged my calves and rested my head sideways on my knees. I kept my eyes on the fire, watching and hoping the flames would leap out and engulf me, as they'd swallowed up Félicité and Félix.

I felt around my neck for Maman's angel pendant, seeking its warmth, and courage. I felt nothing though, and when I couldn't recall where the angel might be, my groping fingers scrabbled at my skin, raking until blood and gritty flakes stained my nails.

My hand dropped. I was too tired to keep scratching; I would find the angel another day. I let my heavy eyes close.

The flames curled about the table and chairs, the bed, Maman's medicinal herbs and flowers. It flung its mighty heat against the walls, crumbling them. The smoke choking me, I ran outside and watched, helplessly, as the fire-devil consumed our home. When, finally, the flames dwindled, I reeled in horror at the two small, blackened skeletons resting in its embers.

A raven circled above me—slow, perfect arcs on extended wings. It swung in curves, faster and faster, carving mad spirals through the air. A ridge of goosebumps prickled my arms, the coldness slithering down my back.

Maman and Papa laid Félicité and Félix onto the back of a cart piled high with other dead children. We all stood and waved as the cart rumbled off, right into the path of an elegant coach the colour of ox blood. The coach thundered into the cart, overturning it. Corpses spilled out. Pieces of Papa's body were strewn across the road.

The raven swooped down from a branch overhanging the riverbank. It began pecking at the bits of my father and I saw it had a jagged scar over its left eye.

'Stop, no stop!' I struck the bird with a stick, over and over.

Morsels of flesh dangling from its beak, the raven thrust itself at my face, pecking at my eyes until it almost blinded me. It flapped its wings and flew off across the river, a basket swinging from its bloodied beak.

The basket fell from its beak into the water, spinning faster and faster on the current. From inside, the small screams, 'Maman, Maman!' weakened as the basket twirled away, beyond my reach.

Breathless, I stumbled, tripping over an open grave in which a skeleton lay.

Rubie stood by the grave—a pretty girl in a red dress. She smiled and walked towards me. I spread my arms, reaching for my daughter. I was about to take her hand when I woke, startled, Léon's hand in mine.

'There's somebody here to see you, Victoire.'

'Who is this?' I did not know this man, or why he stood before me.

'He is the bailiff.' Léon gripped my arm as if he was afraid I would fall over, or perhaps run off.

'Child murder is one of the most heinous crimes known to man,' the bailiff proclaimed. 'You, widow Bruyère, are to be incarcerated for life in la Salpêtrière asylum of Paris.'

As they dragged me off, I had not the slightest idea what the man was talking about.

La Salpêtrière Asylum
1785–1787

20

How odd it was to be still after what seemed like weeks of bumps and jolts. Or was it months, perhaps years, I'd been cramped inside that windowless carriage with so many people and their smells of sweat and sickness?

The coach door creaked open, the bright sky burning my eyes. Hot bits of fire danced in mid-air but I was cold, and shivered beneath my cloak. I reeled from the orange sparks. A man grabbed my arm, his fingers digging into my skin, pinching my flesh.

'Must get away … get outside. Papa says get out, now! Fire's burning. The twins … inside.' I tried to pull away from him, from the flames.

The man sneered. 'Scared of a few autumn leaves, my lovely?'

'Leaves?' Ah yes, I saw then, they were leaves—autumn leaves rocking in the breeze and fluttering to the ground, where they lay still amongst the browned, dead ones.

My hands were smarting. I looked down and saw my palms were grazed and bleeding. Perhaps it had been me, not the leaves, falling to the cobbles as I'd tried to flee the man restraining me.

He dragged me upright and pushed me ahead of him, towards a cluster of dark buildings. The closer we got, the stronger the stench of piss, shit and unwashed bodies flared my nostrils.

'Where am I? Where are you taking me?' My words came out in hoarse, sharp whispers. 'Where's Grégoire? Find Léon, he'll know what to do.'

'Welcome to paradise, my lovely.' The man's breath was foul on my cheek.

He pushed me down into a chair. Why was he binding my limbs to the chair legs? Something moved across my head. I glanced at the floor—at the spatter of cinnamon waves covering the grimy tiles. My head felt different. I shook it and found it light, unburdened.

I hadn't the strength to struggle as the man removed my clothes and shoved me into a wooden tub, nor when he fastened something cold and heavy about my neck.

'If you move a muscle, that iron ring will break your creamy neck,' he said. I dared not move and I breathed so slightly I could barely inhale enough air. 'Have a nice bath, my lovely.'

The shock of icy water hitting my face was so great I did not even cry out. It gushed into my eyes, my nose and my mouth. I tried to breathe, coughing and spluttering. The cold water came again, and again.

'Stop, no! Please!' Still the water hit me.

It stopped, the man unchained my neck and the next thing I knew, a woman was standing over me, holding a chemise and an ash-grey dress.

'Put these on. Hurry, girl. Time to go and meet your fellow lunatics.' She laughed, but I had no idea what was funny.

The man was back, and leading me across a deserted yard entombed in high walls. He hurried me down steps slick with moss, and nodded beyond the wall. 'Shame your room got no river view. Nothing to remind you of home, *n'est-ce pas*, my lovely?'

I didn't know what he meant but I flinched, as we'd reached a deep place where only the thinnest, grey rope of light penetrated. I quivered with the fear, the unknown. Where was the bright sky and those leaves the colour of fire? I was sure I would feel better; understand it all, if only I could get back to the sky and the leaves.

Cries began to beat against my eardrums—sounds so raw with despair I was certain I must be dead, and I had reached some vast hall of Hell.

I was still too terrified to struggle as the man thrust me into a damp room, and a smudgy blot of women with shaven heads. Some were clothed as I was, others stood naked, and thinner than scarecrows.

'Where am I?' I looked about wildly, trying to run from the swarming women towards the only light that came from a barred grid in the door.

'No, no, I can't stay here!'

There was nowhere to go; no way to get out. I backed into a corner, cowering behind my arms across my face.

'Don't take my Rubie ... cold in her basket. Stealing Madeleine's milk.'

I clutched at my breasts, but I held only withered knobs, and I felt again the fierce suckling of the rich, robust infants, sapping my energy and leaving me too exhausted to stand.

'*Plus de pain.* No more bread.'

The women's words mewed softly from some distant labyrinth of my mind I could not reach. I think I moaned.

The man was quickly upon me again, fastening chains about my wrists and ankles, and I could move from the wall only as far as the chains allowed. I caught snatches of his words that meant nothing.

'... mad ... incurable ... drowned ... river ... Insane Quarter.'

'What river?' I gazed about me. There was no river running into this sea of filth.

'No point clawing at the walls, imbecile,' a woman said. 'Nobody will help you in here.'

I stopped. I fought no more, so weak that I slumped to the ground and rested my head on ragged straw, which squeaked with the bustle of small creatures. I didn't know what else to do, so I covered my ears to block out the dipping, mournful cries pulsing from the women's lips—sounds like birds that had lost the nest.

I rubbed my blue clotted arms. My nails were ragged, my hands streaked with blood. What was this blood from? Armand's wound? No, no, I'd stopped the bleeding—used Maman's treatment to stop my husband's blood flowing, and save his life. His leg could heal now and Armand would be well, and everything would be all right.

I will wake soon, I kept telling myself. I'll wake and Armand will be lying beside me.

'Only a bad dream,' he'll say, his gentle smile caressing me, and the day's work done, we'll sit together on the riverbank, the sun tickling our faces, the wind ruffling our hair. I rocked back and forth, waiting to wake up. I think I felt a little better, so I kept rocking back and forth, back and forth.

The man returned. He placed wooden bowls on the floor, threw chunks of black bread beside the bowls and unchained us.

'What is that? Who is this man?' I whispered to a pock-faced woman beside me.

'A keeper. All cruel, evil creatures.' She pointed to my bowl. 'Eat, girl. It's soup. Best keep your strength or your death will be like theirs.' She nodded at two bodies that lay curled and still, their eyes wide as dead fish.

'Slow, cold, agonising deaths,' the pock-faced woman said.

I took the bowl onto my lap, bent my head over the liquid and inhaled a vague odour of something turned bad. I drank it, and chewed the bread.

Once supper—I supposed it was supper—was over, the keeper refastened our chains and stomped off, his heavy boots thudding in my ears long after he'd gone.

There was nothing left to do. 'Armand? Where are you, Armand?' In the glacial damp, I yearned to cling to my husband, to feel his warmth and comfort, but once again, the chains restrained me.

'Do not fret, my dear wife, I'm here,' he said. 'Over here. Yes, right beside you. I'll take care of you, Victoire.'

My eyes darted around the room. 'Where? I do not see you. Armand come back.'

'Shut up, whore!' a woman shouted.

I coiled into the smallest possible ball on the moving straw once more. I shivered in the blue darkness, making odd shapes with my mouth—a strange kind of dry weeping. I recoiled from the creatures that nibbled at my legs, their thin tails sliding around my ankles. I did not think. I did not sleep, or dream.

***

The single cry of a bird woke me. Where is the tree from where it chirps, and the fields, the hills and orchards? There was no smell of damp earth, fresh cut hay or fruit blossom. Then I saw there were no birds at all. The cry into the cold dawn was a woman, who still shrieked as the men steered us all, still half-asleep, across a courtyard.

'Where are they taking us?' I asked the pock-faced woman.

'I already told you,' she said. 'The keepers take us to the chapel for Mass. Mass, every morning. You'll see.'

'Mass? Perhaps Père Joffroy will be there. He'll know what to do. He'll get me home.'

The cold from the chapel flagstones crept through my clogs and the soles of my feet, winding itself around my ankles, and up my legs. It clutched me so tightly I thought I would die of it. I nestled into the women closest to me—a small part of that great, grey, shivering bulk gazing ahead at the altar.

There was a priest, but it wasn't Père Joffroy. Enrobed in purple and gold, this other priest stood at his iron lectern like a great master of ceremony, shouting words I couldn't understand.

I tried to concentrate on the Holy Scriptures. If I could focus on the scriptures, everything would be all right. Things would be back to normal. I recited the prayers, and I sang of the glory of God, though I could barely recall the words.

My eyes were drawn upwards, beyond the cold blue light

that filtered through a high window, to another light. It was the shade of a lemon, and thin as the eye of a needle. I squinted, trying to see it more clearly, not even certain it was truly there. I shut my eyes for a second and when I opened them again, the slice of light was gone.

***

'Health may only be restored through a harmony of blood, phlegm, yellow and black bile,' the keepers said, as they strapped me to the stool. 'This will balance your body fluids and restore your humour.'

They began to spin the stool. 'We must rearrange your brain, put it all back right.' Faster and faster, they turned me. The room flashed by. I was giddy, and bursting from the stool, about to hurtle off and slam into a wall.

'No, stop, please!'

They kept spinning me. My gut lurched and heaved, and when they finally stopped, I clutched my aching head, leaned over and threw my bread up on the putrid floor.

The keepers hurled a bucket of water over me, and the vomit, their sneers as icy as the water.

'*Pitié, pitié*!' I cried, knowing what was coming next—what always came after the spinning stool. My pleas went unheard, and they cocked their lancet device, the trigger firing the spring-driven blade into my veins.

Once they finished taking my bad blood, the blows began.

'Too much black bile,' they said, hitting me over and over. 'Have to beat it out of you.'

I didn't fight; I no longer even flinched, for I was dead, again.

21

Hymn music clanged through the dawn gloom of the chapel, mauve threads of incense smoke twisting up into the cool air. I sang along with the others, my gaze, as always, pulled up to that distant slice of lemon light—an instant of peace through my daily Hell.

The needle-eye light had brightened these past days, and with its glow I'd become conscious of the passing of time, and the daily rhythm of Mass, prayers, blood-letting, enemas, spinning stool.

The fog cleared a little more each day. It swirled upwards, away from me, and from the great oval window of the chapel, that lemony scythe of light spread its warmth through my body.

This morning, the light shone so brightly its glare almost blinded me. I blinked into it, beginning to take hold of the tangled threads of my mind; to weave those unwieldy knots into neater, more purposeful tresses. My lips formed words, then sentences, and I no longer felt the terrible, sharp panic as when I'd arrived at la Salpêtrière; the crushing fright that had made me sweat and scream and tear at my shaven skull.

***

'Why do they shave our heads?' I asked the pock-faced woman, the only one who spoke to me, or made the slightest bit of sense.

'For the vermin, *ma chère*,' she said. 'And they say the wet compresses they use to calm our madness work better on the naked skull.'

'You don't seem mad,' I said.

'I might be as mad as the next woman here, but there are plenty of reasons besides insanity to get you thrown in the dungeons.'

'Dungeons?'

She nodded. '*Les cachots* of la Salpêtrière. Most feared dungeons of them all.'

La Salpêtrière.

From my days at the house in Saint-Germain, I'd heard gruesome stories of la Salpêtrière, and the peculiar warmth of the chapel light burned like a fireball now—a lightning bolt that struck me and left me breathless and dizzy. I finally understood I was imprisoned in the largest and most feared asylum of them all. For what reason though, I had no idea.

At once, my self-awareness became an appalling curse. I wanted to drop onto the dirty straw and scream out my frustration, but I could no longer cry, though the tears choked me as I shivered in that dismal tomb of madness.

'Why do they put us in here?' I asked.

'Oh, for any reason,' the pock-faced woman said. 'Protestants refusing to convert, women reading horoscopes, taking lovers, practising divination, or throwing stones at royal coaches. And, naturally, general madness.'

'How long have I been here, in the dungeons?'

'A month, possibly. You've done well. Most who enter *les cachots* never come out alive.'

I was thankful I had little recollection of that month. 'But why ever should I be sent here?'

'They say you murdered your children ... you went mad and drowned them in a river.'

'Drowned my children!' I squeezed my eyes shut and shook my head like the lunatic they took me for.

The jade green ribbon of river curled between the willows. The shrill songs of birds drowned out the noise of the current and the sough of the breeze. Like new lambs on shaky legs, Blandine and Gustave wobbled towards the water's edge.

'Come back, come back!' I shouted, running towards them, but as I reached them, it all faded to blackness, then nothing.

'I don't know.' I tapped the side of my head. 'It's gone.'

My memories of the misery were not gone though. I recalled how it had crept low in the beginning, so stealthily I hadn't seen it coming. Then it gained on me little by little and, when it was too late, possessed me.

I heard again the demon voices, whispers at first then screeches so loud I wanted to beat my head to get them out. I understood the madness had reduced me to little more than a flaccid, palpitating corpse, no longer commanding any power of thought or reason.

'I suppose I must have been truly insane, for a time,' I said, and while I felt my normal self, there still remained much of which I had no recollection. Something had gouged that terrible day on the riverbank with Blandine and Gustave from my mind.

'Perhaps it would've been better to stay mad?' I said to the pock-faced woman. 'So mad I wouldn't hear these poor wretches muttering nonsense and moaning.'

Surely it would be easier not to see their eyes too—as wide and soulless as felled deer, and to watch them clasping their palms in prayer to a deaf God.

***

As a lucid woman, the keepers' "treatments" seemed more barbaric, and for their entertainment rather than our recovery.

I quickly understood the spring-driven lancet was only one of the horrifying devices they used to blood-let me, but I no longer cried out as the scarificator blades slashed my skin in a mosaic of shallow slits. I said nothing as they drained my blood into a cup. I did not retch on the stench-laden fug of their breath that could have extinguished a candle. I was silent, crumpling to the floor in foetal submission as they beat me, and enclosed me for a time in a solitary confinement box into which the waters of the Seine River rose.

I thought of writing to my friend, Claudine. She would know what to do, or perhaps Léon, or my brother, but in those dreaded *cachots*, we were barely able to get bread, soup and water to survive, let alone ink or paper.

***

Most of the rich Parisians who visited la Salpêtrière in their glamorous carriages with liveried footmen came purely for entertainment, but I sensed many of them also feared us "crazies"—that long-popular equation of mental illness and demonical possession.

Oh yes, those same wealthy people who'd once hired me as a wet-nurse, paid the keepers handsomely for the pleasure of ridiculing me—the freak.

'Here they come again,' the pock-faced woman said. 'Their special Sunday afternoon outing, after feasts of … of what?' She stared at me. 'I cannot remember. It's an age since I have eaten anything besides bread and soup.'

'Oysters?' I said. 'Lamb and green peas, and maybe strawberries?' My mouth was moist with memories of Claudine's kitchen.

Through the barred grid, I watched the keepers lead their guests across the courtyard of the Insane Quarter of the asylum. Their pockets jangling with louis d'or coins, the keepers pointed out to the visitors where they could peer in at us, through the bars.

I recoiled as a man in a beaver fur hat waved his sword, lace frothing from his wrists and neck. Another in a powdered wig poked his cane at me and sneered. The swish of his cape washed cold air over me, and I felt like a monkey in some macabre circus act.

'Come, Jean-Henri,' a woman in a fur-trimmed cloak and fluffy handmuffs said to the sword-waver, her tight ringlets bobbing under her veil. In a dour cold that gripped me tighter than my shackles, I envied the woman her velvet cloak, her full skirt and the lingering smell of her perfume that vied for airspace with the shit and vomit of la Salpêtrière.

The handsome couple moved away, the man swinging his cape, the woman's steps delicate in gem-encrusted slippers. I imagined them stepping into their decorated carriage, the horses clomping daintily off, leaving the asylum far behind.

Our visitors gone, I stared around me, at all those sent here for treatment—the beggars, prostitutes, epileptics, Jews, Protestants, criminals and the thieves; at the presumed witches, magicians, bohemians and idiots. Those women would never recover, but simply die slow, horrific deaths.

I gnawed on my hard bread, thinking of those visitors pausing at a café on their way home for brandy, sorbet or candied fruit, and I felt the surge of fury again; the injustice of it all.

I closed my eyes to the women's vacuous stares, a murmur coming from some distant corner of my rearranged mind.

How dare they keep me trapped in their web of human misery? I did not deserve to be here. Like these women, I could succumb and die. Or I could fight it.

As I finished the last of my soup and crumbs of bread, I pledged to myself I would not perish in the filth of this asylum. I would flee la Salpêtrière. Somehow I'd get back to Lucie, to my brother, my daughter, and to Léon.

22

I held my breath and clenched my buttocks to still my quivering body. I dared not move, nor utter a sound, under the frosty stare of Sister Superior.

The woman took her goose-feather plume and lowered her gaze to the register that, from what I could make out, recorded every detail of life in la Salpêtrière—its rules and punishments, garments and food allotted, animals maintained, vegetables harvested, personnel employed.

'Name: Charpentier, Victoire Athénaïs, widow of Armand Bruyère, merchant and innkeeper,' Sister Superior read in a grim monotone. 'Date of entry to la Salpêtrière Insane Quarter: 8 September, 1785. Age: 23 years. Condition: Alienism of *la Frénésie* type caused by too much moral sensitivity, the listlessness of deep grief, and an imbalance of bile humour. Medical Observations: The effect of this humour has bogged the patient's intestines by slowing down excretions and drying out the brain.'

Sister Superior barely took a breath and her voice never wavered. 'Usual treatment performed on patient for six weeks: copious bloodletting from the feet to the temporal artery. Leeches applied to the anus. Purges, ice baths, spinning stool. Balms applied to the shaven head. Medical Observations: patient appears to have responded to treatment and regained lucidity. Recognises own name.'

She paused, meeting my eyes again as if searching for lingering madness.

Ink flickering across the page, she wrote and read at the same time: 'Date of transfer to Prison Quarter of la Salpêtrière—1 November, 1785. To be held there for life for the crime of murder. Condition: Alienism, diminished to the mild *mélancolie* type.'

Transfer to prison! I could barely stifle my gasp. 'But, but, Sister Superior, am I not to be sent home? I don't recall any murder. There has been some mistak—'

'The prisoner will not speak.' The glacial eyes didn't blink, nor move from mine. 'Otherwise I'll have no choice but to remove her back to the dungeons.'

I clasped my hands, holding them close to my heaving breast. Sister Superior kept writing. My pulse racing, I looked down at the register again, trying to understand, and to find the mistake. There must be one, somewhere.

It was difficult to read upside-down, but it looked like a list of the different asylum dormitories, each bearing the name of a saint—Sainte-Anne: 107 cantankerous old women with canker sores. Sainte-Catherine: 87 deformed girls. Sainte-Magdeleine: 48 epileptics. Les Cachots: 84 violent, crazy women. Logis: 100 incurably insane women and girls. Long lists of women coming from all over the country, it seemed. A shudder bristled through me as I read, in many of the final columns, "suicide" or "death".

'I note you, widow Bruyère, have no particular skills in weaving, spinning, embroidery or lacework,' Sister Superior said, jolting me from my horrified daze. 'As a former innkeeper, you shall thus provide your cooking services to the community of la Salpêtrière.'

She kept on talking, never raising nor lowering her voice; never blinking.

'Nourishment shall be given, as to all prisoners, by soup, bread and water. You will be allotted a blouse, a dress, stockings and a bonnet every eight days. You are to wear your own clogs.'

I had no choice but to bow in submissive assent. 'If I hear

the slightest complaint about your kitchen work, or if you fail to remain silent outside the daily hour permitted for talk, you shall be taken from your cell, chained by the neck to a wooden beam and whipped. You will remain in that upright position for one whole day. If this bad behaviour continues, you will be returned to the dungeon.'

Not the dungeon. Never could I survive another day in such a living tomb. I could hardly believe I'd survived almost two months there. In my weakened state, I felt faint, my legs threatening to fold beneath me.

I said nothing and bowed to Sister Superior, who nodded to two keepers standing by the door.

The keepers hustled me across the icy cobblestones, gripping me so tightly my arms went numb.

'Please, you're hurting me.' I tried to twist away, but they held me tighter.

'Think you're lucky to escape the dungeons, do you, my lovely?' The keeper sneered. 'Those *cachots* that make ordinary folk tremble?'

'She mightn't think herself so lucky once she gets to the Prison Quarter, eh?' the other said with a cackle. They hustled me to walk faster and I stumbled, and fell to the cobblestones, which grazed my face.

After perhaps ten minutes, we reached a building as gloomy as all the others, besides the dungeons, for which there were no words.

'Here we are,' the keeper said. 'The Prison Quarter of la Salpêtrière—your new home.'

'But you forget,' the other one said. 'She needs her flower—our pretty *fleur-de-lys* reserved for murderesses.'

They sniggered as one pinned me down, the other, holding an iron, lurching at me. As the hot iron seared its lily flower pattern onto my left shoulder, the pain ripped the breath from me so that I couldn't even scream, and I thought my heart would stop beating.

'Off you go to the wolves now, my lovely,' a keeper said, pulling me from the chair.

As they bundled me into a room, banged the heavy door shut and slid the bolts home, an icy rush scrambled down my back.

***

Clammy fingers pawed at the shoulders of my prison garb. I winced from the pain of the burn, taking in the vast dormitory in the scant light from a high dormer window.

'Welcome, Victoire. I'm Agathe,' a husky voice whispered close to me. 'You need anything in here, you ask Agathe.'

Smallpox had ploughed the woman's face into deep furrows, and robbed her of an eye. I shrank from her stale breath and the crusty sores that spotted her lips and oozed yellow liquid.

'And we all know what the pretty emerald-eyed Victoire did to end up here, *n'est-ce pas*?' Agathe winked at the group of women surrounding her, her smile mocking. 'Poor drowned little mites.'

I opened my mouth but couldn't think what to say. I tried to recoil from Agathe's moist touch; from the foulness that made my gut heave, but the sharp curves of the woman's nails held me still, and punctured my skin.

I shut my eyes to rid my mind of them, but all I saw was the river flowing faster, higher, the heads of Blandine and Gustave bobbing on puckers of current like flower heads the wind had ripped from their stalks.

'S'pose we all got our reasons for doing what we do,' Agathe went on. 'I myself had the bad luck to marry a gambling drunkard, Victoire. Had to chop him up with his own axe in the end.' Her throaty laugh was snug with phlegm.

With a ragged nail, Agathe began tracing my lily-flower branding.

'Hah, truly one of us!' Her fingertips moved slowly, dipping into the hollow below my shoulder, and following the rise of my breast down to the stippled skin. She grabbed my nipple and twisted.

I cried out and tried to run, but there was nowhere to go, and the stink of the inmates rose as they pawed at me and clung feebly to my dress. I wrapped my arms around myself, choking on my sobs.

'Aw, no need to cry, pretty thing.' Agathe was at my side again. 'Come and meet my friends.' She pointed out two tall women. 'Catherine and Marguerite. They're poisoners, here for life, like you. And here is sweet Toinette, a freethinker, swindler and cheat.' Agathe raked her mouth into a horrible grin as she pointed out Marie-Françoise. 'A knife-wielding blasphemer, and over there is Julie, our little gypsy girl and money forger.'

'Sleep, you whores!' a sister officer shouted from the corridor. 'Bedtime!'

Bedtime? I gazed about me, at the fifty or sixty inmates. I counted only six straw mattresses.

Agathe laughed. 'How many sous you got for me, Victoire? Most expensive bed is next to the window. No money, no bed.'

'Silence!' the sister officer shrieked through the spy hole. 'Next one who makes a sound goes in with the crazies.'

I had no choice but to huddle on the damp straw covering the ground with the other luckless ones without beds. The cold bit at my hands and feet as I lay, crowded in with all those women, yet the pain of solitude wrenched at me as if I were the sole occupant.

The inmates' breathing slowed to gentle snores but, as small things crept and gnawed through the straw beneath me, my eyes stayed wide open, staring into the blue slice of light.

To remain in the dungeons would have meant certain death, but survival here in the prison seemed hardly possible either. I knew, like crops struck by drought, I would quickly wither and die.

***

The chapel bell clanging through the fog signalled the end of Mass. The chill November morning hovered between dawn and day, as two keepers took me to the kitchens for my first working day.

Up to the end of my time in the dungeons, I'd been too ill to contemplate escape; too sick to think of anything besides surviving. Now, outdoors once again, thoughts of fleeing the asylum flitted through my mind.

I glanced around, my brain spinning with ideas to get past the asylum's guard of soldiers and corporals. Perhaps to the left of the main courtyard, via the workshops and housing for the wheelwrights, locksmiths, cobblers and carpenters. Or the lodgings of those who watched over us—the keepers, guards and sister officers. Was there was a way out through the stables or the wheat granaries? Or could I hide in a cart that transported sick women and children to and from the city hospital?

The carts came every day, full of young girls with labels attached to their bonnets, stating their name, age and dormitory. Older women too, were aboard, their labels attached to their right sleeve. In the split second the cart governess might turn her head, I would jump down, unseen, into the crowded Paris street.

I shook my head. The cart governess would never turn her head, constantly watching for women exchanging their labels, ripping them from sleeves, or jumping from the cart. Despair wracked me. For the poor with no money, no connections, escape was unthinkable.

The smell told me we'd reached the kitchen, and I dismissed all notions of fleeing the asylum.

'Peel those vegetables,' a stout woman barked, wielding a knife. 'Then you can stuff the chickens.'

'Marinade the beef!' another barked at me.

'*Non, non,* imbecile, cabbage is not cut like that,' a beak-nosed woman snapped.

More people began shouting orders at me, all at the same time so I could barely understand any of them. The noise was worse than all the bells of Paris clanging at once. I flinched against the din, trying not to retch on the smell of boiled cabbage and mutton fat, or to faint with hunger, which seemed even worse surrounded by food.

'And don't be tempted to eat the slightest morsel,' a sister officer said. 'I'll be watching you, and if one crumb passes those lips, your punishment will be the dungeons for twenty four hours. Understood?'

I nodded. '*Oui*, madame.'

I learned quickly how to make the daily gruel—thin and bland with much the same odour as the drains and the barnyard located next to the asylum orphanage. Once the food for patients and prisoners was prepared, I helped cook the meals for la Salpêtrière personnel, who ate in a vast dining room, and for the few wealthy prisoners who could pay for decent food and water.

Blasts of muggy air and hours of inhaling the smells of untouchable food made my heart beat quick and thready, and many times throughout the long day, my legs trembled and I feared I might collapse. That sister officer's eyes never left me.

***

'*Allez*, lazy whore,' the keepers said when my kitchen day was finally over. 'Back to your cell.'

The scent of woodsmoke prickled my nostrils; the food smells lingering in my clothes taunting my taste buds. I licked my numb lips as I slithered across the icy cobblestones under the keepers' firm grip.

Back in the dormitory, Agathe was beside me again.

'What did you bring me from the kitchen, *chérie*?' she said with her cracked grin.

I shook my head, opening my empty palms.

'What, nothing? Hold the bitch, Marie-Françoise.'

As the tall, God-cursing woman restrained me, Agathe

pinched and twisted my nipples again.

'Stop, please, stop!' I begged.

'Next time you'll bring me something nice, eh, Victoire?' Agathe said, pus leaking from her lip sores. 'A slice of beef or a plump chicken breast, perhaps?'

'Surely you could hide *some* leftovers?' Julie said, her gypsy face locked in a nest of black curls.

'Anything?' Catherine, one of the poisoner women, said.

I shook my head. 'Please, leave me alone. I cannot get you anything. They watch me constantly. All the food, even the scraps, are checked and recorded in the register. I'm s-s-sorry.'

'What a shame,' Agathe said, 'because s-s-sorry isn't good enough.'

I closed my eyes and let her blows batter my body, undefended. Until I could think of a way out of la Salpêtrière, it was easier not to fight.

23

The tawny November fog lifted but the clear, more frigid air of December seemed to freeze in my lungs. Vicious as a keeper's whip, snowstorms beat against the austere walls of la Salpêtrière's vast buildings and outhouses, their grime staining the snow brown.

Throughout that icy winter in the asylum, the mournful nocturnal cries of the desperate grew louder as the cold claimed its victims. They removed the multitude of women and girls who perished, their bodies shovelled together in the foetid necropolis of Paris, like old dogs. I hugged myself and prayed for their wretched souls.

As I diced vegetables, stirred soup and baked meat, fish and dark bread, I often recalled cooking at L'Auberge des Anges. I saw my beloved Armand laughing with the inn guests, pouring his wine. 'A toast to our good health!' he said, raising his beaker.

I smiled as tiny twin footsteps, and those of their sister, Madeleine, scurried about, their shrieks of glee drowning the older voices of Léon and his siblings. I hoped somehow, they had rekindled the spark of L'Auberge des Anges.

What had become of Léon? Remarried, no doubt. Grégoire and Françoise's children—Emile and Mathilde—must have grown so. There would be more children by now. I prayed they were taking good care of my little Madeleine—that she was so entranced with my brother's tales she wouldn't be suffering my absence.

I blinked away the pain that scissored my head when I let myself reflect on all I'd been forced to leave for this prison life.

As I moved through my day, from Mass to the kitchen, then back to the dormitory for evening prayer and Agathe's hell, I wondered how much longer I could continue such an existence.

***

The snow finally melted. I had survived the winter. The distant sun moved closer and cast the asylum buildings in an insipid yellow. From my barred existence I heard no spring birdsong though, as if the birds avoided this forgotten place where trees barely grew, where flowers struggled to blossom and where, behind its sombre facade, the women were abandoned to die.

Most mornings, as the keepers herded us to the chapel, I wrenched my eyes from the grim dormitories that housed la Salpêtrière's orphanage and the school for poor and abandoned children. I feared, amongst the knot of orphans, I might perceive a girl—a lovely child with the same green eyes and cinnamon hair as mine. A girl who was six years old, by the name of Rubie.

That sharp March morning, from my place in the pews of the Saint-Louis Chapel, I couldn't stop my eyes from straying to the lines of children, and their governesses, leading them into the great domed building.

The two ordered ranks, all dressed in white—child brides from la Salpêtrière and child grooms from la Pitié—slowly advanced towards the altar, coming together for *la bénédiction nuptiale*. Against the noise of hymns, the deep stride of organ music, their weak '*oui*' spiralled with the incense smoke, evaporating into nothingness.

In that single morning, I witnessed about sixty such "marriages", and as the newly-wed children departed for the boat at Le Havre, I looked into their frightened eyes, wide with the helplessness of young victims.

No, no, my Rubie cannot be among them, I kept telling myself. She is not being brought up to be placed for work, or married off to populate some far-off colony in Madagascar, Louisiana or Canada.

That afternoon, perhaps because my thoughts were full of Rubie, I yearned to feel the soft innocence of an infant.

'I would like to help out in the nursery,' I said to the sister officer. 'For the break after prayers, until my kitchen tasks resume.'

The sister officer agreed, of course. Continually short of hands, the *nourrices* were not fussy about the help proffered—even that of a woman imprisoned for child murder.

I stood before hundreds of barred cradles aligned in numbered rows. Not a soul cared for these motherless bundles whose wails and whimpers echoed off the bare stone walls. I gaped, too stunned; too sad to speak. I wanted to hold, to love, all of them—these babies of girls who had no money, no standing. No choice.

Moving down a line, from one bundle to the next, I began changing their soiled nappies. The dried excrement and their raw, blistered skin told me the infants were rarely changed.

A *nourrice* instructed me to feed several, from a bottle of milk, which I did, holding them close, cooing soft noises at one nameless cherub face after the other.

'No point getting attached,' the *nourrice* said. 'We only keep them for a week. Then they'll be shipped out to the country.'

'The country?' I said. 'But why?'

'Farmed out to wet-nurses,' she said. 'Though most won't survive the journey—five or six to a basket stuffed with straw, and hitched to a mule.'

I thought of Rubie on those church steps and how I'd imagined matron would simply take her to her foundling hospital and raise her there, and find good parents for her. I knew nothing of this farming out to the country.

My poor Rubie. Never would I have left you in the basket, but what was a penniless, sullied scullery maid to do? No, no, stop. Don't think like that. Rubie has found a good home, a loving maman and papa who dress her prettily on Sundays for Mass and let her wear my angel pendant.

After I fed the babies, I wrapped and lay them back in their stained cots. Some screamed, some cried weakly, others lay still, too feeble to make any noise at all. From the smell, I also knew that several were dead, though nobody had bothered, or had the time, to remove them to some common grave.

I picked up the next baby, a little girl. One arm had wriggled free from the cocoon wrapping. As I touched the hand, tiny fingers closed around my thumb, gripping it with surprising force.

'Petite chérie,' I crooned. 'You cannot be much more than a day old.'

As I stared into her perfect face, the unsuspecting eyes, the unbounded sadness of my own past, and the terrible assaults of prison life, clogged my brain.

I rocked her gently and shut my eyes. The river washed over me, its force sweeping my feet from the murky bed. I tried to clutch at ferns, a rock, a sprig of leaves, but my hands kept slipping, the current dragging me downstream. In their little white shifts, Blandine and Gustave swirled with me.

As my babies disappeared, my eyes flew open and a horrible light broke inside me—a flash so fierce it both terrified and calmed me.

Darkness snuffed out the light—the same creeping darkness that had brought me to the asylum; a sadness so familiar it had seemed almost like a friend I'd clung to in those first terrible weeks of the dungeons. It had somehow been easier, sheathed in madness, than to be lucid, and comprehend the terrifying reality of *les cachots*.

'Poor child,' I whispered to the infant I cradled, seeing at once its destiny laid bare. 'Misery only, watches over your cradle.'

I looked around. The *nourrices* were busy. Nobody paid me

the slightest attention.

'How simple it would be,' I murmured, 'to lift the length of my dress and press it over your beautiful face.' I surged with gladness. 'Would it not be simpler to relieve you of your suffering now, before it only gets worse?'

A sister officer marched up to me and snatched the baby from my arms. 'Time to get back to the kitchen, you.'

***

On that first day of June, the cobblestones trapped the heat and threw up the stench of putrefying food, diseased flesh and unwashed bodies. The whole of la Salpêtrière stank like one great rotted mass.

As they escorted me from the kitchen back to my cell, I watched old scabies-ridden women scraping up scraps of onions and cabbage from the courtyard. The keepers' foetid odour snagged in my nostrils and sweat dripped into my eyes. I ran my furry tongue over dry lips.

'That Diamond Necklace trial is over,' the fat keeper said.

'What happened?' asked the other, thin one.

'It's all here,' the fat one said, flapping the newspaper about with the hand not restraining me. 'Front page news!'

'Well, read it to me, man,' the thin one said.

The fat keeper thrust his newspaper at him. 'You read it.'

'I can read,' I said. 'I'll tell you what it says.'

The fat one shoved his paper at me. 'Go on then, smart whore.'

'"In a sensational trial the thirty-year old con artist and brains behind the Diamond Necklace Affair, Jeanne de Valois-Saint-Rémy, Comtesse de la Motte, was condemned to be whipped and branded in public, then interred for life in the Prison Quarter of la Salpêtrière"', I read. '"After having accepted the *Parlement de Paris* as judges, the Cardinal de Rohan was acquitted, and exiled by the King. The prostitute Nicole Leguay d'Oliva and the charlatan, Cagliostro, were also acquitted. In his absence, after his probable escape to England with the necklace, Jeanne's husband, Count Nicolas de la Motte was condemned to the galleys for life."'

The following day, the asylum quaked with two pieces of news. Firstly, a new Sister Superior had been appointed.

'Some rich old bitch,' Agathe said.

'Only the wealthy and well-connected get that position,' Marie-Françoise said with a sneer.

The other news rippling through the dormitories was of the famous Jeanne de Valois-Saint-Rémy, and her pending imprisonment in la Salpêtrière's Prison Quarter.

'They say she fought so hard when they whipped her that five torturers had to hold her,' Julie said.

'And she writhed about so, the hot iron slipped and they burned the *voleuse* "V" into her breast instead of her shoulder,' Toinette said.

'Bet she's still got them diamonds,' Agathe said. 'I don't think she'll mind sharing some with me, *n'est-ce pas*, Victoire?'

'Or she sold them and we'll get a load of sous out of her,' Marie-Françoise said. The two women cackled and Agathe hacked a gob of green phlegm at my feet.

But none of my fellow prisoners got to meet la Comtesse de la Motte. Two keepers came to our dormitory and hauled me away.

'Where are you taking me?'

The men remained wordless as they hurried me across courtyards into another part of the vast prison, and pushed me into a private cell.

Clothed in a black silk dress, a woman sat on the blanketed bed. How regal she looked, trying to hold her back straight when I knew it must be stinging from the whip burns.

From beneath a dark lace net that covered most of her face, she smiled, stretching one hand out to me.

'Sister Superior informs me you are an intelligent, literate woman, just as I requested. I am very happy to welcome you as my personal maid, Victoire.'

My hand clamped in the warm grip of the most-talked about woman in the country, I sensed a confidence; a subtle power. Bathed in the dark luminous eyes, I glimpsed a hint of the enigma that shrouded Jeanne de Valois-Saint-Rémy.

24

'Why have you never told me of this scandal, *ma chère?*'

I was still far from discovering everything about Jeanne de Valois, but I had learned much about her in the three months as her personal maid. I knew this look, reflected in the mirror, and the way the vein bulged in her temple—the signs that belied her mute rage of all the violations, every malfeasance occasioned against a commoner, which Jeanne seemed to suffer as her own.

As she twisted about to face me, her swathe of dark hair knocked the hairbrush from my hand. The brush clattered to the floor. I bent to retrieve it and began brushing Jeanne's hair again, my strokes charged with rhythm and purpose.

Jeanne clasped my free hand. 'Don't tell me you never said anything because you felt ashamed, Victoire? That you believe the behaviour of this marquis was your fault?'

'Perhaps I never spoke of it,' I said, still brushing, 'because I was trying to forget. I had hoped it would fade with time, but whenever I let myself think back, the memories of those nights are as fresh as ever.'

Barely pausing for breath, I told Jeanne the rest, my voice faltering only when I reached the part about abandoning Rubie.

'I wrapped her in kitchen rags.' I put the hairbrush aside and folded my arms. 'I left her in a basket on the church steps.'

I felt Jeanne's hand on my shoulder. 'I am glad, *ma chère* that you have shared this with me. Now, give me the name of the vile libertine.'

I shook my head. 'Claudine—that's Cook, my friend—said I must not think of vengeance, but how can't I? He strangled a girl. Perhaps if I'd spoken up that maid would still have her life.'

'I understand why you said nothing, Victoire, you needed to keep your position, but that's no longer the case and this depraved man must be stopped,' Jeanne said. 'I am certain you don't wish him to go on murdering innocent girls. Now you must tell me, who is this so ignoble noble?'

'Alphonse Donatien Delacroix, Marquis de Barberon,' I said, through gritted teeth. 'I despise him. I hate all nobles, and what they stand for, but as much as I crave revenge, I fear it is impossible. Claudine says commoners will never triumph over powerful nobles.'

Jeanne tossed her head. '*Ppfft*. Times are changing, *ma chère*. Those aristocrats will soon topple from their mighty pillars, and I am sure, like me, you will be there, laughing when they fall flat on their powdered noses. Besides, there is none more powerful in this country than la Comtesse Jeanne de Valois-Saint-Rémy!'

Her smile, bent with irony, revealed straight, polished teeth. I'd always thought they were so white because of the ivory-mounted brush she used, or the toothpaste, which cost an outrageous three livres. Now I understood they must be the same, expensive porcelain teeth of the Marquis.

She kissed the back of my hand, and rubbed the rough skin.

'Let me smooth those working hands with my special salve,' she said, massaging her rose-scented cream into my skin. 'Then we'll stroll in the courtyard. We must continue your French lessons and try to rid you of that dreadful provincial accent. Besides, the fresh air might colour your cheeks.'

***

Jeanne batted at flies with her walking cane. She twitched her nose at the smells rising from the drains, and the waste rotting in piles in obscure corners. I could almost pretend, on our afternoon strolls, that Jeanne—ever poised and elegant—was a real countess roaming the grounds of her vast country home, and I her dedicated maid.

As Jeanne instructed me on the words and phrases of the language of Paris and the manners of a respectable city woman, I forgot my dormitory cell and the fellow prisoners I had to endure.

'You have never told me your story,' Jeanne said, twirling the cane. 'Everybody has one. Why won't you tell me yours, *ma chère*?'

'Oh it's not very interesting, the usual peasant-girl childhood.' I fingered the lavender and the pale blue hydrangeas, which had folded themselves against the burning heat. The leaves on the sparse trees hung low, the shrubs too looked thirsty, their colour bleached out in three months of scorching sun.

Jeanne hooked her arm through mine and as we walked on, I found myself telling her about the fun of the harvests, Carnival and Saint John's bonfire night.

'My brother, Grégoire and I, and my friend, Léon had our own special place at the river. We'd swim in the waterfall and catch fish with our bare hands.' Remnants of song lyrics, sunlight and raked hay flitted through my mind. 'Maman always warned us the Vionne River could be dangerous. She forbade us to go there.'

'But that never stopped you?' Jeanne said with a knowing smile.

'We'd come home wet through, so she must've known where we'd been, but we were so happy, I don't think she had the heart to scold us.'

'Is your maman still alive?'

I looked away, across to where the Seine River flowed behind the high asylum wall. 'They claimed Maman was a witch and murdered her. She was no witch. Maman was Lucie's healing woman and midwife. My mother was also an angel-maker. As a child, I imagined she performed some magical, fairy-like thing with the tea she made from rue, vervain and her tiny blue flowers.'

I waved an arm in the direction of the nursery. 'Seeing those hundreds of doomed babies in there, I can't help thinking that surely an angel-maker is not so dishonourable after all?'

'A most philanthropic calling in life,' Jeanne said, brandishing the cane again.

'After Félix and Félicité, then Papa died, Maman became … I don't know, sad. A little mad perhaps, as if each separate tragedy swelled into one great crushing wad of grief. She lost her faith in God, and the Church.' I felt for my angel pendant—an instinctive gesture I couldn't throw off.

'*Mon Dieu*, the barbarians,' Jeanne said. 'I assume she had no proper trial?'

'There were never trials.'

'Another victim of our unjust, archaic system, Victoire—the one we must fight to change. And your father?'

'Papa was a carpenter,' I said. As I told Jeanne about the fire that had destroyed our cottage, the agony of that moment still split my heart in two. 'Since a baron killed my father, and of course, those nights in Saint-Germain, I have despised every aristocrat.'

'I know too well life can be unjust.' Jeanne's arm pressed against mine. 'You have borne terrible tragedies. I would like to hope that for the rest of your days, you will experience only pleasurable things.'

'Nice things? In *here*? And they'll never let me out, Jeanne, ever. All that—the peasant girl from Lucie—is so distant, so unreal. It's as if my whole life has been this asylum.'

'How absurd, *ma chère*! As if someone as God-fearing as you could remain in this infernal mosaic of misery, with such a wretched portion of humanity—all the country's mad people and vagabonds, its whores, charlatans and cutthroats. A place of no gentleness, no remedy! Not likely, Victoire, as I have a plan for us. It is proving time-consuming but I will tell you of it shortly. So don't ask questions now.

Jeanne still held my arm as we strolled alongside *le potager* where gardeners were plucking the last of the season's garlic and vegetables for the meals of la Salpêtrière's personnel and its wealthy, paying prisoners, like Jeanne de Valois.

'Don't despair, Victoire. As I said, if my plan succeeds, everything will change. I have privileges and some influence here, but still it will not be easy and requires careful planning. Besides, you need time to learn the ways of the Parisian bourgeois society if you are to blend in once you are free.'

'Bourgeois society?' I said. 'Free?'

Jeanne touched a finger to my lips. 'No questions yet, remember? Now, I notice, *ma chère*, you do not mention your little twins. Naturally, I have heard the talk here, but am I to believe such malicious gossip? How hard I find that, of someone so ... so unstained—a woman who seems not to have a speck of badness in her veins.'

I breathed deeply, the tendrils of melancholy unfurling, wrapping themselves around me again as I tried to recall that day on the riverbank. 'When I think about it, it starts coming back, but before I know what truly happened, it's gone.'

We had reached the Insane Quarter, girdled on three sides by a lofty wall. Through the gate, I could see several women chained to benches, their grey dresses hanging from them like empty sacks. They stared at us with wide, liquid eyes.

As we approached, I shut my ears to their cries, their shrieks, and the soft whimpers of the particularly feeble.

'The dungeon keepers would put us outside for an hour every day,' I said, nodding towards the women. 'To improve our mental health, they claimed. What a joke.'

'Poor, desperate wretches.' Jeanne beckoned me away from them with her cane and nursed my arm closer to her side. 'You know, *ma chère*, whatever you have done, whatever happened at the river with your babes, I'll not judge you. I, of all people, know everyone has their reasons.'

As we walked away from the dungeon women, I saw myself in the orphanage, cradling the baby girl, something urging me to press my dress down over her face. The thought both shocked and terrified me.

'Well I'll not press you now, Victoire, but one day I hope you can free yourself of this terrible secret trapped in your mind.'

'And you, Jeanne, why have you never told me the necklace story? The true story?'

'*Mon Dieu*, that gaudy chunk of jewellery. Well, probably because I was so angry I'd missed my chance,' she said. 'But time has cleared the fog and the future shines bright and sunny, *ma chère*. I will regain my name, and our land.'

She took my hand, fondling my fingers and rubbing my calloused joints. 'But first you must know the beginning, Victoire. Then you might understand why I did what I had to.'

Jeanne sat on a bench and patted a place next to her. 'My dear papa, Henri de Saint Rémy-Valois, was a descendant of the love child of King Henri II and Nicole de Savigny. He was a member of Parliament. I should have lived in luxury, but they stole everything from me.

'Who?'

'The King's guard came and murdered my father, and the Crown stole our property and land.' Jeanne's voice did not waver but from the pulsing vein in her temple I knew she was, as always, masking her fury.

'So instead of an opulent life, we were the poorest of poor. Maman was forced to prostitute herself for our survival, and my siblings and I tramped the streets, begging for charity for the last of the Valois. Poor Maman's heart was broken when she lost my father. She died soon after.'

'So you too, are orphaned.'

'My sister and I were destined for the convent, so we escaped back to our birthplace, Bar-sur-Aube,' she said, 'and found refuge with a family we had known. I never forgot the injustice but I knew that to regain our property, I had to be in royal favour.'

'However does one get the royal favour?'

'I married the nephew of the family, Count Antoine-Nicolas de la Motte, and *voilà*, I became Countess de la Motte.'

'A real count?

'How many of the aristocracy strutting around this country are genuine?' Jeanne said with a smirk. 'What with all those rich bourgeoisie buying government offices, inventing some long-lost noblesse, or the King simply elevating them to the noble class—that new Nobility of the Robe.'

'You got into the royal court with your husband's title?'

Jeanne nodded. 'I hoped to become close to Marie Antoinette and get back what was rightfully mine.'

'Rumours say the Queen ignored you?'

Jeanne flipped her head. 'The Austrian bitch would have nothing to do with me.' Her fingers began tracing a gentle line from my wrist, up my inner forearm. 'All the Queen had to do was notice me, listen to my pleas, read my petition. All the rest could have been avoided.' Her fingertips lingered in the crook of my elbow.

'Then the goose laid me a golden egg,' she said. 'The Cardinal de Rohan wanted to become Prime Minister of France, but when he was envoy to Austria, his personal letters were intercepted. He bragged that he'd bedded half the Austrian court and said Marie Antoinette's own mother, the Empress, had begged him for her turn. Of course, Marie Antoinette blocked his ministerial progress at every turn.'

She dropped my arm and gazed towards the wall behind which the Seine River curled its way through Paris. 'So, we lay there, together, I exploding with intrigue, the Cardinal exploding with lust. I told him I was an intimate friend of Marie Antoinette's.' She laughed. 'Silly, silly courtesans and royals, so caught up in their frivolous, purposeless lives. I assured the Cardinal I would reinstate his good name, and he would become Prime Minister. A kiss, a caress in the right place, and the fool was a kitten in my palm, spooning out louis d'or like honey.' She smiled. 'Money for the Queen's charity work! Though it did get me into respectable society. See Victoire, you can do whatever you like with money.'

'But what of this necklace?'

Jeanne took her cane and marched off. I stood too, and hurried to keep up with her brisk steps.

'All those festoons, pendants and tassels of diamonds. Nothing but an inglorious tribute to the vanity of man,' she said. 'The vanity that began when the previous king asked Boehmer and Bassenge—the jewellers, you see—to create a diamond necklace to surpass all others, as a gift to his favourite mistress, Madame du Barry. It cost two million livres. Can you imagine, for one piece of jewellery, and such a hideous one?' She rolled her eyes. 'Well, it took these jewellers several years and a lot of money to assemble the diamonds, but in the meantime the old King died of smallpox and the du Barry woman was banished from court.'

I nodded. 'Yes, I heard the story of the old King's death.'

'The bankrupt jewellers then tried to sell the necklace to the new king,' Jeanne went on. 'But Marie Antoinette refused because it had been designed for her enemy, Madame du Barry. Well, that was my cue, Victoire. Of course, my scheme was not without risk, but there was every chance I could succeed. I told the Cardinal the Queen secretly desired the necklace. He paid the two million livres to me, believing I would hand the money to the Queen.' She swiped at a fly, fidgeting around my cap. 'I then collected the necklace from the jewellers, who thought I would give it to the Queen, who would then pay them. When the time came to pay and nothing happened, the jewellers complained to the Queen, who told them she had never received or ordered the necklace.' She waved an arm. 'Then followed the *coup de théâtre* which you no doubt heard about.'

'I think the whole of France was talking about it,' I said.

'Well, *ma chère*, you know the rest—how they whipped and branded me and threw me in here. That bitch Queen fixed it all. She will suffer, as I have. I am finished with the rich trampling the poor. And I would hope you are too, Victoire.'

She pointed her cane at a tree. 'Look at those leaves, already on the turn. Do you want to spend another winter here, flirting with death? You are twenty-four, and still ravishing. You may still have a good ten years left, out of this madhouse.'

'I stopped thinking of a life beyond these walls long ago,' I said. 'Nobody could get past the guards.'

Jeanne laughed. 'My sweet love, so naïve. I told you, I have an idea to get past those imbeciles.'

'Visitor for you, countess,' an approaching keeper shouted.

Jeanne raised my hand to her lips. 'Return to the dormitory. It is safer for you if you know nothing. That way they cannot torture you.'

***

So accustomed I was to the shouts, steam and clatter of the kitchen, I'd almost forgotten the daily silence of the cell. Since I had become Jeanne's maid, they only made me cook in the mornings. The afternoons I spent with my mistress, learning the ways of Parisian society. I never questioned why this good luck had befallen me. The wise never asked questions at la Salpêtrière.

The women were hard at work—knitting, weaving, embroidery, lace work and spinning—as they would have been since morning prayers. Sister officers strolled amongst the quiet clot of women, all clothed in identical ash-grey dresses, bonnets and clogs.

Religious in nothing but name, the sister officers tapped their sticks on the stone floor, rapping the knuckles and shoulders of anyone who slackened off from the incessant labour, or who made the slightest sound.

'Don't think your hands will stay idle,' one of them hissed, as

I entered the dormitory. She threw me a pile of cloth. 'No special privileges when you're not with that con woman.'

Agathe raked her festering lips into a smirk and blew me a kiss.

At four o'clock work ceased briefly as we said the rosary and prayed again. A little later, I knew it was five-thirty, because I heard the children and old women outside—the only ones, apart from the insane, permitted to leave their dormitories to take the courtyard air for an hour.

Five-thirty was also the one hour of the day they permitted us to talk, but not to stop working. We were never to stop working except to sleep, eat or pray—that same monotonous cycle.

'How is our personal maid, then?' Agathe twisted my arm behind my back, but I refused to cry out with the pain. 'When are you going to find out about those diamonds?'

'I told you, I am only her maid. I know nothing.'

'Careful, Agathe,' Marie-Françoise said, 'Remember last time you gave her those bruises they locked you in the dungeons with the crazies for two days. Our Victoire is well connected now.'

'But the countess woman must still have the diamonds, or the money,' Agathe said.

'Yes,' Toinette said, 'how else could she afford a private cell, a maid and proper food?'

'And afternoon strolls, outdoors,' Julie said.

I raised my hands. 'Please, I know nothing.'

Agathe sneered and spat a glob of phlegm at my face as the sister officers distributed the evening meal of black bread, *potage* and wine. I dared not wipe my cheek, and the phlegm slid down my face. 'You'll talk, my lovely,' Agathe went on. 'You'll tell me everything before I've finished with you.'

Agathe could threaten me all she liked, but the woman no longer frightened me. Since Jeanne shared her simple, but adequate, meals with me, I felt stronger and more able to bear her intimidation, her beatings, and her resentment of my privileged role.

The meal over, Sister Superior rang the bell for evening prayer and recital of psalms. Afterwards, the sister officers performed their nightly dormitory inspection, checking nobody was hiding anything illegal. At ten o'clock they snuffed out the sole candle.

I lay prone on the straw mattress. There was no room to curl up, though every lonely night I did silently thank Jeanne for buying me this bed by the window. At least I shared it with only two others, instead of the usual five.

I listened to the women's exhausted snores, their shallow night breaths, and I felt their loneliness, their desperation. As I began to drift into my own restless sleep, a single cry from the Insane Quarter broke the quiet. Then another, and another. The cries spread, louder and louder; inhuman shrieks, which penetrated the night silence and rose over the stone walls. Woken by the noise from the lower *loges*, several prisoners cried out, like some instinctive reply to an ancestral code. I clamped my hands over my ears.

The light from the zenith moon slanted through the dormer window, casting criss-cross shadows on the wall. I'd resigned myself to an existence in la Salpêtrière, death my only way out, but as the illusory warmth of that feeble moonlight flooded my face and neck, a glimmer of hope shone through the shadows of desperation. I could almost believe in Jeanne's claim of another life for me beyond the bars.

25

I scuttled through the crisp autumn breeze, across the courtyard, from the kitchen to Jeanne's cell, and tapped on the door.

It opened a crack and I was surprised to see the smirking face of a guard. A muffled giggle and another, deeper voice, came from inside.

One of Jeanne's sleek dresses was heaped on the floor, along with her undergarments. The keeper who had opened the door was reaching for his uniform. The second keeper lay naked, sprawled on the bed beside Jeanne; she too, was unclothed.

Her skin so pale it was almost translucent, Jeanne reminded me of the nymph creature painting in the Saint-Germain house. The dark curls between her thighs recalled to me those grape clusters, draped across the creature like forbidden fruit. I swayed back, averting my eyes from the male bodies.

'What's eating the emerald-eyed princess?' the still-naked keeper said. 'Never seen a cock before? Come here, I'll show you mine!' He laughed, waggling his penis at me.

'Now, now, boys, enough amusement for one afternoon,' Jeanne chided. 'Put your jewels away, get dressed, and come back another day.'

The keepers laughed as they crept away from Jeanne's cell, their hair still dishevelled.

'How can you do that, Jeanne? Surely you cannot enjoy them

… those hideous men?'

Jeanne patted the bed, inviting me to sit beside her. 'Oh it's not too bad. Quite fun, even. How else am I to alleviate prison boredom? Besides, they're my friends now, our allies, Victoire.'

I clasped my hands in my lap. 'Sometimes I wish I was more like you,' I said. 'So free; so unbound by rules and tradition.'

'You may find it hard to believe, Victoire, but I envy you— your morals, your virtues.' She took my hand and placed it on the veined mound of her left breast, over the sign branding her a thief. 'Feel it, *ma chère*. Trace the V with your finger.'

She rolled down my shift, exposing my left shoulder. 'They have burnt you too,' she said, her fingertips tracing my *fleur-de-lys* burn. 'How dare they brand us like common cattle!' Her hand slid down and she rested her palm against my breast, which rose and fell like a river swell. 'Those keepers will pay for that.'

Jeanne sat up and I fastened her stays, helped her put her petticoat on, and the black dress.

She reached under her bed, brought out a wooden box and inserted a gold key into the lock. She flipped the lid and withdrew a small glass bottle, holding it as if it were a diamond.

'What is it?' I took the bottle of red-brown liquid and lifted it to my nose. 'Such a strange smell … sort of fierce and tart, but at the same time sweet and earthy, like cut grass. Oh yes, I remember now, Armand would use this for the calves with colic.'

Jeanne nodded. 'This, *ma chère*, is laudanum—remedy for pain, insomnia and diarrhoea. And, possibly, calf colic.' She took the bottle from me. 'But two or three teaspoons could kill a man … or a keeper.'

'No, but—'

'Don't fret, we're not going to murder them,' she said with a laugh. 'We just want to make them sleep long enough to steal their uniforms and dance right out of la Salpêtrière.'

***

'We leave tomorrow afternoon, *ma chère,*' Jeanne said. 'Our favourite keepers are on duty. Twilight will have fallen before you have to be back in your dormitory—the perfect cover.'

A tingle flitted down my spine. I dared not cry out with joy; dared not hope we might soon be gone from this most ungodly place.

Jeanne took her wooden box from under the bed. She lifted the compartment containing the hidden phial of laudanum and drew out a scroll of papers.

'This,' she said with a smile, 'is your new life. You will call yourself Mademoiselle Rubie Charpentier—I know you like that name. Your father is the recently deceased, and wealthy, Monsieur Maximilien Charpentier.' She handed me two sheets of paper. 'Here are recommendation letters for positions I am certain will suit you.'

'Positions?'

'Why, an independent woman with no husband or lover must work, Victoire! Besides, it will be beneficial for you to mingle with society, get to know people.' She held up one of the pages. 'Here, your literacy skills are commended for work in a printing press. A contact of mine owns it.'

'Why am I to work in a press?'

'You read and write well. Surely you can understand we revolutionaries must print out a multitude of pamphlets to help the people's cause to bring down the monarchy? After the death of your father at the hand of a noble, and then this barbarous marqu—'

'Yes, of course,' I said. 'I certainly do want to fight for the commoners' rights.'

'As I thought,' she said, squeezing me arm. 'Our revolution needs people like you here in Paris. People who are passionate about the cause, and intelligent enough to instruct the minds of others, with the decorum and education of the most educated Parisian woman,' she added, with a wink. 'As for me, I shall continue my own private battle from afar—'

'Afar? You will leave me, alone?'

'I have done all I can in France, discrediting Marie Antoinette's abominable reputation and the Bourbon monarchy even further. Now I must go where the Queen can no longer touch me, *ma chère*,' she said, kissing my cheek.

'But we also hear the Queen's behaviour has improved as she's grown older,' I said. 'That she is generous with money and charity, and devoted to her children.'

'I do concede she is liberal with her funds, and has begun to dress with more restraint,' Jeanne said. 'But that is far from sufficient. Did you know she built a fantasy farm at Versailles, where she plays at being a peasant? Of course, the million francs annual expense of it is met by the public purse.'

'But why would she do such a thing?'

'Oh for the simple reason that it is fashionable among aristocratic ladies to experience a rural idyll whilst remaining cloistered in the comfort of their estates. Many view the Queen as a clueless money squanderer playing at shepherdess—a mockery if you will, of the desperate and inhumane peasant condition. And not to mention those ridiculous, metre-high wigs adorned with jewels, feathers, ships and whatever else tickles her royal twat.' She rolled her eyes. 'Did you ever set eyes on that *pouf à l'inoculation* head-dress?'

'Vaccination *pouf*?'

Jeanne nodded. 'A serpent wrapped around an olive tree stuck on her head. She wore it to boast of her success in persuading the King to be vaccinated against smallpox.'

'I know nothing of any head-dress,' I said, as Jeanne handed me another sheet of paper.

'This second letter recommends you as a reputed chef for a position at *Le Faisan Doré* restaurant. The owner is an ex-lover. He also, is expecting you.'

'You believe I should cook in a restaurant? But can't I return to Lucie? My little Madeleine must be missing her mother.'

'It is my greatest wish to see you reunited with your family,

Victoire, but first you have things to do, business to finish. Besides, don't forget, as an asylum escapee, you'll not be able to show yourself in public as Victoire Charpentier. Now, this restaurant is located at the Palais-Royal and I am certain, once there,' she went on with a knowing smile, 'you will understand why you must stay in Paris for a time.'

'What else do I take?' I asked. 'Not that I have anything to take.'

'Everything you need will be waiting in your apartment. You shall have the address on a slip of paper, once we are beyond these walls.'

'My apartment? You'll not be with me, even for a moment, before you go … go afar?'

Jeanne pressed my hand to her lips. 'You no longer need me, *ma chère*. You must stand alone now; forge your own personal battle, and our country's struggle, but one day, when both of us emerge triumphant, who knows?'

I gripped the letters. 'I'll sew these into my petticoat. The cloth is coarse and thick, and will mask the rustle of the paper.'

Jeanne nodded. 'You learn quickly.'

I stitched the papers into my petticoat hem, feeling Jeanne's eyes on me, as if they were burning through my clothes, searing the layers of my skin. I felt my cheeks blush with the rising heat.

'I shall miss you, my friend.' Jeanne took my hands, massaging them again with her rose-perfumed salve. 'And don't forget to keep these peasant hands hidden within gloves or beneath a muff,' she said. 'People notice such things.'

She leaned close, and her hair, falling against my face, made me quiver. I shut my eyes and suddenly I was, no more, a prisoner of la Salpêtrière.

Jeanne's simple bed became one of oak, carved with angels and inlaid with diamonds. We lay on silken sheets, so slippery the fabric felt damp. Jeanne reached up from our warmth, drawing heavy crimson drapes, concealing us from prying eyes.

I could not see her. I could only feel her and taste her lips, warm and insistent on mine. My mouth was still at first. I think it was the shock of her touch. Then my lips moved against hers, and opened. I felt her tongue, tentative for a moment, then thrusting, exploring the inside of my mouth. It tasted like wine, which made me more and more drunk. I felt dizzy and my heart—frozen for so long—thawed with her heat and gushed like a waterfall from my breast.

She touched a corner of our wet lips, my cheek, my brow, a fingertip trailing across my eyelid. Her hand moved down, across my neck, my shoulders and to my breast.

When Jeanne reached between my legs and her hand began to move, sliding wet and gentle, it was as if she had touched a raw wound, and exposed a nerve. I felt a longing so great, so sharp, it was painful. It mounted and mounted until I thought I would go mad. I feared it might even kill me.

She wrapped her hips about my thigh and pressed over and over, opening me to the throb inside. I think I murmured or groaned, but maybe it was Jeanne.

As she reached to my core, I let the ecstasy swamp me, drowning my every sense, until I burst from her hand and shattered on her wet thigh.

We cried out together, and I barely heard the clanging bell that signalled supper, and the return to my cell.

26

The following afternoon I scurried across the courtyard. Yes, this pale November light would be perfect cover. I glanced about, hoping my excitement, my trepidation, didn't show, but nobody paid me any attention. I tapped on the cell door.

'Good, you are here, *ma chère*.' Jeanne smiled and pressed her lips to mine. I detected no hint of embarrassment about the previous afternoon. It was as if it had been the most natural thing.

A bottle of red wine sat on the commode next to four glasses. Engraved with lovebirds and flowers, the glasses were as delicate and handsome as those of the Saint-Germain house.

'It is so kind of Sister Superior to lend me glasses from her own collection, *n'est-ce pas*, Victoire?' Jeanne wrapped a pale hand around each opaque, twisted stem as she filled the glasses. 'A full-bodied, strong wine you see, to mask laudanum of the deepest red and the wildest odour.'

I held my breath as Jeanne *plink-plinked* drops of laudanum into two of the glasses. 'I'd best not mix the glasses up, eh?' she said, stoppering the bottle just as the tap came at her door.

She opened the door a slit and the two keepers sauntered in like cocks in a hen coop.

'*Eh bien, comtesse*, I see we'll not have to share you this afternoon,' one of them said, grinning at me and groping for my breast. 'If it's not Victoire, our pretty child murderess.'

I tried not to cringe or move. I was even able to smile, as I recalled the small bruise that lay beneath his hand—the place on my breast Jeanne had kissed a little too hard yesterday.

Jeanne smacked his hand from me and mock-frowned. 'Not yet, frisky boy. First we'll make a toast and drink this delicious wine that was so kindly acquired for me.' She handed the glasses around.

'To a most special afternoon,' Jeanne said, as we raised our glasses.

I lowered my eyes from the keepers' lust-darkened gazes.

Jeanne drained her glass quickly, and I supposed she was urging the keepers to do likewise. My stomach was such a tangle of knots I could barely sip mine.

As we had rehearsed, I positioned myself on the bed beside Jeanne, who crooked her forefinger, beckoning the keepers. Slowly we began removing their uniforms. The one before me grabbed at my breasts again.

'Not so fast, *mon garçon*,' Jeanne said. 'Savour the moment.'

I kept glancing at their glasses. Surely they had not drunk enough for the laudanum to take effect. I was petrified they would recognise its pungently sweet smell, its acrid taste. Or worse, that I would have to pursue their lurid advances before the drug worked.

Soon their speech began to slur and their gestures became slow and listless. I felt my shoulders and neck relax as they sank, swan-like, to the floor.

'Quickly,' Jeanne said, the vein in her temple pulsing. 'We don't have long.'

We finished removing the keepers' clothes, and tore off our own dresses and chemises. I kept my petticoat on, with its concealed papers, as we dressed in the keepers' uniforms.

'Hurry, tie my hair up, Victoire.'

I fumbled with Jeanne's hair all the while searching the keepers' faces, certain they would stir any instant.

'My hair … it's not all under the hat,' I hissed.

The blood rushed through me as Jeanne fiddled with wayward strands.

'Now for the finishing touch.' Jeanne reached into a drawer and drew out two moustaches. 'Courtesy of an actress friend.' She pasted one above my lips, then her own. She span around. 'Don't we look the perfect keepers?'

'He moved,' I said, pointing at one of the keepers. 'He blinked.'

'Don't be anxious, *ma chère*, we're going now.'

Her cell was too small to step around the slumbering keepers, so we were forced to step over the prone bodies.

I held my breath, certain the faint sweep of air from our feet would waken the men. My eyes fixed on the dozing faces, I lifted my first foot over. I raised the second one.

Something cold gripped my ankle. I screamed, and Jeanne was yelling and swearing.

'*Merde, merde*! Let go. Let go of me you great oaf!'

The keepers were wide awake, spitting out mouthfuls of the laced wine, and grasping our ankles. In that instant I understood they'd not drunk a drop of the laudanum. The trick was on us. I couldn't move, and Jeanne was still yelling and kicking at the keeper.

He let her ankle go for a second, sprang up and punched her in the face.

'*Foutre de la garce*,' he said. 'Fucking bitch.' Over and over he hit her and swore, until blood streamed from Jeanne's lips.

I tried to rush to her, but the keeper only tightened his grip. Jeanne stumbled backwards under the repeated blows, her lip gaping and red. I saw the rage in her black eyes, each blow fuelling her fury a little more. I feared the vein throbbing in her temple would explode.

'Pig!' Jeanne spat, through bloody lips. 'You'll pay for this!'

He twisted her arms behind her back. 'You take us for fools, Jeanne de Valois, greatest con artist of all time?' He restrained her with one hand. In the other, he held a sodden piece of cloth, stained a reddish-brown. 'Such a shame our handkerchiefs, and not our lips, absorbed that delicious wine—and the purest of laudanum,' he said. 'Apart from that one, delicious mouthful.' He waved an arm at the wine puddle on the floor.

'As if we'd trust Jeanne de Valois, and risk our jobs,' the keeper holding me said. He too, sprang to his feet and twisted my arms behind my back.

'Risk our heads, more like it!' Jeanne's captor shrieked. 'They would whip, torture and break us on the wheel—tomorrow's public spectacle on la place de Grève, if we let la Salpêtrière's most infamous inmate escape.

'Sister Superior will be livid with you, countess,' he continued. 'She will see this attempted escape as a personal slight to the tight ship she boasts.'

'And you,' Jeanne said, her words thick through swelling lips. 'I bet Sister Superior's tight ship pays you keepers no more than a pittance?'

'What are you suggesting?' Jeanne's captor said with a smirk.

'I suggest you both get dressed,' Jeanne said. 'And go far away from my cell, and nobody has any notion of what went on this afternoon.'

The keepers looked at each other.

'I think we could manage that,' the second one said. 'As long as Madame la Comtesse makes it worth our while.'

***

I dabbed Jeanne's lip with cool water.

'Merely superficial injuries,' she said, beating a fist against her chest. 'In here, they cannot touch me.'

'Hush now.' I held the cloth against her lip. 'It must hurt to speak.'

Once the bleeding had stopped, I dressed in my prison garb and sat on the bed beside Jeanne. She drew me close and I felt the rapid beating of a heart and supposed it was mine, but it was

Jeanne's. I began to weep, my tears coming fast, onto her face.

'I'm so afraid,' I said.

'Of what?'

'I don't know. Of never getting away from here. And, at the same time, of one day succeeding, and then being alone, without you.'

'Once on the outside you will find the strength to fight, Victoire. A strength I know is inside you.'

'You have paid the keepers off,' I said. 'But how can you be sure they'll not keep asking for money?'

'Oh, they will, *ma chère*, they will, but we won't be staying here much longer.' She held me at arm's length, and met my eyes. 'You surely don't imagine that little laudanum party was my only plan?'

She sat up. 'Now, help me put my clothes back on.'

'But why didn't you simply give the money to Sister Superior, as you've done since you were imprisoned?' I said, helping her dress.

'I may be wealthy,' Jeanne said, 'but the woman is getting beyond even my means. Aside from the wealth she possessed before acquiring this position—the money that *got* her the position—her enormous income allows her to live in such opulence, *ma chère*.'

'Why is a woman of such wealth obliged to work at all?' I said, smoothing down the full skirt of her *robe à l'anglais*, puffing up the sleeves at her elbows.

'Oh she doesn't *need* to work,' Jeanne said. 'It is simply to maintain her social standing. She loves the power she wields over all of Paris; the people who clamour for invitations to her buffets to play games, dance and sing to grove-filled violin music. And that's not forgetting all the other benefits *la patronne* of la Salpêtrière is entitled to.'

'Like what?' I wrapped Jeanne's soft, full shawl about her shoulders.

'Oh, her chic apartment with its fashionable furniture and

many servants. A vast garden with vegetables and gardeners and, of course, the private coach, horses and coachmen.'

'But however are we to get away?'

'Unfortunately, *ma chère*, we are bound to remain here over the winter. Our chance will come again at *la fête de Carnaval*.' She inhaled deeply. 'And this time, my plan will not fail.'

'Carnival? As if we, in the asylum, will be allowed to celebrate that!'

'Indeed, Victoire. In a recent conversation, our new, well-connected Sister Superior informed me she is to hold a Carnival ball here at la Salpêtrière, before the penitential dullness of Lent.'

'A ball for us—the criminals, the poor, the insane? I can hardly believe such a thing.'

Jeanne shook her head. 'Of course not. Sister Superior would never risk her precious Parisian public mingling with us *idiotes*, *maniaques* and *hystériques*. Apparently though, she wishes for the most presentable of the mad and criminal fiends to be present. She wants to boast to her hierarchy; her fawning society, what a marvellous job she's doing here at la Salpêtrière; how well we are treated, how graciously we are reformed.' She laughed. 'Reform, what a joke! Though I am certain of one thing, Victoire. Sister Superior will make an exception for you and me—for all prisoners offering healthy donations.'

'You can get tickets for us? For *me*? But aren't they worried about prisoners escaping?'

'Of course,' Jeanne said with a nod. 'Sister Superior will take every precaution to thwart escapees who might try and take advantage of the festivities—the usual mounted guard of two corporals and eight soldiers will be increased two-fold. She'll hire extra keepers, spies and so on, but I know she wants this ball to be a special celebration. I think she sees it as the beginning of an enlightened-thinking annual ritual that will mark her as new head of la Salpêtrière.'

I helped Jeanne slip on her shoes. 'The curious public will buy tickets at exorbitant prices,' she went on. 'With the money,

Sister Superior claims she will improve the asylum, get rid of the dungeons and set up proper medical care.' Her fingertips felt like feathers on my cheek. 'Of course, she really only wants to impress people in high places so they compliment her and continue paying her fine salary.'

Jeanne traced around my lips with her index finger. 'This ball is already the talk of the capital, *ma chère*—marquises, countesses, the idle wives of bankers, lawyers and doctors—awaiting this one special *soirée* to escape their dull daily lives. The one night their cheeks will blush, not with modesty or shyness, but with heat and longing.' Her bright gaze held mine.

'The night they can play at being chameleons—throwing aside modesty and pretension—to dance for hours, and speak of men, love and sex. And, as they experience their most depraved desires, they will amass a mind full of memories and pleasures because, Victoire, the night is short. Too soon morning will come and they'll be back to their stifled lives.'

'But however will we escape?' I said.

'Well.' Jeanne's face crimped in a wide smile. 'Fortunately for us, Sister Superior's grand spectacle is to be none other than a masquerade ball.'

27

Jeanne fingered the pale green gown she'd had made for me by a renowned seamstress on the rue de Richelieu. She took a few paces back. 'Always wear this shade, Victoire, with your hair and eyes. Now, you have everything—your letters, your new identity?'

I nodded and finished helping Jeanne dress, running my trembling hands through her silk gown of dark turquoise, shot with gold embroidery.

'Exquisite as ever,' I said, a tingle sliding down the cleft of my breasts. 'Of course,' I went on with a wry smile, 'the countess Jeanne is only too aware of how her costume ripples about her like some gentle sea against the ivory sands of her skin.'

Jeanne laughed and brushed my lips with hers. '*Oh là là, ma chère*, I did say you'd be the next Voltaire, didn't I? Now remember, all you have to do is employ everything I've taught you and, above all, forget you were a peasant from the poor provinces. Dressed as we are, nobody will mistake us for anything but groomed Parisian ladies out for a night of fun.'

She fixed her peacock mask in place. 'Think of it as a final dress rehearsal for your new bourgeois life. Now hurry, Victoire, put your mask on and let's go and dance with the devil.'

We linked arms and stepped out into the cold February evening. We crossed courtyards, hurrying by the different buildings of la Salpêtrière rising so grandly—the gilt dome and marble facades that splendidly belied the catacomb of living bones. By the time we reached the ballroom entrance, I was quivering.

Jeanne squeezed my arm. 'Relax, the night will be unforgettable.'

I inhaled as deeply as my stays would permit, as we strolled along the entrance hallway, through the dim light flickering from gold-painted leaf sconces.

Once inside the ballroom, my mouth dropped open. Black velvet tapestries covered the ceiling and fell in heavy folds to a plush carpet the same bloody hue the windowpanes had been tinted. Six cloth-clad caryatids, one breast exposed, formed a rectangle around the perimeter of the room. Each brandished a burning flambeau.

'Never have I seen anything so magnificent,' I said.

'Yes, Victoire, so bold, so … fiery!'

The chandeliers drew my gaze upwards. Throwing the gaudy masqueraders' costumes into a fantasy of angular shadows, the golden light cast its magic on the women's diamonds and rubies.

'*Oh là là*, such a graceful, macabre lustre Sister Superior has created,' Jeanne said. 'Sometimes I think that woman is madder than half the women here. Come, Victoire, we need sustenance.' She led me through the crowd to the grand buffet at the end of the room.

'I'm sure I'll gorge myself silly on all this food,' I said.

'Tonight is an exception, *ma chère*. Everybody gets to eat the same food, but Sister Superior has planned it all cleverly.' Jeanne nodded at the people behind the buffet table.

'Those women dressed as maids, in white tulle caps, serving drinks, are all sister officers. And those,' she pointed towards the chefs offering sweets and cakes, 'are keepers, watching to make sure we prisoners don't stuff ourselves, or hide food within the folds of our clothes, to remove to our cells.'

'There are the keepers who stopped us escaping,' I hissed. 'The one who made your lip bleed.'

'*Eh oui, ma chère*, I haven't forgotten them.'

'But how welcoming they all are,' I said. 'What a turnaround.'

'Don't fool yourself, it is nothing but an illusion,' Jeanne said, as we found places alongside other guests, on the bench seats lining the walls. 'Tomorrow those smiling keepers and sister officers will be as evil and nasty as ever.' She sipped her wine and bit into her cake.

'Not that we care what happens tomorrow, eh?' she whispered, beneath the cadenced murmur filling the room.

The crowd fell silent as Sister Superior appeared, the hem of her rose-coloured silk gown sweeping across the floor like the sound of rain.

'*Merci à tous*,' she announced. 'With immense pleasure I declare the ball open. Let this spectacle begin—eat, drink, dance and enjoy! And don't forget the mask game. We all must try to guess the identity of each and every guest.'

The orchestra started playing and people began to dance in a swirl of fabric, which glittered and shivered like spring water. The music quickly mesmerised me, as Jeanne swept me onto the shiny floor and I played out all the dance steps we'd practised together—*le menuet, l'allemande, le cotillon*—for when I was a free woman.

We danced on, Jeanne taking the male role, like many of the women, who vastly outnumbered the men.

'The wine, the music, is making me giddy,' I said.

'Keep a clear head,' Jeanne said as yet more people approached us, trying to guess our identities. Jeanne turned away each time, laughing and dismissing the person with some vague excuse.

'Do not remove your mask … for anybody,' she said.

I was breathless, almost delirious, as we spun faster and faster amid the swirling mass. Snakes, bats, felines, sorceresses, princesses, Romans, Egyptians, milk maids and peasants: wealthy Parisians and wealthy prisoners brought together for this night of dreams.

'Nobody can tell who the crazies are. How to guess who

is *folle* and who is not?' Jeanne said as we rested on a bench seat with glasses of squash. 'Isn't that quite the bizarre irony of Carnival?'

'Perhaps we're all a bit mad,' I said. 'When we least expect it, the madness hits us as quickly as lightning strikes a peasant cottage and burns it to the ground. So vulnerable we are, to the caprices of *la mélancolie*—helpless to master wherever it takes us; whatever it makes us do.'

'You're right, *ma chère*, but don't think of such things now. This is the first night of our happier, brighter lives.' She took my hand. 'Let's get away from this crowd for a moment. Come and see some fun things.'

'What things?'

'Oh, Victoire, this is Carnival—a holiday, a game in which we oppose that ridiculous, ecclesiastical ritual of Lent,' Jeanne said with a wave of her arm. 'A time of ecstasy, of liberation. Sister Superior has promised her guests such dens of pleasure and debauchery you could never imagine!'

I followed her down a hallway with several private rooms off to each side. Jeanne went to open the door of the first one.

I laid my hand over hers. 'Must we, really? You said we were to leave tonight. What of the plan, Jeanne, why are we still here?'

'Because, *ma chère*, we must choose the perfect moment. It will come soon enough, just enjoy the ball for now.'

Jeanne opened the door and pulled me inside after her. 'Come on, it will be most entertaining to watch the demons play.'

Muted in sallow candlelight, a tangled silhouette of naked men and women lay sprawled across a Turkish rug, limbs entwined, hands searching, fingers and mouths exploring any available orifice.

From rose and lavender-perfumed incense, smoke curled into the amber gloom. In a darkened corner, three men wearing bull masks bucked, thrust and groaned as horns dug into the soft flesh of their shoulders, their backs.

'Welcome ladies, come and join us,' said a fat woman, fondling the penis of a young boy draped in nothing but a snake stole. 'Keep your masks if you wish, but remove your clothes.' The woman cackled and winked at me as she widened her crimson lips and took the length of the youth's penis in her mouth.

The Marquis of Saint-Germain and the keepers from Jeanne's cell flashed through my mind. I turned and fled from that feverish beat of vice.

I leaned against the wall, my breathing fast and shallow. 'I cannot watch those things, Jeanne. It makes me feel dirty … ashamed.' I lowered my eyes, shuffling the toe of my slipper through the thick red fibres. 'But at the same time, never have I feasted upon such phantasm, or felt such zest. What sort of a person have I become?'

Jeanne placed her hands on my hips. She kissed my ear, her tongue flicking in and out. 'A warm, very lovely woman, *ma chère*. Don't be anxious, it is only a game.'

We returned to the ballroom. The orchestra was taking a break, so we moved to the buffet area for more food and drink.

'I was told she would be here tonight,' we overheard a woman say, who was dressed in an arabesque outfit of flowers and foliage. 'Which one do you think she is?'

'Well, my dear,' a lady dressed as a Spanish dancer answered. 'Nobody has yet unmasked the famous Jeanne de Valois-Saint-Rémy, but I am sure we'll know who she is by the end of the night.' The women glanced about furtively.

'As if, in this huge crowd, la Salpêtrière's most celebrated prisoner might be standing right next to them,' Jeanne whispered. We threw our masked heads back and laughed.

'They say she has hidden many of the diamonds, *and* uses the fortune from the ones she's sold to bribe Sister Superior,' the first woman said, adjusting her hat—an elaborate birdcage in which two canaries twittered. 'Apparently she lives in relative luxury here in the prison building.'

'You heard she tried to escape?' the Spanish dancer said, sipping her wine. 'As if anybody could escape this asylum. I ask you, whatever was the woman thinking?'

Jeanne leaned towards the Spanish dancer. '*Oh là là*, what a thought,' she said. 'To try and flee la Salpêtrière!'

The woman turned to us, wordless. I tried not to gape at Jeanne's audacity, her nerve. As she giggled, took my arm and pranced off into the crowd, I wished I too could treat everything as some frivolous game, relishing the dangerous risks.

***

We danced again. We ate, drank, laughed and kept our masks in place. Finally, the mahogany wall clock began to chime the hour of midnight, its pendulum swinging back and forth with the strangest, deepest clang. So peculiar it was that everyone stopped and listened.

The orchestra paused. I sensed a hesitation; an uneasy break in the revelry, as if nobody really knew why everything had stopped so abruptly. It seemed we were all waiting for something to happen.

'Perhaps the bewitching hour has truly entranced us all?' Jeanne said.

A tall figure wearing an ankle-length black cloak entered the room. Beneath the hood, there appeared not a face, but a dark cowl with white pinpoints flashing from eye hollows. Within its cloak, the figure resembled a skeleton.

I wondered how the costume had been fashioned. Perhaps the skeleton was sewn onto the outside of some dark, body-hugging outfit. So curious was I about the costume that I barely registered the beautifully-carved scythe the figure clutched in one hand.

'Isn't it frightening?' Jeanne whispered, laughing softly, nudging me towards the doors.

'What is it?'

'That, *ma chère*, is *la faucheuse*. The angel of death. Hard to believe it's only a simple dress-up thing, isn't it?'

All eyes had turned to that spectral angel of death, strolling amongst the ball guests as if searching for someone in particular.

Nobody took any notice of a regal lady in a peacock mask, leading another, clad in emerald green, towards the doors.

As the hooded skeleton stalked in beat to the clock chimes—solemn, constant and deliberate—I sensed the revellers did not know whether it interested, excited, or terrified them. They stood still, their whispers lost in the boom of the striking clock.

As the small hand of the clock made its last circuit, a low murmuring rose from the crowd and hundreds of feet began to shuffle on the spot. All eyes stayed fixed on the angel of death, slinking through the crowd.

The black drapes swallowed the dying echoes of the chimes. The angel of death had reached the buffet table, and there it stopped, turned, and faced the line of keepers dressed as chefs. It looked them all up and down, studying each face one by one. I barely had time to recognise them as the men from Jeanne's cell, before I reeled in horror as the figure lifted its scythe and sliced the keepers' heads off in a single swoop.

In the seconds of shock as blood splattered the finery, and the heads and their sappy gore stained the carpet a darker red, the angel of death was gone—simply another masquerader disappearing into the night.

In its mysterious wake, before anyone had the chance to react, Jeanne was rushing me from the building.

Thankfully, thick clouds obscured the moon, shrouding us in darkness, as we gripped each other's hands and hurried across the damp cobblestones, further and further from the ballroom affray.

I soon heard the shouts behind us. 'Quick, catch him!'

Then followed a mass shriek from inside the ballroom. I kept glancing back as I ran. In the distance, people were streaming from the building, stumbling and falling over each other in their hysteria.

Jeanne and I reached the asylum entrance just as the soldier guard must have learned of the ballroom melee. Breathless, we kept ourselves hidden behind a thick stone column.

'We haven't seen him leave via the front gate,' one of the soldiers said to his group.

'He must still be in the grounds then,' another cried.

'*Allez*, we will find this murderous creature!'

'Not likely.' Jeanne stifled a giggle. 'He'll have long discarded his costume by now.'

The soldiers began rushing in all directions, around the vast expanse of buildings. Whilst the tumult and confusion reached its height, Jeanne and I slipped through the unmanned entrance of la Salpêtrière asylum.

Once outside we slowed down.

'Fool, I only paid him to scare the keepers and divert the crowd's attention,' Jeanne said. 'Not to actually slice their silly heads off.' She fingered her lip, which the keeper had made bleed and swell. 'Never mind, we'll lose no sleep over them, eh, *ma chère*? Besides, no time to think of that, we must be gone.'

'I can hardly believe we're out, Jeanne. I am afraid it is a dream and I'll wake any moment, back on my straw mattress.'

'Well you might, Victoire, if we don't hurry.'

A faint breeze displaced the cloud, and the moon's gleaming nakedness illuminated two coaches waiting on the street.

Jeanne pushed her rose-perfumed pomade into one of my hands, a slip of paper into the other. 'Give this address to the coachman. Once I have reached the safety of English shores, I will write to you.'

Jeanne wrapped her arms around me. Moonlight streaming onto our faces, her lips met mine, but she drew away quickly, her kiss brief and passionless.

'No time for long goodbyes, *ma chère*. No, you must not be sad.' She took my hand again, placed a small leather bag in my palm and closed my fingers over it. 'And remember, *bene qui latuit, bene vixit*. My favourite Latin motto: one who lives well, lives unnoticed.'

Without a backward glance, Jeanne hurried into the first coach. The horses' hooves clomped off down the street. They picked up pace. Quicker, fainter, and finally soundless. Jeanne was gone.

My blood beat hard. Everything had changed. I was no longer the shy, ignorant peasant girl. Jeanne de Valois had dragged the flesh from me, tearing it back to the quick, opening me up, and reshaping me into someone new. She had awakened the life in me.

I thought back to the previous afternoon when we had lain together on her bed again, the heat pulsing through my wet thighs. Then tonight, caught up in the whirling crowd, tipsy on the wine, the gaiety, the fantasy, and strung out on the swelling orchestral music, the costumes, I had forgotten those would be our last moments together. No more would I taste the fruit, nor drink in her delicious juices.

I had not realised the price of my freedom would be so high. Already, I felt completely alone.

'Is madame ready to leave?' The coachman's voice jolted me back to the crisp night. I nodded, gave him the address and stepped up into the coach.

I sat down and opened Jeanne's leather bag. My hand flew to my breast as I heard the coachman's whip come down upon the horses' backs. The coach lurched away and I stared down at the bag full of louis d'or coins jangling in my lap.

I did not even glance from the window, as la Salpêtrière asylum disappeared, for I could not take my eyes from the glittering cluster of transparent gems that nestled beneath the bed of coins.

Paris
February 1787–November 1789

28

'Where am I?' I bolted up in the bed. In the bleary moment between sleep and waking, I couldn't remember a thing. I wondered why, beneath the blanket, my fingers gripped a leather drawstring bag as if moulded to it.

In the wan early light, a dark wisp of a girl stood over me.

'Who are you?' I said.

The girl smiled. 'Don't be alarmed, Rubie—'

'Rubie?' My head darted right and left. There was no sign of anybody else.

'You are Rubie now,' she said. 'Mademoiselle Rubie Charpentier. La Comtesse Jeanne sent me to meet you here last night. You were exhausted after the ball. It must have been quite a *soirée*?' She raised her eyebrows, black arcs across skin the colour of ripe oats.

The ball. Swirling, glittery dancers. The heat of Jeanne's touch. Bloodied heads falling to the floor. The stink of death and despair in an icy dungeon. Two little children floating on the crest of a current.

The fug of sleep cleared. Oh yes, I was Rubie Charpentier, Jeanne De Valois's bourgeois Parisian friend—a woman who held herself with such befitting poise and mannerisms, and spoke the language of the capital.

Still clutching the leather purse, I twisted my head about

taking in the strange surroundings: the simple, elegant wooden furniture, the patterned cream wallpaper that gave the room an ambience of soft peace. The green ball gown was draped across the bottom of the bed in which I lay—no straw mattress alive with vermin, but a real bed with curtains, blankets and a pillow. It all made me dizzy.

'But who are you?' I asked the girl again.

'I am Aurore, your maid.' She fetched a tray from a small table by the window and laid it on the bed. 'Because, Mademoiselle Rubie, all fine ladies have maids, and appearances in Paris are most important. Now eat your breakfast. You are thin, and we must build your strength. Besides, you have much to do today I believe?'

I tried not to gape at the croissant, the buttered brioche and blackberry jam, and my eyes closed as I inhaled the delicious, bitter aroma of the coffee.

The girl drew back the green drapes that separated the bedroom from, I saw, the main room parlour, and light flooded the apartment.

The brioche crumbled, soft and moist, on my tongue. I washed it down with coffee, watching the steam waltz and die in mid-air. I could hardly believe, after a year and a half in what must be the direst Hell God created, I was finally free.

But was this true freedom, this pain gouging my breast like the thrust of a nobleman's sword? Jeanne is probably halfway to the great city of London by now, as I hide, utterly alone, in some unknown Parisian faubourg.

I pushed the tray aside, got up, and stuffed the drawstring bag under the mattress.

I crossed to the window, pulled back another of the drapes, and squinted into the watery winter sunlight. Above a jumble of street noise and rumbling traffic, I looked out across tiled roofs and their wayward angled chimneys.

The cold air felt like the iron shackle around my throat again. I touched the skin on my neck, feeling again the shock as the keepers hurled icy water over me. I rubbed at the chill on my arms and turned as I heard Aurore's footsteps on the parquet floor.

She gestured towards a mirrored dressing table. 'Let me brush your hair out, Mademoiselle Rubie.'

'Just Rubie, please.' I shuffled over to the dressing table and froze when I saw the skeletal features staring back from the mirror. It was as if each laborious day—every one of la Sâlpetrière's inflictions—had etched itself into my skin as deeply as the lily flower branding.

'You will regain your looks,' Aurore said, as if she'd guessed my thoughts. 'With fresh air and good food.'

I toyed with a straggle of chestnut curls, which, eighteen months after they'd shaved my hair for the dungeons, almost reached my shoulders. 'My father always said my hair was my finest asset.'

'And it shall be again,' Aurore said, and as she resumed brushing, I was reminded of those afternoons I smoothed the dark hair from Jeanne's white shoulders. I shivered with the love—the longing—I knew I should banish, and blinked away gritty tears.

'Don't be sad, Rubie. La Comtesse wants only your happiness.'

I nodded. 'I know. Yes, I know.'

'Jeanne trusts me,' Aurore said. 'You can trust me too, Rubie. I'm your friend.' The twinkle in her black eyes made me want to believe her. 'Come now, look at your dresses.'

I gasped in disbelief as Aurore showed me an array of garments and accessories. I picked up the large, circular cloak, the velvet fabric as soft as a chick's feathers, the fur trimming silken in my hand. There were cotton caps edged in lace too, straw hats, and ribbons and gloves of every colour, alongside muslin dresses of different shades.

'Everything is magnificent,' I said.

'Not really,' Aurore said. 'Nothing too grand to attract attention; simple enough to blend in with the crowds.'

She fingered a luxurious green gown trimmed in lace, with a white satin underskirt, matching slippers and hat. 'This one though, is for special occasions.'

Always wear this shade, Victoire, with your hair and eyes.

I burned with the thrill of Jeanne's words. Had it only been last night?

I held the green dress up against my thin body. After the drab asylum garments, I felt swathed in glory.

'Yes, I'll keep this one clean and special,' I said, and chose a white dress with a peach-coloured sash for today.

'I'm not very used to wearing a corset,' I said, as Aurore tucked a small packet of fragrant herbs into a concealed pocket, instantly reminding me of my mother.

'Well, you don't have to wear the silly thing if you don't want to, Mademoiselle Rubie,' Aurore said, frowning as she tightened the laces, and squeezing the breath from me. 'You may do as you please now.'

'Well, I will try,' I said, recalling Jeanne's advice about standing tall and confident.

I wanted to tell Aurore that even if we peasants could afford them, corsets were not conducive to hard, physical labour, but I caught the words on my tongue. I had no idea how much Aurore knew about me, and from my days at Saint-Germain, I knew one servant in four was a spy by whose means the most carefully hidden secrets fell into the wrong hands.

Once dressed, I walked across the even tiled floor, gazing around the apartment. Wide beams supported the low ceiling, and my footsteps fell silent on a Turkish rug. The small kitchen had a glazed tile stove, a dry sink, a cabinet, a wooden table and two benches. I ran my hand over the shiny copper kettle and the pans standing on a shelf near the hearth. My cheeks warmed as I remembered my friend Claudine, and the heat of her comforting kitchen, and I clenched my fist to stem my rage against the Marquis de Barberon.

'It's all so lovely,' I said. What luxury, next to the filthy, cramped conditions of the peasantry, I wanted to say. And of course, it could not even compare with the bleakness of la Sâlpetrière, but still I held my tongue.

'This townhouse is owned by a countess friend of Jeanne's,' Aurore said. 'The lady lives in the countryside and only uses the ground and first floors when she comes to Paris to visit friends or shop at the Palais-Royal. This whole second floor is ours.' She smiled, spreading her arms as if for her too, it was all new and beyond belief.

'Now, Rubie, have you all your papers, your recommendation letter, everything you need? We should go soon.'

I glanced at the slight girl. What do you know of things I'll need? Who are you really, and why did Jeanne bring you to me?

She seemed pleasant and accommodating, but Jeanne had taught me to distrust people; to be wary and, I believe, a little cunning. As Aurore busied herself tucking her curls beneath her cap and finding her shoes, I slipped one of the diamonds and several coins from the bag into a concealed pocket of my dress.

I tightened the strings and shoved the bag back under the mattress—better off there than at the mercy of the pickpockets and villains of Paris, or a supposed maid I knew nothing about.

***

The calluses of my working hands concealed beneath the muff, we left the courtyard of the ivy-covered stone building, last season's twigs and dead leaves crunching beneath our feet.

'See, Rubie, we have a separate stairway and entrance,' Aurore said. 'And so you'll not lose your way, you should know we are in the rue Saint-Honoré. Well, actually at the junction of the rue Saint-Honoré and the rue du Faubourg Saint-Honoré.'

The shock of hearing the name of the street that housed fashionable shops on the lower floors brought a wry smile to my lips. Who'd have thought I would live at such an address.

We stepped out into dense traffic, the din almost hurting my ears. Church bells clanged into the cool February morning, and I wondered again, as on my very first morning in Paris, how many bells there could be in one city.

Aurore pushed me against the wall as a cabriolet driven at breakneck speed by a distinguished-looking man flashed past. Instinctively, I grabbed her arm.

Aurore waved her fist. 'Imbecile!'

Just ahead, a cart had lost its wheel and overturned, dumping its load of charcoal across the street. People were shouting streams of obscenities, carts backed up as far as we could see.

Knocked down by the heavy load, a man lay in a puddle of blood. A woman knelt beside him, holding a rag over a gaping wound. My father's dead face loomed in my mind, and I flinched.

'Don't worry, Rubie, accidents such as this are cleared up quickly,' Aurore said. 'They will simply pay the man's family the accepted price for leg injuries and the police will say nothing. That's how it is, our unjust system!' Her dark eyes burned with an anger that unnerved me; a fury I recognised so well.

Aurore held my arm as we picked our way over the mess, swerving, a few paces later, as a maid opened a door and threw slop into the street without looking left or right.

'Idiot!' Aurore shouted at the maid.

Ah yes, the capital was just as I remembered it—noisy, chaotic and unruly.

Aurore steered me down the rue Royale. 'It will be more pleasant to walk along the right bank of the Seine,' she said, 'rather than risk being run down by these mad carriages and hackney coaches.'

We reached la place Louis XV within a few minutes. 'One of the most popular sights for visitors to Paris these days,' Aurore said. 'Like some grand entrance to our great, corrupt city, don't you think, Rubie?'

'My father told us the story of the fireworks disaster here,' I said as we crossed paving stones still glistening with dew, and stopped in the shadow of the bronze statue of the old King.

'The display to celebrate the new king and queen's marriage; the catastrophe people believed to be an ominous portent.'

'Of course I heard of it,' Aurore said. 'An omen that is proving true, *n'est-ce pas*, Rubie? You will discover how our benighted city stinks now, of noble wealth and depravity, like some poisoned beast. In the cafés, people are speaking more and more of equality and liberty. Our monarchs are slipping, slowly but surely, into their graves!'

She scowled up at the equestrian bust of Louis XV—a gesture I thought, once again, uncharacteristically passionate for a simple maid. I imagined I would find out soon enough, what was behind that dark temper, but this morning I had more pressing things to do.

We continued along the Quai des Tuileries, past the royal gardens. The hour of nine chimed as we reached the Louvre, and it seemed those church bells signalled the barbers of Paris into motion, for they all appeared, wig in one hand, tongs in the other, quickly becoming covered in flour.

Women carrying tin urns on their backs sold their coffee for two sous a cup, and waiters from the lemonade-shops were busy with trays of coffee and rolls.

'Breakfast for people living in furnished rooms,' Aurore explained.

We reached the junction of the Quai de l'Ecole and the Pont Neuf. 'I will leave you here, Rubie, to go to the Palais-Royal on your own,' she said. 'I must buy food for us at the market.'

'So you know Jeanne recommends me to work at this restaurant of the Palais-Royal,' I said. 'But do you have an idea why?'

'Jeanne never tells you why,' Aurore said with a grin, 'it's only afterwards you come to understand. Now you must give me money for the food. I'll see you at the apartment later this evening, when my work is finished.'

'Work? But aren't you a maid, Aurore?'

'Well,' she said, the eyes flashing with secrecy, or perhaps delight. 'I was never trained for such a position, but I promised Jeanne I would help you adapt to your new life. My passion lies in the theatre. I'm a vaudeville actress for a theatre company at the Palais-Royal.'

'Vaudeville?'

'Oh, it's a genre of variety entertainment. A series of separate acts really—musicians, dancers, comedian, magicians and acrobats. Walking the high-wire is my speciality. Perhaps you'll watch me sometime, Rubie?'

'Oh yes. Yes I'd like that.'

I hoped my relief wasn't obvious when I understood Aurore would not be staying with me all day. Accustomed to someone barking orders at me, my daily existence carved in the strict regulations of la Salpêtrière, I did feel fearful of being on my own, but I was anxious to go to this jeweller unaccompanied.

Jeanne told me I would find her jeweller on la place Dauphine, at the very western end of L'île de la cite, so as Aurore's jaunty strides vanished into the crowd, I turned and walked across the Pont Neuf. It was frightening carrying around such a diamond and I yearned to be rid of it as soon as possible.

Amidst the hawkers and entertainers, coaches and vegetable carts jostling and locking wheels, I felt the trembling start in my thighs, the mounting panic that someone would detect a peasant girl's ambling gait, her weather-worn face, her simple, uneducated airs.

Any moment someone would tap me on the shoulder. 'Back to the asylum, you cheap impersonator,' they'd say. I hurried on, clenching my hands hidden beneath the muff.

29

Jeanne must have taught me well, because nobody arrested me. Even the legal practitioners descending on the Grand Chatelet criminal court in a black cloud of gowns, wigs and brief-bags, paid me no attention.

A bell tinkled as I pushed the shop door open. I tried to stop the tremor in my hands and the thud of my heart as the enormity of what I was about to do struck me—sell a diamond which, if things had gone differently, may have been worn around the neck of Marie Antoinette, Queen of France.

A short round man wearing a striped suit greeted me. 'Ah, mademoiselle. *Bonjour*. I have been expecting you. Do sit down. And please accept my condolences for your loss.'

'My loss?' I frowned, and the silence that followed seemed long.

'Are you not the only child of the deceased merchant, Monsieur Maximilien Charpentier?' the jeweller said. 'Come to sell the diamond he bequeathed you, under my wise guidance?'

I cleared my throat, hoping he would mistake my blush for rouge. 'Oh yes. Yes. Thank you for your sympathy, m'sieur.'

The man nodded, explaining to me how unwise, and unsafe, it would be for him to keep piles of coins in his shop. 'Besides, such large mounds of coins only serve to expose our country's financial backwardness, *n'est-ce pas*, mademoiselle?'

Anxious not to make any silly blunders, I remained wordless

for a minute.

'*Excusez-moi,* m'sieur?'

'Those piles of metal for which our country's *backwardness* cannot seem to find any paper equivalent,' he said. 'With the wretched messengers bent double under the weight of their bags of money, carting them from strong-room to strong-room.'

I nodded. 'Ah yes, m'sieur, it does seem a little … a little backward.'

The jeweller then explained he would give me a piece of paper instead of money.

'A bill of exchange,' he said.

I finally understood, and I sat there, unmoving, numbed with disbelief at how simple it was to sell a diamond worth more livres than I could probably count.

I could have taken a cabriolet, or even a fiacre, with its higher chassis and glass windows for better viewing, but not having assumed the reflexes of the rich, I left L'île de la Cité on foot. I continued walking back along the right bank towards the Palais-Royal, cowering from careening coaches in shop doorways and porticoed entrances.

As I drew closer to the market, I lifted my dress and stepped over the rivulets of blood streaming from a stinking *boucherie*.

'Charlatan!' a woman screeched, from a crowd gathered around a hawker selling cures for toothache.

'Liar!' another woman shouted, her eyes fiery. 'Get the teeth pulled out, that's the only way.'

Of course, I was relieved I would never have to concern myself over food or shelter, as these people about me, but I felt an odd flatness, which blunted the edges of my elation. I understood that I would have to hide this new-found wealth, always. Never could I have the pleasure of flaunting it, nor forget my riches were ill gotten.

***

I stood beside the fountain in the vast gardens of the Palais-Royal, gazing at the colossal cream-coloured facades. The misery of the poor out of sight for a moment, I could not help feeling lifted by the grandeur of this palace owned by the King's cousin, the Duke of Orléans.

I located *Le Faisan Doré* restaurant midway along the rue Montpesier, and handed the proprietor my recommendation letter.

'And how is our mutual friend?' the elegant dark-suited man asked.

I coloured, unsure what to say. 'She is well, thank you. Very well, monsieur.'

'Yes, I imagine she is,' he said with a knowing smile. 'I do hope the Channel crossing was not too turbulent for her. I am certain she will be happier on the untroubled shores of Great Britain.'

He read my letter and looked me up and down, his manner not unfriendly or leering, simply professional.

'You may start tomorrow, Mademoiselle Charpentier, at midday. And remember three o'clock is the busiest time,' he said, 'when people take their main meal.'

Still unsure why I should work in his restaurant, I couldn't help smiling to myself. Within a few hours, I had become a respectable, working *Parisienne*. Jeanne had sent me here for a reason and I was curious, excited and a little nervous, to discover why.

Perhaps, once I knew, I could stop working as a cook, and use my literacy skills, somehow. But what of my family and Léon, so far away in Lucie? I had to see them soon.

It seemed odd to eat in the restaurant in which I would be working, so I took a table in another establishment further along the rue Montpesier.

Decorated in ancient Greek style, with long mirrors, the café was airy and clean, the high windows sweeping in great swathes of light. I caught snaps of the men's conversation—for the clientele was almost exclusively male—as they sat around marble-topped tables drinking brandy, reading newspapers, or playing chess or dominoes. I noticed their raised eyebrows when one mentioned the words, "Versailles", "deficit", or "Marie Antoinette".

'*La soupe, s'il vous plaît,*' I said to the waiter. I could order anything—everything—on this menu, I yearned to boast to him, but I smiled, coy and unassuming, as was fitting for a lady dining out alone.

Like the other people with this life of leisure, I gazed out into the enclosed gardens. Fashionable men and women in striped silk gowns or the white muslin of the Queen's "milk maids" were gathered in the Valois Gallery on the far side of the garden, and in the Beaujolais Gallery, to my left. I noticed more and more people wore their hair loose and unpowdered these days, and rustic simplicity had evidently become fashionable among the nobles. It also seemed that canes had largely replaced swords, and women had developed a penchant for small yappy dogs.

The irregular-shaped duke's palace stood at the far south end of the garden. Common folk thronged in the low wooden stalls of the Tartar's Camp, from where vendors barked out their wares. I thought of my friend, Claudine, who frequented the Tartar's Camp, and yearned for her friendly face in this sea of strangers—someone to ease the ache of my loneliness without Jeanne.

I beckoned a waiter. 'Please, I need paper and quill, and a reliable messenger boy.'

He dipped his head. '*Oui*, madame.'

My dear Claudine,

I hope you recall your old friend, from Armand's country inn a week south of Paris?

I have been ill for some time and unable to contact you, but happily I am well recovered and keen to rekindle our friendship.

Please find below my new address, and advise me when we can meet at the fountain in the gardens of the Palais-Royal.

With the honour to be your true friend,
Mademoiselle Rubie Charpentier

I folded the paper and pushed it into the messenger boy's palm, with two sous for his trouble.

'Please, it is most important,' I said.

The boy nodded, bowed his head and hurried off through the crowd. I could only hope that when the Marquis or the Marquise intercepted and read it, as they did all servants' letters, they wouldn't guess it was from their long-forgotten scullery maid, Victoire Charpentier, and simply cast it aside.

My hand itched to pen a few words to Grégoire; to let him know I was no longer a mad asylum woman. I wanted to ask after Madeleine and thank him for taking care of her, but I was afraid my brother would never understand any code I adopted to disguise my identity. It might only confuse and frighten him.

***

Perhaps it was the novelty of being free to roam; to have the money to do whatever I desired, that enticed me to stay at the Palais-Royal for the afternoon puppet show.

'*Mr Punch is one jolly good fellow,*
His dress is all scarlet and yellow,
And if now and then he gets mellow,
It's only among his good friends,' sang the boy and girl, beating drums as they strutted up the aisle and onto the platform of the small theatre on the west side of the Palais-Royal.

The crowd hushed as the curtain parted. They began laughing as Punch beat his wife with the traditional stick. I feigned a laugh but I did not find it funny and, beneath my velvet cloak, a chill scrambled along my arms as Punch beat the woman, over and over.

A dog bit Punch, which made the children in the audience shriek. Punch ended up in prison, and I shivered again as he tricked the hangman into hanging himself.

The curtain closed and the boy and girl reappeared with beaming smiles, bowing to loud applause. I left in the crowd's wake, via the rue de Richelieu entrance, hurrying back along the rue Saint-Honoré to the apartment. The bells of Saint-Roch struck five o'clock and the afternoon mealtime calm was broken with the din and chaos of traffic lurching, once again, in all directions.

The shadows shortened and disappeared, and twilight fell over Paris. I caught sight of a sign in a window: Proposed voyage. Monday, February 26 at 7pm precisely, a superb berline with eight new, solid seats, will be leaving Paris for Lyon. Travellers are invited to view it at the following address: M. Brissot, angle of the rue Saint-Denis and the rue Saint-Honoré. This berline transports packages, trunks and other important effects as well as travellers.

I wanted to stay here in Paris to fight the commoners' battle, but oh how wonderful it would be to see Madeleine, Grégoire and his family, Léon too, and L'Auberge des Anges.

Powerless before, to help the inn through financial difficulty, Jeanne's wealth now gave me the means to resurrect it to its former grandeur.

Scenes of the farm, the village, flitted through my mind like the pictures in Maman's book of fables. I longed to breathe the clear air of Lucie, to hear the sough of wheat on a summer wind and to float in the clear waters of the Vionne, rather than swimming naked with all the Parisians in the filth of the Seine River.

Abruptly, I came to a page that was blank—white at first, then darkening as the terrible reality seeped in. Someone had sent me to la Salpêtrière. I wondered why this had never occurred to me in the asylum, when I'd learned how any poor girl could be sent on the whim of family members, neighbours or villagers—badly behaved girls, pregnant or idiot ones, and crazed women whose madness could not be treated otherwise, their devil's curse afflicting the entire family.

Who then, had sent me? I could never believe my beloved brother capable of such treachery, and the cool breeze coming off the Seine bristled the hairs on my nape and whispered a single name in my ear: Léon Bruyère.

Léon must have told the bailiff I was mad; that I'd drowned my little Blandine and Gustave. He'd had me sent to the asylum, left there to rot like some old carcass. In that instant—with the shock of his betrayal—the blood drained from my limbs, the pain piercing my breast like a poison barb. I leaned against the wall to calm my shaking body.

Well, it was certain now—I could never return to Lucie. I walked on, my steps short and shuffling, as if those chains still shackled my ankles. I was not free; I had simply exchanged one prison for another.

30

The early March sun threw weak slivers of light into the parlour. Aurore frowned in concentration, gripping her quill as she painstakingly copied out the words.

'There's soon to be another after-production party,' she said. 'Why don't you come, Rubie? You could meet new people, have some fun.'

'More of your tempestuous political friends?' I blew on my coffee and winked at my "maid". I was still unsure who my pretty friend truly was—the small girl with a big heart and a temper that flared with the slightest kindling. I was certain though, she was no more of a maid to me than I'd been to Jeanne.

'Well why not,' I said. 'Yes, I would love to come to your party.'

Aurore continued writing out the words I'd listed, my reluctant pupil yawning and sighing.

'I'm tired, I can't concentrate,' she said. 'I drank too much tavern ale last night, which is your fault, Rubie.'

'Not everyone reaches twenty-five,' I said with a smile. 'I think I deserved a birthday celebration, n'est-ce pas?'

'Mmn, I suppose,' she said, as I returned to the book I was studying: *The Dark Side of the Human Mind*. I sipped my coffee, the birds outside chirping louder as the morning wore on, as if to drown out the rising din of people, carts and horses.

Aurore flung the quill onto the table, arcs of ink droplets fanning across the page. 'It's no use, I'll never be more than a badly-paid acrobat, pretending to be an actress.'

A frown creased her petulant face as she swallowed the dregs of her coffee, bounced out of her chair and waved her arms. All this melodrama did not surprise me. Aurore was always jumping up and down about something.

'Oh I know what you'll say, Rubie. Compared with the five or six sous those wretched workers earn at slaveries like the Saint-Gobain glassworks or the tanneries, we actresses are well-off, but I'm still poor and I don't want to stay like that all my life.'

'No, of course you don't,' I said, trying to steer the conversation away from money. After several weeks together, I had begun to trust Aurore, but still I didn't know if she was aware of the wealth Jeanne left me. I was never sure whether she was digging for information or if hers were genuine grievances.

'So, if you want to earn extra money copying scripts for rehearsals,' I said, pushing the goose-plume back into her hand, 'you must learn to read and write. And that takes lots of practice. Don't you enjoy our mornings here together, both of us learning our lessons?' I nodded at the pile of books—works on astronomy, science, politics and biology—through which I was striving to become a scholar.

'Yes, I know you are a good friend,' Aurore said with a smile, her teeth bright against honey-hued skin, 'to teach me my letters.'

'Besides,' I said, settling back in my chair as Aurore resumed her writing. 'I'm sure this is why Jeanne brought us together. You helped me when I came to the apartment, now it is my turn to help you.'

Aurore put the quill down again and rested her chin in her cupped hands. 'I've never told you, Rubie, but la Comtesse Jeanne helped me too. She rescued me from the deepest, blackest pit.'

'Black pit?'

'My parents died in a coach accident when I was six. They were actors, and their theatre friends took me in and taught me to dance and sing, and walk the high-wire. When I grew up I became a dancer in the chorus of a small theatre company.

Along with the singers, we were the worst paid, and forced to become spies.' She waved a thin arm. 'We'd sell our information to the police or anyone else hungry and willing to pay for a scandal, but that still wasn't enough to survive.' She lowered her dark gaze. 'In the end I had to do what most girls like me do.'

My hand tightened over Aurore's. 'You don't mean … sell yourself to … *mon Dieu*, I couldn't imagine anything more terrible.'

'The clients would often run off without paying, and beat us. When Jeanne found me, I was bruised from head to foot, and too sick and starving even for rage.' She sighed. 'The hatred came later.'

'My poor Aurore. So Jeanne took you away from all that?'

'She gave me money, and she spoke to a friend who found me a better-paid acting job with a theatre company that had moved from the Boulevards to the Palais-Royal.' She looked around the parlour. 'Jeanne also brought me to live in this apartment … with her.'

'With her? Jeanne li-lived here too, w-with you?'

An entirely different sensation began to creep over my sympathy for Aurore; an oddly sickening thing stained with grief, which stirred low in my gut.

'Oh Jeanne had several residences,' Aurore said, flicking a slender wrist. 'She had to keep moving, you know, while … during that jewel business.'

Her smile rueful, Aurore lifted her gaze to the sun-lit window. 'If they hadn't caught Jeanne and thrown her in that gruesome prison, we'd still be together. At least she helped bring down the Queen,' she said. 'You know, when the Cardinal de Rohan was acquitted, the people truly believed Marie Antoinette perpetrated that extravagant fraud for her own frivolous ends. The people hated her even more!'

I felt as if something was siphoning the life from me, draining me so that I barely heard her words. Jeanne and Aurore together, here. Probably sleeping in the bed I slept in. Had I simply been the next in Jeanne's long line?

'This necklace scandal was nothing short of political disaster for the King and Queen,' Aurore went on, with her raucous chuckle. She slipped her shoes on, to leave for work and I saw she hadn't the slightest notion of the venomous impact of her words.

In a murmuring part of my mind, I'd always suspected I might discover I meant little to Jeanne, while she was everything to me, but in that instant I was numbed. I wanted to cry out but the tears seemed frozen inside—hard little ice chips.

I no longer heard the snorts of horses, the clippity-clop of hooves on cobblestones, the creaking of cart wheels and the shouts of drivers. My world went silent, and through the open window, the sweet fragrance of spring flowers turned sour as they reached my flared nostrils.

Aurore fussed about, tucking her hair under her cap. 'Are you walking with me?' she said, in her joyous lilt.

I cleared my throat. 'N-no you go ahead, I'll walk to the Palais on my own today.'

When I heard the door shut, I crossed to the window, and as the scent of window-box roses and lilies vied with the stink rising from the street, I envied Aurore her skipping steps, as if she hadn't a single care.

As she disappeared onto the rue Saint-Honoré I flung myself across the bed and sobbed into the pillow.

***

After several minutes I heaved my sorrowful self from the bed and drank another cup of coffee. How childish this was, not at all the elegant behaviour I'd worked so hard to adopt.

I should go to the restaurant. If I stayed in the apartment and reflected on Jeanne's falseness, on her flippant juggling of my emotions, I feared *la mélancolie* would creep upon me again— the sadness that seemed ever poised to spring onto my back and wrap its malevolent arms around me for the slightest reason.

Along the rue Saint-Honoré, the Palais-Royal was only ten minutes by foot from the apartment, but I wanted time to think, so I took the opposite, longer way. With its leafy trees and elegant cafés, the Boulevard—city limit before the construction of the hated Farmers-General wall—was the perfect place to stroll, and think.

I dawdled, letting the spring sun play across my cheeks, drenching me with its warm energy. I would not reply to Jeanne's letter. I would leave her stewing in London, writing her nasty memoirs about the Queen. I'd let her wring her hands with worry when she had no news, despite sending me letter after letter wrought with worry.

From the Boulevard, I turned right onto the rue de Richelieu, where Jeanne had had my plush ball gown made.

I walked across the intersections of small streets, where construction work was going on all around. Scaffolding, piles of stone, the noise of stone-cutters' chisels and carpenters' hammers met me at each turn. It seemed every man was a builder's labourer, swathed in plaster dust, his shouts hanging off the dusty air, sweat glistening off thickly-cabled limbs.

Teams of them were tearing down old buildings and replacing them with new ones, in the fragile white stone of Paris, and all at reckless speed to earn the bonus for finishing ahead of time.

I stood with a small crowd witnessing a complex operation with a boulder. Accompanied by the labourers' curses and shouts, the great stone crashed to the ground, and as the noise drummed in my ears for minutes afterwards, I thought of Jeanne again. The vibrating void of that resonance filled with all she had given me—a decent prison life and the means to escape it, education, clothes and a comfortable apartment, not to mention money and, of course, the diamonds.

If it wasn't for Jeanne de Valois, Agathe and the other women from that foul prison cell would have beaten me to death, or I'd have perished from the cold or sickness, my nameless corpse shovelled into some communal tomb.

I understood Jeanne was what the great thinkers—our philosophers—meant when they spoke of free spirits; a woman who belonged to no one. Especially not to me. A woman who could change her circumstances, her lover, as readily as she exchanged one silk dress for another.

I recalled our conversation about how dissimilar we were; how she lived free from the chains of tradition and morality, and how my existence seemed bound in the disciplines of my upbringing. I remembered how we'd envied each other.

I hurried away from the crowd, my steps lighter and quicker as I approached the Palais-Royal, and slipped in via the Richelieu entrance.

As I secured my apron and began marinating meat and dicing vegetables, I still felt the pang of losing Jeanne, but my loss was tempered as I recognised the sweet balm of true friendship.

***

'A brandy for me, *s'il vous plaît*,' a businessman said.

'A pot of your finest tea over here,' another asked.

'Champagne,' said a woman in a great plumed hat.

From the kitchen of *Le Faisan Doré* I listened to them all snapping orders at the waiters.

I glanced out from time to time at the habitual customers: well-dressed men from the Paris Mint on the Quai de Conti, business papers overflowing from their pockets, ladies gossiping over wine, their wide skirts spilling beyond the chair edges. The stock-exchange dealers were there too—those men who came thrice daily to sit in their private room to drink brandy and gamble their money away. I could tell immediately whether they won or lost, from their expressions.

There were the circles of men too, who sat all day reading the public papers, all of which could be found in the restaurant. They judged the latest plays and argued loudly about the actors.

Amidst one such group debating the current news, a pastime that occupied many throughout the day, I finally saw him.

With his rose-coloured satin suit embroidered in silver, his hooked nose and the small scar on his left temple, I could never have mistaken the Marquis de Barberon.

The hatred filled me as swiftly as a drunkard fills his beaker with cheap ale. I froze in the doorway, clutching my apron, my breath coming in short, sharp bursts.

As I backed out of sight, I saw it all as clear as the Vionne River in spring—why Jeanne had sent me to the Palais-Royal. As the Marquis chatted and laughed, vaunting his gleaming porcelain teeth as he took pinches of snuff from his decorated box, the coldness vanished and warmth swept in.

The rising heat gripped me and a hundred thoughts collided in my brain. Laudanum—remedy people relied on for wasp stings, menstrual cramps, insomnia and all other ailments— seemed my only option. A few drops in his meal, but how many?

I recalled our dismal failure when Jeanne and I attempted to drug the asylum guards. As for the dose large enough to kill a man, I had no idea.

There was the risk too, the Marquis might detect some odd, bitter aftertaste. If he suspected anything was amiss with his food and discovered me, they would whip me, and hang or burn my body or break me on the wheel.

No, I didn't want my revenge on the Marquis in such a fashion. As I prepared the veal dish scented with saffron, for the afternoon meal, I knew I wanted him to see me; to know the identity of his aggressor and why he was facing such an agonising death, however that might be. I had to see regret in those red-rimmed eyes, to smell the terror on his breath, to watch him drop to his knees and plead for his life, as he pissed all over his satin breeches. Something such as this required careful planning; I could not be caught.

Quaking with nerves, with terror, and delight, I could hardly cook that afternoon. My mind chopped over my revenge—

mixing, basting and stirring until it rose perfectly, and tasted far sweeter than the meringues and lemon pie I prepared for the diners of the *Le Faisan Doré* restaurant.

31

I'd been gone from la Salpêtrière a month when spring flung her freshness across Paris. Even though the sun warmed my cheeks as I waited in the Palais-Royal gardens for Claudine, I hunched my shoulders against the snap of breeze.

I stood in the thin shade of a chestnut tree from where I could observe people approaching the fountain. I almost took my freedom for granted now, but still I couldn't help assuming the role of watcher.

Well-dressed ladies bustled in and out of arcade shops, buying silks and muslins. Men strode from others that boasted surgical and astronomy instruments, and toys whose fashion would be dead by the end of the day. There were no sounds of the blacksmith's anvil, the clog-maker's or tinker's hammer, for the Palais-Royal was an elegant, expensive place, its prices triple that of elsewhere. But people still flocked, those who loved having everything they desired under one roof.

As short and round as I remembered her, Claudine approached me, her smile spreading as wide as her arms.

'Finally we meet, my child.' She kissed me easily, lavishly, like a true Parisian. 'How lovely you are still.' She cupped a palm under a wad of my wavy shoulder-length hair, which I wore in the latest style of loose ringlets, adorned with ribbons.

'I knew it was you, in your note,' she said. 'But why the secrecy, why do you call yourself Rubie? And what of Armand

and his son, Léon, and your children?'

I hooked my arm through Claudine's. 'I work in a restaurant here at the Palais-Royal now, so why don't we walk somewhere else, away from prying ears, and I'll tell you everything.'

We left the fancy palace crowd, and its aromas streaming from the cafés and coffee-roasters, and strolled along the rue Saint-Honoré.

'Losing Armand was a catastrophe,' I said. 'I had grown to love and respect my husband, and what he meant for my life as a free woman. When he died, *la mélancolie* came upon me, so slowly at first I barely noticed, until it choked me like some malignant disease. Then it was too late.' I took a breath. 'Finances too, became so dismal we had to close the inn.'

Claudine squeezed my arm. 'Poor child, I have heard *la mélancolie* is an evil thing once it comes on you.'

I nodded. 'So evil that I cannot even recall the terrible day *la Vionne violente* stole my little Blandine and Gustave.'

'The twins drowned? *Quelle tragédie!*'

I glanced away so she might not see the pain in my eyes. 'Worse. They claimed *I* drowned them. They sent me to la Salpêtrière.' I waved an arm eastward, across the river, in the direction of the asylum.

'Someone as good and God-fearing as you could not commit such a crime. I will never believe it.' Her probing eyes studied me. 'But you are quite sane now, my child?'

'Oh yes, lucid enough even to escape la Salpêtrière.' I held up a palm and dropped my voice to a whisper. 'Don't ask me how; it is safer you know nothing.'

'Escaped la Salpêtrière! But nobody … nobody besides the necklace conwoman has escaped that place,' Claudine said. 'Aren't you afraid somebody will see you, have you arrested and sent back? You know we Parisians are a curious lot, and quite suspicious.'

'I was terrified at first,' I said, 'but I barely even glance over my shoulder now. People are too busy with their lives to bother with me.'

'Well I am relieved you are safe,' she said, patting my arm.

'Let's walk along the riverbank,' I said, steering Claudine away from the grimy, outstretched palms of beggars.

We continued along the right bank, the breeze snapping at my ankles as we paused on the Notre Dame bridge, watching rafts float firewood down the murky Seine.

'Wood,' Claudine said, shaking her head, as men waded into the muddy water, unloaded the precious fuel and carried it ashore on their backs. 'One of the most extravagant things in Paris these days, my child. Twelve sous for a log no longer or thicker than a man's arm. Can you imagine that?'

'Yes, I've heard,' I said. 'Everything is so expensive these days.'

'So, tell me about this restaurant position of yours,' Claudine said, hooking her arm through mine as we moved off towards the working class faubourg of Saint-Antoine.

'Thanks to your culinary skills I've become quite the renowned cook at *Le Faisan Doré*,' I said. 'I am appreciated for my—*your*—buttery *potage au cresson*, sautéed veal in Madeira sauce and, of course, *haricots verts au vinaigre*.'

Claudine puffed up at my compliments. 'I am surprised you are working in *Le Faisan Doré*. Why would you return to the Palais-Royal when you know too well the Marquis frequents that place more than his own home?'

'He stole my innocence.' My voice was tight and low, as a cluster of cloud obscured the sun and the chill seized me.

'Ha! As I suspected, my child. You return to the Palais-Royal with your mind full of revenge.' Claudine's eyes grew wide. 'You should banish this foolish idea. The Marquis knows people in high government places; you'll be in the pillory in no time.'

'I must do it for Rubie, for myself, for all those other girls, to stop hi—'

'Speaking of those other girls,' Claudine said. 'I had not planned to mention this, as I wanted to preserve your sensitivity, but I believe now it is my duty to tell you.'

'Tell me what?'

'Of the tragedy.' She took a breath. 'Our latest scullery girl—Margot, poor sweet child—was a victim too, of the Marquis. When Margot's child was born she tried to get money from the Marquis.' She rubbed her fleshy arms. 'Naturally that didn't work so Margot wanted revenge, as you do. And now, this very afternoon, they will execute her. You must come with me.'

'But I'm not like most people, Claudine. I cannot bear to watch innocent people treated with such brutality. I loathe public punishment, and flee those macabre spectacles. Why should I go?'

'Firstly, it will ease my suffering to have your company on such a painful occasion,' Claudine said, 'but I hope it will also serve to chase these silly ideas from your mind, Victoire.'

'All right, I'll come with you,' I said, glancing around. 'But please call me Rubie now.'

'Thank you, your presence will console me.'

Claudine took my arm again as we walked down the rue Saint-Antoine, passed the glassworks that made mirrors. 'And please, my child, no more talk of vengeance. It only blackens the soul. Besides you don't want to end up in the Bastille.' She pointed at the black shapes of the walls and turrets of the fortress, which towered the three-arched Saint-Antoine city gate.

'The cells underground run with water, and are alive with rats,' she said. 'If you're poor, that is.' She tapped the side of her nose. 'Of course, the rich can pay for beds with proper curtains, and bring their cats in to keep the vermin down.'

Lucky prisoners like Jeanne de Valois, and their personal maids. A nervous hum stirred within me, at this talk of prisons, and as the sun broke through the clouds my feet began to ache.

I glanced about for a street vendor or a decent café, and chose a clean, well-lit, but unpretentious establishment opening onto the Boulevard, from where pedlars showed off their wares.

As Claudine and I enjoyed our simple, but tasty meal of cheese, liver *pâté* and salad, a man climbed onto a crate and began addressing the patrons in a clear voice.

'In this spring of 1787, our country—twenty six million citizens—has reached the brink of the most profound revolution of modern times. The royal government has fallen into dire financial crisis. The only feasible alternative for Finance Minister Calonne was to raise taxes.'

The speaker paused for breath, the crowd of diners silent, all eyes fixed on him.

'At the opening session of the Assembly of Notables last month, Calonne proposed a uniform tax across the kingdom—a fiscal policy that would apply to all equally.' He punched his fist in the air.

'No more tax exemption for the clergy and the nobility!' a man shouted.

'Hear, hear, equality for all!' I cried, along with the others.

Claudine stared at me as if shocked at my outburst.

'But our King claims the divine right to govern, and has refused to yield any of his authority,' the orator continued. 'Public affairs are at an impasse. Urban and rural workers feel trapped in poverty. The cost of rent and basic commodities rises, while their incomes remain static, or decline even.' As he shuffled his orator's pose, I thought of my father narrating his tales.

'And now they are building that loathed Farmers-General wall to collect royal taxes,' cried another café patron. 'With rich tax farmers pointing their guns at our heads while they search us, and imprison uncooperative citizens in a flash. Those rich bastards should be the ones in prison!'

'Hear, hear!' I cried again, and that time Claudine joined in.

'The *savants* are predicting a bloody cataclysm, a Pandora's box of grievances about to burst open!' the orator concluded, jumping down from the crate.

As the crowd whistled and applauded, I felt a lust budding inside me—the shoot of that seed sown in my childhood. Nourished and nurtured on unjust tragedies, it pushed itself from its dormant earthy bed and flourished now, in the light of day.

'Our commoners' battle is fast approaching, Claudine,' I said, 'hammering on sides of the hated Farmers-General wall.'

***

The church bells pealed out the hour, and as Claudine and I neared the Hôtel de Ville, I could smell the excitement of the crowd gathered on la place de Grève for Margot's execution.

'Day after day they come, vying for the best spots,' I said, motioning at the people—parents with children, sedan-chair carriers, cobblers and mud-brushers. 'You'd think they had better things to do.'

'Ah, it is their only entertainment, my child.' Claudine's words came out in broken-up whispers.

'Here she comes!' cried a rough-faced woman who stank of fish.

A roar rose as a cart rumbled onto la place de Grève carrying Margot—a thin girl in a brown smock girdled at the waist. Her hair had been savagely cropped, her arms secured behind her back. I didn't understand why they'd tied her hands, she was hardly about to run off. Margot stared straight ahead at the stake, her eyes rigid with terror, her breaths coming in ragged gasps.

I held Claudine's hand, felt her start to shake, and my own limbs trembled. 'Are you certain you want to stay and witness this terrible murder, of an innocent girl?'

'I promised Margot I would come and pray for her soul,' she said with a curt nod.

'What's the girl done?' someone asked.

'Killed her bastard,' said a fishwife woman standing nearby. 'Girl's a scullery maid at the house of a noble. Claims the lord was the bastard's father and asked for money. Course, the lady of the house threw her and her bastard into the street.'

The *poissarde* seemed to be enjoying her rapt audience, and raised her voice. 'So what did the silly girl do? Cut the baby's throat, the little murderess!'

'The poor girl had no choice!' I shouted to the people about me, the blood fizzing in my veins. 'She's the victim. You should be sorry for her, and angry that we can do nothing to fight these nobles!'

'What would you know?' the woman snarled, looking me up and down. 'You don't look like no poor girl to me.'

'Stop, Vic-Rubie,' Claudine said her hand tight on my arm. 'We didn't come here to argue with the likes of *poissardes*.'

'Whatever the reason, she must've been mad to kill her child,' another woman said.

Mad to kill her child. Kill her child.

Images filled my mind, of a fast flowing river sweeping away everything in its murderous path—twigs, leaves, dead animals, and small, screaming children.

As they tied Margot to a beam and the priest stood before her, brandishing a crucifix, I felt the heat of rising fury, as if it would explode from me. As the darkly-clad executioner pulled a hood over her terrified face, and tied it around her neck, I wanted to shove the people aside and push my way up onto the platform, and free the girl. Amidst the murmur swelling from hundreds of throats, and rising to a hideous bellow, I felt faint. People pushed and shoved me, straining their necks as they clamoured for the first glimpse of the flames.

My mother's words echoed across the years.

Watch, Victoire, this will teach you a lesson.

Yes, Maman, I yearned to tell her—the lesson that there is no justice; commoners are powerless against the mighty aristocracy.

As the executioner lit the kindling beneath Margot, the repugnance ignited inside me, spreading like an uncontrollable blaze.

'Come on, Claudine, you don't want to stay any longer, surely?'

'See what will happen to you, my child, if you insist on this idea of revenge,' Claudine said, as we hurried away from the leaping flames and the frenzied cries of the crowd.

'The Marquis cannot get away with what he does,' I said. 'But you don't have worry for me, the asylum taught me to be shrewd and sly. They'll never burn me at the stake.'

Claudine and I walked back to the Quai des Tuileries without a word, for I could not find words for how bereft, and enraged, I felt.

Night had fallen when I kissed Claudine goodbye, and she stepped into a cabriolet to return to Saint-Germain. I waved at the disappearing vehicle and my gaze turned to the rising moon—a slim waxing crescent above the city dust. The bells of Saint-Roch Church struck the hour, a madman's shriek punctuating the low drone of a day's end.

As I turned into a dark narrow street to reach the rue Saint-Honoré, a soft, croaking noise seemed to rise straight from the dank cobbles. I stopped still as if struck, tremors of fear rippling through me.

I knew that sound, the sad croak of the Night Washerwoman who'd killed her infants. Now I knew the tale was simply a means to incite children to hurry home after dark, yet my pulse galloped. Perhaps it was the execution still unsettling me still, or was it something that plunged deeper—that day on the Vionne with Blandine and Gustave?

I looked around for a lantern-man, not only to light the way to my door, but to protect me against the thieves and muggers skulking in the darkness. It was too early for the lantern-men though, who didn't come out until after ten, supplementing the hanging street lanterns with their welcome cries of, 'Here's your light.' I quickened my pace through the blackness.

The croaking noise grew louder, and I stumbled over the prone figure of a man. I cried out, and stared at the motionless man, whisky vapours hot on his rasping breaths.

I almost laughed with relief as I hurried away from the drunkard, though my pulse quickened again, as the fog closed in on me. Relieved to be home, I almost ran into the townhouse courtyard. An ominous sort of quiet, though, hung over the stone walls, the creeping ivy-like fingers reaching blindly into the darkness.

No welcome candlelight shone from the second floor. Aurore was not home, which was usual, with the late theatre hours she kept—the girl whose friendship and cheeky smile continued to comfort me beyond those first lonely weeks out of captivity.

I hurried up the steps, lit a candle and immediately saw the letter lying on the small parlour table, addressed to Mademoiselle Rubie Charpentier.

I recognised the bold, flourishing hand, sat in an upholstered armchair by the candlelight, and unfolded Jeanne's letter.

My dear Rubie,

I hope this letter finds you well and happy. You will be pleased to hear I have arrived safely on the other side of the Channel, and let me tell you that never were two neighbouring cities—Paris and London—so utterly different. Nature has contrived a moral separation too, which goes even deeper than the physical boundary dividing them.

I reread her words, trying to decipher what she was trying to tell me. Moral separation? Surely she can't be referring to us—to her and me?

Anyway, all talk of separations aside, Rubie, I wanted to thank you for our wonderful time together in Paris. Didn't we have such fun at the ball? I will remember our last, angelic dance for the rest of my days.

It must still be cold in the capital, so don't forget to keep your shoulders covered, you don't want to catch a chill. Besides, you know I cannot bear those new dress styles, with the shoulders dropping right down, revealing a woman's bare shoulders. Some things I believe we should keep hidden from others, n'est-ce pas my sweet lily flower?

And I'd like to remind you too, Rubie of another purpose of your stay—to amuse yourself with anyone you desire.

The page quivered in my hand. Jeanne was urging me to

amuse myself with others, with ... with men! Despite my efforts to forget our love, I still ached when I imagined her with someone else, and I saw how readily she was casting me off into the beds of unknown men.

I also knew she was right; this is how it must be.

As for me, ma chère *Rubie, I pass my days happily pursuing a newfound delight for story-telling. I am working on a kind of fairy tale about a wicked queen and a blighted woman, who brings the queen down, in the end. I am confident many will be eager to read my enchanting story.*

I look forward to your reply, Rubie, and don't forget to tell me when that black furniture arrives, the one you ordered. I am certain it will well suit your new lodgings.

I have the honour to be your friend,

Madame J. Collier

That black furniture. I knew she was referring to the black cabinet—*le cabinet noir* division of the police who read and copied private letters.

'You're too clever for all of them, my Jeanne.' I laughed aloud. 'Madame J. Collier indeed!'

The sallow light tapered and flickered, throwing angular shadows across the walls. I hugged the letter to me as if, through the ink and paper, I could feel Jeanne's caresses again.

I tucked her letter close to my breast and went to prepare supper, planning my reply laced with the coded secrets of sweet, noble revenge.

32

I tucked the last stubborn chestnut curls under the dark wig Aurore had lent me from the theatre wardrobe. I checked my face in the kitchen mirror, and saw excitement, and nervousness, but I was certain no one would recognise me beneath my disguise.

I threw my mantle across my shoulders and crept from the back entrance of *Le Faisan Doré* around to the front, and joined the crowd in the Western Arcade of the Palais-Royal. Hundreds of people strolled beneath the ordered rows of trees in the gardens—favourite *rendez-vous* of nobles, bourgeois, artists and free thinkers. Many more—dark Africans, turbaned Indians and wealthy businessmen—lurked in the shadows of the arcades, in the shops and restaurants.

I threaded through the people, towards the theatre, beneath the tiny lights coming from windows above the arcades, from where the Palais-Royal indulged every taste from gambling club to gaudy brothel. As I reached the theatre, the shops began to close their shutters.

Amidst the smells of powder, the shuffle of feet and the rustle of cloth, I squeezed into the theatre. I gazed up at the wealthy women in their private boxes, reclining on cushions with their spaniels, their foot-warmers and their pet imbeciles with spyglasses, informing them who was in the audience and on the stage. I could have afforded the yearly rent on a private box, but the chatter and gossip of the pit was so much more interesting than the bored, idle chatter of the rich.

I joined the fidgety pit audience, the engraved handle of my pistol pressing cool and hard against my flesh. I'd wondered wherever I could procure such an item, but purchasing a pistol in Paris had proved as simple as selling diamonds. Money, it seemed, could buy whatever a woman desired.

'I have the perfect model for madame,' the dealer had said, showing me a tiny pistol. 'Look at its mock ivory grip and gold-toned barrel, such elegance, *n'est-ce pas*, madame? Very light to carry too, and easily concealed under a lady's muff. That's why we call it the muff pistol,' he said, and explained how to fire it, as it must have been obvious I had never used such a weapon.

I flushed with pride as I watched Aurore amuse the audience with cartwheels, handstands and backflips across the stage. As always, she exuded boundless energy, passion gleamed in her black eyes and a roguish smile kinked her lips.

Then came the acts of her variety entertainer friends: The Strongest Man in the World, The Rubber Lady, and the flamenco dancer from Spain—a land far to the south whose exotic dancers we were just discovering.

I felt safe, hidden beneath the wig, though I still trembled as I searched the faces of the audience for a man with a beaked nose and a scar on his temple. I would be so disappointed if the Marquis didn't come tonight, though Claudine did assure me he frequented most post-production theatre parties.

The crowd was hushed as a drum roll heralded Aurore's high-wire act. She appeared from the wings, proud as an eagle in her figure-hugging outfit of sparkling gold. As she sprang onto a platform I was so breathless with her beauty I almost forgot the reason I'd come tonight.

A trumpet sounded from the orchestra and Aurore stepped onto the tightly-stretched wire. The audience held its breath, the silence charged with anticipation, perhaps a hint of fear, as she held her body rigid. Like the outspread golden wings of an angel, she stretched her arms and, with silken ease, slid her feet across the wire.

On the orchestra's final note, Aurore smiled, her teeth glinting in the footlights as she leaped down onto the stage. She waved and threw kisses to the audience and we all rose in a roar of applause.

I clapped louder and faster than anyone, the last vestiges of possessiveness over Jeanne winging from me as entirely as a fledgling fleeing the nest.

***

Aurore had said to meet her in the palace hall, where her theatre company was renting a room for the party.

Breathless from the glitz, the excitement, the trepidation of the night, I stepped into the vast room. Hundreds of candles in sconces around the walls lit the mass of revellers chatting in groups or dancing in colourful swirls to the beat of tambourines.

I glimpsed Aurore across the crowd, her curly head thrown back as she laughed with her theatre friends, the babble of their voices rising above the music.

'You were magnificent,' I said, kissing her on both cheeks.

She grinned, dipping her head and took two glasses of wine from the tray of a passing waiter.

'Come, Rubie, let me introduce you to my friends.' She handed me a glass, took my hand and giggled. 'How funny you look with black hair. Nobody would ever know you.'

As Aurore whirled me through the dancers, greeting her fellow entertainers, and accepting compliments with her mischievous grace, I spotted him.

In a black silk suit of the finest quality, the Marquis de Barberon was drinking brandy with a group of distinguished-looking people dressed in the latest style—the women in narrow-waisted full skirts and towering hats adorned with feathers and silk ribbons, the men in embroidered pastel coats with matching breeches.

I stayed close to Aurore, chatting about the performance with a circle of admirers. From the corner of my eye, I observed the Marquis. How to get near him without any obvious manoeuvring? I burned with the glow of vengeance and, beneath my scarlet robe with its coquettish black lace trim, the pistol rested comfortably against my thigh.

'There's someone I know from the restaurant,' I said, drawing away from Aurore.

My hands clammy, I strode—seductively I hoped—towards the Marquis. As I reached him, I bent to retrieve my handkerchief, which had fallen to the floor beside his leather shoes. As I straightened, with languid grace, I brushed my fingertips along the back of his hand, feeling the hard gold of his signet ring.

I stood upright, looked into his face, and saw in the flare of his nostrils and the quiver of his lip, that the Marquis had understood my brief, but unmistakable invitation.

I smiled, trying not to recoil from the touch of his skin and the lecherous grin leaking across his ruddy jowls. I breathed too, to stop myself from shaking, terrified he might recognise me.

As his gaze travelled across my body and hovered over my breasts—the place where he'd once fondled my angel pendant—I knew he had no recollection of me.

The Marquis bowed. 'Since madame almost knocked me down, I think I deserve the pleasure of her acquaintance?'

'Certainly, monsieur.' I stretched my hand, sheathed in black lace, for him to kiss.

'And such an elegant gown,' he said, his eyes already stripping the robe from me. I tried to ignore the sickness rising from my gut as his lips lingered, his tongue flicking, snake-like, over my gloved hand.

A smatter of powder from his wig had whitened the silk on one shoulder, and I brushed it off, giving him an almost imperceptible nod in the direction of the garden. With a gentle swing of my hips, I walked away, certain the Marquis was following me.

My fingers damp around the pistol hidden, once again, beneath my muff, the blood thundered in my head as I held the Marquis's clammy hand, feeling the familiar bump of his signet ring.

We were outside the party hall, and he almost skipped alongside me, his breaths short and fast, as I lured him further and further from the crowd, beyond the light of the oil lamps, and into the darkest reaches of the grove.

As we slid through the trees, I saw other couples had the same idea. A woman was leaning against a tree trunk, her skirts lifted high, her thighs wrapped around a man thrusting into her, and grunting. A little further on I glimpsed a woman's bare breast, milky white in the pale moonlight. Another woman kneaded her flesh, her tongue toying with her lover's nipple. The woman gripped her partner's head, her head arched, her moans softly ecstatic, in the darkness.

I thought of Jeanne, which both calmed and spurred me on, in my deadly mission.

We hadn't gone much further when the Marquis grabbed my shoulders, turned me to face him, and pushed me up against a tree trunk.

'It seems you want this as much as me, lovely lady,' he said, ripping open his breeches, and I almost fainted at the sight of his swollen penis jerking free of its cloth restraint.

As he went to lift my skirt, I flicked out my hand that held the pistol. The weapon gleamed in the moonlight as I levelled it at his face.

'Don't scream,' I hissed, gracing him with my loveliest smile, enjoying the raw fear springing to his eyes. 'Or I'll explode your ugly face.'

His lust quickly paled to shock. 'W-wha, what?' He frowned, his intent gaze searching my eyes.

'Monsieur does not recognise me?'

He shook his head, still speechless.

I ripped the dark wig off and shook out my hair. 'Perhaps now, then?'

He kept staring at me, then slowly, like the ticking hand of a clock approaching the hour, I knew he'd understood the woman before him was no elegant lady offering her body, but the girl who'd cried herself to sleep in his attic bed.

'Ah, the sweet scullery maid,' he said, his tone mocking. He looked down his hooked nose and sniffed at me as one might some diseased dog.

'You wouldn't dare pull the trigger,' he said with a laugh.

'Oh believe me, I would. I'd do it for me, and for my daughter—the bastard child you forced me to abandon. And for the girl you raped and strangled; for Margot, burned! I'd kill you for my father, and for every other crime you rotten aristocrats have committed against commoners.'

My trigger finger itched. I felt I might explode with the desire to watch him suffer and die. I should hurry though, anyone could come along.

Pull the trigger. Come on do it. Now, before it's too late!

My fingers clenched the trigger, paralysed.

In the instant I stood still, willing them to work, the Marquis lunged at me. He knocked the pistol from my hand and wrapped his hands around my neck.

My loathing fuelling me, I lifted my knee and thrust it into his groin.

The Marquis yelped like an injured dog and reeled backwards, tripping over a fallen branch. As he sprawled on the ground, I kicked him hard. Twice, three times, harder and harder.

I cast about in the dark for the gun, but couldn't find it.

The Marquis lurched upright.

'Vile pig!' I hissed, as I turned and fled.

'Fucking bitch!' he screamed. 'I know who you are, you murderous slut. I'll find you. You'll not stay alive another week on the streets of Paris!'

His voice faded as I ran, faster and faster, the panic unfurling and making me shake with a violence I couldn't control.

A shot rang out in the darkness. The Marquis must have found the pistol. People appeared from the shadows, shouting and stumbling in all directions. I hoped they would assume I was fleeing, like them, from an enraged noble firing a pistol blindly into the night.

Was he following me, shooting as he went? I didn't dare slow down to glance over my shoulder. I flicked my tongue over my parched lips. On I ran, the scent of perfumes, of wig powder and body odour catching in my throat.

It seemed I'd never reach the exit, but finally I hurried past a watchman, dozing under a pair of oil lamps burning on the wall, and out of the Palais-Royal.

My chest heaving, I waved my arms wildly at the first cabriolet, and slumped, breathless, beneath the hooded cab. The driver cracked his whip on the horse's back and as we sped away from the palace, the Marquis's words hammered in my head in perfect cadence with the horses' hooves.

I know who you are. You'll not stay alive another week on the streets of Paris.

33

Several weeks after my failed attempt on the Marquis's life, I opened the townhouse door to Claudine.

She cleared her throat. 'Mademoiselle Rubie Charpentier, *s'il vous plaît*.'

I took her arm and drew her inside. 'I'm happy to see my disguise is a success, Claudine.'

'Oh, it's you, Vic … Rubie! What is this scarlet hair?'

My friend's brow was still wrinkled as she followed me up the stairs and into the parlour. 'Your note asking me to come arrived two weeks ago,' she said. 'I'm sorry I couldn't get away before. The Marquis has been in such a state.'

I pursed my lips in mock pity. '*Oh là là*, poor dear fellow.'

'I knew you were full of vengeance,' Claudine said. 'I just prayed witnessing Margot's execution would bring you to your senses. Obviously not.'

We sat at the parlour table, facing each other. Claudine folded her arms across her hefty bosom, and I slumped over my crossed arms.

'Well maybe it did,' I said, 'since I couldn't do it in the end. I wanted so much to pull that trigger, but things—voices, pictures—flashed through my head, and stopped me, my mother's voice mostly. I saw myself convicted by the *Parlement de Paris* like Margot, and burned on la place de Grève … I saw my little Madeleine left motherless.'

'Well the Marquis is still stamping about the house, shouting about his old servant, Victoire Charpentier, who tried to murder him. I overheard him speaking with the Marquise. Through his government contacts, he has obtained a *lettre de cachet* from the King, ordering your imprisonment and, surely, execution!'

'But we both know Victoire Charpentier no longer exists,' I said. 'However could he find me, Claudine?' I touched the scarlet curls. 'Especially with this new hair?'

I served Claudine her coffee. She was looking around the parlour room. It seemed now she'd said her piece, she had the time to eye the soft furnishings, the simple, though elegant decoration—the unmistakable whiff of wealth.

'Such comfortable lodgings, my child. Far beyond the means of a lowly peasant girl.' The little raisin eyes narrowed. 'Have you become a mistress, a kept woman?'

I glanced up sharply. 'What must you think of me?'

'What else am I to think?' she said with a shrug.

'Don't ask about the apartment, Claudine. One day I hope it will be safe to tell you everything, but it is not what you think. I have no lover. Oh no, quite the contrary. I am so very much alone.'

'You must then, banish this vengeance, which weighs you down, my child.'

'But surely you understand why?' I said. 'Certainly, I should have thought of another method. I don't know what … what temporary *lunacy* possessed me to contemplate murder, because I am convinced not the slightest trace remains of my brief affliction of madness, but the Marquis cannot keep assaulting women with impunity.'

I thumped a fist onto the table. 'I have to stop him. For the girls of his past, for Margot, and for those to come, justice must be done.'

'Praise the Lord you didn't succeed,' Claudine said. She drained her coffee and stood. 'I can't linger, my child. I have to get to the market for vegetables and meat. So, what will you do now? Of course, you can never return to *Le Faisan Doré*, but poor country girls need some sort of income. Those without rich lovers, that is.' From Claudine's reproachful look, it seemed she still believed I was a kept mistress.

I accompanied her outside, the summer heat surging in as soon as I opened the door. 'Don't worry for me. My maid, also an actress in fact, has helped me find new employment. I work for a theatre company at the Palais-Royal now, copying scripts for the next day's rehearsal. All this writing has made me keen to invent my own scripts, and I feel this is what I was meant to do; why my mother taught me the letters.'

'But surely it's dangerous for you to be at the Palais-Royal?'

I smiled, patting my scarlet curls. 'Even you must admit, this disguise is effective. My actress-maid is a makeup adept. She taught me theatrical tricks to change the contours, even the colour, of a face.'

Claudine's eyes widened. 'You *wanted* to go back to the Palais-Royal. You still have revenge on your mind, *n'est-ce pas*? You must stop!'

'He has to be punished,' I hissed, waving her away. 'Please don't worry for me.'

My friend shook her head, her face grim. 'I can do, or say, nothing more for you. You dig your own grave.'

Her shoulders hunched over her stout body, Claudine strode off across the courtyard without looking back.

***

'It's no surprise the assembly of notables baulked at Calonne's deficit,' cried the orator addressing the Palais-Royal crowd. 'Since the very assembly is composed of the system's social and political elite!' The man stood on the sun-drenched café terrace, one foot placed before the other, just like my dear father.

'But Calonne's tax reform plan was our only solution,' another man shouted. 'He even had the King's backing.'

'Perhaps,' the speaker said, 'but the people still suspect our enormous financial strain was Calonne's fault.'

I sat in the shade of the chestnut trees, listening to the debate about the exiled finance minister. Since I no longer worked in the restaurant, I enjoyed spending many hours in the cafés listening to the speakers—the perfect place to continue my education and remove myself, as far as possible, from my peasant-girl roots.

I was enjoying a glass of wine with a refreshing *soupe aux cerises,* and tinkering with my plume, jotting thoughts down as the muse came, when a man stumbled over a chair leg. He almost landed in my lap.

'Goodness, *excusez-moi,* madame,' he said in a strange, accented voice. 'How clumsy of me.' The tall, angular man repositioned his hat. He took my book he'd knocked to the ground, and placed it back on the table.

'Are you hurt?' I asked. 'Please, if you need to sit down.' I gestured at the empty chair opposite me.

'Why thank you, madame.'

I dipped my head, curious about the peculiar accent as the man sat.

'A popular spot, it seems.' As he waved an arm across the crowded café and nodded at the speaker, I saw he held his right wrist awkwardly, as if it had been injured and never healed properly.

'All the cafés are crowded these days,' I said. 'Especially when there is talk of political and financial trouble.'

'Yes, certainly,' the man said, glancing at the title of my book he'd knocked from the table. 'Ah, *The Social Contract.* Does madame find it of interest?'

'Oh yes, very interesting. Rousseau argues against the idea that monarchs were divinely empowered to legislate,' I said. 'That only the people have such an all-powerful right.'

'I hope to read it myself, shortly,' the man said, eyeing my paper of scribbles. 'So, you write too, as well as read, madame? May I be so bold as to ask about what?'

'It is a script,' I said. 'For a play. About oh, lots of things—class differences, the health of the mind, women's rights.'

'The rights of women? Well that is a very bold thing to write about. Alas,' he continued, shaking his head. 'Even though I have learned to speak your lovely language, I remain the awkward novice at writing it.'

I tapped the end of my quill against my bottom lip. 'In what language do you write then, monsieur?'

'Why English, naturally, madame. I am American. Please let me introduce myself.' He stood and tipped his hat to me. 'Monsieur Thomas Jefferson, ambassador to the French Court.' He took my hand and kissed the back of it.

'Mademoiselle Rubie Charpentier, playwright,' I said, feeling the heat of the day heighten in the flush of my cheeks.

'Well, perhaps the delightful Mademoiselle Charpentier would care to share a cup of the famed mocca they pump up through the columns of the Café Mécanique?' He raised his eyebrows. 'Purely to observe this engineering ingenuity, of course.'

My blush deepened and I lowered my eyes, fidgeting with my papers and shuffling them about on the table.

***

My dear Madame Collier,

I am happy to hear you have arrived safely in London. Sorry for my late reply, but I have been busy visiting all the sights of the capital you recommended.

I understand why you advised me to eat in that particular restaurant of the elegant Palais-Royal, which the people call the capital of Paris—the greatest bordello in Europe—where any desire can be had from the most depraved debauchery to the heights of learning about physics, anatomy, poetry … anything the heart desires. Naturally, those of the noblest tastes frequent it.

Some say the Duke of Orléans transformed his palace into the centre of Paris's political and social intrigue simply to get back at the King and Queen, who constantly suspect him of anti-royalist sentiment. I suppose however, standing so close to the throne, it is natural our rulers treat him as treacherous, hypocritical and selfish.

Despite his outward scorn for Marie Antoinette's lavish, immoral lifestyle, I see the duke as a man of the people, in touch with their moods and concerns.

I have been attending the theatres of the Palais-Royal, admiring our mutual friend's acting talent, though I think most of the scripts are trite, ridiculous even, which has led me to doodling with my own ideas.

So, my friend, you are not the only one writing stories. It seems as if my entire repressed lifetime has found release in words. As we enter the height of summer, in this new age of enlightened thinking, of questioning our archaic social mores, I see prose as the ideal vehicle to impart my ideals to others.

An incident, which may have reached you on the English shores, inspired my first play. At a Palais-Royal party, an attempt was made on the life of a certain marquis. It was not apparent why this elegantly-dressed woman failed to pull the trigger. Possibly the disciplines on which she was reared held her back, who knows? I suppose, fundamentally, we can't change. We can merely present varying public facades, which remain, in essence, superficial.

Anyway, all scandals aside, my friend, I must tell you of an event you may find exciting, I certainly did.

Several weeks ago I met a most charismatic gentleman in a café. It transpired he is Monsieur Thomas Jefferson, American ambassador come to Paris to negotiate trade treaties with the European powers.

I could hardly believe a man of such importance took the time to speak to an ordinary woman such as myself. Apart from being an amateur architect, he is also an avid reader and theatregoer, and we had an interesting conversation.

Since then, despite his time and presence being in such demand, we have spoken together over coffee one morning, and agreed to help each other: I am to teach him to write French and he will help me learn English. All you have told me about Great Britain inspires me to visit one day, so I am keen to learn the language. Anything English is also very fashionable in Paris, and we're all becoming, as Monsieur Jefferson says, Anglomaniacs!

I am quite excited to meet him again. After all, you did urge me to make the most of my stay in Paris, and amuse myself!

I leave you, my friend, with that last thought, to return to my script.

By the way, you didn't mention your husband in your last letter. I trust he is well?

I have the honour to be your friend,
Mademoiselle Rubie Charpentier

34

'I imagine you've heard about the death of the princess?' I said to Aurore, as I drew back the pastel green drapes, a blast of summer sun flooding the parlour.

'You mean Sophie-Beatrix?' Aurore placed a fresh fruit salad on the table. 'Yes, we hear every last thing about our loathsome Queen.'

'The child hadn't even reached her first birthday,' I said, sweet flesh spurting into my mouth as I bit into a cherry. 'Her poor mother, there is nothing more tragic than the loss of a child. Apparently the Queen is devastated and spends hours weeping over her baby's body.'

'Poor mother?' Aurore's spoon clattered to the table, chunks of plum and strawberry flying about. 'How can you feel sympathy for that hateful Austrian, whose face is set in stupidity and contempt for us, her diamonds flashing like naked blades? All she does is hurtle our country closer and closer to financial ruin.'

'I understand how you feel, Aurore, I too have seen the Queen's scornful face in street processions, but even so there is no worse tragedy. And for that, Marie Antoinette has my empathy.'

'Well I for one am glad we don't see much of her anymore,' Aurore said. 'And on the odd occasion she does go outside Court, she is met with silence, or hisses. The public simply shun her these days.'

'I wouldn't venture out either,' I said. 'If all those insulting pamphlets and songs going around the cafés were about me.'

'She deserves it.' Aurore finished her fruit salad, and stood to get ready to leave for the theatre.

'Wait, I have something to show you.' I placed a stack of papers in front of her. 'My first play.'

'What's it about?' Aurore said as she flipped through the pages. 'You know I cannot read well enough to understand this.'

'The oldest of themes—the poor fighting against the rich. Satire, Aurore, social messages disguised in simple drama. I know you cannot read perfectly, but I hope this will spur you on to learn more. For if you can't read the script, how will you play the leading role?'

'Leading role?' She frowned. 'You know I only do vaudeville—the high-wire. I don't play real parts.'

'Don't you want to become a famous, well-paid actress?' I said, lifting my eyebrows. 'I am sure my play will cause such social rumblings, you cannot help but be noticed.'

***

My dear Rubie,

What marvellous news you send me, especially about the distinguished American gentleman, whose attentions are, I imagine, in great demand.

How exciting also, to hear of your play. One day I'll be back in Paris and take great pleasure in watching your works.

You ask after my husband. I have no idea where the scoundrel is. Run off with another of his women friends, I suppose. His female entourage seems to think he's in possession of some great wealth, though I have no idea why. How disillusioned they'll be, when they discover he has nothing, and is as poor as the next person. My husband was always too stupid to hang onto any sort of wealth.

Never mind, you know I never really loved the man. Besides, I now have a new, and admirable, lover. Having suffered himself, at the hands of those who wield the power, he is a great inspiration for my writing.

So the rumours were true about the Marquis de Calonne, finance minister exiled to Great Britain, taking up with the infamous woman of the necklace affair. I smiled to myself. How typical of Jeanne.

I continue to enjoy my stay in London, with its offerings of domestic bliss and peaceful conduct. Of course, the French could also enjoy such things if only they would give over these silly games of luxury and appearance, which are simply a waste of energy and money.

The English seem happy too, with their government, which, while still enforcing the law, respects the rights of the people. They have finished with civil disorder and emerged triumphantly enlightened from their crises. Enlightenment, that's what we French can learn from them.

I continue my story-writing with delight, and will shortly publish the first one.

I have the honour to be your friend,

Madame J. Collier

I refolded the letter. Enlightenment. Yes, Jeanne, how I craved for that too, almost as much as I hankered for justice.

***

'Let us celebrate the Assumption of Mary,' the parish priest cried, glowing in his holiday vestments of gold embroidery.

The stifling August heat had done nothing to deter the crowds. My companion, Monsieur Jefferson and I managed to find a spot in the dappled shade of a linden tree, but the sweat still trickled down my neck, and the sun scorched my head through my straw hat.

'It's like being back in my village,' I said. 'Every August 15 we celebrated the Festival of the Blessed Virgin. Our priest always reminded us she is as important as God.'

Monsieur Jefferson waved away a humming bee. 'And what village might that be, Mademoiselle Charpentier?'

I stirred the gravel with the toe of my shoe. 'Oh, it is about a week from Paris, if your coach is a good one and doesn't break down or have an accident.'

As the priest continued, I was reminded again of Père Joffroy's cassock dancing about as he waved his arms at his congregation.

'Having completed the course of her earthly life, the Virgin Mary was assumed, body and soul, into heavenly glory!' the priest cried.

His voice rising with his conviction, I felt a pang of yearning for Lucie, and a deep ache for Madeleine, but I could not forget Léon's treachery—what prevented me from returning.

As I waved away the flies and heat with my fan, squinting against the scorching sun, I vowed one day, despite Léon Bruyère, I would find a way to return to those earthy tendrils binding me to Lucie-sur-Vionne.

The ambassador and I had taken his private coach earlier to attend a play at a *château* just outside Paris. We'd not planned on participating in these celebrations, but caught up in the fervour, we joined the people lining the street cheering and clapping as an effigy of Our Lady and the Divine Child rumbled along on a cart heavy with flowers, ribbons and fruit.

'You French certainly know how to celebrate,' Monsieur Jefferson said, smiling down at me. I didn't think I'd ever met a man as tall as he, or as well mannered, and I felt quite safe, by his side.

'Feast days take up almost a quarter of the year,' I said. 'Well, they did in Luc … in my village. It was a time when everyone forgot their worries in food, dancing and telling tales.'

I gazed across the vast swampy marshland in the distance, the rural scents of fresh hay, of flowers and sun-baked earth catching in my nostrils, even though we were but a short distance from the stink and filth of Paris.

'You're certain you don't want to attend the sermon?' Monsieur Jefferson asked, as we stepped back into his coach for the ride home.

I shook my head and settled into the leather seat. 'At one time I would have entered a church with pleasure, but not now.'

'At one time?' he said, as we swayed to the soft thud of the horses' hooves on the baked ground. 'What changed?'

'No single thing,' I said. 'Life, I suppose, growing up.' Of course the well-brought-up daughter of deceased silk merchant, Maximilien Charpentier mentioned nothing about prison, and how that alone hardened and changed a person, and made them question the ways of God.

'And education,' I went on. 'Like you, Monsieur Jefferson, I am a great reader. Recently I managed to acquire a copy of *Le Dictionnaire Philosophique*, which has been most instructive.'

'But isn't that banned in France?' he said. 'All copies burned on town squares?'

'Not *all* copies,' I said with a smile. 'I have a special book trader who, for a good price, seems able to procure whatever reading matter you desire.' I leaned closer to my companion. 'I heard it whispered in a café—the author is our own Voltaire.'

Monsieur Jefferson nodded. 'Ah yes, I have read his works. So, how does it appeal to you?'

'I think it is his scepticism,' I said, as the coach rumbled on. 'How he believes in a God; in a religion without church or politics. And while I do retain my faith in God, I now see the Catholic Church as a hypocritical and sometimes harmful institution—a place where the feeble-minded worship a piece of bread!' My mind clouded with the memory of my father's battered body, of my mother being dragged, screaming, across the muddy riverbank, her eyes wild and searching me out, her hand pressing the angel pendant into mine.

My fingers strayed to my neck, feeling for the little bone carving as if it were still there. Even in its absence, I felt the warmth prickling my fingertips, the comfort stealing through me. I concentrated on that strength to calm my voice.

'My m-mother was ex-executed for doubting the existence of God.'

Monsieur Jefferson's brow creased. 'How tragic.'

'Like Voltaire, though,' I went on, 'for some people I believe organised religion is necessary. When disaster strikes, it is often a person's only consolation.'

The smoke raged in my nostrils again, and I cringed from the lightning, the soaring flames, the twisted wood and two small, blackened skeletons. 'Oh yes, Monsieur Jefferson, the Church has its place but I, personally, have no need for it any longer.'

I realised then, the smoke I smelt was no memory. Great brown palls of it curled into the sky from somewhere in the distance. As we approached the city gates, I craned my neck, but could see nothing. It was probably just another shop fire.

A green-coated clerk stopped us at the toll gate, or *barrière* as we now called them, since building on the hated Farmers-General Wall had started.

'Anything to declare?' The tax farmer stared at us, and must have realised it was Monsieur Jefferson in his private carriage, because he merely nodded and waved us through the toll gate.

'He dares not search us for taxable goods,' I said, squinting into the fierce ball of setting sun throwing its orange-grey haze over the city. 'Oh the advantages of being important, unjust as that is.'

As we approached the Pont Neuf from the left bank, to cross the river and reach my apartment, the coach jostled with others down the narrow streets.

'I was brought up an Anglican,' Monsieur Jefferson said, 'and while I consider myself a Christian, I have come to view the Church as the principal agency enslaving the human mind. I firmly believe separation of church and state is a necessary reform of this religious tyranny which punishes and denies rights to those who are not of that religion.'

As he slapped a palm on his thigh, the first cries reached us, and the streets thickened with people running, shouting and brandishing stones, clubs and pikes.

'Whatever is happening?' Monsieur Jefferson said, as the knot of angry, shouting people forced the coach to a complete halt.

'I have no idea.' The smell of smoke grew stronger, the noise of rising shouts, and a growing unease pulsed through me. 'But I am going to find out.'

'No.' Monsieur Jefferson laid a hand on my arm in gentle restraint. 'It may be dangerous to leave the carriage.'

I shrugged him off. 'Don't worry for me, monsieur, I just want to know what's going on.' I stepped down into the furious mob.

'What's happening?' I asked a young man with wild hair and unkempt clothes.

'The people are rioting, madame,' he said. 'The King has banished the Parliament of Paris, because the judges refused to register his corn trade edict. They knew it would only bring about even more taxes!'

'Come back inside,' Mr Jefferson said, his voice urgent, as more and more people carrying rudimentary weapons squeezed past the coach, shrieking and charging towards the Pont Neuf to join the commotion. The horses pawed and snorted, their soft brown eyes filling with panic.

The crowd became so thick we reached an impasse. 'We'll have to continue on foot,' I said. 'We have no choice.'

'Well hurry then,' Monsieur Jefferson said, as the angry crowd swept us along. 'The French Guards will soon be here. We don't want to get caught between the police guns and the rioters.'

We rounded a corner and it only got worse as we came upon a square, thick with choking smoke, the noise of a heaving mob deafening. We began coughing, and clamped our handkerchiefs over our faces.

Monsieur Jefferson pointed to the blazing effigy. 'Who are they are burning?'

'Madame de Polignac I think, despised favourite of the

Queen and governess of her children,' I said, trying to push away from the confusion. 'New pamphlets have been printed these last few days, even more virulent than usual, against the Queen. I'm certain it's Marie Antoinette they really wish to burn.'

'Come away, quickly.' Monsieur Jefferson started to drag me through the seething crowd, as the first shots rang out. The French Guards must have arrived.

I jumped at the sound of more gunshot, louder, closer, and a hot numbness stopped me.

I felt nothing, apart from a slow trickle from my left shoulder. I glanced down and saw the gaping rip in the cloth of my muslin dress. From a small, dark hole, blood flowed down my front, quickly drenching my dress. The strength drained from my legs, and the pain came, lancing me with its ferocity.

'My God!' Monsieur Jefferson's eyes widened. '*A l'aide, à l'aide!*' he shouted. 'She's been shot.'

As I sank to the cobblestones, a vision of the Marquis stained my mind. I thought it odd his face was the last thing I would see. He'd never found me, with my clever disguise. On the other hand, nor had I been able to stop his abuse.

'Mademoiselle Charpentier, stay with us, keep your eyes open,' Monsieur Jefferson was saying. I opened my eyes to slits, felt him pressing on my shoulder and I saw his hands were stained red and shaking violently.

People hovered over me and through a gap in the circle of faces, the blue sky turned a dirty grey. I wanted to tell them to move back; that I couldn't breathe with them all crowded around me, but no words came.

I couldn't get any air in. I started gasping. The voices became fainter. They faded to silence. The ring of faces was a blur, and gone.

The sky turned black.

35

My eyelids hung heavy, as if insistent fingers were tugging on them. Drenched in a quiet peace, the room smelt like a mixture of wood, lemon and polish. The edges of the dark furniture, the wide, crowded bookshelves and the cream drapes were smudgy, as in a dream. I had no idea where I was.

I turned to the window. A girl with skin the same dark colour as the turbaned men I'd seen at the Palais-Royal, sat in a chair, sewing cloth by the light. As I squinted through the window beyond her, onto what looked like a great expanse of land, a knife-like pain rippled through my shoulder.

The girl stood and smiled. 'You're awake now, ma'am. Don't be afraid, I is Sally, Massa Jefferson's slave girl, and this is his home, the Hôtel de Langeac.'

The girl's English was quite different from Monsieur Jefferson's—more the slow, sad lyrics of a ballad, the words rising and falling with the heave of her breast.

'Rest, ma'am, you is safe now,' she said, patting the bed covers.

I glanced down and saw a wad of cloth covered my shoulder and it streamed back—the riot, the smoke, the blazing effigy, the crack of a pistol.

I summoned my rudimentary English skills. 'Where is Monsieur Jefferson?'

'Massa negotiating good prices for whale-oil and salted fish.

He tell me you to stay put in bed while I is goin' to market.'

I felt giddy, and rested my head back on the pillows.

As the girl left the room, I tapped my fingertips over the wound dressing. My hand froze. The prison brand! Monsieur Jefferson must have seen it, when he pressed on the wound to staunch the bleeding. He would know he'd been frequenting a branded killer.

My mind worked fast, like a rising scream. He'd realise I had escaped from a prison—murderesses either die in custody, or are executed.

I felt the panic mount, the sensation of being snagged in a net. The ambassador had always been amiable, and the politest of men, but he was also fiercely law-abiding. He would never let an escaped prisoner remain on the loose. That's probably where he was now, telling the police.

I had to get away before the maid returned. I swung my legs over the side of the bed. My gaze blurred, the wound smarted, and I lay back on the pillows. I still felt giddy, and the furniture and the window frame stayed hazy. They must have given me something to calm me, and the pain. Laudanum, perhaps.

I eased myself upright again, casting about for my clothes. I couldn't see my robe anywhere; besides, part of it must be ripped to shreds. Perhaps that's what the dark girl was sewing. I looked around again. Draped over a tapestry chair was a muslin dress similar to mine, in pastel green. A sash of a darker green lay beside it, with my straw bonnet.

I slid from the bed. Wincing against the bolts of pain, I used my right arm to drag the dress over my chemise. I slid my shoes on and crossed to the window, hoping I might recognise something. The room looked out onto a well-tended garden of plants, flowers and some strange-looking corn ears. They must be from the seeds Monsieur Jefferson told me he'd had sent from America—his beloved American corn he couldn't find in France.

There seemed to be nobody around, but still I crept from the bedroom. Apart from some distant clanging of pots, there was not a sound. I eased down the staircase, gripping the rail both for support and to stop myself shaking. Elegant paintings graced the walls, and through a doorway, I glimpsed a pianoforte and a music stand. I opened the front door, cringing as it creaked. I looked about me. Still nobody. I skittered, as fast as my ungainly legs could bear, across the pristine courtyard, and out of the huge iron pavilion gates.

It was still early but already hot, the Boulevard trees drooping, the sun blinding me as I stepped into the street. Once outside, I saw Monsieur Jefferson's residence was located about halfway up the Champs-Elysées, adjoining the Grille de Chaillot. A little further along, I recognised the toll gate under construction, soon to replace the Grille de Chaillot as one of the city limits. At least I knew where I was.

I hurried away on shaky legs, my head swivelling from left to right, scanning the street for a tall man or a small dark girl. It was, indeed, only a short distance back to the rue Saint-Honoré, but I had no energy, and soon my head started spinning. I licked my dry lips, regretting not having drunk something in my haste to leave.

As I reached the stables of the Comte d'Artois, which were being built on the corner of the rue de Berri and the rue du Faubourg Saint-Honoré, I began to lurch like a drunkard. I kept stopping, leaning against a wall to get my breath and clear my head. The pain seared through me like a burn, and a spot of blood blossomed on my left shoulder. Despite the heat, I shivered, and sweat slid down my back.

Everything around me—trees, people, buildings—seemed suspended in fog. I feared I would pass out, and as I stumbled into the courtyard of the townhouse, never could I recall feeling so relieved to be home.

'*Mon Dieu*, what's happened to you, Rubie? You're so pale.' Aurore took my arm, helped me into the parlour and onto a chair. 'I've been worried, no news for two days, and I had not the slightest idea where to look for you.'

She placed a glass of water on the table beside me, which I gulped down.

'I was shot.'

Aurore's hand flew to her mouth. 'Oh no! The Marquis?'

I looked up sharply. I'd always suspected she knew about that monster.

'No, not him. At least I don't think so. I'm fairly certain this scarlet hair is enough to deceive such a stupid oaf. I was caught in the cross-fire of the riot the other evening.'

'I was there,' Aurore said. 'And we've not finished rioting, Rubie! Now you lie down and let me take care of you. Sick and weak as you are, you'll be no help for our fight.'

***

Two days later, a messenger arrived at the apartment with a sealed note.

My fingers fumbled with the seal as I recognised the shaky scrawl of Monsieur Jefferson.

My dear Mademoiselle Charpentier,

I was both shocked and surprised to learn you had left the Hôtel de Langeac in your delicate condition. I know nothing of your circumstances but I think I am a good judge of character, and believe you to be an intelligent and honest woman. I can only surmise you had good reason to flee my hospitality, the privacy of which I will respect.

I coaxed your address from your actress friend, Aurore, at the theatre. Please don't be harsh on her, she was quite reticent to divulge any information, but I assured her I meant you no harm and merely wanted to ask after your health.

After the shooting, when you lapsed into unconsciousness, I was fortunately able to stop the bleeding, transport you to my home and call the barber-surgeon.

He said you were lucky, that the bullet only nicked your shoulder. He says the wound is large, and thus you will have quite a scar. However, I'm certain you'll not be too dispirited about such a scar, given your life was spared. I only hope your injury heals without complication.

I hope once you are recovered, we can continue our mutual language lessons. My French writing slowly improves (as you can see!) though nothing as remarkable as your progress in the English language.

Not wishing to trust the post office, where every spy reads one's letters, I have placed this note into the trusty palm of a personal messenger.

Take great care, Mademoiselle Charpentier, in these troubled times.

Your most obedient and humble servant,

Monsieur Thomas Jefferson

I took a fresh sheet of paper, dipped my plume into the ink and replied to Monsieur Jefferson, expressing my interest in continuing our lessons. I apologised too, for fleeing his hospitality, excusing my hasty flight as some laudanum-induced confusion, which had manifested in inexplicable panic.

When I'd finished writing, I sat back and smiled. I patted my heavily-padded injury—the pistol brand that, in baring my flesh to the world, had effectively camouflaged the old one.

36

My dear Madame Collier,
Please excuse the hiatus in correspondence. Unfortunately I was shot during the Paris riots, which, as you might know, lasted from August until October last year. I consider myself fortunate the wound healed without complication, thanks to our mutual friend, who nursed me back to health. Beneath that tempestuous, wildcat exterior, she truly is a sweet, nurturing girl. I am as proud as you must be, to know her.

By some quirk of chance, the wound has completely covered the unsightly birthmark you recall I had on my left shoulder. Next summer, and for all the summers to come, I am finally free to wear daring dresses with plunging shoulders and neckline!

We are glad spring has arrived because winter was the coldest any living person could recall. I did not venture out much, preferring to stay warm inside, continuing both my studies of the books you recommended, and my script writing.

The Seine was a solid sheet of ice. What a novelty, at first, with all the children skating about like mad things, but the gaiety didn't last. With the ships impaled on the ice, the grain rotting in their holds, goods could not enter the city—no cloth to be dyed, no skins to be tanned, no corn.

The price of a loaf of bread rose to fourteen sous and all the vagrants hung around the markets in the late afternoons for the free bread, though they had to fight off the fierce housewives first.

People wandered aimlessly, looking more and more starved, mainly the lower class Savoyard labourers. As you know, these people make up more than a quarter of the population, so you can imagine the atmosphere of misery and desperation.

Even the rich seemed dislocated. When they stepped down from their carriages, over the frozen corpses littering their fashionable streets, they'd pull their cloaks about their faces, to keep both the stinging cold from their cheeks, and the miserable sights from their eyes.

I believe I would not stay in Paris if I weren't passionate for the commoners' cause. Despite my hesitation in returning to Lucie, I constantly feel the tug of my childhood village; the pull of my daughter. But I know my place is, for now, here in the capital.

Did you hear that in January, the Parliament complained to the King about his lettres de cachet? *It is likely they will be banned. I imagine all those people having such letters out against them with be sighing with relief.*

I know your affairs keep you in London for now, but sometimes I think how wonderful it would be to have you visit, especially as we are about to witness the birth of a new nation. Only four days in the diligence, and you could be here!

Lessons with Monsieur Jefferson continue; he remains both a scholarly and amusing acquaintance. He also frequents the theatres of the Palais-Royal, and I don't know how he managed it, but he had my script submitted to the reading committee of one of the companies. I was so excited when they accepted it, and it won the approval of the censor. Roles were cast, work began immediately and the premiere is next week! I can hardly believe my good fortune. Our mutual friend will play the leading part. Of course, I wrote it with her in mind. As you know, she generally plays minor roles—maids, slaves, and the like—so this may be a great chance to advance her career.

I have the honour to be your friend,
Mademoiselle Rubie Charpentier

***

Snug against the chill spring evening in her lioness costume, Aurore paced the length of her cage, her hips jutting in erotic thrusts with each languid step. Her chocolate brown eyes—devoted and sensual—never left her master's face.

In the first act of *Les Barreaux de la Liberté*, my audience travelled to an exotic jungle, and witnessed the capture of wild beasts most had never seen—monkeys, gaily-coloured birds, a zebra, a rhinoceros, even a condor.

In Act II, the audience swayed and rocked with the animals as they took a torturous boat trip to France. The audience were sad when the condor died of starvation and was thrown overboard, and when the ship's crew roasted three of the monkeys for dinner, they booed and hissed.

Now, in Act III, the surviving monkeys, the birds, the zebra, even the rhino, were performing backflips, cartwheels and walking on their hands across the stage to entertain their owner, Lord Frisson, who had brought them to his *château* ten leagues south of Paris.

The audience laughed at the beasts' antics, and Lord Frisson and his aristocratic entourage twittered and whispered from their seats on the right-hand side of the stage. Left-stage, at the back, Aurore the lioness kept pacing, gazing in rapture at Lord Frisson.

The audience shrieked with laughter as the monkeys stopped their acrobatics, darted at Lord Frisson's group, jumped on their heads and ripped their powdered wigs off. They dissolved in tears of mirth as the monkeys began shitting on the nobles' heads.

Monkey excreta sliding down his face, Lord Frisson leapt from his throne-like chair and chased the monkeys, yelling and waving his fist, and trying to stamp on them with his great hunting boots. The monkeys shrieked, darting back and forth across the stage.

'Free me from this cage, my Lord,' the lioness called. 'I'll save you from those disgusting monkeys. I shall rip them apart for you.'

'But you are a wild and dangerous beast,' Lord Frisson said. 'How do I know you'll not devour *me*?'

The lioness gave a sensual thrust of her head. 'Haven't I proved to be his Lordship's most loyal, entertaining companion, since our arrival here?'

The monkeys were still charging about like mad things, ripping the clothes from Lord Frisson's friends, who stood trembling in their undergarments.

Lord Frisson turned to the audience. 'Can I trust my lovely lioness?'

'*Oui, oui*, let her out!' the audience cried.

With a melodramatic gesture, Lord Frisson swept Aurore's cage open and, with a giant leap, the lioness's great jaws clamped around Lord Frisson's head. Her teeth began tearing him apart and Lord Frisson crumpled in a bloody heap to the stage.

As the curtain fell at the end of the first week of my debut play—*Les Barreaux de la Liberté*—the audience stood, cheering, clapping and stamping their feet.

I felt I'd been holding my breath in anticipation the whole way through. Naturally, I was aware the playwright whose works were performed on Parisian stages required a thick skin to survive the catcalls and whistles of the parterre, or the gibes of the critics and reviews. I breathed out with relief, the apprehension seeping from me the louder they cheered.

The actors removed the head section of their costumes and bowed low and long, the audience even cheering the shat-upon "nobles". I couldn't stop beaming, and my smile was especially wide for Aurore.

From my vantage point in one of the theatre boxes, I saw Claudine in the pit, still clapping. In another private box, across from me, the Marquis de Barberon was frowning and shaking his head in what looked like shocked disgust. As he pushed aside the lackey who attended his box and stormed out of the theatre, I laughed aloud.

***

'How clever you are, my child.' Claudine kissed both my cheeks. 'From the moment that girl walked into my kitchen, I just knew she would make something of her wretched life.' She gave me a mock-frown and hissed, close to my ear, 'once she banished those silly ideas of revenge.'

'Oh but I am getting my retribution, Claudine,' I said, thinking of the Marquis's noble displeasure. 'And it is proving far sweeter and more satisfying, disguised in stage costumes.' I took her arm. 'Now come along, I want you to meet Aurore.'

I looked up to see Monsieur Jefferson loping towards us. He tipped his hat to Claudine.

'Congratulations, my dear Mademoiselle Charpentier. The critics are raving and the pamphlet reviews positively glow,' he said. 'How well you evoke this new, gruesome obsession noble Parisians have developed for foreign animals.'

'The leading lady deserves the praise,' I said. 'She's the real star.'

'Oh your lioness certainly is the talk of the Palais-Royal theatre buffs,' he said. 'But surely the writer and producer of "Cage of Freedom" deserves acclaim too? You know what they're calling you now? *L'Enchanteresse Rouge.*'

I laughed to cover my blush. 'The Scarlet Enchantress ... how nice. Listen, we're all celebrating at La Taverne. Will you join us?'

'I'd be honoured, Madame the playwright.' He waved at a group of distinguished-looking people. 'I must speak with some acquaintances first, then I'll join you.'

'The gentleman is taken with you,' Claudine said as we strolled off. 'If he wasn't a foreigner, or an *Anglican*, he'd be quite a suitor for the sophisticated Mademoiselle Rubie Charpentier.'

'Oh no,' I said as the stream of people propelled us toward the Palais-Royal restaurants. 'The ambassador socialises in far greater circles than I.'

I patted Claudine's arm, hooked through mine. 'But I've come to learn it's better to have certain people as friends, than never to know them at all, *n'est-ce pas?*'

In the ruby light of the tavern, everyone raised their glasses, fizzing with champagne.

'A toast to the Scarlet Enchantress!' they cried. 'To *Les Barreaux de la Liberté!*'

'To the lioness,' I said, lifting my glass to my leading lady, and bursting with a delight I thought I'd never know.

'To Aurore!' cried the actors, stagehands and sceneshifters.

Aurore's face turned an even darker shade as she dipped her head. 'I couldn't have done it without the Scarlet Enchantress.'

Once the excitement over the success of *Les Barreaux de la Liberté* died down, talk in La Taverne turned to the usual topic.

'Paris has become a furnace of politics,' Monsieur Jefferson said. 'Men, women and children talk of nothing else. It feels the entire country is on the eve of some great revolution.'

'But it is, monsieur,' said a man in a dark suit. 'And things like this,' he said, waving a pamphlet with the headline, *Memoirs of la Comtesse Jeanne de Valois*, 'will serve to bring the Queen down even more.'

I inhaled sharply.

'The first of what is apparently an endless stream of accusations against Marie Antoinette,' the man went on, waving his pamphlet.

'Everybody who is *anybody* is talking about the memoirs,' a woman in a mauve gown said. 'And it is rumoured the countess was assisted by her current lover, the exiled former Finance Minister, the Marquis de Calonne!'

Mock-gasps and laughter rang out across La Taverne. Under fire of all the excited breath, it seemed even the candles quivered in their sconces.

'What's so humorous, Mademoiselle Charpentier?' Monsieur Jefferson asked, as I tried to cover my smirk.

I giggled, which might have been the effect of the champagne. 'I think Jeanne de Valois is a brave woman to fight for what is rightfully hers, ripped away by our pitiless monarchy.' I waved my glass at the ambassador to the French Court. 'Even though they were possibly doomed from the moment they stepped on the throne, Marie Antoinette has, largely, brought all this upon herself.'

Monsieur Jefferson's eyebrows twitched. 'Yes, well, everyone is entitled to their opinion, madame.' He turned and strode away from me.

Aurore frowned. 'What's wrong with *him*? Surely he knows our opinions on the monarchy by now?'

'Yes, I thought so,' I said. 'But still, I should have held my tongue.' I placed my glass on the table, as the champagne turned sour in my mouth.

37

The leaves of the tree-lined street already showed the first tinges of autumn colour. They rippled with birdsong and the afternoon breeze, as if the sparrows and blackbirds were competing for centre-stage with the hammering and shouts of workmen, the creak of carts and the rhythmical *walop, walop* of horses' hooves.

As the coach set me down in the rue d'Artois, I glanced over my shoulder, up and down the line of elegant homes. In this peaceful residential quarter, laid out beyond the Boulevards less than ten years ago, I was not afraid. I could relax the heightened awareness with which I walked the city streets since the second wave of riots that summer of 1788.

Everybody was on guard in the city. People watched each other, sometimes out of simple curiosity, but more often out of malice. Two people could not whisper together without a third craning his neck to hear them. Spies haunted the alleys and arcades, stood in the long lines for bread, eavesdropped on *poissardes* and prostitutes, and followed the prices of sugar and soap. I also knew I had been lucky to escape death from one bullet; I surely would not survive a second.

A maid opened the door and admitted me into the home of Madame Sophie Gilbert. In the centre of a stylish drawing room, surrounded by a group of women, Sophie reclined in a milk bath.

This was very different to the traditional salons I'd heard of—the assortment of liberal anglophiles, their glamorous wives and mistresses, and ambitious young men meeting to discuss the latest books, plays, affairs, and above all, politics. *Chez* Madame Sophie Gilbert, there was neither the whiff of an aristocrat, nor a male, in sight.

'Ah, our star has arrived.' Sophie smiled and beckoned me closer. 'The Scarlet Enchantress. Sit down, relax, Rubie.' She gestured around the room of women, who all seemed to boast the easy bourgeois friendliness and confidence of philosophical thought. From the way they perched on the edge of their chairs though, there seemed too, an air of uneasy discontent and restrained energy about them.

'Feel free to say what you want, Rubie,' Sophie said. 'Whatever burns inside your breast.' She laid a palm in the cleft of her own, naked breasts, rising from the white bath like islands in a sea of milk. 'We are safe from censure here, and spies too, who have become so virulent as to poison even the most private and friendly of gatherings.'

She raised a leg from the milky water, resting her ankle up on the edge. 'We prefer a more relaxed atmosphere,' she said. 'Freedom from the binds of whalebone stays encourages open speech and thought, *n'est-ce pas*, Olympe?'

The woman she referred to as Olympe laid a hand on Sophie's cheek and stroked the pinked flesh.

'Metaphorically and literally,' Olympe said. She moved back from Sophie, handed me a glass of wine from a tray and patted a place beside her on the sofa. 'I for one am thankful those ridiculous corsets are finally going out of fashion. How barbarous to wear something that impedes a woman's breathing and deforms her chest.'

'My sister lost a child because of tight stays,' a dark-haired girl, Manon, said. 'The midwife said the corset squeezed the life out of the infant.'

'So you believe we should all follow the advice of Rousseau—

that prophet of naturalness, of sensibility?' said a tightly-stayed woman with a hooked nose and such an array of feathers spilling from her hat she looked like some great bird perched atop the tapestry armchair. 'And have our children run around wild, barefoot, and half-naked?'

'Rousseau rightly said it is better for our children to wear loose clothes so as not to constrict their growing bodies,' Olympe said. 'Even if the man did dare to argue women should be educated for the pleasure of men!' She rolled her eyes.

Manon pursed her lips in mock-concern. 'And, of course, if the corset were banned, that would eliminate the moral problem of displaying one's bosom so prominently.'

I laughed along with the others, hoping I appeared as relaxed as they seemed. We drank more wine and helped ourselves to sugared cakes the maid placed on a glass table.

'Enough of corsets, I'd like to learn more about our new guest.' Manon leaned towards me. 'Our successful Scarlet Enchantress.'

I blushed, staring at my gloved hands. Even though the women here were all commoners, like me, and Jeanne's rose-perfumed salve had worked wonders, I still preferred to hide my peasant-girl hands. 'I never expected my plays to be so popular. It's as much a surprise to me.'

'I loved your second one—*Nuit Tranquille*—wasn't it?' the bird-woman said. 'About the peasant boys crouched by the Count's pond, bashing those noisy frogs to death. You certainly portray the quaint peasant life so cleverly, Mademoiselle Charpentier.'

'*Merci*, madame.' I bowed my head, wondering if my brother, Grégoire, and the other boys of Lucie thought it quaint when they were forced to stay out in the cold night, killing all the frogs so the count and his noble entourage might enjoy a croak-free slumber.

I drank more wine and kept the smile pasted on my lips.

Olympe frowned at the bird-woman, some distant relative of Sophie's apparently, visiting Paris. 'In my cousin's village,' she said, 'the peasants *are* forced to perform such ridiculous tasks for their lords.'

The bird-woman laughed. 'Oh surely not, Olympe, your cousin's been telling you stories!'

'Don't you understand?' Olympe went on. 'Plays such as *Les Barreaux de la Liberté* and *Nuit Tranquille* are celebrated for their social messages. That's why the aristocracy are shocked, and why we cheer so.'

The bird-woman sniffed, her whole face deepening to the same shade as her rouged cheeks.

Olympe gripped my forearm. 'But you must be careful, Rubie, not to overstep the limits. I have heard murmurs of threats against you. Nobles hate to be teased. They feel it is their right alone, to make fun of commoners.'

'I appreciate your concern, Olympe,' I said. 'But I have no reason to be afraid. My works are purely light entertainment. Nobody can claim any direct attack upon their person.'

Sophie laughed. 'The perfect satire, n'est-ce pas, my dears? So what else are you working on, Rubie?'

'I have an idea about a boy who catches a rabbit on the land of a baron and puts it in a hutch to amuse his dying sister,' I said. 'The boy is then imprisoned.'

'But the peasant child should know it is illegal to catch game on the baron's land,' the bird-woman said. 'It's obvious the bailiff would imprison him.'

'The problem is,' I said, 'the rich and poor view each other as utterly alien beings. The rich see the poor as barely human— savage beings for whom it is certainly not worth stopping one's coach if they'd had the bad luck to be run over—while the poor view the rich as frivolous, mannered and cruel.'

'These attitudes must be stopped,' Olympe said, 'as must the unfair privileges of the nobles and clergy, if we are ever to exist in harmony.'

'I have another idea too,' I went on, 'for something concerning the Church—an affront to its political power and wealth, and its suppression for the exercise of reason.'

'Oh, I can't wait,' Sophie said, smoothing milky liquid along an outstretched leg. 'But surely that's a direct attack on the Church?'

'People should be free to follow whatever their heart, and head, tells them,' I said. 'Without fear of reprisal or punishment.'

'Well, we commoners certainly are making our claims heard,' Olympe said. 'Rioting against the privileges of the nobles and clergy this summer gone, from Brittany right down to Pau. It's vital we have a more rational and efficient government.'

'The Estates-General meeting, where these grievances booklets from all over the country are to be presented, will get us out of this dire political and financial crisis,' Sophie said, shifting in her bath.

'The rantings of illiterate villagers are not likely to have much influence,' the bird-woman said, sniffing again.

'The grievances booklets certainly will be heard, madame,' Manon said. 'They'll expose the unfair advantages of the aristocracy and the clergy, and suggest remedies for their representatives to implement.'

'What infuriates me,' Olympe said. 'Is there will be no women present at this Estates-General meeting—we who, in this time of general revolution, should have so much to say, so many abuses to combat, yet we dare not raise our voice in defence of our cause.'

'Don't be ridiculous, Olympe,' the bird-woman said. 'Women have never been admitted to the council of Kings and republics. It's an inconceivable and pretentious thought.'

Olympe shook her head. 'So you are satisfied with the woman's motto—work, obey and shut up?'

'Surely today's enlightenment has demonstrated the absurdity of that?' I said to the bird woman. 'A system of centuries of ignorance, when the strongest made the laws, subordinating the weakest?'

'Besides, we've seen that women can hold the reins of

government with skill and wisdom,' Olympe said. 'Look at Elizabeth, Queen of England, Tsarina Catherine II, and Marie, Queen of Portugal. Why not in our country, too?'

'But women *are* involved in the pursuit of this limitless hope of happiness which grips our nation,' the bird-woman insisted.

'Perhaps,' Manon said. 'But only on behalf of our husbands, brothers, lovers and sons. Women, in fact, have no real voice.'

'That is because we are not educated,' I said. 'Women need an education if they are to have a credible voice.'

'It's a shame you weren't here for our last meeting, Rubie,' Sophie said. 'We spoke about a conduct book: *Letters on the Improvement of the Mind* by Hester Chapone, in which she argues for a programme of study for women.'

'She also emphasises that women should be considered rational beings and not left to wallow in sensualism,' Olympe said.

'I'm certain,' Sophie said to me, 'as your works deal more and more with the rights of the female, it will greatly interest you, as will a similar one, of which I propose we speak today: *Thoughts on the Education of Daughters*, by another Englishwoman, Mary Wollstonecraft.'

'*Thoughts* is excerpted in this English language magazine,' the bird-woman said, holding up a copy. 'Oh, but maybe you're unable to read English, Mademoiselle Charpentier?'

'My private tutor says I am becoming quite proficient,' I said and, ensuring my smile was full of grace, added, 'perhaps you'd like me to read it to everyone?'

The bird-woman shuffled her wide bottom, pursed her crimson lips, and handed me the magazine, from which I read, albeit haltingly.

'*Thoughts* is a conduct book encouraging mothers to teach their daughters analytical thinking, self-discipline, honesty, and marketable skills in case they should need to support themselves,' I read. 'Her aim is to educate women to be useful wives and mothers because it is through these roles that they can most effectively contribute to society. Much of the book criticises what Wollstonecraft considers the damaging education usually offered to women: artificial manners, card playing, theatre going, and an emphasis on fashion. She endorses breastfeeding—'

'*Oh là là, quelle horreur!*' the bird-woman exclaimed. 'That's what wet-nurses are for.'

'So you don't mind your husband using you as a receptacle for his self-gratification?' Olympe said. 'Impregnating you every year, wearing your body down little by little with one pregnancy after another? Why even the poorest of the poor are inherently intelligent enough to realise breastfeeding stops pregnancies, thus preserving their health as far as possible.'

The bird-woman shuddered. 'The very idea of an infant suckling one's nipple doesn't bear contemplating.' She stood. 'Now, please excuse me, ladies, but I must depart early.'

As she kissed our host, still in her bath, and the maid saw her out, I thought nothing more of the bird-woman—Sophie's distant relative whose name I'd not even learned.

'But while conduct books such as these have helped develop a specifically bourgeois ethos challenging the primacy of the aristocratic code of manners,' Olympe went on. 'They also constrict women's roles. They encourage us to be chaste, pious, submissive, graceful and polite.' She spread her arms. 'Where, I ask you, is the individual, thinking woman in all of that?'

'Exactly,' I said, finishing my cake and wine. 'The educated, thinking woman—that is what we must address.'

Sophie emerged from the bath, glorious in her pink-scrubbed flesh. This was evidently a sign the salon was over, as the women stood and began pecking each other on both cheeks, as Sophie wrapped a gown around her nakedness.

I lingered a moment after the others left. 'Thank you for an enjoyable afternoon,' I said.

'I hope you'll come again, Rubie,' she said with a smile.

I nodded to the maid as she let me out the door, stepping into the twilight of the rue d'Artois. The five o'clock after-meal din had calmed—the moment the entire city seemed gagged by some invisible hand. A strangely quiet moment, it was also notoriously the most dangerous time of day when thieves and muggers skulked in the darkening streets before the night watch was about.

I looked around me. Nothing and nobody, the calm broken only by the noise of the drizzly rain.

As an upholstered carriage drew up in front of me, I was certain I glimpsed the bird-woman in her feathered hat, slinking away into the street shadows. Whatever was she still doing here?

The coach door opened and a man in a black cloak stepped out, his hat drawn low over his face. I didn't know him but in those seconds, as he stepped towards me, fear prickled my senses and I knew he meant me harm.

'I've finally found you.' His voice was tight and husky, his hand firm on my arm. 'The Scarlet Enchantress.' He tightened his grip as the rain fell harder and his hand slipped on my skin. 'I'd like a word, about your plays. Causing quite a scandal amongst the nobility. We cannot have that, can we?'

'It's purely entertainment, nothing serious!' I tried to fight him off, and scream, but as he placed his free hand over my mouth, the shriek died in my throat.

'I am far stronger than you, madame. Don't waste your energy struggling.'

His grin spread into a leer as he shoved me into the carriage. 'Besides, after I've finished with you, you'll need all your energy simply to survive. That is, if I let you live.'

38

My abductor spoke to the coachman in clipped tones as the coach lurched off into the rain, gathering speed, and careening along the narrow streets. The blinds were drawn, but I could picture the startled people, carters and dogs leaping from its path.

'Where are you taking me? What do you want?' My arms flailed as I tried to writhe from his grip.

'Keep your mouth shut, whore.' He reached back in a wide arc, his hand clamping down hard on my face. I was too shocked to retort, the fire in my cheek burning as fiercely as my pride, as he roped my wrists together.

The keepers of la Salpêtrière, binding my wrists to the spinning stool, loomed in my mind. As the other prisoners had taught me, I pressed a thumb into the opposite palm.

'And that's only Act I, *ma petite enchanteresse*,' he said, his face so close to mine I could tell from the sun-creases and the hard jowls, he was simply a common, dressed-up thug. 'You'll think twice about what you put on stage next time. Or perhaps you'll never write again, if I cut those hands off.'

I glared at the stranger, hardly believing what was happening. Of course, I was aware of murmurs of threats against me. What playwright isn't? But not for a minute had I taken them seriously. My anti-aristocracy satire offended certain nobles— the Marquis amongst them. Had he learned the identity of the

Scarlet Enchantress, and sent this thug for me?

I recalled the bird-woman lurking in the shadows of the rue d'Artois, and wondered at her involvement in this. Doubts, questions, hurtled around my brain, as deeply as the fear that sliced into my thoughts.

Unbalanced, the rocking movement hurled me from side to side of the carriage, as the horses galloped on. My bladder threatened to burst and a band of tears formed behind my eyes. Whatever happened though, I would never show fear—or tears—to this man.

'There won't be any nobility left soon,' I shouted, over the noise of the rain on the carriage roof. 'The poor are starved, the people of Paris are restless. The days of the aristocratic sweetness of living are numbered.'

The man withdrew something from his pocket. 'I said shut your mouth, filthy whore.' His knuckles white, gripping the handle, he touched the blade of his knife to my chin.

I inhaled sharply, shrank away, and collided with the carriage wall. I was certain I could have wriggled my hands from their binds, but for what? To have him tie me up again? No, better to wait for the right moment.

The man smirked and lowered one shoulder of my dress. I dared not move, or breathe.

'I told you, no point fighting me,' he said, as he traced circles around my breast with the tip of the blade.

He thrust a knee between my thighs and I stumbled backwards, landing hard on my hands. I tried to scream, but over the noise of the rain and the horses' hooves, I knew it was nothing but a token protest.

His hand dropped to his breeches. A wad of hair came loose from his ponytail, and fell across his leering face. As the hard, shiny cock burst from his breeches, images of the Marquis clouded my mind, and I felt my blood as cold as marble.

He pressed himself between my legs, his fingers fumbling to raise my skirt. I tried to kick out but my skirt folds hampered me. He grabbed my raised foot. I bristled as he ran his hand up my leg and wrenched my skirt and chemise aside.

I felt his hardness about to break me apart, and with all the strength I could muster, I let my bladder go in a hard stream. I felt not a trace of humiliation, only a silent thrill of power as copious amounts of pee—an entire afternoon of wine and tea drinking—covered his hand, his cock, and the smart leather seat of his carriage.

'Bitch,' he said quietly, with far more menace than his previous shouts, 'you'll lick up every drop.' A darkness crossed his features and he glared at me with such rage I thought he would kill me right then.

I said nothing, as I wrestled with the ropes behind my back, slowly—silently—freeing my hands.

As he jerked away from me, holding his pee-soaked hand as far away from him as possible, I brought my knee up, hard, into his groin.

The man gasped and reeled backwards, wavering about the carriage. I grabbed his walking cane and whacked him on the side of his head. My breath coming fast, I hit him over and over until he let out a muffled grunt, and lay still. From the gash on his temple, a thin curl of blood snaked across his half-closed eye, down his cheek and between his parted lips.

I inhaled deep, hiccupy breaths, unable to move for a minute. With shaky fingers, I reached over and felt about the man's neck. The pulse still beat strongly.

'Stop, coachman, stop!' I hammered on the carriage wall. 'There's been a … an accident!'

My shouts must have scared the horses, their sharp whinnies and the coachman's curses as he urged them on, swallowing my words.

I perched on the edge of the seat and peered around the blind. The coach was approaching an intersection, and I felt the horses' slowing down. At the driver's shout, the horses' pace slackened further to turn the corner. I flung the door open, and tumbled out into a muddy puddle.

I gave a short, sharp scream, leapt to my feet and fled into the blur of the night, through the steadily falling rain.

I had not gone far when, in the pools of lamplight, a young man strode towards me. He held an umbrella so low, shielding his face that he almost walked straight into me.

'Oh, madame, I am so sorry, I didn't see you. Did I hurt you?'

'No, I'm fine,' I said. 'Really, just fine.'

In the pale light, his eyes met mine. 'You do not seem all right … you look troubled and … and quite dishevelled.'

'I am quite well,' I said. 'I only want to get home, out of this rain.'

'But, whatever are you doing out alone, on such a grim night?'

'My … my carriage broke down,' I said. 'I thought it would be quicker to walk home.'

'Well perhaps I can ensure madame reaches home safely?' he said, holding the umbrella over me.

'No, really, I will be all right. Can you just tell me where are we?'

'The rue Neuve Des Petits Champs,' he said, pointing down the street. 'You're not far from la place Louis-le-Grand.' He thrust his umbrella at me. 'Keep this at least, so you'll not get soaked.'

Relieved it was only a short walk from la place Louis-le-Grand to the rue du Faubourg Saint-Honoré, I took the umbrella. 'Thank you, you've been very kind,' I said, hurrying away.

Perhaps it was the *contrecoup*—the terror of what the kidnapper would have done to me, and my miraculous escape—that stopped me, as I reached the square laid out during the reign of Louis XIV.

I thought about soaking the man with my pee, and cackled loudly, like some mad woman. I thought of the rain too, which had come like a blessing, camouflaging a urine-soaked dress.

Ideas rushed in; notions I pictured so clearly on a stage, and I yearned to note them all down right then. I tilted my face to the inky sky, and closed my eyes to the rain coursing down my cheeks. I trembled with the cold, the fatigue, the shock, but a new, raw energy infused me; an even fiercer determination to wreak my vengeance the best way I knew—behind a theatre curtain.

I opened my eyes and pointed the umbrella at the moonless sky. My fingertips rubbed the place on my breastbone where Maman's little bone pendant had sat. I felt the absent angel folding me into her maternal wings, sheltering me with her warmth on that wet autumn night. I shivered, but inside I was dry and warm.

***

The following day, Monsieur Jefferson stood in my doorway.

'What a surprise, monsieur,' I said. 'To find you here. I've not seen you since our celebration for *Les Barreaux de la Liberté*. I assumed you were still angry with me for lashing out at the monarchy?'

'Excuse my absence but I've been busy, as always,' he said. 'I just came to tell you not to worry yourself over our last meeting. I was not angered but you understand, as appropriate to my diplomatic status, I must be seen to preserve the character of a neutral spectator, particularly in the presence of all those people—stagehands, scene-shifters—and a restaurant no doubt seething with spies.'

I nodded. 'I understand, especially about spies. I'm certain one of the women at the salon I attended yesterday was a spy, and led me to the kidnapper.'

'You were kidnapped?' The Ambassador's eyes widened. 'But … are you unharmed? What did this man do with you?'

'By a great stroke of luck, I managed to get away,' I said. 'But thank you for asking, I am unharmed and quite recovered.'

'Oh dear, I should have known that might happen,' he said. 'Theatre and libertinage are amongst the greatest of French passions these days, and no celebrated playwright can hope to remain unnoticed for long. This type of incident is common, and liable to recur. Have you considered protection?'

'I appreciate your concern, Monsieur Jefferson, and yes, I have hired a few thugs of my own, for when I go out unaccompanied.'

'I am relieved to hear that. Now, so you are aware, Mademoiselle Charpentier, you may be frank about the royals with me. I believe the French Court's overindulgence, especially Marie Antoinette's, is both ridiculous and scandalous. It is no wonder they are the butt of such slanders unimaginable in any other Kingdom.'

'Yes, incredible, isn't it?' I gestured into the apartment. 'Would you like to come inside, or do you prefer the doorway?'

Monsieur Jefferson shook his head. 'Thank you, but I have pressing business.'

I couldn't resist a smile. Ever charming and concerned for the welfare of others, the ambassador remained, as usual, elusive.

Monsieur Jefferson dipped his head, took my hand and kissed the back of it. 'I hope to see you shortly, Mademoiselle Charpentier, perhaps to accompany me to another play in the countryside?' He backed away to his waiting coach.

'Yes, I'd like that,' I said. 'And thank you for coming.'

***

Dear Madam Wollstonecraft,

I hope you don't think it forward or impolite of me to write.

I recently had the pleasure of reading your book, Thoughts on the Education of Daughters. *As a Parisian playwright known as the Scarlet Enchantress,* Thoughts *greatly inspired me both for my stage scripts and for these times of ardent zeal in which I live, as well as for the education of my own daughter, Madeleine.*

I cannot agree with you more that, in general, women remain silly and superficial, and could achieve far greater things if men stopped denying them the right to education. We must convince them to view us as human beings deserving of the same fundamental rights as them.

This autumn I made some new acquaintances—women of the same mind as myself—with whom I meet from time to time to discuss the important role the well-educated wife and mother must play in the downfall of our archaic governing system.

That is why I intend to be here, Madam Wollstonecraft, for every battle ahead of us—as the voice of women, the nurturer of a fledgling nation.

With the honour to be,
Mademoiselle Rubie Charpentier

39

The winter and spring of 1789 passed in a kind of tremulous expectation, like a sunny morning before an afternoon squall. On May 4th, it seemed every Parisian was talking about the meeting of the Representatives of the Estates-General at Versailles, who would bring their *cahiers de doléances*—grievances booklets—to the Assembly.

Several days later, when the first eyewitnesses returned to Paris, Aurore, Sophie, Olympe, Manon and I jostled with the crowd in the gardens of the Palais-Royal, craning our necks to hear the first-hand reports.

'This meeting will have changed everything!' Aurore said, bouncing with her usual excited energy. 'No longer will we have to live with this unjust, corrupt system we have borne for so long!'

'It won't be that simple,' Olympe said. 'This is only the beginning of a long and bloody journey for us commoners.'

'Such a pity there were no women amongst the Representatives,' Sophie said.

'Women weren't allowed,' Manon said, with a scowl.

'To quote Rousseau: "Man is born free, and is everywhere in chains",' I said. 'Should it not be: "Man is born free and woman is everywhere in chains"?'

'But I heard a woman did write one of the grievances booklets,' Olympe said. 'How I would love to meet her, and kiss her for her bravery.'

'What did the booklets say?' a man shouted, as the eyewitnesses appeared.

'Will something be done about our grievances?' another cried.

'All three estates expressed their loyalty to and love for the King,' one of the eyewitnesses said, 'but declared that absolute monarchy is obsolete. The booklets also demanded the church and the nobility pay their share of taxes and justice be less costly, the laws and punishments more humane.'

'Hear, hear!' shouted the crowd.

'You are wrong to rejoice,' a noble-looking young man cried. 'All this will be the source of great misfortune to France.'

'Ah, go hang yourself,' someone said and several people laughed.

'Hang all the nobles!' Aurore shrieked.

'Temper your rage, Aurore,' I said. 'It will only cloud your thoughts and lead to reckless actions.'

'Shouldn't you be the one concerned about recklessness, our Scarlet Enchantress?' Sophie said. 'After that frightening kidnap attempt, of which I am mortified. Aren't you afraid someone will silence you for good?'

'Perhaps you won't invite spies to your salon next time?' I said. 'Don't worry, I don't blame you, she was a clever woman to deceive us all. Besides, the incident was nearly eight months ago and, thanks to my two guards, there's not been a whiff of trouble since.'

'The Archbishop of Aix spoke for the clergy,' the eyewitness went on. 'He even produced a mouldy piece of bread to show what the poorest people have to eat, but a deputy of the Third Estate—a young lawyer called Robespierre—overshadowed him. He suggested the Archbishop tell his fellow clergy to join forces with the patriots, and if they wanted to help they might give up some of their own luxurious ways of living.'

'I know this Robespierre,' a man said, his ragged hair

streaming in the breeze. 'We'll hear more of him, depend on it.'

'Most of the *cahiers* listed the same grievances,' another eyewitness explained. 'Taxation, road-repairing duty, hospitals that no one can reach though we pay for them in taxes, billeting troops and their horses, ineffective policing.'

'The greatest grievance, by far, was hunting rights,' the first man went on. 'To see a furry feast scampering across a field and to know catching it means death by hanging is more than hungry peasants can bear. If the local lord spends his time in the city or is not a keen hunter, his domain might be overrun by game. The people want the right to hunt; they want freedom from poor soil and hailstorms, fire and flood, from wolves, and famine!'

'What of the booklet written by this heroic woman?' Olympe called out.

The man cleared his throat. 'Yes, well, it seems this certain madame had the nerve to appeal for representation of woman, by women, in the Estates-General!'

'He looks as shocked as if she'd requested to bed the King,' Manon said.

'And whoever would want that?' Aurore said. 'When everyone knows the King is a hopeless fuck!' The women dissolved into peals of laughter.

***

Dear Miss Charpentier,

I am acquainted, in fact, with your satirical works, and it is with great pleasure that I received your letter and learned the identity of the Scarlet Enchantress. I am humbled too, by your compliments on Thoughts, *and pleased it has inspired the social messages inherent in your plays.*

I admire your choice of career as an author, although it is a radical one, with few women attempting to support themselves as such, or even daring to pen the things we do. Men regard a writing career for a woman as precarious and improper, a notion which

I find ridiculous. We should have the right to voice our opinions as they do.

As much as I respect your choice of profession, I do fear for you, Miss Charpentier. You will create male enemies, as I have, who will want to silence your voice. However, I am sure you feel as I do—if we ignore their threats and hold our plumes steady, we can become the first of a new genus of women for the future.

I imagine you too, have suffered at the hands of men, dear Miss Charpentier. The germ of my battle was seeded during my childhood, suffered at the hands of a violent father who beat my mother in his drunken rages.

On another issue, we were saddened here in Great Britain, to learn of the little Dauphin's death from consumption. While I can appreciate this was a disaster after his long-awaited birth, and sympathise the loss of a child, I do find it shocking that the passing of his sister, Sophie-Beatrix, was met with the indifference of both the Court and her family. Is it inconsequential to be born, and die, a female—two sexes the creator formed from the same mould, who worship the same God? Why is it that one sex has everything and the other nothing? This can only be another bad omen for Marie Antoinette.

I sincerely hope our correspondence continues. Please keep me abreast of the progress of your enchanting works, as well as the political and social situation in your country.

I hope to visit France in the near future, and would be delighted to make your acquaintance.

I have the honour to be,

Mary Wollstonecraft

As I folded her letter, my mind drifted back to the villagers of Lucie huddled around Armand's warm hearth, listening to my papa tell us of the terrible omens surrounding Marie Antoinette. I envied my young self—my blithe insouciance of the foreboding in my father's fireside tales.

40

July 12, 1789 hailed so bright and sunny, I could never have imagined the torrent of darkness and death that would rain down over the following days.

The gardens and café terraces of the Palais-Royal were more crowded than usual, as Aurore and I sat amidst people eating ice cream, buying bouquets of flowers and watching magic lantern shows.

The sun burned down on us and, through a magnifying glass directing its noon rays onto gunpowder, the little cannon fired. Men flipped the lids of their watches to check they read midday precisely, as a man leapt onto a nearby table.

'Last winter was the worst we have known,' he said. 'The harvest was disastrous. The Seine froze. The peasants, the city people, have nothing to eat. Are we going to sit by and let the monarchy starve us to death?'

He waved his fist, his next words drowned in the thunder of applause and cries of, '*Non!*'

I recalled the cold, hungry winters of my childhood and I hoped the famine had not hit the people of Lucie-sur-Vionne hard.

'The Estates-General meeting achieved nothing!' the speaker said.

'Hang all the tax farmers!' a man cried. 'How dare they tax food so, in this time of famine?'

'The Farmers-General wall is but a noose around the neck of our starving city!'

The raucous discussion continued as a stream of freshly printed pamphlets was passed from hand to hand.

'How many more can they print?' I said, as we skimmed through the pages propounding the ideas of a new declaration of rights, new conceptions of national sovereignty and France's need of a constitution. 'Every hour seems to produce another one.'

'About ninety new ones last week I heard,' Aurore said. 'The more the better!'

'And isn't it amazing that while the press teems with the most lawless and rebellious articles,' I said, 'the Court takes no steps at all to restrain this extreme licentiousness of publication?'

A young man with a yellowish complexion and long curly hair sprang onto a table in front of the Café du Foy.

'I return from Versailles,' he cried. 'The King has displayed his treachery in sacking the reformer, Necker. This dismissal is the Saint Bartholomew's tocsin of the patriots!'

A hush fell over the crowd, all eyes drawn to the speaker.

'Who is this man?' Aurore said.

'Camille Desmoulins, I believe,' I said. 'A lawyer living in poverty but passionate about the political changes with the summoning of the Estates-General.'

'The regiments of the French army—twenty thousand Swiss and German mercenaries—with which the King has surrounded Paris,' the young man continued, 'will come from the Champs-de-Mars this very night to crush the city and slit our throats!'

A collective gasp rose from the grounds of the Palais-Royal. Drinks were spilled, tempers flared and the sun blazed down on us like some great, inflamed wound.

'Do we simply allow these Germans on horseback to herd us like pigs in a pen, then massacre us *en masse*? We have but one thing left to do. Fight!'

Camille Desmoulins seized a leafy twig from a chestnut tree

and, fastening it to his hat, chanted, '*Aux armes*! *Aux armes*! Let us all take a green cockade, the colour of hope!'

'To arms, to arms!' everybody shouted, as Camille Desmoulins leapt from the table into the embracing arms of people growing hoarse from shrieking and cursing.

'Here, Rubie,' Aurore said, ripping a branch off, along with the hundreds of others, and thrusting it at me.

'Pikes to be had. Get your pike!' someone shouted, and a crack of musket fire startled me.

A drum began to beat a hard, hollow note, filling me with expectation, and trepidation. Revolutionary ideals shouted from a café seemed suddenly tame compared with the harsh reality of what we were about to start.

That evening, Aurore and I watched from our window as a great, marching army thudded along the cobblestones, the wind tugging away the smoke streaming from the burning *barrières*. In that instant, watching the striding mob, I wondered just how far my patriotism could stretch.

'All this savagery,' I said. 'It is hard to bear.'

'I thought you wanted to fight too?' Aurore said.

'Yes ... yes I do, but this senseless brutality rips me apart.'

'I don't understand you, Rubie. I thought the flame burned inside you as fiercely as in me? This is all we've heard and talked about for so long. It's happening now, and all you want to do is hide in our safe apartment?'

'I do want to fight,' I said. 'I do, really, but I just ... I don't know.'

'Well you can hide under your cosy bed if you want, but I'm going out there!'

Aurore banged the door shut and disappeared into the heaving mass of people on the rue du Faubourg Saint-Honoré.

Darkness fell. Growls of thunder rivalled the crack of gunfire, the smash of breaking glass and the bark of orders. The heat did not abate until sometime during the night when the storm broke, veins of lightning illuminating the devastation of the city's rampaging army.

I had always loved the summer storms of Lucie; the freedom of the wind sweeping away the suffocating air—the same air we'd been breathing all summer, but this storm terrified me.

I fell into my bed and in my restless slumber, I dreamed someone was stabbing Aurore with a bayonet. Torn and bleeding, she lay on the filthy ground, people trampling her in their frenzied march to destroy the city.

'Don't walk on her!' I shouted. 'Stop, you'll kill her.'

Nobody took the slightest notice of me, and in their noisy wake I saw the crowd had crushed my little friend to death.

***

The following night I woke to Aurore shaking me, her black eyes aflame, her uncapped hair a dark tangle.

'Come on, Rubie. Get up.' She told me the storm had lasted all that previous night, and the next day, hammering on windows and doors like nothing in living memory.

As I slid from my bed and rubbed my eyes, I became aware of another kind of din hammering the city—the tocsin.

Largest bell in Paris, the tocsin's urgent cadences warned of disasters, fires and any other emergencies. This time I knew, immediately, why it was ringing.

'Hurry, Rubie. We are going to search for arms,' Aurore said, preparing a snack of bread and cheese. 'We need weapons to defend ourselves.' She downed a beaker of ale and shovelled the food into her mouth.

Sweat prickled my brow. 'Of course I want the same things as you, Aurore, but you know the bloodshed unsettles me so.'

'Rubie, this is *revolution*. There has to be death and destruction!'

'But surely there is a better way?'

Aurore shrugged. She took my arm and by the time we were on the street, it seemed every church bell in Paris had joined the tocsin, their incessant clanging beating with the same, frantic rhythm as my heart.

'Stay close to me,' Aurore said, gripping my hand as the force of the crowd snagged us, the din of the tocsin raising the hairs on the back of my neck. 'Are you all right, Rubie?'

I nodded as we continued on, all walking together—the working class rabble of the faubourg Saint-Antoine, the lawyers and clerks, the brewers, drapers and tanners, the coachmen and prostitutes. Scoured by rumour and precarious unease, our numbers only swelled more as night relinquished to dawn. I thought I caught a glimpse of Sophie, Manon and Olympe at some time, but the crowd was far too dense to reach them.

Empowered by the strength of our numbers, I felt my anguish fade for a brief moment, as we marched into the overcast morning of July 14th.

By six o'clock, our seething arms-hungry crowd had reached Les Invalides, and I was relieved when the French Guards peacefully seized the guns, pikes and sabres, and several pieces of cannon from the arsenal within the old veterans' hospital. Nobody was hurt.

'There is no ammunition!' Aurore shouted, along with several others.

'*A* la Bastille!' people began chanting. '*A* la Bastille!'

Aurore's eyes gleamed with that potent combination of resentment, patriotism and the desire for change, as the excited mob propelled us down the rue Saint-Antoine.

'We want the Bastille!'

While their shouts fuelled and thrilled me, they sent bolts of terror through me too, as I moved with the crowd, like some carousel abandoned to centrifugal force, towards the old fortress.

'Surrender the prison!' the people shouted, gathering before the Bastille as early daggers of sunlight sheared the dirty brown underbellies of clouds.

'Remove the cannons!'

'Release the gunpowder!'

'Get the Governor to withdraw the cannons!'

Two men chosen to represent the mob entered the fortress to negotiate.

By mid-afternoon, when nothing had happened and people were pawing the ground like restless horses, the crowd hacked down the drawbridge chains and streamed, unimpeded, into the undefended outer courtyard.

I heard shouts from the roof. The panic rose in my chest.

'They're going to fire on us, quick run!' I grabbed Aurore and tried to push our way back through the crowd, away from the prison, but we were trapped, unable to move any which way.

The garrison began firing. I shut my eyes and held my breath.

I expected, any second, the hot burn of a bullet would throw me to the ground. Flambeaux blazed, fanning the shrieks of terror and pain as more and more bloodied bodies crumpled around us. Clouds of gunpowder smoke burned my eyes, almost blinding me. I clutched Aurore's dress, whimpering like a child as we crouched and cowered in what were the most terrifying moments of my life.

As much as I had yearned for things to change—for an improvement to the commoners' lot—never had I wished for that change to wash in on such vast rivers of human blood.

It was over quickly. Our brave French Guards massacred the garrison and the Governor of the Bastille, de Launay surrendered, his face an ivory-pale mask of terror. The crowd tore and spat at de Launay in his grey frock-coat, clubbing and kicking him to the ground.

Faint with horror, my mouth dropped open as a man stepped forward and drove his bayonet into de Launay's stomach. He withdrew the bayonet and the Governor staggered upright, only to stumble onto the point of another weapon.

Someone hammered at the back of his head with a lump of wood, another dragged him into the gutter. I glanced around wildly, helpless to stop the grisly attack. I grabbed Aurore's arm again as a third man fired shots into the Governor's smashed body, and when he finally stopped twitching, a wild-looking man flicked open his knife, strained the corpse's head back, and began hacking at his throat. I turned from the gruesome scene, clutching my heaving belly.

I tried again to find a way through the crowd; away from the sickening butchery. It was impossible, and besides, I was certain Aurore would never agree to flee. Her eyes shining, she seemed bewitched, energised, by the bloodthirsty recklessness.

'The Bastille, symbol of our intolerable regime, has fallen!' the people shouted, parading the Governor's head around on a pike.

Our revolution had received its baptism in blood, and I felt too shocked to cry; too stunned to feel anything. I did not even know what I should feel—joy, triumph, sadness? Perhaps a mixture of all of those.

'We've beaten them, we've beaten them!' Aurore cried, joining the throngs of people dancing, kissing, drinking wine and cheering, tears of mirth streaking the grimy sweat on their faces.

'Yes,' I said. 'And whatever happens now, things will never be the same.'

***

More and more people massed around the burning fortress, smoke flapping into the grim sky like a hero's flag. Whole families streamed onto the streets. They brought their children, their dogs, to see the fiery spectacle.

I watched Aurore, caught up in the dancing, chanting revellers, and still I could not entice her away from that bloody, triumphant scene. I was about to leave on my own when I heard, amidst the din, a voice calling.

'Come, Rubie.'

I spun around, wondering whoever was addressing me. My eyes scanned the knot of unfamiliar faces, but besides Aurore, I knew nobody. I heard the voice again. 'Rubie.'

Whoever would be calling me? Still I recognised no one, then I glimpsed the face of a young girl wearing a scarlet dress, and my hand flew across my mouth.

She was some distance away, but I could make out the cinnamon-coloured curls. My own ten-year old face. I could have sworn too, she was wearing a necklace—a small angel carving perhaps, threaded onto a strip of leather. I felt giddy, and held Aurore's arm to stop myself fainting.

The girl had turned from me and was vanishing into the crowd. I started pushing people aside, stepping on feet, shoving my way through the throng.

'Rubie, Rubie, wait. Wait! Don't leave me again!' I thought I would burst with desire, with hope, and with the fear I wouldn't reach her.

Like the river in a summer drought, the girl receded from me, further and further. Then she was gone.

41

Dear Madam Wollstonecraft,
    I was overjoyed to receive your reply.
    I imagine you heard we patriots won our first revolutionary victory when the Bastille fell? As terrible as it was for me to witness the death and destruction, I know we must continue to fight, to be part of the women's voice of Paris.

Of course, this also inspires me to write more deeply on our female fate, and I am happy to report the plays of the Scarlet Enchantress continue to be successful, despite these turbulent times.

To refer to your comment, I too felt sorrow for the Queen, at the death of the Dauphin.

However, contrary to popular belief, I believe Marie Antoinette did grieve deeply for her daughter, Sophie-Beatrix. Whatever mistakes she has made as Queen of France, she is a bereaved mother. I cannot forget that.

In your wish to keep abreast of our political situation, I inform you our King has capitulated and even wears the tricolour cockade now: blue and red for the colours of Paris, and white for the Crown. The Assembly has drafted a Declaration of Rights of Man and Citizen, which spells freedom from oppression, arbitrary arrest, the presumption of innocence in criminal proceedings, freedom of religion and opinion, and the equality of all before the law. Access to the judicial system is to be free. Judges no longer purchase their functions but are now appointed based on merit, and commoners are no longer barred from any profession.

As wonderful as all this sounds, Madam Wollstonecraft, women appear to have been excluded as far as equality goes. Still we have no voice. Still we work for less than half a man's wage. Still we cannot vote. Still we are inferior!

I had the great pleasure recently, of reading your book— Mary, A Fiction. *I so admire your heroine's strong opinions, her independence and capability to define femininity and marriage for herself.*

I hope this letter finds you well, and I look forward to your reply.

With the honour to be your friend,
Rubie Charpentier

***

After the fall of the Bastille, I no longer had reason to fear the Marquis or his wife, or any other noble. The *ancien régime* was finished, the privileges of our feudal society abolished, and it seemed we were embarking on a new era of happiness and liberty.

As odd as it felt to stand again under the coach porch on the rue du Bac, I was quite unperturbed, knowing the Marquis was no longer even in Paris. I toyed with a loose red curl, realising I did not need my disguise now. Perhaps I would keep it though, proud as I was to be known as the Scarlet Enchantress.

A maid opened the door and the minute I stepped inside, I sensed everything was different. Only a scatter of servants remained; none wore livery and the Marquis de Barberon's coat of arms had been erased from every surface. There was no cloying scent of the Marquise's floral perfume and the air seemed to resonate with an odd, quiet emptiness.

Claudine's kitchen, however, was the same gleaming haven I recalled. Roux was asleep on a cushion in his favourite chair.

'*Dieu merci* you are safe, my child.' Claudine's sturdy hands gripped my shoulders. 'I was so afraid for you and Aurore. We heard hundreds were killed and maimed at the Bastille.'

Claudine pushed the scowling, tail-swishing Roux from the chair, and I sat as she started brewing tea. Roux immediately jumped onto my lap and curled up again.

'Still the best mouser in Paris?' I said, stroking the orange fur. 'You said in your message the Marquis and his wife have gone?'

Claudine nodded. 'Fled to some family estate in the country. The servants could have gone too, but what would I want with a new place at my age? Marie went, but she's young.' She sat opposite me. 'Oh I know everybody is jumping with joy, embracing strangers in the street, young girls wreathed in orange blossom in thanksgiving for the Bastille's fall, but what of an old woman, Victoire? Can I call you Victoire again?'

'Yes, well …. yes, but what do you mean, what of you?'

'The house is to be rented to new people,' she said with a sigh, 'and I have no idea what will become of me; of those left inside it.'

I laid a hand on my friend's arm. 'I'll never see you without food or shelter. How could I forget all you did for an impoverished scullery maid?'

Roux lifted his head for me to tickle under his chin. 'Speaking of food, I don't know what to make of these rumours of the King and Queen withholding bread from us, to crush our spirit of revolt,' I said. 'There's talk of a women's army marching to Versailles.'

Claudine filled two teacups with the fragrant, steaming liquid. 'I imagine you and Aurore will be marching with them?'

'Aurore certainly,' I said. 'But the savagery sickens me. You know how my parents suffered at the hands of a violent, soulless system. This callous use of force sits uneasily in my mind.'

I slid the teacup towards me. 'And as much as that boils my blood, and makes me want to fight against it, I cannot condone such barbarous cruelty.'

'I understand, my child, your nature is not one of violence.'

'Anyway,' I said, 'I didn't come to talk about that. I've come for another reason—something important.'

As Claudine blew on her tea, I told her about seeing Rubie at the Bastille celebration, and how I'd tried to follow her, and lost her in the crowd. 'I'm sure it was her. She had my face ... she wore the angel pendant. She was wearing a red dress.'

Claudine frowned. 'A red dr—?'

'Oh I know that doesn't mean anything. It's just that I have always imagined her in a red dress ... her name, perhaps. But it *was* Rubie, I know it!'

'But of all the children in Paris, my child, all the orphan—'

'They called her Rubie, Claudine. I know it was my daughter.' The hot tea scalded my lips.

'You and Aurore must have been exhausted. You'd not slept or eaten. You were probably seeing things that weren't there. The mind plays trick—'

'My mind was quite clear. I know what I saw.' I sipped my tea.

'I went back to the church where I left her basket. I met the priest there—the brother of our priest from Lucie. He told me they took Rubie, like all abandoned babies, to the foundling hospital at L'Hôpital Général de la Salpêtrière! You can imagine the shock when I discovered my Rubie had been in such a terrible place.' The cup shook as I put it back on the saucer. 'I've seen the orphanage nurseries there. I know how those wretched infants are neglected, so many of them simply left to die.'

'Did you discover what happened to Rubie?'

'I knew I wouldn't find out anything about her at la Salpêtrière, they'll have destroyed all the records. Besides, even though the prisons were opened and the prisoners freed after the Bastille fell, and I have all but erased those dreaded underground dungeons from my mind, I don't want to revisit what memories I have the misfortune to hang onto.' I scratched Roux's head.

'Ah yes, I understand,' Claudine said. 'The mysterious asylum escape.'

I waved an arm. 'Nothing too mysterious really—I managed to flee that Hell with another prisoner I was lucky enough to befriend—a generous woman who left me funds to keep me more than comfortable. That's why I can help you, and Aurore. There are enough livres for all of us. So, now you know everything.'

Claudine refilled my cup. 'Well I am relieved to learn you're not some man's mistress, being paid for your services.'

'I told you I had no lover, Claudine.'

'I thought you might be keeping it from me. You've been secretive about so much. So, yes, now I know everything, but you know nothing of Rubie, and for that I'm sorry for you, my child.'

'Oh I can imagine what happened to her,' I said. 'A *nourrice* from the orphanage nursery told me they keep the babies a week, then send them out to wet-nurses.'

'Ah yes, I have heard of this plight of our foundlings,' Claudine said. 'It is a sad thing, Victoire, but most of those babies never survive the journey.'

'But Rubie did! I saw her. She's alive, here in Paris. And I'm going to find her.' I finished my second cup of tea. 'After all, doesn't anything, and everything, seem possible in this new era of happiness and liberty?'

***

On that October morning, three months after the fall of the Bastille, an uneasy calm hung over the streets of Paris. It was as if the prison storming had been only the first small wave of discontent, and that some great seism was gathering force, ready to break apart and swamp the entire country.

I had not found Rubie. The words of all the people I spoke to echoed in my head like one continuous drumbeat.

Perished … dead … deceased.

I was almost convinced my daughter hadn't survived her journey from the orphanage to the wet-nurse. Claudine was right, in the fug of my exhausted brain the night the Bastille burned, I had simply imagined Rubie.

Dawn was quiet and chilly, the little shops still shuttered, as Aurore and I joined my salon friends—Sophie, Olympe and Manon—and the rest of the women marching along the slop-damp cobbles to the low beat of a solitary drum.

When it came light, there were still no coaches or presentable souls about, besides a few clerks hurrying to their offices. All the gardeners though, mounted on their nags, baskets empty as they headed out of town, gaped at the communal stride of hundreds, perhaps thousands, of women.

'Neither our mayor, Jean-Sylvian Bailly, nor General Lafayette can ensure we have bread!' Olympe, our self-elected representative, proclaimed to the group who had gathered in front of the Hôtel de Ville. 'They are withholding bread to crush our spirits!' She flung an arm in the direction of a bakery shop, and its "No Bread" sign.

'String them up from the streetlights!' a woman shouted back.

'Since the men of our city are unable to put bread on our tables,' Olympe continued, 'the women of Paris will march upon Versailles and demand bread.'

'Let's go and see the baker, and the baker's wife!' a woman shrieked.

A hail of cheers and applause smothered her words, children blew bugles and rang bells, and an even greater knot of women assembled in the Tuileries gardens.

The sky turned dark and cloudy as we marched along the Cours de la Reine with our makeshift weapons: pitchforks, broomsticks, pikes and swords. Six drummers headed our procession, alongside two women riding on cannons. We all boasted the tricolour cockade and carried leafy branches, as we had three months earlier when we took the Bastille.

'Are we truly going to fire cannons on the palace?' Aurore said.

'Of course not,' I said with a wry smile. 'We have no powder.

They're only for effect.'

'What a pity,' she said. 'How I would love to see the Austrian whore blown to bits!'

Aurore reminded me of that enraged lioness from *Les Barreaux de la Liberté*, back arched and tail swishing. 'However can I calm this hate you carry inside?' I said.

'I'll be calm the day I see the Queen's head roll,' Aurore said, striding out ahead as we approached the *Barrière des Bonshommes* tollhouse.

'We certainly must fight for what is rightfully ours,' Olympe said, 'but like a woman, Aurore, who uses her head, and not like a man, who uses only his stiff cock!'

Laughter and giggles rose from the crowd as we marched on, through steadily falling rain.

Dusk fell and Sophie handed around hunks of cheese and cold meat, and that rain-drenched food seemed the best thing I'd tasted.

Flanked by friends, I couldn't help feeling imbued with their energy and determination throughout that rainy day, but as we approached the royal palace, my foreboding grew.

'If slander and malice could kill, blood would flow knee-high in this place,' I said.

'With no one spared the treachery and deception, least of all the King and Queen,' Sophie said, as we plodded on, cold and drenched, down the broad alley leading to the palace.

'Look, they've drawn the gates across the entrance,' Manon said. 'They must have had word we were coming.'

'Good, let the Queen tremble in her golden nightgown,' Aurore said. 'Let her shit herself with fear!'

We all laughed—a shivery laugh—as we joined in the chant from the palace gardens: '*Du pain, du pain, du pain,*'a monotonous drone against the cold drizzle.

A group of fifteen chosen women, Olympe amongst them, disappeared into the palace to appear before the King, to voice the grain-hoarding rumours.

When we heard nothing from inside, a band of women, more agitated than the rest, broke off from the crowd. Brandishing their clubs and meat-cleavers, and calling for the blood of the Austrian whore, they stormed into the palace.

'We'll fricassee her liver!' a woman shouted.

'I'll make lace out of her bowels!' Aurore shrieked, joining the angry mob.

'No, don't go inside, it's too dangerous.' I tried to clutch onto Aurore's sleeve, but she shrugged my hand off and I could do nothing to stop her belligerent determination.

Musket fire rang out from within. I jumped, a hand over my breast.

'Please, let Aurore be safe. Let them all be safe.'

'She'll be all right. Aurore's a fighter,' Sophie said, swiping a hand across her brow and streaking it with dirt. Her dress clinging to her drenched skin, she looked a very different Sophie to the one who received her friends from a milk bath.

We heard more shots, and reeled back in a great human tide as the bloodied bodies of several women were thrown out into the courtyard.

I gagged on my meagre stomach contents, as we picked our way through them, searching the lifeless faces.

'None of them is Aurore or Olympe,' Manon said. 'They're not here. They must still be inside.'

'I'd so hoped this could be peaceful,' I said. 'That we could voice our concerns in serenity.'

'Serenity?' Manon shook her head. 'No, Rubie, the women are too angry, and starving.'

Everybody joined in the chant for the King to show himself, '*Le Roi, le Roi!*'

The King appeared on the balcony and smiled down on the crowd in the palace courtyard. He promised bread to his loyal subjects, and there rose a cheer of '*Vive le Roi!*'

'How absurd,' I said, 'that we cheer when some of us have already fallen.'

'*La Reine au balcon, la Reine au balcon!*'

The Queen stepped onto the balcony in her night-robe. I tried not to smile with the irony as I recalled my childhood dream of meeting a real princess. Marie Antoinette's face a chalky mask, as if frozen in terror of her people's hatred, I was certain the poorest peasant girl wouldn't dream of being this princess.

We all knew Marie Antoinette loathed the Marquis de Lafayette, regarding him as a symbol of the revolution, but the General stood by her side—a liberal aristocrat with the unenviable position of reconciling the mob and the Queen.

'Shoot the whore!' a woman cried. People pointed muskets and pikes at her.

For minutes, the air was taut with nervous tension and an expectant kind of silence.

Lafayette remained still, though obviously aware he would be forced to shield the Queen if the people started firing. Then in a dramatic, unprecedented gesture, he turned, took her hand, bowed low and kissed her fingertips.

'*Vive* Lafayette!' the crowd shouted.

For no other reason than perhaps impressed by her bravery in the face of a hated crowd, everyone rose in a collective roar, '*Vive la Reine!*'

Marie Antoinette seemed to fall against Lafayette with relief, before a bodyguard ushered her back inside.

The King agreed to move the royal family from Versailles to Paris, and most of the women began the long trudge home to inform the Parisians of the King's promises of bread.

'Where's Aurore?' I said. 'And Olympe? We can't go home until we find them.'

'They'll be here somewhere,' Sophie said, as we hurried about the palace gardens, calling their names.

'They can't have gone far,' Manon said. 'This is where all the action was.'

Each of us ran in a different direction, our search becoming easier as more and more women left, marching back along the wide alley, chanting, 'Here we have them—the baker, the baker's wife and the baker's little apprentice.'

'Perhaps they're still inside?' I said, feeling my panic unfurl again.

We still had not found Aurore and Olympe by the time the last soggy footsteps of the women faded, along with the words of their new song:

> *To Versailles, like graggarts,*
> *We dragged our cannon.*
> *Although we were only women,*
> *We wanted to show a courage beyond reproach.*
> *We made men of spirit see that just like them, we weren't afraid;*
> *Guns and musketoons across our shoulders...*
> *I hope we can meet up one day.*

We found Olympe, her dress torn and splattered with blood, thankfully not her own.

'I lost Aurore in the stampede to get to the Queen,' she said.

'It's dark now, and we're exhausted,' Sophie said. 'We should bed down here in the corner of a stable for a few hours. We have a long walk home.'

'I will hire a coach to get us home,' I said. 'One long march is enough for me.'

Olympe nodded. 'Yes, but still, we have more chance of finding Aurore in daylight.'

Even as I wanted to keep searching, I knew they were right. We would never find her in this gloom, and as we huddled together on some straw in our damp clothes, the dull ache tore at every part of my body.

Where ever could she be, my little friend? My breaths came fast and shallow, as I dropped into a listless slumber, hoping Aurore had found a dry spot in which to sleep.

***

A strange quiet reigned over the palace of Versailles when I woke. It seemed that great pitiless sprawl had been abandoned, leaving only a straggle of ragged women and the ghosts of kings long gone.

I stepped over the sleeping figures of my friends, and left the stable to find a place to relieve myself. I ducked into the thick of a row of bushes and, as I lifted my dress, I saw her.

Aurore lay on her side as if she'd rolled, and come to rest against a large stone. Her sodden, grime-streaked dress was entwined about her muscular acrobat's limbs, her arms flung to one side as if she were reaching out to an applauding audience. My cries strangled me as I stared at the dark puddle of blood framing her charcoal-coloured curls in a macabre halo.

The pain in my breast knocked me to the ground, and the blood in my veins seemed to set to stone. Unable to wrench my eyes from Aurore's lifeless gaze, I lay on the ground clutching my dress and howling like a wolf that had lost her cub.

42

My dear Jeanne,

As you can see, I do not bother with the disguise of any coded names. The Cabinet Noir *exists no more.* Besides, since Aurore's death at the hands of the palace bodyguards, I am too tired and saddened by everything to worry.

My tempestuous wildcat is gone, and a quiet emptiness and sadness shrouds the apartment.

Aurore's murder, coupled with our revolutionary battles, and my desperate failure to find Rubie, who most likely met the infant death of countless foundlings, has siphoned the zeal from me.

They are still calling me the Scarlet Enchantress, but my plume hovers above the blank page, my mind a void. I can barely muster the force to nourish and drag myself through the day, let alone pen scintillating dialogue. I fear, as another winter sets in, la mélancolie *has struck me again.*

My fond acquaintance, Monsieur Jefferson, returned to America in September. I have neither the spirit nor the vigour for my salon friends right now. I feel like an old woman of forty-seven rather than twenty-seven.

So, in an effort to combat this profound sadness and solitude, I have decided to leave Paris and return to Lucie.

With the news that the Queen was conspiring with the local nobility to massacre the peasants and break the power of the Third Estate, I am anxious for the well-being of my village. It will also lift *my spirits to see my brother again. I feel it is a lifetime since I saw my brother, and even though she has been in caring hands, I ache to see my Madeleine again.*

While the opening of Paris prisons and the release of the prisoners has rendered me free, and no longer fearful of return to the asylum, I am concerned the entire underworld of Paris—prisoners, beggars, thieves and murderers—has all made south. People say that during this past summer, these thugs were crouching in the forests, biding their time to seize crops, slaughter beasts and burn every deed proving the existence of a family's feudal rights.

It is as if the initial triumphs of our revolutionary battles have warped minds; swelled them into flaming wounds, and this underworld can think of nothing beyond recklessly looting and pillaging everything in its path.

We heard in some villages, they put all the women and children in the church, the tocsin to be sounded in the case of attack. Personally, I could think of nothing more likely to cause panic and fear than being shut inside a church with the incessant clanging from the belfry above my head.

What happened in Paris will happen throughout the country. My place is no longer here, Jeanne, I must return to Lucie and continue our revolutionary battle from there.

Of course, I have thought about the traitor, Léon Bruyère who interned me in la Salpêtrière. However, I will not be obliged to return to L'Auberge des Anges, or speak to him again. Apparently all Church property is to be passed to the nation, so I shall simply acquire some small abode in which to reside. Besides, why should that man stop me from returning to my village?

Certainly, I remain bound by the chains of my sadness, but I am free at least, to be, once more, Victoire Charpentier. I think, along with the country air, reclaiming Madeleine and assuring myself Lucie was spared from these brigands, will be a great comfort and give me inspiration to pen further scripts.

Since anti-aristocracy satire is, thankfully, a thing of the past, I shall now put my mind to evoking the plight of women—a subject

that remains close to my heart.
  Forever your loyal friend,
  Victoire Charpentier

∗∗∗

'The diligence leaves tomorrow,' I said to Claudine. 'I've written to Grégoire, telling him of my return.'

'Your brother will be pleased to see you after such an absence,' Claudine said, as she crossed to the stove to brew tea.

I threw her a rueful smile. 'And to learn his sister is no asylum madwoman.'

'Of course I'll miss you, but I understand why you must leave. Everything has taken its toll—the search for Rubie, Aurore's death, this violent revolution. You are whey-faced and drawn, my child. Once you return to Lucie you'll perhaps find the gladness inside you again.'

'Yes, this fear of rogue bands sweeping the countryside may well have been born on rumour's breath,' I said, 'and spread by all our fears, yet I must reassure myself.'

'I'll miss you too,' I said, as Claudine sat opposite me.

She shrugged me off with a wave of a pudgy arm. 'Do not worry for me. The new people here—a successful banker and his wife—are pleasant and happy to keep me on, as well as my …' Claudine bent to pat Roux, weaving between her ankles and rubbing his cheek against her leg. 'My new beau.'

'Your beau?'

'Ah, you never thought an old thing like me would get myself a man, eh, my child? He was *le majordome* at another defunct noble home further along the rue du Bac. Now he is the butler here.' She winked. 'You would do well too, Victoire, to find someone to stop this sadness that keeps haunting you.'

I smiled as she poured our tea. 'I'm glad for you. You deserve the happiness of a good man.'

I slid the daily newspaper from my bag. 'I want to show you

something before I leave.' I smoothed the newspaper out on the table.

'In October, a *Second Memoir Justificatif de la Comtesse de Valois de la Motte*,' I read, 'much more barbed and venomous than her first, was rushed to the printers. Another direct attack on the Queen by Jeanne de Valois, it has stirred the mobs to a new frenzy. Some say of the countess: "Madame de la Motte's voice alone brought on the horrors of July 14th and the storming of Versailles in October, with the slaughter of troops by the Women's Army".'

I sipped my tea. 'And here is a quote from the countess: "From the moment of my arrival in London, my only thought was to publish my justification. I too would have preferred to spare the honour of the Queen, and I tried to warn her Majesty that I was in possession of certain letters incriminating her and exculpating me. All I asked in return was restitution of property rightfully mine, seized to enrich the King's coffers. I never really considered the French court would capitulate, and besides, my main goal was public vindication. So, to this purpose, I eagerly took up my pen, denying my body nourishment and sleep until my memoirs should be ready for publication. Five thousand copies in French have now come off the press and three thousand more in English".'

I refolded the newspaper. 'It seems the readers of England and France can't get enough of the countess's memoirs.'

Claudine drank her tea, her eyes narrowing in the wise look I knew so well.

'Ah, I begin to understand, my child. This countess was a prisoner at la Salpêtrière *n'est-ce pas*? One of the few who succeeded in fleeing the asylum prison, along with her personal maid?'

'Didn't I promise to tell you everything once it was safe?' I said, kissing my friend goodbye.

With promises to write, I left Claudine, sliding a healthy sum of cash beside her kettle.

***

Beads of November rain, so fine they were barely visible, wet my face as I stepped up into the diligence.

The horses clomped off and I took a last look at bleak, wet Paris. Despite our revolutionary jubilation, something had vanished from the streets.

For one thing, there were fewer coaches, the thoroughfares bare of all but trading vehicles. Most of the bright cafés and small shops had boarded windows, with "To Sell" or "To Let" signs, and while many people still walked about, there were fewer loiterers, and most seemed intent on their business. The elaborate coaches and the magnificently dressed folk who'd ridden in them had clothed the capital in the kind of enchanted, fairy tale glitter I'd only dreamed of in books of fables. Now it looked just gloomy. With their martial air, the National Guard patrolling the streets did nothing to improve this drabness. At least they were protection against thieves.

The rain fell steadily, coursing in muddy channels down the street as we passed the Palais-Royal. Perhaps it was the absence of the Duke of Orléans and his household, who were in London, or that trade was slow, but the palace wore a forlorn, abandoned appearance.

The windows were shuttered, the paving full of puddles, the grand gates closed, with only the side gates open to admit people to the gardens and arcades. A circus after the circus is over.

As the diligence rumbled away from the *barrière* tollhouse, I left Paris with the odd feeling I would never return.

I ignored my fellow passengers, staring at the naked trees lining the streets, their limbs hanging at strange angles, and dotting the fields like scarecrows, as we rode away from the city. I felt as desolate and bare as those autumn trees.

Across a field, some sort of raptor was perched atop a dead tree, still and patient. I watched the mighty bird glide down onto an unseen carcass—a magical show against the silken backdrop of rain.

I turned from the window and caught the leer of a fat man in a dark suit, seated beside me. He leaned closer to speak, his rank smell catching in my nostrils.

'Going all the way to Lyon, madame?' he said.

I straightened my back and gave him a small nod, regretting this price I had to pay for travelling without a male escort. I glanced across at the woman opposite me, and envied her, journeying with her husband.

'I hope none of those brigands are hanging about to steal our valuables,' the dark-suited man said, a little further on, as the diligence stopped at the bottom of a hill. 'All sorts of whisperings of bandits robbing and raping everything along the road,' he went on, as we all descended and began walking up the slope, to save the horses' energy.

'Perhaps madame would care to walk alongside me,' he said, his buckteeth giving him the comic air of a piglet. 'For protection against such thugs?'

I was tempted, as I thought of the diamonds sewn into the hem of my dress.

'Thank you, but no,' I said, and at each night stopover, I avoided lingering in the common room of the inn, ordering dinner to be brought to my room. I also knew the spies, thugs and thieves of Paris travelled in many guises.

Lucie-sur-Vionne
November 1789–July1794

43

As the coach neared Lucie-sur-Vionne I grew more restless, though as I glimpsed the view of Lyon, and Mont Blanc with its familiar crown of snow, I did feel the muscles in my neck and shoulders loosen.

As I stepped from the carriage, the Monts du Lyonnais, more purple than green in the autumn light, stretched along the valley like maternal arms, and la place de l'Eglise hummed with the usual noises—the anvils of the blacksmith and the clog-maker, the bark of dogs, the quack of ducks, the bustle of people around the fountain and the warm, floury scent of the bakery. Save for the absent equestrian statue of King Louis XV, it seemed unchanged. No sign, here at least, of any pillaging or burning.

In my city clothes, and swinging a parasol, I couldn't help but notice the villagers' garments of coarse cloth dyed from oak tree bark, their sandals, clogs, or plain rope wound around their feet. This obvious display of poverty was something I had forgotten in Paris, where the poor did not appear so destitute in their left-over garments from the rich.

I looked around at all that was familiar but seemed oddly alien, my gaze resting on the great granite facade of Saint Antoine's Church. What had become of Père Joffroy when the clergy lost everything—our poor *curé*, who'd always been so kind to me?

I glanced across the fields, the woods and hills, inhaling the scent of rotting leaves, of damp earth, and the silvery chill that heralds snow—all that grounded me to this land. I realised how accustomed I'd become to the crowded city conditions, and how I'd missed this wide expanse of clean, fresh countryside.

I also understood I was no longer the naïve peasant girl, and wondered how I would see these simple folk now, and what they might think of me. Would they look upon me as a mad asylum woman, with suspicion, and fear?

I didn't relish their curious gazes immediately, so I hurried from the square, almost running up the hill towards Grégoire's cottage, and to Madeleine.

As I neared the crest, I saw a woman shuffling along, ahead of me. She carried a basket in one hand, and cradled an infant in the other. I recognised her as Noëmie, the poor woman from the woods to whom I'd lent tools.

I recalled how she'd reminded me of the witch-woman I was so afraid of, and how I learned the painful way those accused of sorcery are rarely witches.

'Noëmie,' I called, skipping a few steps to catch up to her.

Noëmie twisted around and I saw she was still lean, but pink-cheeked, and quite different from the desperate, bedraggled woman from before.

'Madame Victoire? You are … you have come back to Lucie?' Her gaze travelled from my powdered face, across my fine clothes, and down to my embroidered slippers. 'I am pleased to see you looking so … so fine.' Her eyes flickered across my flame-coloured hair.

'You look in good health too,' I said. 'It seems *la chance* has shone upon you?'

'My sons and my husband—no longer a journeyman I am pleased to say—found work this past season. We have built our own cottage on the riverbank, not far from your brother's new home.'

'And that is just where I'm going,' I said, linking my arm through Noëmie's. 'Let's walk together. I am so keen to see my brother and his family, and my little Madeleine. How grown up she must be now.'

We took the track that skirted L'Auberge des Anges and led through the woods, towards the river. Noëmie and I swished through the carpet of autumn leaves, under the boughs of grand oaks with their ivy-strangled trunks. I lifted my hood and drew my cloak around me, against the chilly fog; against anybody from L'Auberge who might see me.

We reached the top of the slope and even as I averted my eyes from the Vionne River, I saw it all again—the whorls of current, small heads bobbing up, down, up, down, in the hollows. Then there was nothing, except the lusty cries of Noëmie's child.

'Ah, he is a hungry boy, this one,' Noëmie said. 'I must stop and feed him.'

We sat together on a boulder and Noëmie latched the baby onto her breast, who soon made contented, gulping noises.

'I am happy to see you back in Lucie,' Noëmie said. 'I tried to tell them you didn't drown your little children; that you are a good, kind person, but they wouldn't listen to me. They thought because I was a poor beggar, I must be mad too.'

'You told them?' The confusion swamped me again. 'But how do you know? And why did they all believe some diabolical thing had stolen my senses, and I killed them?'

'Because I saw what happened,' Noëmie said, swapping the baby to the other breast. 'I tried to tell them all, but nobody—'

'What did you see, Noëmie?'

'You must have dozed off,' she said. 'I came upon you just as your little girl stumbled, and fell into the river. I was too far away to help, and I saw her brother run in after her. So young, but he must have sensed she was in danger. You tried to save them both, but the current stole them away before you could reach them. A terrible tragedy, Madame Victoire, but it was an accident.'

Her words shocked me into silence, and I could not reply for a minute.

'Why can't I remember a thing then?'

Noëmie shook her head, her nutbrown eyes wide with pity. 'Perhaps it is too awful for your mind to hang onto such a thing?'

I suddenly felt weary, my legs so heavy I could barely move them.

'Thank you,' I said, smoothing clammy hands down my cloak-front. 'Thank you for telling me the truth.'

'I kept saying it was a mistake,' she said, 'that you weren't evil or mad, but nobody would take notice of a crazed witch-woman from the woods. After you ... when you left, they put up a carved cross for your little ones—your brother and Léon Bruyère—on the slope above the river.'

I had to get away; to move. Sitting still like this, it was harder and harder to breathe. I must see this cross.

'I should hurry to Grégoire's,' I said, trying to keep my voice steady. 'They will be waiting for me.'

'Take care, Madame Victoire. You must come and drink some tea with me soon. I will show you our new cottage.'

'Y-yes, I-I'd like that,' I said, reeling away from Noëmie and her child.

Staggering like a drunk, I followed the cord tugging me to the Vionne—a thread from the same skein that had entangled my mind when the river stole Blandine and Gustave.

My pulse quickened as I caught sight of a stone cross a little further along.

My trembling legs folded to the damp earth beside the small memorial. With a fingertip, I traced their names, in the heart shape carved into the stone.

Blandine
Gustave
1785

Yes, an accident but they were my children, my responsibility, and I felt the stinging barbs of guilt as surely as if my own hand had held Blandine and Gustave under the water.

How could I let them drown? How could I do such an evil thing? A bolt of heat struck me, and a shudder of cold. The darkness flooded in and clutched me so tightly I couldn't get my breath. I lay on the ground, my fingers clutching the cool stone.

I struggled upright and onto the path I knew so well. My breaths coming fast and shallow, I followed the curve of willow trees until I reached my special place on the riverbank. I slumped down on an icy rock.

'Just a few minutes … a quick rest to gather my senses.'

The wind gusted from the Monts du Lyonnais, sighing chill and weary on my face. The valley, clothed in moss greens and browns, rose vast and harsh around me, the rotting smells of autumn scenting the air moving back and forth in quick tides.

A blackbird carved mad spirals through the air, bands of grey light silvered the puckered surface of the water, and the longer I sat there, the more the murmur of the water bubbling across stones was like a beckoning voice.

***

Blandine is thrashing about, a netted butterfly, her eyes wide with a child's instinctive fear. She reaches out, tries to catch my skirt, and my outstretched hand. I am so close that her fingertips brush mine, then a burst of current carries her beyond my reach and her little hands flail, grasping at cold water.

Blandine's face turns the dark hue of a winter sky, her eyes balls of glass, her white shift dancing a lazy liquid waltz. Gustave's wails are so loud they might be heard all through the woods and up to the village. Or perhaps the screams are mine.

I wheel around to him, paddling against the drift towards me.

His face twisted in terror, my son reaches out, desperate to grab hold of me. His head sinks below the water, and I fight its tug, my heart beating in a frantic panic.

The water pulls stronger than me, and Gustave too, remains just beyond my reach. My son's face disappears for the last time, and I am powerless, watching the river carry off my silent angels.

***

Without thought or sensible reflection, because I was far beyond that, I stood and walked into the water without a trace of fear.

I couldn't feel its coldness; could not feel anything, as my feet slid across its slimy bed. I waded in deeper until the water swirled my cloak about me like clothes drying in the wind, and the circle of current held me there.

A hoarse, croaking noise startled me. I looked up and saw the Night Washerwoman amongst the willow branches—ghost of the mother who had killed her children. Dark and hulking, she was bent over a rock, scrubbing their little shrouds.

'Come and help me, Victoire.' The voice came from the depths of the black hood shadowing a face puckered with grooves. 'You must, or you too, will be covered in the blood of your children.' She cackled, revealing a toothless mouth, and I knew the Night Washerwoman had trapped me, and I could not escape her.

I had won some battles in my life, but I was powerless to fight this conflict rampaging within me. Death was the only reprieve for such a sin; relief from the bondage of my mind. If left to live it would ravage me to the core and consume me like a malignant disease. I could not let such a demon survive in my unwilling body.

My heartbeat steady, I propelled myself through the water, watching the bank recede, until I reached the deep centre where my feet no longer touched the bottom.

'Please let me go.' I sank below the surface and once in that dark, secretive underworld, as the coldness seeped into me, I groped about my neck for the bone angel. Where was it? I thought of all the women who'd worn it before me, and I fancied the water lapping over me to be their cries of pain; their tears of grief. Their spirits were calling me to join them. The current closed over me, holding me tight and carrying me towards them.

With a last glance upwards, in a shaft of wan light, I glimpsed a scarlet smudge on the riverbank. Was it a girl in a red dress, her hair streaming like the tail of a fox on the run?

My head broke the surface. Chest heaving, I gasped for air. She smiled and raised an arm in a wave.

'Rubie!' In sharp, panicky bursts, my arms cut through the water towards the bank.

As I got closer, the red blur became more and more hazy, vanishing, and when I neared the edge, there was only her outstretched arm.

I gripped the muddy bank, and reached out to the hand, to the clicking, urgent fingers.

'Take it,' a voice said, though I could not see from where the sound came. 'Hold onto me, I've got you, Victoire.'

Strong hands held me under my arms, hauling me from the icy water.

I pushed the tangle of hair from my face, and the last thing I saw before the ashen light darkened to black, was the gaunt gaze of Léon Bruyère.

44

A gentle voice tugged me from the nightmare of glacial water, the current trapping me, my life eddying away. I sat up on the straw mattress, gazing about the same room I'd once shared with Armand Bruyère.

'Ah, you're awake.'

'Léon? What ... how did I get here? When?'

'You don't remember?' As he sat beside me on the bed, I expected to inhale his familiar scent of earth, hay and horses but Léon smelled more like damp and mouldy linen—the musty smell of an unaired house.

'Only yesterday,' he said. 'I saw two women walking along the path beside L'Auberge. I recognised Noëmie but the other one ... I noticed the way she walked—that so familiar walk. She seemed different, so much more ... more *sophisticated*, but still I was certain.'

He took my hand, rubbed my knuckles with a calloused thumb. 'I followed you; saw you at the memorial, then when you walked into the river ... I couldn't let you do it.'

I slumped back on the pillow. 'I couldn't live with myself; with what happened to them. Noëmie told me it was an accident, but still ...'

I swung my legs over the side of the bed. 'Madeleine ... and Grégoire ... they will be so worried. I must go to them!'

A panicky sensation set my heart racing, and it all rushed

back—Léon and his treachery, but now he'd brought me here, I burned to know why he'd sent me to such a gruesome asylum. I wanted to stare into his dark eyes; to tell him he was wrong, and make him shake with remorse and shame. The anger bloomed, and I started to tremble with every terrible memory I thought I'd banished.

'So, you see,' I said, shrugging his hand off. 'I was not the mad murderess you banished from Lucie five years ago—mad enough to have me locked up in God's worst Hell!'

Léon's face darkened, as if in shadow. 'I did not know what to do. You were so … so bereft. For the melancholy to strike you as it did, everyone said evil had possessed you. They said there was nothing to be done when a person gets in such a way, and I had to send you away to drive the wicked madness from you.'

'Only fools equate madness with devilry, Léon! I would have died in there, if I hadn't escaped. La Salpêtrière does not make people better. It is simply a place to forget them.'

I jerked away from his hand hovering over my arm. 'When I realised it was you who sent me there, I never wanted to return to Lucie, and I definitely never wanted to see you again.'

'They all said you drowned Blandine and Gustave in a moment of insanity,' Léon went on. 'A madness demon that terrified us all. Nobody believed the rantings of the beggar-woman, Noëmie. We did not know what to do.' He sighed and ran a hand through his dark hair. 'It was not only me who decided, but I beg your forgiveness.'

'Absolution is not that easy,' I said. 'It takes time, that is, if it ever comes. But all that—the madhouse—is over now. So much has changed. I've changed. Our *country* has changed.'

Léon waved a thin arm. 'Yes, nothing will be the same, after the looters.'

'Looters? You mean they came to L'Auberge, those brigands everyone has so feared?'

'No, not brigands. Those stories were not much more than the mindless panic of the people. Just common thieves, but as you will see, when you're well enough to get up, the result is the same. They took everything—the crops, the animals, the furniture, even the food from our kitchen. Late hail-storms destroyed the harvest and we are destitute. We shall all be dead before next spring.'

'We?'

'There is only Adélaïde and Pauline left, besides me. The others are dead from hunger, or sickness, or I don't know what.'

Léon's face seemed to twist in pain as he gazed out the window, across the Monts du Lyonnais. 'The farm is mine but I am unable to provide for or protect my sisters, as I promised my father. They are frail and too afraid to leave the house.'

'I am well enough to get up now, Léon, and I want to see what they have done to Armand's farm; to our inn.

***

A blanket curled about my shoulders, I stood with Léon in the u-shaped courtyard, staring about at the decaying buildings of L'Auberge des Anges.

The shutters were either closed or hanging from their hinges, the paint worn and peeling. The fields and orchard lay fallow and untended. The short, expectant barking of hounds was eerily absent; no quacking ducks or clacking hens.

I looked upon the ruins, my breaths shallow leaps catching in my throat. I shrank into the blanket but the chill crept inside the folds and beneath the layers of my clothes.

I shuffled across the cobbles to the stables. No grain, no hay and no corn. Sacks, wooden barrels and containers lay sideways, ploughs, forks, and other implements strewn about, twisted and broken. I felt as if something had struck me down—a corpse whose blood had marbled.

It was silent too, as if when the looters left, the people—Léon and his sisters—had also been swept away with the life and glory of L'Auberge des Anges.

The shock and sadness stilled me, and in the frigid silence descending from the hills, tears leaked down my cheeks.

The dun daylight faded to dusk, and the bell of Saint Antoine's clanged low and strong across the valley. I nodded towards Grégoire's cottage. 'How is Madeleine? I am anxious to see them all.'

'Your daughter thrives with her uncle and aunt,' Léon said. 'You will see she is a happy child and doesn't seem to have suffered your absence. They have another new baby too, just a few weeks old. An especially joyous occasion after the last child was born dead.' He shook his head. 'Not having children is my great regret, Victoire ... amongst others.'

'Grégoire will be waiting for me,' I said and, without a backward glance, I walked away from Léon, who seemed as forlorn and wasted as L'Auberge des Anges itself.

***

After several days of Françoise's tasty cooking, I felt recovered from my icy dip in the river.

I sat at the cottage window, Madeleine perched on my lap. Shy at first, with only snaps of memories of her mother, she now sat easily with me. I couldn't stop stroking her dark curls, and smiling at my daughter who'd inherited her father's pleasant, easy manner.

Madeleine laughed with her cousins, Emile and Mathilde, as Grégoire narrated one of our father's tales.

'Look, Papa,' Emile said. 'A pretty bird.' He pointed outside, to a robin redbreast, preening itself on a branch.

'Why is his chest red?' Madeleine said.

'Well,' Grégoire said, 'at the Crucifixion, a robin was removing the bloody thorns from the head of Christ and a drop of his blood fell on the bird's breast. Quick, before he goes, let's make a wish for the first robin redbreast of the season.' They joined hands and shut their eyes, and a second later, the pious bird spread his wings as if gathering their wishes into his scarlet breast, and vanished into the autumn gloom.

My brother nodded beyond the window, to L'Auberge des Anges. 'Such a wretched sight.' He took the new baby from her crib, and cradled his daughter. 'After all Armand Bruyère's kindness towards our family, to you, Victoire.'

Grégoire handed the baby to Françoise, who nestled him against her breast. 'If it wasn't for that man's generosity,' he went on. 'I wouldn't have this cottage. I would never have become the master carpenter I am today.'

I smiled at the baby's lusty suckling noises and recalled those happy times with Armand. I fingered the diamonds, which still lay snug in the hem of my dress.

'Well, Grégoire, perhaps it is time to repay his generosity.'

I closed my eyes, picturing the inn as it had been in its prime: a welcome beacon beyond thick woods, the glowing candles and burning hearth beckoned the worn traveller. As their horses approached, sweat-sleek and panting with thirst, the scent of rosemary and lamb reached the tired man's nostrils. He sniffed and caught a whiff too, of firm, baked vegetables and the sweetly bitter vapours of coffee. Once inside, he was welcomed with a smile, a beaker of wine and a warm, clean bed.

I breathed easily, above the receding tide of melancholy that had almost drowned me. I understood it was not only Grégoire and Madeleine who'd brought me back to Lucie, but the Inn of Angels, which thread through my veins as richly as my own blood.

45

'You'll have food in the kitchen again,' I said to Pauline and Adélaïde. 'And linen and blankets. Even new beds.'

'Ducks and hens too?' Pauline, said, clapping her hands in excitement.

I nodded. 'And you'll have your horses, pigs, cows and sheep,' I said to Léon, who couldn't stop grinning. 'We'll rebuild the stables, the granary ...'

'But, Victoire, however can you—?'

I held up a hand. 'I said not to ask me about that. The funds are my business. You just get to work, we'll need a long list of things to order.'

'And make plans for the new inn!' Adélaïde said her eyes bright for the first time since I'd arrived back in Lucie.

'We will also need firewood, candles and cooking fat for the winter,' I went on. 'Work shall start as soon as spring arrives.'

'You'll stay here on the farm now, Victoire with me ... with us?' Léon said, his cheeks turning crimson. 'After all, this is your home. This is where you belong.'

'Our brother never took another wife,' Pauline blurted out.

Léon glared at his sister but Pauline carried on. 'He always said you were the only one.'

'I am not doing this for Léon,' I said. 'But for the memory of his good father, and what we once had together, but I suppose it is easier if I am here ... purely to oversee the work, of course.'

***

My dear Madam Wollstonecraft,

Please excuse my lapse in correspondence, since my first letter when I arrived back in Lucie.

The farm and inn renovations have occupied me, banishing much of the heaviness that sat like a stone in my breast after the death of my dear friend at Versailles—a similar melancholy to the one you describe as your own enemy.

The women marchers are proud of what we did, and I am pleased to report that in the first issue of Les Etrennes Nationales des Dames, *Marie De Vuigneras—the brave woman who wrote a grievances booklet—hailed the women of Paris for proving they are as courageous and enterprising as men.*

"We suffer more than men who, with their declarations of rights, leave us in the state of inferiority and, let us be truthful, of the slavery in which they have kept us so long," she said. "If there are husbands aristocratic enough in their households to oppose the sharing of patriotic honours, we shall use the arms we have just employed with such success against them."

Our rebuilding work here began three months ago and is almost complete. We hired many workers and spent a pleasant spring surrounded by hammering, jovial shouts, and people whistling the infectious song, which has become the rage of the whole country:

Ah! Ca ira! Ca ira! Ca ira!
Les aristocrates à la lanterne,
Ah! Ca ira! Ca ira! Ca ira!
Les aristocrates on les pendra!

The inn looks splendid, with its whitewashed walls and exposed beams, and we have many guests for whom I cook and make jam, spirits, cheese and bread. I burst with gladness and pride as I see L'Auberge des Anges restored to its former grandeur.

Thankfully, The Great Fear that swept France after the

Bastille fell last year quickly petered out into oblivion, the panic disappearing as swiftly as it came. And, despite this bloody revolution in which our country is gripped, we do feel relatively safe in our beds here in Lucie.

Because the Assembly needs money to bolster finances, it has issued bonds called assignats, *representing Church lands, to patriots who wish to acquire them in return for ready cash. Later, when the actual land and property is distributed, we can exchange the* assignats *for the land. So, under this scheme, I shall purchase the quaint estate of a bishop with the view of setting up a theatre company this coming summer. My enthusiasm has propelled me into penning another script, which speaks of the health of the woman's mind—a subject that you can understand is close to my heart.*

I do hope you will grace us with a visit when you finally decide to cross the Channel.

As you see, I am glad to have the liberty to take back my true name.

With the honour to be your friend,
Victoire Charpentier

Quiet footsteps approached from behind. I knew who it was. After six months of nourishment, work and easy sleep, Léon was once more the sun-bronzed, muscular man. His earthy smells set my nostrils quivering, as I felt his hands on my shoulders.

'How well you write, Victoire. How much you seem to know about everything.'

'I have read books,' I said, my back still turned. 'Many books. Also, the people are so very different in Paris. They hanker to know about everything; to talk of things besides cattle, crops and the latest rumour. They want to know about life beyond our world.'

'Yes, you are worldly now; so different from the people of Lucie,' Léon said with a wry smile. 'They could hardly believe their eyes, to see such a transformation, especially as they imagined you still in the asylum.'

'Oh I know that! They didn't even try to hide their suspicion, their wariness, in the beginning, did they?'

'Forgive them,' Léon said. 'They have accepted you, welcomed you into their arms again.'

'But it took them six months,' I said. 'Six months of proving I was rid of the madness, and sane enough to restore an entire farm.'

Léon held my chin in his hand, lifting my face to his. 'For that, I am eternally grateful, but please, forgive me too. Now come on, it's late and time to sleep.'

The brown eyes brightened, inviting, but my pulse didn't gallop with yearning, my loins remained cold and no shivers of lust twitched my shoulders.

I shook my head, just enough for Léon to understand.

He dropped my chin and rubbed a palm across his brow. 'I hoped now, perhaps ....'

He stared out into the soft darkness folding across the countryside. 'I thought, now it's coming warmer, we might go to the river together? We could go to our special place. You remember it, don't you?'

'Of course I remember.'

'We'll swim again; catch trout with our bare hands. At least we'll not be breaking any laws now.'

'That never stopped us, eh?' I said. 'But you know how I feel about the Vionne River.'

'I will be with you. You see, you'll be all right with me.'

'Perhaps one day, but it still fills me with such dread. I cannot think of going near it after ...'

Léon sighed. 'It's not the river, is it? It is me you don't want to be with. I am sure I will go to my grave without your pardon.'

'It is not a simple matter of forgiveness,' I said, taking his hands in mine.

'It is something much more ... things I cannot explain, and I don't even understand myself. Well, anyway ... since my return, you know I have been working on the play for this summer, but I also decided I would write about my life. I do not know if it's interesting enough for anyone to want to read, and it is not a story I can talk about, but one I can readily lend to paper. I am certain it will help if I can … if I can write it all out of me—the twins, the asylum, what I tried to do at river.'

'And I would learn to read if only to know that story,' Léon said. 'I know the first part, naturally, but you say so little about when you left, and your life in Paris. It's as if I hardly know you.'

'Well if I had stayed in Lucie,' I said, releasing his hands, 'and never gone to the asylum, I wouldn't have been inspired to write. I would not have spoken the English, or even the French, language, or learned the ways of the middle or noble classes. I'd never have acquired such an education at the Palais-Royal, on the streets and in the salons. And I certainly would never have stormed the Bastille.'

I reached up and touched Léon's cheek, my fingertips lingering on his weathered skin.

'So, by some quirk of destiny, rather than forgive, it seems I have a lot to thank you for.'

46

I lay on my bed and watched the autumn dawn come clear, the orange glow spreading across the horizon above Mont Blanc's snowy helmet. It was still a strange feeling, two years after my return to Lucie, lying in the bed I'd shared with Armand, thinking of all that had happened since that time I had so yearned for Léon. How ironic that our love might now have flourished if the soil hadn't dried up; if the roots hadn't rotted beneath us.

I thought of Jeanne too, still poisoning the Queen with her words, as the sky came alight and the farm rose to life. I heard Madeleine's joyful squeals, in the kitchen with Pauline and Adélaïde, the cows lowing to be milked, a pig grunting and the dogs' occasional barks—the start of a typical day.

I splashed water on my face, ran a brush through my hair and caught it up under a cap. I brewed coffee, ate some bread and cheese, and sat at my desk.

The birds carolling beyond my window, butterflies quivering, I dipped my quill into the ink. I began writing the latest chapter of my memoirs, trying to recall each event, every different person who had moulded me, like soft clay, into the person I'd become.

When I finished, I blew on the ink and placed the pages on top of the pile.

'Letter for you,' Léon said, as I stashed my papers in the

carved wooden chest Grégoire had made for my writing things.

I smiled as I recognised Claudine's writing—a smirk that died on my lips as I read her terrible words.

My dear Victoire,

It is some months since I have written and I hope this letter finds you well, my child.

Everyone in Paris is talking of a piece of news in The Chronicle *and I felt you would want to know immediately.*

It was reported that on August 23 of this year, 1791, Jeanne de Valois-Saint-Rémy, Countess de la Motte, died after falling from the balcony of her London hotel room. She was buried in St Mary's Churchyard, Lambeth, on August 26.

Some say she met her death by accident, others believe she was killed by royalists, and still others are convinced she was trying to escape debt collectors.

Of course, there is the other rumour too—that it is someone else buried in St. Mary's and the countess has simply disappeared.

Whatever the case, I suppose we will never know the truth about that mysterious woman!

Jeanne dead! It seemed impossible. She had always struck me as too clever, too good for something as banal as death. The grief settled like lead on my breastbone, as I continued reading.

I am well pleased to hear you still bask in the success of your new theatre company and that your plays are enjoyed by a wide audience. Such a great chance you are giving the villagers of Lucie, especially the women, of pursuing new and exciting actress lives. And, as you say, it cannot be a bad thing that brings visitors, and money, to a village in these difficult times.

Your ever loyal friend,

Claudine

47

I did not learn the truth about my dear friend until three years later. When the letter arrived, I cried out in surprise.

My dear Victoire,

In the pursuit of your success as the Scarlet Enchantress, I am not sure you have time for a thought for your old friend.

I think of you often, and the days we spent together at that unique Parisian establishment. You must be glad that bloody revolution is, finally, over. Not that the Queen can harm us any longer, n'est-ce pas? Ha!

Contrary to the Queen's, my head remains firmly on my shoulders. True, I was injured, and incapacitated for some time, after an unfortunate accident, but I am now healthy and happy, living a peaceful existence in a cottage on the shores of the Crimea.

The people here are charming, the men especially, and we all have such fun when I amuse them with my tales of masked balls, jewel thieves and daring prison escapes!

I do hope to see you again one day, ma chère *Victoire. Time and events have cruelly separated us for too long.*

Your dear and sincere friend,

Jeanne

I laughed aloud as I folded the letter.

'Ah yes, my friend … too clever for death.'

***

The summer sun painted the countryside in rich shades of green and blue, white clouds drew bold gestures in the sky and everybody on la place de l'Eglise laughed and chatted, celebrating the death of Robespierre.

The scent of pies and cakes drifted from the baker's oven, the smell of fresh fruit and sizzling sausages rippling on the soft air. The blacksmith's son played a flute, his brother juggled, and Madeleine chased about with the other children and the yapping dogs.

The girl who stepped down from a carriage stood still amidst the crowd. I stared at her, and my hand flew to my heart when I saw the necklace she wore was an angel, carved from bone. A few years older, but it was the same girl I had seen the night the Bastille fell—the child I had so desperately tried to find.

I think the girl became aware of me, because she smiled and took a step towards me, her hair curling in pleats, like the tug of wind on the river.

'*Bonjour*, madame,' she said. 'My name is Rubie Charpentier. I've come here to find my mother.'

She too, must have noticed the resemblance—the same small features and heart-shaped face rimmed in hair the hue of chestnuts—and understood who I was, because her eyes widened and she inhaled sharply.

Neither of us moved or spoke at first, and I reached for her hand.

***

In the shade of a willow, we sat together on a rock beside my favourite spot on the Vionne River—the place where the water cascades over a stony ridge into a wide, deep pool.

Over the gentle rush of the water and the *tick-tick* of insects, the air hummed with my timorous expectation. But it was not uncomfortable, as if we'd always sat here—my daughter and I— and it was the most natural thing.

'How did you find me, Rubie?'

'With the letter you left in my basket,' she said, without a speck of scorn or accusation in her voice. 'That is how I knew my name and who I was. I had wondered for a long time about you—the mother who left me this.' She fingered the angel pendant, turning it over in her small hand. 'Finally I found someone to read the letter to me. Then I went to the rue du Bac, knocking on all the doors, and met Claudine.'

'How is my friend?'

'She's old, but her health is good. She sends her love and hopes you are well. She and her charming husband were kind, taking me in. She cooked delicious meals, said I needed fattening up, and gave me money for the fare to Lucie.'

'Yes, she helped me too,' I said with a smile.

I hesitated, unsure I truly wanted to hear the truth, which could be nothing but grim, but I couldn't help myself, I wanted to know everything about my lost child.

'What about before, Rubie? Before Claudine took you in?'

Rubie's eyes clouded, and she looked across the water bubbling across the stones, folding over ferns, twigs and errant flower heads as if taking them on a whim, not quite knowing why.

Perepp, perepp, pereep, a bird sang. *Coop, coop, coop*, another answered, each note clear and defined.

'I was too young to remember before Madame Coudray,' she said. 'But she took children into her big house in an alley near the rue du Faubourg Saint-Antoine.'

'I know that place. I went there, several times. To think I was so close …'

'Madame Coudray really did try, but she had so many young ones to care for, and a drunkard husband who would knock her to the ground, so she was ill sometimes and found it hard to look after all of us. But I got to sleep on a mattress with the other girls, not on the floor, and we were warm … mostly.' She spoke rapidly, hardly taking a breath, as if getting it all out at once would mask the bleak truth. 'Well, sometimes it was a bit chilly in winter, but not too many of the little ones died, only about three or four each year.'

Mon Dieu. I could picture the swarm of children lying on the straw, dirty, undernourished and huddling together to leech out the slightest bit of human warmth from the next person—like my la Salpêtrière prison dormitory. The breeze brought a gust of coolness to my face, and the guilt prickled me again.

'I'm so sorry, Rubie, I never wanted you to live like that. I truly had no choice. The Marquis would have thrown us both on the street. We'd both have died—'

'I know,' she said, laying a hand on my forearm—this sensitive girl who had everything to blame me for, and nothing for which to thank me. She squeezed my arm, as if it was I who needed comfort and reassurance. 'But it truly wasn't so bad, Mam—'

She stopped, a smile curving her lip. 'I practised saying "Maman" with Claudine, but should I call you that?'

I took her hand—a rough, scarred little hand that revealed all she was reticent to tell me—and brought it to my lips. 'I am not certain I deserve such a title, Rubie but I'd be ... I'd be honoured.'

'That's good then, Maman.' She smiled, as if pleased at the sound of it. 'So, as I was saying it was really not too bad. I had friends—Louise and Belle. We were always together, sharing our secrets, and one day we decided poor Madame Coudray really did have too many children, so we ran away.'

'Ran away? And lived on the streets?' I recalled, with horror, the filthy beggar children who skulked in the dankest alleyways of the capital, and under bridges, with drunk old men.

'It was not easy at first, but we got used to it. Louise became an expert at getting food and clothes for us. Belle always seemed to have a lump of firewood to keep us warm. I was the best pick-pocket of us all.' Rubie laughed, but her grey-green eyes seemed heavy with the memories of all the tricks and ploys she'd been forced to master to survive.

'Where are your friends now, Louise and Belle?' I kept

reminding myself to slow down, not to overwhelm Rubie with my eagerness to know everything at once.

'Gone,' she said with a sigh. 'Dead from some sickness or other ... I don't know what.'

She turned her face to the sunlit crowns of the Monts du Lyonnais that blanched the blue from the sky. I knew she was trying to hide her pain and I yearned to fold her in my arms and squeeze away the ache and hardship of fifteen years.

'I'm so sorry,' I said, my hand reaching across, gently, tentatively sweeping loose strands of hair from her face. 'I hope you will make many new friends here in Lucie. You would like to stay *n'est-ce pas*, Rubie?'

She nodded. 'That would be nice, Maman, if it is what you want.'

'Of course! Nothing would delight me more than to have you here with me, and with your half-sister, Madeleine. She's a sweet girl and will love you.

'I imagine Claudine told you about your father?' I said, not sure I could bear to hear more about her childhood.

'I'm glad to say I no longer have a father,' Rubie said. 'I would not have wanted one like him, anyway, even if he had survived the revolution.'

'The Marquis is dead?'

The breeze strengthened, rustling the willow leaves, and a crow flapped away, cawing a bleak *ark, ark, ark.*

'He and his silly wife,' Rubie said. 'Claudine told me they fled Paris, just after the Bastille fell.'

'Yes ... yes, I knew that.'

'Their countryside estate was attacked and burned down during *la Grande Peur*,' Rubie went on. 'They returned to Paris in disguise but someone recognised them—the sister of a scullery maid the Marquis had burned at the stake. They were both guillotined, without a trial.'

I stifled my laugh. The Marquis's death was possibly the only one I could celebrate. I had long since gained my revenge through satire and personal success, but there was nothing like death, for ultimate vengeance. And I was pleased poor Margot had finally reaped her own, albeit posthumous, revenge.

'The Marquis de Barberon was not a father to be proud of, Rubie.'

'I do not care a bit. I have a mother I'm proud of.'

'Proud of *me*?'

'Claudine told me about the Scarlet Enchantress, and how she made a success of herself, even though the odds were against her. I only wish I could read the plays.'

'I'd love to teach you to read and write,' I said, feeling almost dizzy with the joy, the gladness, and realisation, in that instant, for whom I'd penned my memoirs. 'That's if you'd like me to?'

'Oh yes, I would like it very much. Claudine told me about my grandmother too,' she went on. 'Your mother, and how she was a midwife. It seems such a noble profession. I would like to become a midwife too … one day.'

'But you shall, Rubie! You will do whatever you want.' I couldn't stop smiling, and I saw my mother again, bustling about the village, birthing babies and tending the sick. I recalled sitting on her lap, her smell of musk and lavender in my nostrils, as she read from *Les Fables de Jean de la Fontaine*, and following each magical word and dreaming of princesses and fortune. 'Your grandmother would be so pleased to know your wish.'

As the sun poured down onto the countryside, we were quiet—a small span of moments in which I felt the passionate happiness of which I'd only dreamed.

I stood, brushing leaves and bits of dirt from my skirt. 'You must be thirsty, hungry and tired, and there's so much to show you. And you must meet Madeleine and your cousins, and see your new home—L'Auberge des Anges. There's my theatre company too, and the village, and oh, everything!'

I reached across and took hold of the angel pendant resting against her pale skin, my fingertip tracing the halo, the wings, the streaming gown. I rubbed the carving, the old bone warming beneath my thumb and forefinger.

'I prayed this angel would keep you safe on your journey, Rubie.'

'So it did, Maman.'

'It sent you the force of all those who wore it before you—the spirit of the women of L'Auberge des Anges.'

'What kind of bone is it?' Rubie asked.

'Oh, probably seal or ox, or walrus tusk, or perhaps even mammoth bone.'

'Mammoth! How thrilling.'

As Rubie laughed, I felt the angel burning my fingertips, branding me with the energy of all those who had left my world. The spirits of angels lost, but never gone.

Author's Note

This is a work of fiction, a work that combines the actual with the invented. All incidents and dialogue and all characters, with the exception of some well-known historical figures, are products of the author's imagination and are not to be construed as real. Where real-life historical figures appear, the situations, incidents and dialogues concerning those persons are fictional and are not intended to depict actual events or to change the fictional nature of the work. In all other respects, any resemblance to persons living or dead is entirely coincidental.

Acknowledgements

My grateful thanks to the following people, without whom this book would not have been possible:

Lorraine Mace, Gillian Hamer, JJ Marsh, Barbara Scott-Emmett, Catriona Troth, Tricia Gilbey, Sheila Bugler and Sharon Hutt of the Writing Asylum for expert advice and support; Pauline O'Hare for the Barry's tea, for weeding the garden and for always being there; Judith Murdoch for her wisdom and expert editorial advice; Claire Morgan and Gwenda Lansbury for their input on early drafts; Jane Dixon-Smith for her wonderful design; the very helpful people from Araire (historical research group of Messimy, France); and Jean-Yves, Camille, Mathilde and Etienne Perrat for their infinite patience with an absent wife and mother.

Thank you for reading a Triskele Book

If you loved this book and you'd like to help other readers find Triskele Books, please write a short review on the website where you bought the book. Your help in spreading the word is much appreciated and reviews make a huge difference to helping new readers find good books.

Why not try books by other Triskele authors?
Choose a complimentary ebook when you sign up
to our free newsletter at

www.triskelebooks.co.uk/signup

If you are a writer and would like more information on writing and publishing, visit http://www.triskelebooks.blogspot.com and http://www.wordswithjam.co.uk, which are packed with author and industry professional interviews, links to articles on writing, reading, libraries, the publishing industry and indie-publishing.

Connect with us:
Email admin@triskelebooks.co.uk
Twitter @triskelebooks
Facebook www.facebook.com/triskelebooks

Other novels by Liza Perrat

Wolfsangel
Book 2 in *The Bone Angel* series

Available now as print and e-book.

Amazon: myBook.to/WolfsangeleBook

Smashwords: https://www.smashwords.com/books/view/363451

Kobo: http://store.kobobooks.com/en-US/ebook/wolfsangel-2

Nook/Barnes & Noble: http://www.barnesandnoble.com/w/wolfsangel-liza-perrat/1117076332?ean=2940150281158

Seven decades after German troops march into her village, Céleste Roussel is still unable to assuage her guilt.

1943. German soldiers occupy provincial Lucie-sur-Vionne, and as the villagers pursue treacherous schemes to deceive and swindle the enemy, Céleste embarks on her own perilous mission as her passion for a Reich officer flourishes.

When her loved ones are deported to concentration camps, Céleste is drawn into the vortex of this monumental conflict, and the adventure and danger of French Resistance collaboration.

As she confronts the harrowing truths of the Second World

War's darkest years, Céleste is forced to choose: pursue her love for the German officer, or answer General de Gaulle's call to fight for France.

Her fate suspended on the fraying thread of her will, Celeste gains strength from the angel talisman bequeathed to her through her lineage of healer kinswomen. But the decision she makes will shadow the remainder of her days.

A woman's unforgettable journey to help liberate Occupied France, *Wolfsangel* is a stirring portrayal of the courage and resilience of the human mind, body and spirit.

Indie Book of the Day: http://indiebookoftheday.com/wolfsangel-by-liza-perrat/

Josie Barton (TOP 500 AMAZON REVIEWER) Best books of 2013: http://jaffareadstoo.blogspot.co.uk/2013/12/books-in-my-year-2013.html

Wolfsangel Editorial Reviews

'A heart-stopping novel of love, betrayal and courage which will leave you shaken and profoundly moved.' … Karen Maitland, bestselling author of *Company of Liars*.

'… one of the best books I have ever read.' … Kimberly Walker, reader

'… captures the tragedy of betrayal and the constancy of hope. It brings home to the reader that choices made in youth, cast deep shadows. A superb story that stays in the mind long after the final page.' … Lorraine Mace, writer, columnist and author of *The Writer's ABC Checklist*.

'A beautifully laid-out spiral of unfolding tragedy in German-occupied France; a tale of courage, hardship, forbidden love and the possibility of redemption in times of terror.' … Perry Iles, proofreader.

Blood Rose Angel
Book 3 in *The Bone Angel* series

Available now as print and ebook.

Amazon: myBook.to/BloodRoseAngel

Smashwords: https://www.smashwords.com/books/view/581151

Barnes & Noble: http://www.barnesandnoble.com/w/blood-rose-angel-liza-perrat/1122873896?ean=2940151046091

1348. A bone-sculpted angel and the woman who wears it--heretic, Devil's servant, saint.

Midwife Héloïse has always known that her bastard status threatens her standing in the French village of Lucie-sur-Vionne. Yet her midwifery and healing skills have gained the people's respect, and she has won the heart of the handsome Raoul Stonemason. The future looks hopeful. Until the Black Death sweeps into France.

Fearful that Héloïse will bring the pestilence into their cottage, Raoul forbids her to treat its victims. Amidst the grief and hysteria, the villagers searching for a scapegoat, Héloïse must choose: preserve her marriage, or honour the oath she swore on her dead mother's soul? And even as she places her faith in the protective powers of her angel talisman, she must prove she's no Devil's servant, her talisman no evil charm.

Bibliography

Many fictional and factual books, films and other material were useful in creating the atmosphere of Spirit of Lost Angels.

Books:
Anderson, James M.: The French Revolution
Doyle, William: The Oxford History of the French Revolution
Hibbert, Christopher: The French Revolution
Janin, Jules: The Dead Donkey and the Guillotined Woman
Lever, Maurice: Beaumarchais a Biography
Mercier, Louis-Sébastien: Panorama of Paris
Moore, Lucy: Liberty
Rice, Howard C, Jr.: Thomas Jefferson's Paris
Rattner Gelbart, Nina: The King's Midwife
Robb, Graham: The Discovery of France
Xenakis, Mâkhi: Les folles d'enfer

L'Araire booklets (Groupe de Recherche sur l'histoire, l'archéologie et le folklore du Pays Lyonnais):
Foires et Marchés en Pays Lyonnais: N° 148 — March, 2007
Soins et Santé en Pays Lyonnais: N° 157 — June, 2009